SILVER

A NOVEL

DYLAN THYER

c

ISBN (Hardcover): 979-8-9923616-0-5
ISBN (Paperback): 979-8-9923616-1-2
ISBN (e-Book): 979-8-9923616-2-9

Book design by Christian Storm

To my wife Anh for her unwavering support.

CONTENTS

PART II

PART III

SILVER

OUT TO PASTURE

Two dozen head of Black Angus pushed their way around the feeding trough, while the sunset cast radiant orange and pink across the sky. Nat Fuller got an accurate count of the herd, her eyes focused on a patch of matted ground. A month earlier, she had lost a heifer there. Disgustingly mutilated by an animal. Sheriff Mills had come by to check out the scene. He had been working a murder case down the road—not to mention a few FBI, and then a host of the Kansas state bureau. Everyone had gathered to gawk at her slain cow.

That seemed like a distant memory.

Mattfield's police had their hands full once more. Last night saw the most horrific tragedy for this community since the Civil War.

Dread had taken up residency across the county. What was this world coming to? Nat felt lucky to be old. A sense that something just isn't right in the world these days. Like it had fallen into the Devil's hands. Twisting and contorting the standards of good and evil. Thirty years ago, people knew the difference. Wicked hearts were prevailing. Proof only the good die young. Each day pushed the boundaries of what people would tolerate. The leaders installed a system to punish and control. A reluctant populous sat back and let it consume them. Weak men created hard times. These are the birth pangs of hard times to come.

Living alone on a farm in rural Kansas had its challenges at her age. Luckily, neighbors still turned out to help one another. Nat would do the same for them.

It'd been the way of life since the land was settled. There were far fewer genuine neighbors since the city folk began to flee from the hellholes they voted into existence. Avid white-tailed deer hunters gobbling up land just to use it for one week of the year. They continually drove up the price of an acre year after year. Which was ideal, except Nat meant to never sell. She wished to die on her farm whenever the Lord saw fit. No need for a will. What family she had left could squabble over the remains.

Content that her herd was fed and accounted for, Nat went to the house for the evening. The first rule of owning livestock: They eat before you do. This time of year, bales of hay would feed them through the winter. The cows' evening snacks in the trough kept them comfortable with her presence. Nat could inspect them each day for illness or injury. A small price to pay. When it came time for them to be shipped to the sale barn, she could easily fool them into a pen.

On the stroll to the backdoor, she noticed the full moon rising in the east. Nat kicked off her boots inside the French doors before making a beeline to fridge.

Leftover enchiladas, oh joy, she mused.

Nat pulled them steaming from the microwave and sat at her dining room table. The yard light out the backdoors flickered on. With the remote, she turned on the small television mounted on the wall. News reporter Lily Roth was on scene. "Another development in the Jackson Road murders. We are currently south of Mattfield, where the sheriff and his deputy were involved in a shootout earlier this afternoon."

"Good Lord, Carl," Nat said, turning the television off again. What the hell was going on around here? As if dead kids weren't bad enough.

Suddenly, her front door shuddered from an impact. Startled, she dropped her fork mid-bite. Her temper flared as she marched into the living room to give whoever it was an earful. Checking the time on her phone, she then threw it aside onto her favorite recliner. "Oh, I oughta kick your ass, hittin' the door to my house like that! Do you have any idea what time it is!?" Nat fumed, but when she opened it, no one was outside.

She ran her fingers along four scratch marks that tore through the door's white paint. Nervously, Nat peaked around the front yard, but there was no sign of life. Not a vehicle in sight.

That's unusual. It was hard to imagine a prank in times like these. What on earth would leave those scratches in Kansas? Nat bolt locked the front door shut. She had never locked the door in all her years, but these weren't normal times. Better to be safe than sorry.

Suddenly, her cows in the back pasture raised the alarm in distress. Preemptively, Nat rushed to the closet and grabbed her semi-auto 12-gauge shotgun, loading buckshot as she headed to the backdoor. Nat swung the door open to see a tall, shadowy figure standing just outside the radius of her yard light. "Hey! You are trespassing! You the one that killed my heifer? Made a big mistake stepping foot on my property!"

The figure didn't answer at first, silently studying her as Nat ranted. Then, a low rumbling growl came forth. Nat's heart rate skyrocketed to the point she nearly fainted. She realized what stared at her in the dark was not human. Instinctively, she aimed the shotgun. It stood upright like a person, but much taller.

Has to be a bear, she surmised. *What else could it be?*

With a sudden burst, the beast charged toward her. Recoil jolted her body as Nat fired a shot. Retreating into the safety of the house, she secured the door shut behind her.

I have to call the sheriff.

Nat remembered leaving her cell phone in the living room. Taking heavy breaths to try and slow her heart rate, she went to call for aid. As soon as her back turned away from the doors, they exploded inward. Glass and debris filled the air around her as she fell hard onto the linoleum. Losing her grip on the shotgun, it slid out of reach, catching on the living room carpet. The creature towered over her as she tried to scream. Fear prevented any audible noise from escaping her lungs.

That is no bear.

Nat crawled frantically for the gun, but a massive foot pinned her down. Hooked claws burrowed into her back. A humanlike hand engulfed her head from behind. Its claws slid onto her face as it started to squeeze.

Nat Fuller felt her skull crack under the pressure.

PART I

1

WELCOME HOME

The metro area faded away. Rolling grass hills frocked with groves of trees became the scenery. It stayed this way for an hour as the truck barreled south down the highway. Leaving what was his home for seventeen years, Brett Adams turned his half-ton pickup into the drive of a little white farmhouse. He was shocked and upset when he found out in his senior year of high school that his mom was moving him and his younger brother to the country, leaving behind his friends and the place he had grown up and thrived. This was the biggest change his life has ever had. Now he would have to try to make new friends and fit into a rural school, which contrasted greatly with what he was accustomed to.

It was a personal hell for him and his brother to be caught up in his parents' marriage woes. Brett and his brother, Dalton, would be the ones paying the price.

Brett was turning eighteen in November. Athletic build, blond hair, and blue eyes. Six feet tall, skinny, muscular, and lanky. His mom was always telling him he should eat more. He excelled at track and field, opting out of all other sports after his junior year to focus on the one he thought he had a future in. School work never could keep his attention; he especially had a hatred for math. He had a modest GPA of 3.54 and got a twenty-three on his first try with the ACT. He struggled with what he wanted to study in college, but he felt there was plenty of time to figure that out.

His grandfather lived out there in the country, but that was all the exposure he and his brother ever got. They had come down to visit his mom's dad for a few of the big holidays over the years. When they were younger, they would stay with their grandparents for a week, occasionally during summer break from school. Now, Easter, Christmas, and Thanksgiving was pretty much it for visiting the area, which he was not mad about—Brett much preferred life in the suburbs. There was never a lack of things to do in the city. You could go bowling, to a movie, or out to eat without traveling more than ten minutes. Out here, some of those things were a luxury you would have to travel half an hour for. Going out to eat would mean hitting the local bar or diner. That's all there is.

He did love his grandfather, though. To his parents' protests, his grandfather had always let Brett and Dalton run wild over the years. They never enjoyed more freedom than when they visited. The only time Brett had ever got to shoot firearms was at his grandfather's house.

His grandpa, Walt, had been an Army Reserve vet and a truck driver before he retired. Now he spent his days managing his ten-acre plot outside of Mattfield. Just him and his dog, Buck. Buck was a healthy, plump yellow lab. Mellow and laid back, never getting excited about anything besides truck rides and dinner time.

Brett's grandma had been gone a few years now, after a brief battle with pneumonia. The heartbreak his mother suffered paved the way for the marriage problems his parents faced. His father was a successful businessman who spent a lot of time on the road, much to his wife's protests. They started fighting more when the family was together. Things devolved over time and his father committed the ultimate betrayal: having an affair while away. Although his mother could not bring herself to file for divorce, she was willing to split the family apart by separating from Michael, and moving back to her hometown.

Walt, at age seventy-four, looked well for his age. He had some gray hair on the sides of his head, but mostly it still clung to the light brown it always had been. He stood tall at six feet, with a round belly. Because of his height, he did not look unfit. He got plenty of exercise walking with Buck every day around his property. He kept his plot of land manicured, and he had made it into a beautiful homestead in his retirement years. Walt loved guns and had an arsenal in his collection. Although he complained about it not being cost effective anymore, he would teach Brett and Dalton the art of reloading spent rounds during holiday visits. It was their grandfather's favorite way of recycling.

If he was being generous, the big town that everything revolved around for rural folks was Mattfield, KS. It had the honor of being the county seat hosting the courthouse, jail, and police station. Situated outside the western edge of town, this is where he would be attending his senior year at Mattfield High School with his brother—eighth grade through twelfth, all in one building. Just under three hundred students in all. It was a place where everyone was into each other's business. Hell, if you messed up or got in trouble, your parents would know before you got home. It was that way *before* cell phones.

The town was steeped in rich early American history. Native Americans inhabited the lands the town were founded on. Starting out as a coal mining outpost, it snowballed into a prominent Midwestern city—from serving as a hub on the underground railroad for slaves escaping from neighboring Missouri to being part of the border war during Bleeding Kansas. Those events culminated in the Civil War, in which the town's population took part.

The town cemetery has a section for the Union soldiers, buried there with a historical marker bearing their names. The city hit its peak population after World War II. Though Mattfield had seen a decline in businesses and residents over the decades, new life had been breathed into the community over the last five years.

Mattfield was now a prominent farming economy in the modern day. All the farmers sold their harvest at the local agriculture co-op. Two large grain elevators loomed over the southern side of town. Cattle farmers were abundant.

Almost everyone had some form of livestock. If nothing else, owning cattle was an easy tax write-off for the mostly lower middle-class families.

It really upset Brett that he would be starting over again as a senior at a new school. It became overtly angering when he thought about doing that again the following year, when he would hopefully be off to compete as a track athlete in college. He resented his father, placing the blame on him for ruining their family, causing them to have to move to redneck central.

He had barely spoken to his father in the last few months. He had not felt the need or desire to speak with him anymore. His father chose a whore over his family, as far as Brett was concerned.

His mom, Julia, had taken a job at the local hospital in Mattfield as their new nurse practitioner. It was a rural hospital, mainly for simple medical ailments but sometimes emergencies. Most major injuries or medical complications would earn you an ambulance or Life Flight ride to Kansas City or Joplin, MO. Which one you ended up at depended on the life-threatening nature of your condition. Mattfield sat evenly between them.

It felt like moving to the edge of the civilized world, but Julia was highly qualified for the job, having worked in a few big hospitals over the years, so Mattfield Hospital was happy to have her joining their staff.

Brett was always teased about his mother by his friends for being attractive. That was a weird concept for him to deal with. His mother had shoulder-length dirty blonde hair, although she would tell Brett and Dalton they were going to turn it gray quite often. Her face was warm and inviting, with round cheeks and a perfect smile. Julia dressed modestly during family outings. Brett saw her wearing scrubs for work more often than regular clothes.

Dalton could not be more different from his brother. He was a skinny kid like his brother, but he didn't get into sports. He was very pale in complexion compared to Brett; most of the things he enjoyed were better done inside. His hair was a shade darker brown, and he was two inches shorter, but there was a chance yet that he would get a little taller before he was done growing. He wasn't as strong-framed as Brett, but had definitely come into some strength with puberty.

Dalton elected to wear reading glasses when at school, even though the eye doctor had told him his vision was acceptable. Brett believed his brother was striving for a scholarly appearance. The baby of their family, he always obeyed and seemed to actively avoid trouble. His relationship with their father had not seem impacted like Brett's. Dalton seemed unfazed by the move. The public schools in the city made him feel disenfranchised. Dalton loved classes and learning new things in general. He never could get into all the crazes that would come and go with his generation. Making connections with people was not something that came naturally to him. He just could not relate to most of the other kids his age, so moving to a new town and school did not burden his social life. Honestly, Dalton was not leaving much behind in the city that he could not easily replace in Mattfield.

Brett pulled into the circle drive of his new home for the first time. The U-Haul was already backed up to the front door of the country house his mom rented for them. It was a white, two-story house sitting right along a chip and sealed county road. The house appeared much older than the home he grew up in, but had been well taken care of. The yard had a few strong oak trees casting their shade in the August heat, and a detached garage that sat off to the side, the same shade of white to match the house.

The yard around the property caught Brett off guard. He had never had a yard in the city. This property had two acres of freshly mown grass around the house and garage. Interspersed with the trees, it was beautiful. Besides the occasional car that passed by on the road, it was peacefully quiet out here.

Around the perimeter of the yard was a plastic white picket fence. It looked cheap if you got up close, but at a distance, it made the property visually stunning. On the outside of that was a tall grass prairie. The dry brown grass danced in the southern wind, swaying back and forth. The only thing stopping it from going on forever were the tree lines in the distance, dividing fields from neighboring properties.

It was just before noon, the August heat sweltering—the dying gasp of summer in Kansas. In a month, the rain would return and the cooler air from the north would settle over the plains. Kansas had a way of making people beg for a cooldown in the summer, then look for the warmth to return in the winter—weather that changed on a dime. If you didn't like the temperature outside, you could always find someone to tell you, "Wait a few hours."

Brett brought his truck to a stop. Swinging open his door, he stepped down onto the gravel drive. Grandpa Walt was there helping his mother, Julia, unload boxes from the U-Haul.

"We were starting to wonder if you were going to show up," Walt quipped.

"Yeah, yeah," Brett replied as he approached the back of the box truck. He climbed into the back and grabbed one of the heavier boxes.

Julia and Brett walked past each other, going in and out of the home. "I know this is different, but I really think you are going to like it here," Julia said to him. She had a look of mixed emotions on her face. She was well aware he did not want to move out here.

"As long as you are happy, right?" Brett threw back at her rhetorically. They'd had this conversation a dozen times already.

Dalton was in the kitchen unloading some boxes. "Mom said we get the two bedrooms upstairs. They're basically identical, so I just put some of my boxes in the one on the right," his brother said amicably.

Brett nodded. He was simultaneously struggling with being helpful and not wanting to be there at all.

On this next trip to the U-Haul, Brett made sure to find some of his boxes. His grandpa and mom were in the living room, positioning a coffee table. He shot up the stairs with his possessions to go see the new living space. At the top of the stairs was a short hallway with a door to the left, right, and center. He surmised their shared bathroom was the center door. Setting the boxes down, he opened the door on the left. To his surprise, the room was spacious.

This is larger than my old bedroom, he thought.

His bed was already in there. He picked up the boxes and set them back down on the bed. He had a small closet, but it was enough space for him. Brett walked over and peered out the windows in his room. They overlooked the backyard, a bird's-eye view out into the flowing fields of prairie that bordered them. Certainly not unpleasant scenery, and a far cry from their house in the city, what with houses stacked together as close as they could be built.

Brett and Dalton grabbed the last few boxes out of the U-Haul.

"Alright, boys, the hard part is over," Julia said. Brett was sure the hard part was just beginning. "You boys head into town and get something to eat. Your grandpa and I will go turn in the U-Haul," Julia added.

"The diner has pretty good food. It's where all the farmers get lunch," Walt added, closing the back of the U-Haul.

"A burger sounds good right about now," Dalton said, looking at Brett.

"You'll want to go to the bar, then," Walt said.

"I'm down for that," Brett replied.

Julia climbed into the driver's seat of the U-Haul and pulled away from the house. Their grandpa followed behind in her Chevrolet Trailblazer.

Brett and Dalton hopped into his truck and pulled out of the drive behind them. They rolled the windows down, cruising down the country highway. The hot air tussled their hair as it moved across their faces.

"It's not going to be that bad," Dalton told his brother.

"Easy for you to say. I don't want to live out here," Brett replied.

"How is it easy for me? It's not our fault and we can't change it. We're doing this for Mom," Dalton snapped back.

"She's having a mid-life crisis and dragging us back to where she's from. This isn't our home."

"You know how many people this happens to? Because it's a lot. Marriages statistically don't work out. I don't think I'll ever get married," Dalton reasoned.

Brett was getting angry just thinking about their situation. "Oh, I blame Dad, for sure. He's the one who caused all this trouble. But we didn't need to move to the sticks. The city is a big place. Us moving here was all Mom's doing."

"Like I said, we can't change it. Maybe they'll work things out."

"Yeah, maybe. In the meantime, let's split, move the family, and see if that doesn't help fix things," Brett said, gripping the steering wheel tighter. He shot his brother an angry glance.

"You aren't going to make anything better being an asshole."

"Well, like you said, it's not our fault, but it feels like we're the ones being punished," Brett replied, trying to bring the conversation to a close. He already struggled with trying to block it out of his mind. The last thing he wanted to do was rehash the situation.

He reached over and twisted the knob on the stereo, cranking up the music. "Dragula" by Rob Zombie was on the radio. Something about rock and metal always helped alleviate his anger.

They glided up to a stop sign. Turning right, they crossed the bridge over Coal Creek and into Mattfield. Though it was an old town that predated the Civil War, it was a beautiful place, nestled along Coal Creek in the hills of eastern Kansas. The town was well kept, clean and, above all, safe. Most crime in the county came from low-income adjacent towns where drug addiction had run rampant.

Brett turned left onto the main drag through historic downtown Mattfield, standing tall, with old, orange brick buildings lining both sides of the street. The bar was tacked on the west end of the hundred-year-old buildings. A mismatched navy blue tin building, the most cost-effective build these days. Not exactly suitable for being situated in tornado alley, but that's what insurance was for.

Brett drove all the way down Main Street, past the courthouse, police station, and brand-new jail. As they approached the eastern edge of town, they saw the hospital their mom would be working at. It wasn't anything to be impressed by. A large, single-story building, it was nothing like the hospitals the city boasted.

Brett flipped a U-turn and headed back to downtown Mattfield. Driving back through the large buildings, he admired the businesses on both sides of the road: computer repair; coffee shop; hair salon; thrift store; real-estate; a lawyer's office; the post office; and a hardware store, all nestled inside the old buildings. Brett parked in the last open diagonal parking spot in front of Hopper's bar.

Across the street to the west sat the fire station. The doors were open to show off the three large, red fire trucks stored inside. Rural communities like Mattfield had all volunteer fire fighters. The tax revenue for small towns wasn't enough to have full-time paid professionals on staff, leaving it up to ordinary citizens to undergo the training and help their community out when the need arose. Structure fires were rare, so they mainly did battle with grass fires that could be quite dangerous in the dry, windy, summer conditions.

"I'm starving," Dalton said as they opened their doors and stepped out onto the blacktop. They headed into the bar. It felt awkward to Brett going into a bar, being underage. Bars in the city were not like this. They had Buffalo Wild Wings and other businesses that felt more family suited. There were rows of booths against the walls and a row of tables running down the middle. A bar area sat off to the left of the front door. A girl sat alone at the countertop, reading a book. She immediately caught Brett's attention.

"Let's sit at the bar," Brett blurted out to his brother.

Dalton turned his head to look at the bar area. "Of course that's where you want to sit."

"Dude, shut up," Brett fired back. He wasn't able to look away, though.

The girl's long black hair glistened as it flowed down her back. She looked about their age, but Brett couldn't fully tell with her back turned. They approached the bar and Brett, pushing his nerves down, was able to ask, "Hey, is anyone sitting here?" He pointed to the seat next to her.

She turned to him and their eyes locked. She was more beautiful than he had imagined. Her green eyes melted through him. She flashed a pearly white smile, appearing taken aback. She was sporting a summer tan.

Must spend a lot of time at the lake, Brett concluded.

It did not look like a fake tan to him. She had a strong, athletic physique and a smooth, perfect complexion.

"I'm here by myself. Have a seat," the mysterious beauty invited.

Brett swiveled the bar stool around and crawled into the seat next to her. He extended his hand, introducing himself, "Hey, I'm Brett. We just moved here."

She reached over with a shy look and shook his hand. "I'm Cassie. I'm not new here."

That made him smile. She reached across in front of him and shook Dalton's hand, too. "I heard we were getting some new people at school this year."

"You heard that?" Brett said, raising an eyebrow.

"Everyone knows everything around here," Cassie said, and giggled. "Are you a senior this year?" she asked.

"Yeah, I'm a senior. Dalton here is a junior," Brett answered. He looked at his brother, who rolled his eyes.

"Nice! This is my senior year, too," Cassie said excitedly.

Maybe this whole relocation wasn't going to be the end of the world, after all, Brett thought.

His first day in Mattfield, and he was already awestruck by one of his classmates.

He glanced down at the book she was reading. *State of Fear* by Michael Crichton. "How's that book?" Brett asked.

"It is fascinating. Seems relevant to the world these days, too. He is, by far, my favorite author." Cassie was enthusiastic talking about it.

Not only was she the most beautiful girl he had ever met, but she had good taste, too. "*Jurassic Park* rocks," he replied.

That made Cassie light up. Her smile made it impossible for him to not smile, too. He was not the best at talking to girls, but so far, this had been one of those rare occasions where it was going smoothly.

There was an awkward silence saved by the waitress. "What can I get you boys to eat?" she asked.

Brett hadn't even picked up a menu yet. To save face, he quickly replied, "I'll just have a cheeseburger."

Dalton had been looking the menu over while his brother was enamored. "Same, no onions."

Brett glanced over to the bar door as it opened. A group of teenagers walked in.

"Cassie!" a girl exclaimed. There were five teens in total. Cassie twirled around and went over to greet them. Brett couldn't help but notice the three guys and two girls in the group. He started to feel a little disheartened. He was the new guy now, and they all had established relationships. He wondered if he'd even be able to fit into a group that has grown up together.

One guy—a tall, muscular black kid built like a linebacker—was staring at him. Just the sight of him made Brett feel a little inferior. The guy imbued masculine strength. He was standing tall with his chest pushed out, wearing a medium T-shirt when he clearly could wear a large comfortably. He strolled over and stuck his hand out. "Marcus," he stated.

Brett reached out and shook his hand, each squeezing tightly, though Marcus was clearly stronger. "Brett. Nice to meet you," he managed, trying not to grimace from the handshake.

Marcus relented, giving his hand back to him. "Two-a-days are getting ready to start. You trying out for the football team?" Marcus ribbed.

Everyone knew small towns did not have tryouts. They need everyone they can get to show up.

"I haven't played football for a few years," Brett replied, feeling more and more insecure by the second.

"We need a cornerback if you decide to play," Marcus said, holding his gaze.

"I'll keep that in mind," Brett said with his chin up. Was he being insulted? Was Marcus being genuine? He didn't know.

Marcus turned around and walked back to his friends. They were all chatting and laughing. Brett just sat uncomfortably now, anxiously awaiting his lunch. He heard Cassie call out, "Hey, new kids, we're going to the lake. You guys are more than welcome to join us."

"We'll meet you out there after we finish lunch if that's alright?" Brett answered.

Dalton rolled his eyes.

Cassie strolled back over and held out her phone.

Brett punched in his phone number confidently.

"I'll shoot you the address," Cassie said with a wink.

Marcus put his arm around Cassie as they all exited together.

Brett looked down, confused. *Are those two together? Was she flirting with him?*

Dalton quipped, "Classic."

"Just shut up," Brett muttered. Looking over, he saw the book Cassie had been reading lying on the countertop. He got a glimmer of hope back. "Looks like we have to go to the lake."

After they had finished with their lunch, Brett—with Cassie's book in hand and his disgruntled brother loaded back up in his truck—went to have a look at their new high school. Brett was surprised it was outside of town altogether. Even more concerning to him, it looked more like a jail than the town's jail did. The place only had a few tall, narrow windows in it. Making a loop around the parking lot, Brett checked his phone. A text message with an address sat waiting.

"Not as bad as you thought it was going to be here, is it?" Dalton said, smirking.

Maybe his brother was right. He had only been in Mattfield a few hours and he'd met a girl he was excited about. For the first time in months, he could momentarily repress the negativity he felt toward his home life. Being around his mom always brought out the resentment he was harboring. He couldn't see a way past it. The rage he felt against his father, who remained in the city, was even worse.

"Let's go to the lake. We don't have to stay long," Brett said.

"Alright, whatever," Dalton agreed.

Entering the address, they were only a few minutes away. The lake sat nestled in the hills south of the town. Not knowing what to expect from a country lake, Brett was taken aback when it came into view. Pleasant homes surrounded the shores of the large body of water.

"Who would have thought?" Dalton said, wide-eyed.

Driving on gravel roads, they wound through the hills. These roads weren't on a grid. It felt more like driving in a maze.

Getting here is one thing. I just hope we can make it out again, Brett thought.

The GPS brought them to a log cabin perched above the lake.

"Wow, I like our new friends," Dalton said, impressed.

They had never been to a lake house before. Cassie's book in hand, Brett and Dalton approached the front door. Laughs were heard coming from the back of the house.

"Let's go around," Brett said.

Walking beside the cabin, the brothers descended a hill to a rock patio. The patio had a bricked-in fire pit surrounded by furniture. A two-story dock sat over the water. Their acquaintances were bobbing in the lake.

Cassie noticed them first. "Hey, you guys came!" she shouted.

"This place is amazing," Dalton replied, stating the obvious.

"Thanks!" a new girl said. "It's my parents' lake house. I'm Bethany, by the way. You met Cassie and Marcus. This big fella here is Bradley. Quarterback Luke and his girlfriend, Erica, they're juniors, but they're alright," Bethany added, introducing the group.

"Dalton. I'm a junior, as well," he said with a halfhearted wave.

"You playing football?" Luke inquired.

"Me? No. I don't think either of us are," Dalton replied.

"No football for you, Brett?" Marcus asked.

Brett felt it was more than just a genuine question. "I'm thinking about it," Brett shot back.

"What is there to think about?" Marcus pressed.

"I don't know. We just moved in today. Haven't had a chance to get settled yet," Brett answered. He felt the passive aggressive behavior coming from Marcus.

"Just asking," Marcus said, giving a coy smile.

"Anyway, we just wanted to stop in and say hi. Cassie, you forgot your book." Brett held it up.

"Oh, did I?" Cassie said sarcastically. "You can set it on the couch. I'll make sure to get it this time."

"Will do. Look, it is nice to meet you all. We don't know anyone down here. Inviting us was cool. Be nice to do this again when we have swim trunks on. There's a lot of stuff to unpack back home, so we probably should get going," Brett told the group. He wasn't feeling the social setting.

"You guys just got here," Cassie replied, frowning.

"No, he's right. Our mom will need help," Dalton backed him up.

"Alright, guys. It was nice to meet you both. And welcome to Mattfield!" Bethany yelled enthusiastically.

Everyone said goodbye, exchanging waves. The brothers marched back up the hill to the truck.

"I'm surprised you want to go home," Dalton said.

"I don't. But I don't want to stay here, either. I don't know what I want anymore," Brett replied. Back in the truck, they headed to their new home.

Pulling back into the driveway, Brett thought with displeasure, *Home sweet home.*

Their mom's vehicle was back in the driveway. She was most likely unpacking. Brett pulled up to the detached garage and parked in front of one door. Shutting the truck off, he sighed.

Dalton opened the passenger door, saying, "Come on."

Brett hesitated, then got out and followed his brother to the front door.

They pushed their way inside and were greeted by Julia. "Hey, how was the food? You mind setting up the TV in the living room?" she kindly requested.

Dalton responded, "Eh, a cheeseburger is a cheeseburger. Kind of hard to mess that up. Yeah, I can get the TV ready to go."

Brett looked at his mother, who was holding a stack of laundry. "I'll be upstairs," is all he could bring himself to say to her.

He marched up to his bedroom, making sure to slam his bedroom door shut behind him. He grabbed the boxes of his belongings and moved them to the floor. Throwing himself down on the bed, he wrestled with his thoughts.

He kept replaying his meeting with Cassie and wondered if the attraction he felt was mutual. He wondered about Marcus. *Are they a couple?* After a long while, his mind finally exhausted. Brett fell fast asleep.

The bedroom door sprung open, startling him awake. It was dark outside. He pulled his phone out of his pocket; it was past ten thirty. He hadn't meant to sleep this long. Over five hours had gone by. Dalton approached his bed.

"What's wrong?" Brett asked drowsily.

"Listen," Dalton stated flatly.

Brett listened. He heard a raucous cackling outside. There was an abundance of high-pitched howls, yips, and growls in what sounded like a chorus of nightmarish children, dancing in the dark. The maniacal laughter came from all sides of the home. It was unsettling. *How many of them are out there?* Brett pondered.

"What is that?" Dalton quivered, visibly distraught. All Dalton had done was defend moving to the countryside. Now he stood scared on their very first night.

Brett was too groggy to process a way to be nicer. He bluntly told Dalton, "Those are coyotes. Welcome home."

2

FRESH START

Julia Adams headed out the door on her way to work just as the sun was peeking over the horizon. As soon as the sun kissed the Kansas earth at first light, it was like an oven being turned on. The month was but a few days old, so the miserable conditions were here for a few more weeks, at least. The media was always on and on about climate change this time of year. She was afraid to say it out loud, but in her forty-four years, she didn't think the weather had really changed much at all. Some years had more mild seasons, some harsher. Maybe more people felt the same as her, but they were also afraid to say it. Just wasn't worth the risk of being verbally attacked. Self-censoring out of fear had become a real problem across the world. Such a volatile time when someone was just as likely to physically assault you if your ideas weren't in sync.

Carrying her purse and an insulated cup of coffee, she had to consolidate her items to one hand to get the door to her Trailblazer open. She slid her coffee cup into the snug cup holder and hit the push-button ignition. The vehicle came to life with a hum. Julia immediately kicked on the air conditioner. The car read eighty-four degrees outside. No thank you. She slipped the car into gear and headed out of the driveway for work.

Luckily, her boys would be starting school in a few days. Leaving teen boys at home alone was always a gamble. They were old enough to know better and dumb enough to get into trouble. Dalton was a good voice of reason out of the two. Not a flawless record, but about as good as can be hoped for.

Brett, on the other hand, was angry and bitter. He had stopped communicating with Julia. Her heart felt the sting, knowing how much resentment Brett held. Teen boys can have irrational anger and aggression to begin with. Julia knew he was justified to an extent. She was already second-guessing upending their family life in the city. This move was what she needed. Julia needed space to breathe, time to reflect, to forgive, and ultimately decide what came next. What better place to heal than getting back to her roots?

Julia grew up in Mattfield and she owed who she became to this small town. She hoped her eldest son could forgive her as Julia tried to forgive his father. Moving the boys away from the home they knew and the lives and friends they had made for themselves was a selfish thing to do. This was Brett's senior year. Pulling him to a new place this year grieved her conscience the most.

Julia was at a crossroads in life. Michael, the love of her life, had betrayed their marriage vows. To have and to hold, in sickness and in health, till death do you part. Michael crushed her faith and trust. He was already not present often enough in her eyes. The boys needed their dad as much as she needed her husband.

Michael traversed the country, rubbing elbows with business leaders and Congress members to benefit his company's bottom line. Julia was proud of his success and the money he brought to the table for the family. As the boys grew and Michael progressed in his career, it became less and less sustainable.

Their relationship soured for Julia with the passing of her mother. She wasn't prepared for the loss and needed support. Support she did not receive from her husband. Not only did her mom pass unexpectedly, it left her father, Walt, all alone. She carried the weight of dividing her attention between the needs of their boys and her father. Julia was stretched thin.

When Michael was home, they began to clash over the lack of his presence. Then he came clean. He had been having an affair. Michael clearly felt guilty confessing to the betrayal, but Julia couldn't find forgiveness for what he had done. She cut her husband out immediately, although in her heart, Julia was not able to file for divorce. Not yet, anyway.

Julia turned her eyes to Mattfield. The opportunity to be closer to her father. The ability to be unencumbered as she strived to make sense of it all. It felt like running away from the problem, but things were only going to devolve further without a shift. The hospital happened to have an opening in her field. The stars aligned, so Julia jumped at the chance.

Michael had hurt her deeply, and now he would suffer the consequences. He was supportive of the move, showing understanding and true regret for his actions. He knew he might have done irreparable harm to his family. When marriages fall on hard times, the kids take on part of that suffering. They don't understand as teens.

Julia and Michael decided to set the boys down and talk to them like adults. Michael let Brett and Dalton know that the blame fell upon himself. Dalton showed some resentment toward his father's actions. Brett became enraged as Julia and Michael talked to him. They had seen the sparks before in him. Brett was a passionate boy. Ever since that day, his rage had not been dulled toward either of his parents. Brett felt cheated, distraught, and abandoned. Julia knew it would be a long road to repair the relationship she shared with her son.

Lost in her thoughts, she had spaced out on the drive to work. Time to get life back on track. She was in complete control now. Julia crammed in some positive thinking as she parked in front of Mattfield General Hospital.

The hospital was much smaller than KC Regional, where she'd spent the last decade. More personal, as well. Almost every patient who came in to the hospital here would be a local. Seeing her patients out and about at school functions or the grocery store was going to be a culture shock. Small-town life had less separation and less privacy. This is right where Julia wanted to be. The busy city life could wear you down. There was always someplace to be, an invitation to something you didn't want to attend, and distractions on every corner. Julia's stress level and anxiety had already dropped dramatically after settling in to the new house. Breathing just felt freer in a small town.

Julia grabbed her purse and coffee. The humid air brought her back to the world around her. It was only a short walk to the staff entrance door. With a swipe of her security badge, she watched the green light on the lock flash, allowing her to enter.

The hospital interior sported white tile floors and white walls etched with cedar trimming. Inside, the temperature was a reasonable seventy degrees. The facility was well maintained, keeping it fresh and new.

None of the traveling doctors would be in today, leaving Julia in charge of patient care.

Taking a large gulp of coffee, the first person came into view. Sitting behind the receptionist's desk, Kari Sears called out, "Good morning, Julia! Ready for your first day? If everyone shows and nothing crazy comes up, you will be seeing fourteen people today."

Kari was visibly younger than Julia. Her lips shined bright red with lipstick. Her face was pulled tight. She had obviously used Botox. From the tone of her white skin, Julia could only assume Kari fake baked when she tanned. She wore black leggings and a purple long-sleeve shirt.

"Good morning!" Julia replied. "I am ready to kick things off. Who do I have first?"

"Sheriff Mills is coming in for a yearly checkup. Busy guy, so he likes to get in and out as early as he can," Mrs. Sears informed her.

"Perfect. I haven't seen Carl in quite a few years." Julia looked forward to catching up with the old man.

She proceeded to her office, entering through the open door and placing her items on the desk. There was a knock on the door behind her.

"Hi. You must be Julia. I've been looking forward to meeting you. My name is Debra White." Debra's hand extended as she introduced herself.

Julia shook it. "Hi, Debra. I heard a lot about you when I did my interview for the position."

"Hopefully only the good things," Debra said, and laughed.

Debra's demeanor was genuinely pleasant. She had shoulder-length jet-black hair, and was dressed in black scrubs to match. Her muscular arms jumped out at Julia. Someone in health care who practiced what they preached. Julia respected that. Debra was shorter than her by a few inches.

Julia smiled back. "Everyone said this place doesn't work without you."

"They just butter me up because I have been stuck pulling the night shift for three months," Debra replied. Debra wouldn't admit it, but those months were taking a toll on her, Julia reckoned.

"I'd be happy to take some night work so you can see the sunlight," Julia said.

Debra smiled. "Really, the night shift around here is a bit of a joke. This place hardly sees any action. Small towns go to bed at ten. Usually an old-timer, if anything, with high blood pressure or a heart attack scare."

"I can live with that," Julia replied.

"Well, it was nice meeting you. Time for me to get out of here. I hear my bed calling my name," Debra said with a wave as she left.

Julia called out behind her, "See you this evening!"

Julia's assistant, Tucker Ross, who preps rooms and patients, arrived at her door a few minutes later. "Hello, Mrs. Adams. Sheriff Mills is here and ready to be seen, room two."

Tucker was a twenty-year-old man, working hours in the hospital in preparation for med school. He was heavier set, clean-shaven, and white as a sheet. The youngsters were a mixed bag. Everyone must learn medicine starting somewhere. Julia remembered being that way, as well. They could be a little sparky and energetic for her liking at this age. She might be calling him doctor someday if he made it through all the schooling, testing, and residency.

"Thank you," Julia said, giving him a nod of acknowledgment.

She scooped up her laptop and headed down the hall. She reached out and gave a rap of her knuckles on the door that read "2" on the outside. Warning knock over, she swung the door open and closed it behind her.

Julia started the ball rolling. "Mr. Mills, it's wonderful to see you! I understand you try to get in and out early. Can't blame you there. What brings you in today?" There was a countertop in the room with a sink, latex gloves, and tissues. Setting her laptop down, she leaned up against the counter to engage her patient.

"That's Sheriff Mills to you," he said with a grin. "Town's happy to have you home, Julia. As much as I hate going to the hospital, it's apparently important to have you guys around."

"Sheriff Mills, it is, then." Julia smiled. "If you don't mind me saying, I figured you'd be retired by now."

Mills nodded. "Between you and me, I'm planning on retiring end of February. Put a lot of thought into it. Just time to hang it up."

Julia was a little shocked to hear it from the sheriff himself. Mills has been a part of the police force in some form her entire life. "Everyone says when you know it's time to trust that feeling," Julia replied. She had a little sadness in her voice. Things would feel foreign without Mills involved in the Mattfield police force. The torch would finally pass on to the next generation after many decades of service.

"You do know. Wife and I want to get out and see the world before we can't anymore," the sheriff replied. "I tell you, the older you get, the more things hurt. Body isn't recovering like it used to. Burying more friends. The world is changing so quickly now, feels more like being left behind."

Julia was in awe at the honesty the sheriff showed her. "I haven't been back in Mattfield long, but it sure feels the same to me. How is Martha doing?"

"She was smart enough to retire as soon as she could. She watches a lot of videos online, making a list of all the places we need to see. I hardly recognize the people around town now. Have never met a lot of them. Homes are selling for way more than they're worth. They still get bought. California, North Carolina, Minnesota. People flocking from all over the country, scooping up our properties. Able to sell their homes for a small fortune and raise our property taxes here," Sheriff Mills lamented.

Julia knew that type of house buying was happening in Kansas City, but hadn't realized the small towns were being affected so heavily. "Can't blame them for leaving California," she joked, trying to lighten his spirits.

"No, that place has gone to hell," Mills chuckled. "How are your boys doing? I heard from your father just the three of you moved down here."

"Michael and I ran into some marriage trouble after Mom passed away. Hard to keep things private in a small town, especially when it's your own dad talking. My oldest, Brett, I think he hates me for moving us here. It hasn't been as hard on Dalton." Now Julia felt like the one sharing her struggles with life, but talking with Mills felt safe to her. The old man had a lot of years and wisdom under his belt.

"Nothing stays secret around here for long. Marriage trouble ain't as bad as finding out married couples you have known for years are secretly swingers," Mills quipped. "Just give the oldest boy time. This community tends to grow on people. Boys his age already cause trouble without going through what your family has. Some never grow out of it—my jail's full of them."

That shook Julia a bit. She truly hoped Brett could forgive her and his father with time. Hopefully, Mattfield was as promising as the sheriff believed.

He'd also happened to drop in that there were apparently swingers in Mattfield. She pushed that puzzling thought out of her head.

"Thank you. It has been tough on me. I ran home when my marriage ran into trouble. Pulled the boys away from what they've known their entire lives. Just putting the pieces into place now, hoping they'll fit," Julia said. Her eyes started to water, but she resisted the urge to cry. Instead, she opted to lower her face to mask the pain. "Anyway, you probably want to get going. Did you have any concerns today for your checkup?" The tears were successfully choked back and Julia pivoted back to nurse practitioner.

"My health has been kind of boring the last few years. A good thing, I guess. I usually just get a blood panel done to make sure all that looks up to snuff," the sheriff replied as he stood up from the patient bed he had been seated on.

"I was going to insist on that, but you beat me to it. I'll have you go down the hall and the nurse will steal some blood. If you have any concerns before you head out to see the world, don't put it off," Julia instructed.

"Yes, ma'am. It was nice chatting with you this morning, Julia. Sure are glad to have you back. If you and the boys need anything, you let me know. If your boys are causing trouble, I'll let *you* know." Mills smiled as he opened the door. He paused as he was exiting and made eye contact with her. "A word of advice, if I may. Keep your head up. I can tell you're strong just by looking at you. Raising two boys on your own is tough work. Just know," the sheriff paused for a second as if choosing his words wisely, "I've been married forty years. The only way it works is a lot of forgiveness and a lot of grace." Mills tipped his head and walked out.

Julia walked over and shut the door. Tears flowed down her cheeks. Unable to choke back her emotions any longer, she slid down the door, sobbing. There she sat on the floor, hands covering her face. This was just the beginning of the first day. Would it get easier than this? Was everyone going to have sage advice to share with her about marriage? She thudded her head back against the door, then let her arms fall to her sides.

Forgiveness only got you so far. If she could easily forgive Michael, she'd happily still be in the city at their home, and Brett wouldn't be angry with them. Julia felt such resentment for Michael one moment, then guilty the next. She knew life wasn't about what was fair.

Making the choice to move was the right decision. Happiness was never the reason for moving. It didn't feel like running away, either. Room to heal, room to grow. This was what she had to do. If for nothing else but her own sanity.

Keep your head up, she thought. *The only way forward is to keep your head up. Time away is valuable.*

Maybe time would allow her to forgive Michael. Or maybe her love for him would die completely.

Julia took a deep breath. Climbing to her feet, she walked over to the counter. She leaned over the sink and turned on the cold water. She splashed the frigid water onto her face. It was therapeutic. Grabbing a handful of tissues, Julia dried her face.

Everything will work out the way it's meant to, she told herself. *One day at a time.*

Turning off the water, she exited the room en route to visit her next patient.

The rest of the day went by smoothly.

One emotional outburst—not too bad, she thought.

Rural medicine should have been something she considered taking up sooner. All the patients had welcomed her to town. The sheriff wasn't wrong, though; she really didn't know any of the patients. Mattfield had changed. The demographic, anyway. People move, but the feel of the town seemed in line with what she remembered.

Minus the swingers—that was new.

Finishing up patient notes in her office, she heard Debra's voice out in the hall. Time flies. Julia scooped up her belongings and shut the office door as she exited.

"Welcome back. I hope you slept well," Julia greeted Debra. "I thought about it today some, and I would love to pick up some night shifts for you. I can go ahead and get that on our schedules."

Debra lit up with excitement. "You do not know how much that would mean to me. I would love to see the light of day—at least for a solid week."

"Let's make it happen. Any week in particular you want?" Julia offered.

"Well . . . I know you have high school boys, So this may be a big ask, but would you be willing to take homecoming week? If not, I understand, but it would mean a lot to me," Debra answered kindly.

Damn, Julia thought. She really wanted to be present for her boys. What if one of them got nominated for homecoming king? Then there was the dance after the football game. When Julia made the offer, she hadn't considered the consequences. Now she'd painted herself into a corner. Debra deserved the daytime shift and, of course, there was always a trade-off involving family.

Julia wrestled with her emotions without letting her expression show her disappointment. "I will take homecoming week for you." The words parted from Julia's lips, stinging the whole way out.

"Thank you so much. You're a lifesaver," Debra said.

"Well, that's the job," Julia replied, smiling. She was getting better at concealing negative emotion.

Is that a good thing? she wondered.

Debra laughed at her response. "I better make my rounds and start getting everything settled in for the evening. Have a good night!"

"Have a good night, Debra," Julia replied as she walked past her and out the door into the August heat.

It wasn't like she had just been outsmarted or defeated, but Julia felt immediate regret. She was going to miss the boys' homecoming. Those are moments you can't get back. Julia swung the door open on her vehicle and crawled in to what felt like an oven. Sitting and baking in the sun all day, she would hate to guess the internal temperature.

"Thank God for air conditioning," Julia said as the vehicle roared to life. She had the AC cranked up and roaring like a jet engine. She pulled out her phone and called her dad over the car's Bluetooth system. Julia started the journey home as the phone rang through the speakers, awaiting an answer.

Walt answered jovially, "Hello."

Julia couldn't help but smile at how friendly her dad always answered when anyone called. "Hey, Dad, just left work. Did you check on the boys today? Hopefully there's still a house standing to go home to."

"Oh, they're good boys. I stopped by around noon and the house was still there. They were inside playing video games. Said they didn't want to go outside because it was too hot. Back in my day, we hauled hay in this weather. Tractors didn't have cabs on them, didn't know anyone who could afford one. We weren't allowed to sit around," Walt rambled to his daughter.

"The world has changed a lot," Julia replied. "The last twenty-five years alone, it's changed a hell of a lot. Barely get kids to go outside and play anymore. Thank you for stopping in and checking on them. I worry a lot. These last few weeks have put them through the ringer."

"School is about to start. Those boys will be fine," Walt reassured her. "Soon enough, they'll be making friends and chasing girls. The good things in life tend to make you forget about the bad. Give them a few weeks to assimilate into Mattfield and things will be back to normal."

He was right. Once the school year kicked off, they would both get caught up in it all. They always had each other's backs, minus occasionally trying to kill the other.

"Thanks, Dad. Day started off not great. Chatted with Sheriff Mills. He was my first patient this morning. Got me feeling a little down. The rest of the day, I started to feel like this is where I'm supposed to be," Julia confided.

"You in trouble with the law already? I thought you outgrew that," Walt jested. "You knew it was going to be tough starting over. Give your family time and grace to adjust. Things are going to get better," he finished.

Julia turned the car into the driveway and parked in front of the garage next to Brett's truck. "Well, Dad, I just got home. I'm going to make sure the boys are alive. I'll talk to you tomorrow."

"Alright, you have a good night. Keep your chin up," Walt said warmly.

"Good night," Julia said, nodding to herself as she ended the call.

It was good to be home. Julia was well compensated for her work hours, but the days were long.

She collected her belongings and exited her car. One last stroll in this heat. Fall was around the corner and she could not wait for sweater weather. She pushed her way inside, then hung her purse and keys on a coat hanger to the side of the entryway. "Boys, I'm home," her voice rang out through the house.

Dalton came flying down the stairs to greet her. "Hey, Mom! How was your first day?"

"Oh, it was alright. Where's your brother?" Julia asked.

Dalton turned around and pointed up. "Brett! Mom's home!" Dalton hollered.

Footsteps rumbled as Brett made his way down the staircase. "It's about time," he greeted his mom.

"Yeah, well, some of us have to work to feed our families, don't we?" Julia fired back. "What do you guys want for dinner?"

The boys looked at each other and both exclaimed, "Pizza!"

"Go figure. Alright, I'll throw a pizza in the oven," Julia said, heading toward the kitchen.

Brett followed behind her. "Hey, I'm going to play football this year. These country kids won't like me if I don't play."

"Oh, I didn't think you liked football," Julia replied.

"I don't, really, but I have to try and fit in out here."

"Look, don't do something if it's not what you want to do. You'll make friends, regardless," Julia told him. She was happy he was engaging with her. They had not talked about anything for a while now.

"I didn't want to move to the country, but here we are," Brett fired back. The tone of his voice was meant to sting. "So while I'm doing things I have no interest in, I guess I'll play football." With that, he had already turned and exited the kitchen, followed by the sound of his feet gliding up the staircase.

Julia just had to bear the blow. The glimmer of hope the conversation at first sparked had immediately died.

As she was sliding the frozen pizza into the oven, she had a startling realization. Brett was going to be on the football team. Her eldest son's senior year, he would be on the field for the homecoming game. Julia suddenly felt even worse for taking the night shift that week. The fresh start she envisioned for her family in Mattfield was feeling more like a battle.

A battle she was quickly losing.

3

FOUNDATION

Dalton awoke and sprung out of his bed. The first day of the new school year had finally arrived. He was ready to see what Mattfield High was all about. Hopefully, he could make some quick friends. He needed someone else to talk to besides Brett. His brother had been a completely different person ever since their parents split. Almost impossible to be around after their mother relocated them to the country.

Dalton combed through his closet and drawers and put on an outfit he felt suitable for first impressions.

Brett had decided to play for the football team, so he was already ahead in getting acquainted with new friends. Luckily, two-a-day practice in the August heat had taken a lot of the fight out of his brother. It was a good distraction for him. Plus, he knew Brett had his eyes on a girl they met the day they moved to town.

Dalton grabbed his new maroon backpack. He had taken some time last night to fill it with the school supplies he would need, which wasn't a lot. The school would issue each student a laptop today. He loved physically writing compared to typing everything. He wondered if he'd been born too late sometimes. Computers had taken control. Super computers were the future. It all just felt so artificial to him. Virtual over physical reality.

Dalton dragged his class schedule off his dresser as he exited the bedroom and made his way downstairs.

"Good morning. Ready for the big day?" Julia greeted him.

"Morning, Mom. Ready as I'll ever be. Tired of sitting around the house."

"I made you some bacon and scrambled eggs. Eat real quick and I'll drop you off on my way to work," Julia said cheerfully.

Dalton swung his backpack strap over the back of a chair and sat down at the table to eat. "Do you hear the coyotes at night? Man, they're creepy," he said before chewing on a slice of bacon. It was like having little girls surrounding the house at night and laughing. The worst you got in the city was a car alarm or sirens.

"Yeah, I hear them. They're nothing to worry about. The trade-off for all the man-made noise in the city is the sound of nature," his mother reassured him. "I doubt you ever see a coyote out here. They're like medium-sized dogs. Plus, people shoot them, so they avoid us at all costs."

Dalton hadn't thought of it that way. He complained to himself about everything over relying on computers. Car alarms and sirens fall into the same category. Real versus artificial. He just needed more time to desensitize to country life. Sounds were abundant here. Natural sounds like cicadas buzzing, birds singing, and leaves rustling in the wind. He just didn't know why one of them had to be evil-sounding dogs that only come out at night. In his fright the first night, he heard them and woke up Brett, then he had googled "coyotes." He thought they looked like wolves. It was good to know they didn't pose a threat.

After he had finished shoveling the rest of the scrambled eggs into his mouth, Dalton put the plate and fork into the sink. "Alright, mom, it's go time," Dalton said, swinging his backpack over his right shoulder.

The drive to school was only ten minutes from their home. Dalton couldn't help but think back on living closer to his school in the city, but it took longer to get there. The nerves of the first day in a new place started kicking in as his mom brought the car to a stop in front of Mattfield High.

"This place looks like a prison," he said, sharing his brother's sentiment. He observed that it was all a single-colored, tan stone. Besides the glass entryway, the building sported only a few windows in the front, a massive single-story complex that stretched outwards in multiple directions. The area he could only imagine being the gym was twice as tall as the other walls, with no windows. A line of kids was unloading from school buses and vehicles in the parking lot, streaming inside like ants.

"Well, it actually was originally designed to be a high school for ten years before being converted into a prison to house overflow prisoners from other places. That was over fifty years ago." His mom laughed. "In the last ten years, they've done a lot of upgrading to the place."

"Great, I'm off to prison. Always thought it was going to be Brett," Dalton said, stepping out of the car. "Thanks for driving me. I hate the bus."

"Don't you worry; it's a small school. You'll see your brother a lot. You boys look out for each other," Julia added as she put the car back in gear.

"Yes, Mom. Have a good day at work," Dalton replied, and shut the door. The Trailblazer accelerated until it turned onto the highway and zoomed off back to Mattfield.

Dalton turned his attention to the front entrance.

Here we go, he thought.

Jumping into the line of ants, Dalton funneled toward the glass front doors and into the building. The school did look a lot nicer than he had imagined from the outside. Through windows in the doors to his right, he looked into the gymnasium. It was brightly lit with LED lights, new black aluminum bleachers, and the shine of the freshly polished basketball court. The gym doors burst open as a stream of football players who just finished morning practice blended into the crowd. He joined their march farther into the school complex, passing the offices where the principal and the rest of the staff was housed. Next up was a wide-open cafeteria with white, octagonal tables surrounded by navy blue plastic chairs.

As he walked, Dalton got hit with a shoulder square in the back. "Hey! There you are. What class do you have first?" Brett quizzed.

"Some things are the same here as our other school. Football players use too much Axe body spray. I've got Kansas history first. What about you?" Dalton fired back.

"Not too late to join the team. I'm off to English 101, doubles as college credits. Not a great way to start the day off," Brett said, disappointed.

Dalton noticed his brother's eyes dart toward Cassie, coming toward them. "I'm going to leave you to it. We have the same lunch. I'll catch up to you then."

He heard his brother greet Cassie behind him as Dalton navigated onward.

The school had two hallways branching off from the cafeteria, both running in the same direction. The bathrooms, library, and a classroom were positioned down the middle of the hallways. At the end, it made a ninety-degree turn toward the other hallway, forming a rectangle to traverse around to all the rooms. The classrooms in this part of the building were on the outside perimeter of the rectangle hallway.

Dalton made a full loop, exiting the cafeteria down the left hallway and coming back to the cafeteria down the right hallway. Most of the classes he had with block scheduling would be right here in the two hallways. He scheduled an ag class, which would be in a separate building outside the gym, and a physical education class for some fun and exercise.

Starting down the left hallway again, Dalton wandered into the third classroom on his left. Mr. Kincaid's classroom was decorated with posters of historical figures and quotes. Dalton immediately noticed a poster of Winston Churchill on the back wall. Mr. Kincaid had good taste. Dalton had done a report on Churchill and had a lot of respect for the man.

The classroom desks were laid out in a grid. Six rows of five desks each faced a white board that stretched the length of the room. Mr. Kincaid's desk was positioned beside the classroom door. The room had a solitary rectangle window in the center of the outside wall. It allowed a glimpse of the outside world, and for some of the sun's morning light to spill into the room.

Seats in the classroom were filling up quickly as students flooded in through the open door. Dalton grabbed a seat in the second row from the front, slinging his backpack off and tucking it between his feet. His seat was right next to the teacher's desk. He took notice of the poster over Mr. Kincaid's, a print of the painting *Tragic Prelude*, the most famous image of John Brown.

"New kid, yeah?" a voice said behind him.

He turned around to address them. "Hey, my name's Dalton." He extended his hand.

"Henry," the student replied, reaching out and shaking Dalton's hand.

Henry was a scrawny, pale, freckled ginger kid. His deep orange hair was kept short with a fade cut. He was so pale, Henry's pearly white smile was made less impressive by it. Henry wore blue jeans, dirty square-toed cowboy boots, and sported a plain brown T-shirt.

"We don't get many new kids around here," Henry said.

"My family is from Mattfield. Mom's side, so we're coming home," Dalton replied. "My brother is mad about it, but I like it here."

"Is Brett your brother?" Henry asked.

"That's the one," Dalton said.

"We're on the football team together. He's pretty good. Told us he didn't play football at his last school. I'm glad he's on our team. You should join," Henry said excitedly.

"It's not really for me, but I'll think about it," Dalton answered honestly.

What is this, a cult? Everyone keeps asking.

He knew it wouldn't kill him to play football. A school this small, it was all hands on deck with getting as many kids to play as possible.

A middle-aged, average-sized man walked into the classroom, the door swinging freely shut behind him with a slam. He had a shaved head, a pair of low-profile glasses, and a goatee. Mr. Kincaid wore light-brown dress shoes, khaki dress pants, and a red polo.

"Welcome back to school. I know you are all so happy to be here and starting with me this lovely morning. Welcome back to my classroom for most of you. If you don't know me, I am Mr. Kincaid. This semester we'll be covering Kansas state history. The world will tell you we are a flyover state. We sit in the heart of the United States. There is no better place on earth. Abilene, northwest of here a few hours, is the geographical center of the lower forty-eight states." His voice was soft but assertive. Dalton knew immediately this man was a passionate teacher.

"Now, there won't be much learning today because, as you know, this is a short week. How nice of them to break you guys in slowly by starting school on a Friday. That said, I've got slips of paper in a jar on my desk. You'll each be drawing a topic. These topics have to do with subjects we'll be covering this semester. So, I'm going to write them on the whiteboard. You guys line up and draw a topic. Next week, you will each be responsible for a five-minute presentation on the topic you draw. When you get your school-issued laptops today, you can use PowerPoint, but it is not a requirement."

Dalton, being the closest to the jar, was the first in line. He reached in and pushed the slips of paper around with his fingers before making a selection. Returning a few steps to his desk, he unfolded the slip of paper. MATTFIELD was scrawled across it. A presentation on Mattfield? The prospect didn't excite Dalton.

He turned his attention to the whiteboard to see some of the other available topics. Mr. Kincaid had already written "Bleeding Kansas, Jayhawkers, Bushwhackers, strip mining, the Underground Railroad, the Battle of Mine Creek, the Native American relocation, Dwight D. Eisenhower, Amelia Earhart, Zebulon Pike, and John Brown" on the board. Dalton was intrigued by what this semester had to offer.

Everyone finished drawing their topics and returned to their desks. Mr. Kincaid then read each topic and wrote down the students' names who'd drawn that slip of paper. Dalton watched as the whiteboard filled up with names.

Henry had drawn Edmund G. Ross. Dalton had never heard of the man.

"Mattfield?" Mr. Kincaid called out.

"That's me," Dalton answered.

Mr. Kincaid turned and stared at him for a second. "Dalton, right? Dalton, why don't you stand up and introduce yourself, and tell the class a little about who you are." Mr. Kincaid motioned with his hand for him to stand up.

The pain of being the new kid at school. Dalton sighed as he stood up. "Hey, everyone, I'm Dalton, obviously. My family just moved from the city. It's a lot different here. Not what I'm used to, but change can be good, and I like it so far." With that, Dalton immediately returned to his seat.

"Good. Thank you, Dalton. You drew Mattfield. If you like history at all, you'll enjoy that. We had a small Civil War fort here. The cemetery has a section for soldiers who died in the Civil War. Mattfield served as a hub for the railroad and on the Underground Railroad for runaway slaves. The Osage were forcefully relocated to this area before being pushed farther south into Oklahoma. Putting together your presentation, you'll learn a lot about the community you've joined," Mr. Kincaid said enthusiastically.

"People from other parts of the country can say a lot about Kansas being boring in modern times, but we're all here because of the important historical events that happened all around us. It is the foundation our lives are built upon.

"That's all I have for today. You can hang out and catch up until class is over. The tech guys should be coming by to check out laptops to everyone for the school year. Keep the noise down."

"Man, first day of school and we already have homework," Henry said.

"They never waste much time, do they," Dalton added.

"Any idea who Edmund G. Ross is? Never even heard of this guy." Henry held up his slip of paper, looking confused.

"No, but you're going to fill me in next week," Dalton replied with a smile.

That made Henry smile back. "Yeah, I guess so."

The classroom was full of huddled students, chattering. The door swung open as the tech guys rolled in the laptop carts. One by one, the class had their names called and a laptop checked out to them. Just like that, the room went silent again as everyone went from chatting to surfing the web.

Dalton thought about that for a few moments. What a curious place his generation was in.

Well, he might as well get a jump on his project research with everyone else being consumed, Dalton decided.

He opened up the web browser and typed in "Mattfield, Kansas history." He skipped over the Wikipedia entry, opting for a personal blog of research history someone had done themselves. He opened a Microsoft Word document to take down the notes he found relevant to his project.

The Kansas–Nebraska Act of 1854 opened up the settlement of the Kansas Territory. Mattfield was founded by Howard Mattfield in 1855. It was founded on land belonging to the Osage Tribe, who had been relocated to Kansas in 1825. Residents of the town harbored slaves fleeing north as a stop on the Underground Railroad. This led to bloodshed with western Missouri in the period known as Bleeding Kansas. Kansas was recognized as a Union state in 1861. During the Civil War, Mattfield suffered two attacks from the Confederacy on the same day in 1864 as they fled south from a defeat at the Battle of Westport. With the South's surrender, the Civil War came to a close in 1865. Mr. Kincaid wasn't lying. This town had a ton of history running through its veins.

The Native American history of the area ran deep from being multiple tribes' historical lands to lands they were forcefully relocated to as the settlement of the United States continued to push westward. War between tribes. War with European settlers. Epidemics of small pox decimating their population. The United States government eventually moved the tribes that called the Great Plains home farther south into Oklahoma after years of broken treaties. Unfortunately, they encountered more troubles once they were relocated there.

A loud ring cut the quiet pecking of keyboards. Dalton shut his computer and tucked it into his backpack. One class down for the day. He wondered how much homework the first day would bring.

The mad dash for the hallway and the temporary freedom of walking to the next classroom ensued. He waded out into the hallway and moved with the chaotic flow of students toward biology class.

After Mr. Kirk's biology, he was on to computer science with Mrs. Bourdon. Finally, the next stop was lunch. He intended to sit with Brett, but his brother was busy socializing with some of the football guys.

"Hey, sit at my table. I'll introduce you to my friends," Henry invited as they stood in line shuffling toward their allotted portion of food.

"For sure. I've never been the new kid in school before. Not many people have talked to me yet," Dalton confided.

"Yeah, it's different around here. A lot of us grew up together or played sports together since grade school," Henry explained, emphasizing the fact that many of them are actually related. "They'll warm up to you. This is more like joining a family than a new school. Less than three hundred of us in this building."

"Wow, the school I went to in the city had more kids than that in just my class," Dalton said, surprised.

"Everyone will know everything about you here. It kinda sucks. Your family will know about it before you get home," Henry expressed. "Unfortunately, it is what it is."

That concept was odd to Dalton. Things in Mattfield were a lot more personal. There was no concept of privacy. At the same time, it made him feel some type of way about not just being a face or a number. A whole community would be invested in you.

School lunch started out on the right foot with pasta. Although it was never enough food for a high school–aged boy. Dalton carried his tray and took a seat with Henry and his friends. He picked up what Henry had mentioned: these guys were all tightly knit. They all had long histories together. Indeed, some of them were related. Two of the guys, Trey and Larry, were second cousins. The physical resemblance between the two was vast, but the way they talked with each other, you would assume they were brothers.

The table laughed and joked with each other. Dalton was included in the conversations and it all started to feel natural to him. Before lunch had finished, the group dubbed him "city boy." There were a lot worse nicknames one could get in high school, so he was fine with it.

After lunch was ag sales class. All the rural schools had agriculture classes, apparently. A third of the school participated in the FFA organization, which was great for developing skills you would need post high school. You could take ag classes like sales or leadership without being in the FFA, but the two went together seamlessly.

Dalton left his first ag class intrigued by the idea of getting more involved. PE class followed that. Finally, his class schedule rounded out the day with trigonometry. As much as some of the other subjects in school fascinated him, math was not one of them. Not that he was bad at math; it just never held his attention.

Today marked the end of Brett's two-a-day football practice. He'd have practice after school every day during the season. Dalton convinced his grandpa to give him a ride home from school until he could get a vehicle of his own. Exiting school at the end of the day was the polar opposite of entering in the morning. With the sound of the final bell freeing the students, they erupted from the school exits like lava from a volcano. Spilling out into the buses and the parking lot. They had only been back a single day this week, but the excitement of a weekend without classes was already upon them.

Dalton spotted his grandfather's slate-colored Chevrolet 1500 parked in the mess of cars. He jumped into the passenger seat, securing his backpack with the newly issued laptop on the floorboard. "Hey, Grandpa, thanks for the ride. From all the cars and trucks out here, it looks like I'm the only one not driving to school," Dalton said, shutting the door behind him.

"I try not to come this way when school's getting out. It's like prisoners escaping, the way some kids drive out of here," Walt jested. "How was the first day at the old school?" With that, the truck wove into traffic and made it out onto the highway.

"Different, for sure. In a good way, I think. Everyone here knows each other so well. I think I started to make some new friends." Dalton tried describing his thoughts as best he could.

"Good, good. You can make friends for life in a school like this. A few of these kids who have grown up together since kindergarten even get married," Walt shared. "Meet any girls yet? That homecoming dance will be here before you know it."

"I got put next to a girl in biology class. Sara, she was nice. Seems to gossip a lot, though. Other than that, a lot of people have started to call me 'city boy.'" Dalton was flustered.

That made his grandpa laugh. "Well, you're a country boy now. Half of them kids live in Mattfield. I'd tell them you're more country than they are," Walt advised.

Dalton shot back, "I'm not trying to get beat up." He knew his grandfather was joking, or at least half joking.

For the remainder of the trip, they talked about home life and how Brett and his mother were doing. Dalton had never lived near a grandparent before. Conversations with his grandpa made him feel like he'd been missing out on that connection for years. Part of who he was and where his family came from was represented in Walt.

Walt turned his truck into the driveway of the white house with the white picket fence, which was strangely starting to feel more and more like home. When the truck came to an abrupt stop out front, Dalton opened his door and grabbed his backpack. "Thanks again for the ride, Grandpa."

"It's no big deal. I like getting to spend time with you. Gives me something to do besides going to the local watering hole. Same time on Monday?" Walt asked.

"Same time on Monday. Maybe I drive next time?" Dalton figured it was worth a shot.

"I don't see why not. I've lived a long enough life." Walt never ran out of jokes.

"See you on Monday." Dalton shut the truck door and headed inside the house.

He walked straight to the living room, unzipping his backpack and sliding the laptop out. Taking a seat on the couch, he thought how nice the cool furniture felt. Brett was probably miserable in pads and a helmet right now.

On the screen, he clicked on the open web browser tab where he'd been gathering information for the Mattfield history project.

The Native Americans were relocated to Oklahoma in 1870. Glossing through the town's history, the momentous events in Mattfield really started to slow down. Tornado damage in the 1930s. A handful of bank robberies over the 20th century. For a town that was involved in pivotal events in the Civil War era, Mattfield started to fly under the radar. There was enough information to easily put together a five-minute presentation, at least. All of this from a single source.

Deciding to be thorough in his research, Dalton scanned more Mattfield search results. One caught his immediate attention as he scrolled. "The Hidden Events of Mattfield." As much as he hated stuff that freaked him out, the headline was intriguing enough for a click. This was also someone's blog post. Getting into the weeds a little on reliability, but maybe a fun tidbit could be found for the presentation.

Dalton read the blog, trying to glean anything that stood out. The post was wordy at first, making sure the reader knew it was a big deal that a cover-up took place.

Sometime after the close of the Civil War, there was an unexplained rash of grisly deaths in Mattfield: people, cattle, and horses mutilated. Speculation of the events being so violent in nature that only a large animal, not native to the area, could be responsible. Some immediately blamed the Indians who lived nearby. Others, with the bloodshed of the Civil War still fresh in their minds, immediately placed blame on western Missourians. What was described as a large black dog was spotted numerous times in the area surrounding Mattfield. The events happened for two months, taking the lives of eleven people, all of whom were buried in the Mattfield cemetery, the dates on the tombstones matching up to the events in question. A man was arrested, stood trial, and was sentenced to death for the crimes.

A serial killer in Mattfield? Dalton was shocked. What he read next was more shocking. The man, as the story goes, couldn't die. After many failed executions, a group of men from the town took him away on horseback. They all returned later that day without the prisoner. The men never spoke of it again. The few months of newspapers reporting on it were missing from the historical record at the library. The only newspapers missing from the historical records were April, May, and June 1869.

This blog was definitely creeping Dalton out. Especially being home alone. It also made him want to look further into the information presented. The missing newspapers were easily checkable. So were the graves at the cemetery. Although the names weren't given for the deceased, there was an established time frame in 1869 to identify them. Of course, none of that would confirm a brutal killer murdered them. Brett liked weird stuff like this. Maybe he would want to help with research.

The blog presented a lot of mystery with no answers. Most of the information was collected from old-timers willing to tell the ghost story. Dalton wondered if his grandpa knew anything about this. He also wondered if it was weird to ask someone about an alleged murder spree.

He finished skimming through the blog. To his surprise, there was another weird incident recorded—about a house in the countryside somewhere around Mattfield known as the Indian House. This one had an image, too. A black-and-white photo of a two-story stone house, easily a hundred years old. The yard of the house, situated on a hilltop, ended with the drop-off of a rock bluff. Dalton imagined the house was haunted from the day it was built. Shortly after the home was completed, it was abandoned. Family after family tried and moved on from living there. Stories persisted about the ground itself being cursed.

Then, in 1999, a married couple with their young son from North Carolina purchased and moved into the home. The father made his money as an author. That family stayed in the home for almost two years—until their young son went missing. Shortly thereafter, the parents also disappeared. Obvious theories exist about the parents being responsible for the death of the boy and fleeing justice when the walls closed in. The blog post finished the story, explaining no remains or evidence of a crime involving the boy had been found. To this day, the federal authorities had not located the parents.

Dalton exited the web browser and shut his laptop. That was enough horror stories for one day. The blog had just enough details to make his imagination run wild in the worst possible ways. He hoped someone else would be home soon so he wasn't sitting around alone.

Maybe old towns like Mattfield had a strange story or two attached to their history. Historical places did tend to have ghost stories. A town that could serve as a hub on the Underground Railroad would've been experienced in keeping secrets that were in Mattfield's roots. But covering up murders was an odd thing to do.

Did those roots extend into blood-soaked ground?

4

SNIPE

Sweat streamed down Brett's face inside his football helmet. His eyes felt the burn of the salt. Helmet and pads were doubling as an oven for the early August practices. A miserable experience.

Brett was loving every second.

At his previous school, he would have been a fairly average player. Here at Mattfield High, he was standing out. Two-a-day practice had ended yesterday. Sadly, they were back at practice on a Saturday morning. His coaches wanted to make sure they were all ready to go for the fast-approaching season opener.

Football gave Brett the break he wanted from his home life. A release for his pent-up aggression and pain. Although he would never admit it to his mom, Mattfield was better than he imagined.

Brett was playing wide receiver on offense and cornerback on defense. Football at a 2A school meant everyone pulled double time on both sides of the ball. The team had few backups at its disposal. There were pros and cons to it. You had to be in better shape to make it through a full game, but playing positions that mirrored each other was beneficial in understanding and improving your game. Falling asleep at night would no longer be an issue. Both positions did a lot of full throttle sprinting.

The roles also guaranteed physical contact. Escaping exhaustion was impossible. Endurance was the key. Brett knew by season's end, this would be the best shape his body had ever achieved. He was thrilled to try and maintain his newfound ability into track season.

Practice always closed with a two-minute drill. All the players that started on the eleven-man offense would go against the depth players on defense. In two minutes, they'd drive the field and have to secure a score. Failing to do so resulted in extra sprints before leaving practice. Once that outcome had come to fruition, the roles were reversed. Not securing a stop also brought extra sprints at the end of practice. So after a full two-hour practice, the players had to play with the lights out during the drill or suffer the consequences.

The possibility was always on the table to double up on sprints by not being successful on either side of the ball. Most of the starters on offense started on defense. The drill forced them to push through any moments of weakness. This was a grueling drill with dire consequences. You couldn't look weak in front of your teammates. Getting the blame for end-of-practice sprints was not an honor any of them desired. A mentally and physically brutal affair meant leaving your selfish desires behind and making sure your team succeeded. Today marked the first time the starters rallied to victory on both offense and defense. A monumental task achieved.

Brett, although new to the school and the team, had emerged as a leader. The rage from his personal life was turning into a noticeable advantage. Football was his outlet. Passion translated into a physical sport was paying dividends. To tune out his unhappiness, he put everything into being a monster on the field. With that fire, he was gaining respect. His teammates and coaches had taken notice.

Head Coach Keith Sparts blew his whistle, signaling the team to gather to him. The players referred to him as Coach at all times out of respect, whether on the street or at practice. Coach had a massive physique, towering over most at 6'4". A former college football linebacker and all-American in Division II football playing for the Pittsburg State University Gorillas. Any dream of furthering his career ended with a knee injury, causing him to miss any opportunities post college ball.

Sparts returned to his hometown of Mattfield and joined the police department. Working his way up to the second in charge as undersheriff. Coach was thirty-four years old, and seemed to excel at whatever he put his efforts into. He was a leader of young men. A shining example to his community of dedication and success. Brett and his teammates would run through fire for the man.

The players gathered, taking a knee in front of Coach and his assistants.

"Progress, boys," Coach began. "This is the payoff to two-a-day practices. What you accomplished today shows you are learning and getting better. Now, it wasn't always pretty. You have a long way to go yet. Football isn't about looking pretty. This season is a marathon, not a sprint. Going forward, we'll have a game every Friday night, and that'll be our gauge for how we continue to improve. From now on, practices will be Monday through Thursday. Those are our only days to get better. Saturday mornings we'll watch the previous night's game film. This is it. We're out of the fire and into the furnace." Coach's voice boomed. "I'm proud of how much some of you have improved over last year. We don't get the luxury of extra bodies. Becoming a finely tuned machine is our only option. Freshmen, it can be overwhelming. Continue to work hard. Everything gets earned on the field, not given."

Brett and his teammates looked around, giving the freshman nods of approval. Signifying to them they were on the right track. "As your coaches, we are the ultimate authority. With that, we like to nominate a few of your peers each season to be the leaders of the team. These leaders will guide you, push you, and pick you up when you fall. Leadership comes with its fair share of responsibilities. You are the rule to your teammates, not the exception. You look out for them on and off the field. Football is important, but so is your education. Eligibility for football means getting good grades. Picking your season captains means they are no longer your equals. The burden on them is to make sure all of you become the best football players and students you can be. The role requires accountability, and we expect it. Us coaches may approach one of our captains and set them to task on one of you. Nothing is ever personal here. If you approach criticism as an opportunity to improve, you are setting yourself up for success."

Sparts took a breath, then continued.

"Marcus, you have stood out on and off the field each season. Now, as a senior, it is time for you to take that next step up," Coach proclaimed. "Your teammates look up to you and the example you provide them in striving to be the best you can be. Stand up, Marcus. The coaching staff recognizes you as one of this season's team captains."

Marcus stood up proudly to roaring applause and congratulations from the team. Brett knew as soon as the coaches announced the plan for captains that Marcus would be one. As much tension as there was between them, Brett knew he was a leader.

The group quieted down as Coach continued.

"Captains remain standing until you are all announced. Bradley, stand up. Having big physical players at the line of scrimmage is integral to a team's success. As the left tackle guarding the quarterback's blind side, your job may be the most important there is. Flipping to defense and filling the void as a run stopper, this team doesn't operate without you. Us coaches name you as a team captain."

Just as for Marcus, celebration broke out among the team. Brett could see how much the recognition meant to Bradley. His sweat-beaded face glowed with pride.

"Alright, settle down," Sparts commanded. "We've got one more captain for the season. As you all know, we keep the captain's positions to the seniors on the team. Our quarterback this year is only a junior. That position is the most demanding of all. Leadership is the quarterback. We recognize this so no one feels disappointed. After much discussion, us coaches have decided we are sticking with precedent, only having seniors be team captains. Brett, stand up."

There was a palpable silence amongst the group. Brett confusingly stumbled to his feet.

What the hell is happening? he thought.

He made eye contact with Marcus, who was glaring at him. "This is unconventional because you are new to Mattfield. We don't have a lot of knowledge about you outside of football. But what you have done and the determination you have shown is what led us to this decision. We think your tenacity is unmatched. When we look at you, we see a leader. Brett, you are the third and final team captain."

Brett looked at Coach in disbelief. As with Marcus and Bradley, everyone erupted into cheering. He noticed it wasn't as enthusiastic, but better than imagined.

"Captains, we'll meet daily before practices and games. Good practice everyone. Remember the rules. No partying. Enjoy your weekend. Get your schoolwork done. Big week coming up against the Blue Jays. Go get cleaned up," Coach finished, bringing practice to a close.

Brett unsnapped his chin strap and slid his helmet off his head. A gust of air moved over his face and drenched hair. He was sure the breeze was warm, but after being in a helmet for a couple of hours, it was refreshing nonetheless.

Angling for the locker room, Brett began a slow walk, trying to process the shock of it all.

A hand slapped against Brett's back. "You are a good pick for captain," Henry acknowledged as he jogged past toward the locker room.

"Thank you," Brett called out as Henry moved away from him.

Brett was rethinking how he had been approaching football. What did his coach see in him as a captain? Conflicted by the feelings of the leadership role he was now thrust into, he felt the weight of responsibility. Having the coaches acknowledge him was an honor. Especially Coach. Brett knew going forward he would have to focus on playing football for different reasons than why he had gone out for the sport—a sense of duty to the entire team instilled through a simple promotion.

Marcus and Bradley walked up beside him on the long march. "Well, captains, it's our duty to make sure no one parties tonight," Marcus said with a smile.

Brett could sense the opposite of that statement was being implied. "What do you have in mind?" he replied uneasily.

"We like to go out country cruising. Get a couple of trucks full of people and drive around the dirt roads. We can avoid cops that way. They ruin all the fun," Bradley said.

"It's about time you came out on a Saturday night with us. If you are going to be a real captain, you better be able to hang," Marcus followed up.

"So, what you guys do for fun around here is drive around in the country-side?" Brett tried to sound enthusiastic, but he didn't get how it was supposed to be fun.

"As captains, we want you to prove you belong here," Bradley jabbed.

"Just come out with us tonight. We'll meet in the school parking lot around dark." Marcus ended the conversation as they opened the locker room door and headed inside.

Country cruising was a weird concept for Brett. Was that code for something else? He was tired of being an outsider here. It was clear nothing was going to change unless he engaged his peers.

Brett hit the showers and changed back into his street clothes. Bagging up all his dirty football gear to take home and wash.

Brett threw the bag of sweaty gear in the bed of his truck. His mind now pivoted toward the day ahead. Meeting up with Cassie for lunch was the most exciting prospect. They had fast become close with each other. He had feelings for her already. Was it mutual? He could only daydream about that. Priority number one was not messing things up. With a little time to burn, Brett ran home to be certain he was presentable.

A food truck was in town serving up a selection of BBQ in the grocery store parking lot. Cassie had agreed to meet him there for lunch. Brett whipped in to an open spot. Looking out the passenger window, he saw Cassie already waiting at a picnic table. The owner of the food truck brought a few picnic tables with umbrellas to set up. He appreciated being able to eat and not get scorched. Brett hustled over to her. "Sorry, I hope you haven't been waiting long."

Cassie was wearing a pair of dark-tinted Ray-Ban sunglasses. She smiled at him. "No worries, I haven't been here long. How was football practice? This heat is awful." Her smile was infectious.

"Practice was great. I got named a team captain today. I don't really know what to think about it," he told her honestly.

"Team captain, that's fancy. Be happy about it. Coach doesn't do things willy-nilly," Cassie shared.

"I am happy for sure. I don't know about the other guys. Some of them were just as surprised as I was." Brett found it easy to confide in her.

Cassie lowered her sunglasses with a finger. "Marcus will get over himself. You're the biggest threat he's faced here. He's used to being the golden boy."

Brett found himself surprised at how easy their conversations were. Sometimes he felt like Cassie was reading his mind. "I'm not trying to be a threat. He is a great football player; everyone loves him. Coach made him a captain, too, of course."

"Marcus and I dated a few years ago. He dates around with a lot of girls from different schools. Even though he won't admit it, he still likes me. Most of the girls in school would date him in a heartbeat. I won't. It's one of those want-what-you-can't-have things, so you're a threat."

Brett absorbed what he had just heard and let it sink in. Marcus likes Cassie? He had the impression everyone was just close friends in the group. His mind was racing. Brett tried his best to hide it from his face. Did Cassie just confide that she has feelings for him? They had only gotten the chance to see each other a few times. "I guess that makes sense," Brett mustered.

She was smiling at him again. "That's all you have to say?"

"No, I just . . . I don't know." In Brett's mind, he sounded foolish.

"I see what Coach sees. You're a good one, Brett. Don't let Marcus scare you," Cassie said.

Fireworks were erupting in his head. Cassie clearly noticed that Brett had taken a fast liking to her. Knowing those feelings were mutual melted away his plan of being calm and collected. "Thank you. That means a lot coming from you. I like you. Meeting you on the first day I moved here was the best thing in a long time."

Brett loved seeing her smile at that. "Slow down, city boy. Let's get some food," Cassie said with a laugh.

She instantly brought him back down to earth. "Yes, I'm starving," Brett agreed.

They ordered pulled pork sandwiches from Butt Rub's Food Truck.

For such an oddly named vendor, the food was pretty good, Brett thought.

Trying to be a gentleman, he bought Cassie's lunch. He consciously reminded himself not to talk with a full mouth. Impressions were everything.

"Marcus and Bradley invited me to go country cruising tonight." Brett showed confusion in his voice, hoping she could enlighten him on what that even was.

Cassie laughed. "That's what we do around here. Drive around on dirt roads, seeing what kind of trouble we can get in. You should go with them. They probably want to see if they can scare you. You've never been, so I'll let the rest be a surprise."

That wasn't the reassurance he was looking for. "Okay, I'll go, but that answer doesn't make me less worried," Brett said, shaking his head. What was he getting into?

"Say what you want about how they have fun. Better than out drinking or doing drugs," Cassie offered in justification.

Fair enough, Brett thought. "When you put it like that, I'm all in on country cruising," he replied. "Do you want to come with? I'm not even sure if I can invite someone, but I'd like to go with you."

"Hate to shoot you down, but I made plans with some of my friends tonight. You can text me and let me know how it's going," Cassie offered.

Brett was a little disappointed. He was looking for every opportunity to spend more time with her.

Slow down, he told himself.

"That's okay. You'll hear all about it," he said, smiling at her. He felt goofy, but he was nonstop smiles around her. "Thanks for getting lunch with me today."

"Girls don't pass up free meals—you'll catch on. Besides, I knew it would devastate you if I turned you down. Our first date, yeah?" Cassie flirted.

First, he became a football team captain. Now the girl he met a few weeks ago and caught feelings for felt the same way toward him. Moving to Mattfield was suddenly looking up.

Brett always swore he was unlucky. After today, though, he might find actual gold at the end of a rainbow. "First date sounds good. I'm cool with that," Brett acknowledged in disbelief. Maybe everything that happened in his family was for a reason.

"I have some stuff to get for my parents while I'm in town. You have fun tonight with the guys." Cassie gave Brett a hug goodbye. "Probably just ride along since it's your first time or you'll end up getting lost, or worse. Some of those roads get crazy. A few are dead ends, even."

He agreed with that, and she left him sitting in the shade alone.

What a day it had been, and it was only half over.

Brett arrived back home after the short drive from town. His mind was ablaze with emotions. Anger he felt toward his parents was subsiding. For the first time in weeks, he looked forward to telling his mom about things happening in his life.

Brett grabbed his bag of football gear and took it in the house. The air conditioning sent a shiver down his spine. His mom was sitting in the living room, reading a book. Heading to the laundry room and stuffing all the smelly football gear in the washing machine was priority. He set it for an extra-long wash cycle, then joined his mom in the living room. Brett sat beside her on the couch.

Still feeling conflicted inside, he didn't know where to start, but he embraced the feeling of opening up and talking. "It's been a crazy day, Mom," Brett started.

She looked taken aback. Their conversations had been few, short, and cold as of late. "Are you okay?" Julia asked.

"Better than okay. I thought I would hate moving to Mattfield. My senior year, you know. I left all the friends behind from the city. We still text and play games online and I really miss them. I didn't think I belonged here. Trying to make new friends and start over was a lot. Besides Dalton, I couldn't see how anyone would care I was here."

Brett could see his mother was sad, but also glowing. This meant the world to her. He was finally having a non-hostile conversation.

"Your grandpa told me it would take you boys time. I know this move is hard on you. It was not fair to you, Brett. You need to understand, I have friends I miss, too. We all left a life behind in the city to move here. I didn't want to hurt you. Believe it or not, this has been difficult for me, too. Even though it was my decision, I think about whether I made the right choice every single day. I refuse to talk down about your father to you, or blame him. It was his actions and my reaction. We are here because of both your father and me. He's just not here to be on the receiving end of all the bitterness. It brings me joy to see things going well for you." Julia was tearing up.

Brett took his time to process what his mother was sharing. Not once had he considered how she'd felt about the move. He just assumed this was exactly what she wanted. "I am mad at both of you, but with everything going so well for me here, I'm working on that. I'm a transplant during my senior year. The day we moved in, Dalton and I went to the bar to get something to eat. I met a girl there, Cassie. It's early, but things with her are . . . easy. I don't know, but it's going well.

"I went out for football so I wouldn't have to be here at home. I didn't want to be here. Today, Coach made me a team captain. Only three of us got to be captains; I still can't figure out why I was one of them. I have been playing well, but to be a captain in a new school? Most of those guys grew up together and I barely know them."

His mother's face changed. She looked overjoyed—a sense of pride, even. "All

I want is for you to be happy. I am proud of you. Most people aren't able to look at themselves the ways others see them. Which is humility, and that is a good thing. Just know, Coach picked you to be a captain for a reason. That's a substantial responsibility, one I know you're capable of. I'm also happy you met a girl you like. I would love to hear more about her. Country girls, you need to watch out. They'll steal your heart," Julia replied.

"She's working on it," Brett said with a laugh.

His mom was a country girl, and it definitely worked on his dad. For a while, anyway.

"Some of the football guys invited me out tonight. We're just hanging around Mattfield. Is it okay if I go?"

"Of course, just don't get in trouble or do anything stupid. Also, take your brother along," Julia said.

"Mom, they invited me. I don't even know if I can bring someone else," Brett tried arguing.

"Well, he's your brother, so they'll get over it. I am happy life here for you is improving, but don't throw your brother to the side. You don't want to look back one day and regret not spending more time with Dalton. Family will always be around for you when no one else shows up," Julia lectured him.

Brett was not willing to plead the case any further. "Yes, Mom, okay. I'll take him with me."

"Besides, he is less prone to do the stupid things that *you* do to get in trouble," his mom said with a laugh.

He left the couch, shaking his head, then charged up the staircase toward his bedroom. Passing by Dalton's room, Brett saw his brother sitting in front of his computer. Leaning into Dalton's room, he announced, "Hey, we're going out with a few of the football guys around dark."

Dalton turned toward him. "Have fun with that," he said lazily.

"Mom says you have to go, or you're sleeping outside with the coyotes tonight," Brett shot back.

Dalton rolled his eyes. "Alright, fine, I guess I'm going. By the way, I found some stuff about Mattfield you'd be interested in."

"Town haunted?" Brett asked sarcastically.

"Maybe, but I found this blog. Some weird stuff happened here in the past. Needs to be researched further." Dalton was serious.

Brett didn't know what to make of his brother's vagueness. "A blog? Come on, you can't believe everything you read on the internet, dude. Crazy people are a dime a dozen. Just look at the news."

"I know that. I'm not stupid. The blog had enough information that we could look into it. Probably just a few hours and we'd know if it was bullshit or not," Dalton said.

For whatever reason, Brett got drawn in to dark and unexplained things. Although he was getting the impression most stories were just that—stories. Dalton fed his brother's obsession with the weird of the world. Brett had to part ways with his belief in Bigfoot, though. It just wasn't logical anymore. A giant ape running around in North America with no proof in this day and age. What if Bigfoot was a shape-shifter? The thought crept into his mind.

"You can run what you found by me tonight. If it sounds legit, we'll look into it. I'm going to get a nap in," Brett said as he walked over to his bedroom.

Lying down on his bed, he thought about the rush of excitement happening in all facets of his life. Falling asleep usually took an hour of wrestling with his thoughts. Tossing and turning to get comfortable. Today, he fell asleep with ease.

When Brett opened his eyes again, he sprung to life. Looking out his bedroom window, the light had dimmed as the sun was setting. He felt more confident about country cruising and the adventures tonight had in store.

Dalton appeared in the doorway. "You sleep like a girl."

"Whatever. I don't remember seeing you at two-a-day practice all week."

"Our parents need one kid without brain damage," Dalton said, smirking.

Dalton was never much of a risk-taker. Brett had always been curious about how differently they approached life.

The brothers made their way downstairs together. After rummaging in the refrigerator, they settled on slapping together turkey sandwiches. Brett was hungry enough, he didn't care about yet another sandwich on the day.

A sandwich day, he mused.

Brett's phone buzzed with a text message from Marcus. All he sent was, "It's go time."

"Alright, Dalton, we gotta get moving," Brett told his brother. As they headed to the front door, their mom was waiting for them.

"Remember, use your brains. God gave them to you for a reason. If you go to jail, I'm leaving you there," Julia said.

Brett knew she meant it. He could totally picture getting left in a jail cell by his mom. It was always reassuring knowing that his dad wouldn't leave him locked up, but Dad wasn't a part of their lives anymore.

"We'll be extra careful," Dalton promised.

"What's the worst that could happen?" Brett added. In reality, he was unsure about what the night would present.

Julia shot him a quick glance. "Go have fun. I'd like you home by eleven. Midnight at the latest. I mean it."

The brothers both gave her a hug and headed out the door.

Once inside the truck, Brett shared, "I'll be completely honest with you. We *could* go to jail tonight. Nobody has told me anything about what the hell we're doing. They keep calling it country cruising."

"Luckily for you, jail can't be much worse than staying at home," Dalton replied with a grin.

Brett sped down the highway with the windows down, 98.9 The Rock blaring from the speakers. It was by far his favorite station from Kansas City. By some miracle, it came in clear as day in Mattfield. One less thing he had to leave behind.

Dalton turned off the radio mid-chorus in Creed's "Arms Wide Open."

"Come on, I love that song," Brett said, annoyed.

"Long story short," Dalton began, "I got a history project on Mattfield. This blog I found talked about murders here a long time ago, and the town covered it up. Then, like over twenty years ago, a family living in a house disappeared. The police never found them."

"What? How does that make any kind of sense? How long ago were these first murders?" Brett asked. He was hoping there was at least more to the story.

"I just needed to grab your attention, or you would turn the radio back on," Dalton explained enthusiastically. "So, from what I read, right after the Civil War, eleven people got viciously murdered in Mattfield. No pictures or anything. All the newspapers from when it went down are gone, even though the library keeps records of all that stuff. The best part is, they arrested a man and convicted him for the crimes—a man the blog said could not die. No joke, that is word for word. Some members of the community took him away on horseback and returned without him."

Brett was instantly into the story. "What do you mean, not able to die?"

"No idea. That's all they said about it. An undying man. Okay, and then another story. In the early two thousands, maybe late nineties, a family moved into a home around here somewhere. They all vanished without a trace," Dalton added.

This was all a lot of information to think about. Brett wondered aloud, "So, are the events connected?"

Dalton looked at him like he was a moron. "I mean, around a hundred and twenty-five years apart. The cases differ completely from each other. I don't think so? The blog was just highlighting a few weird stories from Mattfield."

"No, yeah, that makes sense. You think we can do our own research? See if it checks out?" Brett tried to recover.

"Newspaper records and the cemetery are both public. Easy to find clues. I'm not going to the cemetery alone. I thought we could ask these guys tonight. They all grew up here. If anyone knows the stories, it's them."

"This is our first night hanging out. I don't want to be asking them about strange things you found on a blog."

Pulling into the parking lot, Brett drove to the huddle of trucks in the corner. He wasn't aware of how many people were going out tonight. He parked beside a red, lifted Ram 2500.

Dalton quipped, "Think he's compensating?"

"How about we not get our asses kicked tonight, okay?"

They joined the huddle of guys in front of the parked trucks. "Man, why didn't you tell us you were bringing your brother? Anybody have room? Marcus?" Bradley said, annoyed.

"I want the city boys riding with me tonight. I have a lot to teach them," Marcus announced. "Looks like two trucks tonight. Let's hit the gravel."

Brett knew the red Ram truck belonged to Marcus. He couldn't wait to see the look on Dalton's face. As they opened the doors to get in, Brett whispered to his brother, "Still think he's compensating?"

Dalton whispered back, "You have to be shitting me."

"Brett, I want you riding shotgun. Dalton, you're riding bitch tonight," Marcus said.

Dalton riding in the back middle seat amused Brett.

Marcus twisted the key and the hemi engine roared to life. Luckily, his friend, Henry, was on one side of him and the team quarterback, Luke Gill, was on the other. The nightmare scenario would have been getting squeezed between two of the linemen.

Sitting in the passenger seat, Brett saw the wooden handle of a knife sticking up between the center console and Marcus's seat. Marcus caught him checking it out.

Grabbing the handle, Marcus slid it out of its leather sheath. "Grandpa gave me this knife. I don't go anywhere without it." He held it by the blade so Brett could grab the handle.

The knife was beautiful, but clearly antique. Its blade was long and slender, the color dark gray—aged iron, Brett guessed.

"This is one of the coolest knives I've ever seen," Brett marveled.

"Blade is pure silver, believe it or not. Grandpa thought it was an Indian artifact, at first. Turns out after doing research, it probably came to them from the
French or Spanish hundreds of years ago," Marcus proudly said.

Brett put the knife back into Marcus's hand; Marcus slid the knife back into
the sheath beside his seat.

"Any requests for where we go tonight, or you just along for the ride?" Marcus
tossed out.

Without hesitation, Dalton asked, "I read something about the Indian
House? Do you know where that's at?"

Brett turned and shook his head at his brother. "What's the Indian House?"

"Do we know where it's at?" Luke said as he laughed with Henry and Marcus.

"It's close. We'll go there first," Marcus obliged.

They gunned it out of the parking lot onto the highway. This truck had genuine power. They traveled less than a mile and turned onto the first gravel road.

"Believe it or not, it's a few miles down this road," Marcus said.

The truck tore down the road. Each edge had a ditch flanked by never-ending
barbed wire fences. Brett felt nervous at just how fast they were moving. The
moon was full tonight, so at least there was some visibility outside. Out his passenger window, there was nothing to see but empty pasture. It kept his focus on
the road ahead, illuminated by the truck's headlights.

"How fast are we going?" Brett was curious.

"Oh, about sixty-five right now. You ever drive on gravel?" Marcus replied.

No wonder it felt like flying in a plane. The truck felt like it was just drifting
along through space. There was a looseness to it. Brett was having a difficult time
imagining it was safe. "To my grandpa's house a few times," Brett responded.

The truck flew toward a ninety-degree right turn in the road. Marcus slammed
on the brakes to make the angle. Just as the truck steered into it, he hit the gas
again. Brett grabbed the handle over his door to hold on. Marcus slid the truck
through the curve and got it barreling back straight again. Within two hundred
yards, the road did the same thing to the left. Naturally, the lifted truck went
drifting around it, as well. Dalton remained speechless but had sheer panic on

his face.

They cruised through the dark countryside, once again coming to a sharp curve and heading off to the right. Brett was quickly getting the feel for why country cruising was so popular. There was nothing out here to stop you from driving as you pleased. Something about high speed on the gravel roads entailed a feeling of freedom. He was certain what they were doing was dangerous, but the unbridled thrill he felt eclipsed his worry.

The truck rocketed up a steep, tree-covered hill. If not for the full moon, the trees would have created a suffocating layer of darkness in the world around them. The truck lunged onto the top of the hill for a short while before starting the plunge down the other side.

At the bottom of the hill, Marcus mashed the brakes again as water sprayed up over the windshield. He flipped the wipers on, then off again.

"No bridge?" Brett said, startled.

The truck climbed the next hill now. The creek made its path through the middle of the two.

"Nah, around here they don't build bridges at every creek," Marcus explained. "They call them low-water crossings. That one there you just drive across the creek bed. Some of them they put concrete in the bottom so it's paved, but the water runs on top of that so you still have to drive through it."

This was a whole other world—not even that far from where Brett lived most of his life. He found himself in an entirely new realm. No stoplights, no traffic, and apparently not a lot of bridges. The rural area was eliciting an aura of fascination in him.

Marcus slowed the truck at the top of the hill and turned sideways on the road. The headlights shone through two green, tubed gates chained together in the middle. Standing in the middle of a barren yard was a two-story stone house.

"That's the Indian House," Marcus said. "No idea why it gets called that. There were a lot of Native Americans living in these hills back in the day. You know, so I assume. People say it's haunted. Nobody has ever been interested in living in it since the last family disappeared. Needs torn down if you ask me."

Dalton sat forward between the front seats, staring at the house. "That place looks haunted."

"You guys ever been inside?" Brett asked them.

"Hell no. You couldn't pay me to go in there," Henry said.

"I'm not into freaky shit like this. I don't remember the last time we even came out here," Marcus added.

"After seeing it in the dark, I can't say I blame you," Brett replied.

"All good on seeing this little hell on the prairie?" Marcus inquired.

"I mean, it's on a hill, but yeah, I'm good now," Dalton remarked.

"Man riding bitch has jokes. I see you," Marcus said. "Someone get Bradley on the phone. We'll keep cruising and try to meet up with those guys."

The truck drifted and sped through the grid of gravel roads. You could only go so many miles before intersecting a paved county road or highway. It was like a system of veins running atop the earth, access roads and dividing lines carving up the tracts of land. During the cruise, the guys all made small talk and joked with each other. There was never any music played, just the roar of the Hemi.

Brett lost any sense of where they were. Too many twists and turns. Marcus had been driving them around for over an hour at this point. Brett saw a truck up ahead, stopped on the road. It was Bradley's blue Toyota Tundra. Brett rolled down his window as they slid up beside the parked truck.

"About time you guys caught up with us," Bradley said in his gruff, country accent.

"Someone had to show the city boys how we do things out here," Marcus called out across the cab of the truck.

"Speaking of which, we just saw a snipe up here in the ditch. These city boys haven't caught one before," Bradley said, grinning. "What do you say, Brett?"

Brett looked at Marcus. "What is he talking about?"

"Oh, a snipe. That's a big ground bird we have around here. We consider catching one a rite of passage. You're probably not cut out for it, man—honestly," Marcus told him bluntly.

Brett knew they were mocking him. If Bradley could catch one of these birds, he sure as hell could. "If you guys can catch one, I definitely can," Brett declared.

Marcus and Bradley exchanged a look with each other, as if communicating telepathically.

"Well, alright, then," Bradley said in support.

"They're a big, black bird. Long legs, can't fly. Hard to miss. Should be easy for you. This is a two-man job, though. Go stand in the ditch behind the trucks and we'll chase it to you. We use flashlights—it startles them. Unless your brother wants to help you?"

"I'm fine in the truck, thanks." Dalton had zero interest.

"Alright, Brett, just you, then. Hop out and get in place before we move into position."

Screw it, Brett thought. *Hopefully, catching a snipe will help people see I'm not just a city boy. Even better, maybe I'll impress Cassie.*

He hopped out of the truck and walked down into the ditch. The moonlight made everything easy to see once his eyes adjusted. "Alright, I think I'm in place!" he hollered to the trucks. What kind of technique did you need to scope up a bird? Brett didn't know, but he was determined to be successful.

Marcus leaned over and shouted out of the Ram's passenger window, "Hey, man, one more thing you need to know."

"Yeah?" Brett called out.

"Snipes aren't real, dumbass!" Marcus yelled.

With that, both trucks shot off down the road. Clouds of dust filled the air, blocking out any visibility. The taillights vanished into the gravel dust.

Brett clambered out of the ditch, waving his hands. "Wait, guys!" he shouted. Within a minute, the sound of the truck engines had disappeared, as well. "Shit," he said.

Why did he have to fall for such a stupid prank? Brett pulled his cell phone out. No service.

Great. Now what? he thought.

Lost, alone, and in the dark. After five minutes passed just standing in the road, he got the feeling they weren't coming back. Another five minutes went by, and he was almost sure of it. From his best guess, the trucks were heading east. He started walking in the direction they went. At some point, he would at least find a paved road.

Brett kept a careful eye on his phone's service. Thirty seconds of service was all he needed. Make a distress call if necessary. Those guys must have known there was no cell phone service out there.

Brett came upon his first intersection. The top sign read "Jackson Rd." and pointed north and south. He had apparently been traveling on "600 Rd."—the east and west sign. Another sign sat on the left side of the road, pointing north read "Coal Creek Rock Quarry 1 Mile." That meant he was farther out in the countryside than he expected.

He stood at the crossroads, checking his phone again, but still no signal. Brett noticed what time his phone screen showed: 11:17. At this rate, he was going to be late getting home. Anger boiled up inside him.

Then, to his surprise, he heard a vehicle gliding on top of the gravel. Standing at the intersection, he spun around, determining the vehicle was heading at him from the south.

Thank God, he thought. *The guys are coming back.*

From the sound of the vehicle, it was hauling ass; it had to be them. Brett saw a pair of headlights come into view. He waved his hands in the air a few times. The truck was barreling toward him. They were not letting off the gas. At the last second, Brett dove out of the road. With a roar, it passed by like a bullet. Dust rolled in the air all around him once more.

Picking himself up off the ground, he swiped at the dust that covered his clothes. His anger turned to a seething rage. There were minor cuts on both of Brett's forearms, seen from trickles of blood in the light of the full moon. The truck that almost ran him over was much older than any he saw in the school parking lot. As far as he was concerned, this was Marcus and Bradley's fault for abandoning him out here. Not knowing what else to do, Brett trudged on eastward.

Bugs' singing reverberated in his ears. Walking was not calming him down. Every step he took escalated his desire for revenge.

Peering at the phone screen, it read 11:41. Brett knew it was unrealistic to think he'd make it home before midnight.

A thundering boom echoed across the prairie, freezing Brett in his tracks. He felt the faint pulse of an explosion in his chest.

What the hell could that have been? he wondered, pushing down the sudden surge of panic welling up inside. He took off walking, faster this time. Brett barely covered any ground before finding himself frozen again. A distant howl drifted in the air, sending a shiver down his spine—a haunting sound to a lost boy. He stared back over his shoulder. Instincts and fear begun consuming his brain. There weren't any wolves in Kansas. He knew this. And whatever could produce a howl of that magnitude was no coyote or dog.

So what else could it be?

Brett began a slow run down the road, heart pounding with enough alarm that he was becoming lightheaded, crossing two more intersections in less than fifteen minutes. Each intersection he knew was a mile apart.

Finally, he calmed his nerves enough to slow down to a fast walk. To his right, Brett observed a row of round hay bales running parallel to the road. When the wall of large bales ended, he got blinded by a bright light. He immediately dropped to the gravel road.

The light vanished just as quickly as it had hit him.

Seeing spots in front of his eyes, Brett could make out the front of the red Ram truck tucked right at the end of the hay bales. Raucous laughter rang out of the truck cab.

"We were about to go home without you. What the hell took you so long?" Marcus asked.

Brett jumped to his feet and charged toward the driver's door. Ripping the door open, he got his hands on Marcus and dragged him out onto the ground. He was not in control any longer. His right hand clenched into a fist as he swung. Marcus looked stunned as the punch connected with his face.

In an instant, Marcus rolled Brett and locked him in a submission choke hold. "State wrestling champ, bud. You need to settle down. It was just a joke," Marcus said in Brett's ear.

"I almost got run over, you piece of shit," Brett said through gritted teeth.

Marcus released his hold on Brett. They both staggered to their feet. "I'm sorry. We should've come back and got you," Marcus replied, sounding sincere.

"Whatever, man. I was *this* close—" Brett shouted, holding two fingers close together, "—to lying dead in a ditch back there. I'm bleeding, and it's after midnight, when I was supposed to be home! You left me somewhere with no phone service. Not a clue where the hell I'm at. I'm done with you guys. Take us back to my truck."

"Okay, okay. Get in. I'll take you back. We didn't know someone would try to run you over," Marcus said, trying to calm Brett down.

The truck ride back to the school parking lot was dead silent. Not satisfied with the one punch he landed, he didn't feel like adding to the shame of the whole situation by bringing up the explosion and howling, so Brett just kept quiet.

Arriving at the parked trucks, everyone quickly unloaded. Marcus was trying to make amends as Brett exited his truck, slamming the door behind him.

The brothers loaded into Brett's truck and sped home.

"I tried the whole time. They threatened to drag me out and leave me, too," Dalton said, disheartened.

"I'm not mad at you," Brett reassured his brother. "Mom is going to be pissed. It's almost one in the morning."

"I've got your back. It wasn't our fault."

After making record time, Brett and Dalton rushed inside the house.

Their mother was sitting on the couch, waiting for them. "What did I say? I tried calling both of you. I've been sitting here worried sick," Julia chastised.

"Mom, the guys took us out where we didn't have phone service, and left Brett," Dalton explained.

"Brett, you're filthy. Is that blood on your arms? What were you guys doing?"

Julia interrogated.

"Dalton's telling the truth. I got tricked. They left me behind in the middle of nowhere. No signal on my phone. So I just walked until I found them. The guys thought they were playing a joke," Brett said. He wasn't in the mood for any of this. All he wanted was to get cleaned up and go to bed.

"We'll talk more tomorrow. Don't plan on going out anytime soon," Julia scolded as she headed off to her room.

Brett made his way upstairs, heading straight for the bathroom, running warm water in the sink to clean up the cuts on his arms. He felt bad about being late. Bad about not being able to text Cassie.

Country cruising was fun until it wasn't.

Pulling his cell phone out to send Cassie a text message, Brett saw he had one from her. Due to the lack of service, his phone hadn't received it until just a few minutes ago. She'd texted him, "Heads up, don't get tricked into snipe hunting."

Brett stared at himself in the mirror, defeated.

5

MUTE

"In Jesus' name, amen," Minster Frank Walsh concluded his Sunday sermon. "Next week we will continue our Bible series on the Epistle to the Hebrews. Specifically, we'll delve into Hebrews 11:1-7, focusing on unwavering faith in God and what it means to put that faith in action."

Carl Mills and his wife, Martha, got up from their seats along with the congregation. They slowly moseyed out into the lobby of the First Baptist Church. Groups of people huddled around each other, chatting and laughing. An electric atmosphere filled the lobby.

"How does brunch at the diner sound today? I don't feel like cooking," Martha asked her husband. Martha had recently retired from her job as the secretary of Mattfield's grade school. She got offered retirement three years early and jumped on it. The Mills' children and grandchildren all lived out of state. Martha looked forward to being able to spend more time with them. She pictured selling their home and traveling as much as possible once Carl retired in a few months.

She was a short lady at 5'2". For a decade, her haircut of choice was a bob cut, which she kept up on dying blondish brown to mask the gray. Martha felt young at heart, but the mirror always reminded her otherwise.

"Oh, the diner sounds fine to me, dear," Carl replied. He didn't care what they did for breakfast as long as there was coffee. Carl was foggy before caffeine in the mornings. Carl smiled, waved, and shook hands as he ushered his wife toward the door. Martha was chatty with everyone. Besides trips to the hair salon, she had little interaction with people since retiring.

After breaching through the crowded space, Carl pushed through the double doors leading outside.

Pulling out his cell phone to change the setting from Do Not Disturb, Carl noticed a list of missed calls. Highly unusual for a Sunday morning—or any morning, for that matter. Four missed calls from Keith, his undersheriff; two from county officer Erica Ames; and another two from dispatch. "May have to take a rain check on brunch," Carl consoled his wife.

An unmarked black Chevrolet Tahoe came flying into the church parking lot.

What on earth had happened? Sheriff Mills started getting concerned.

The Tahoe pulled up beside them, coming to a sudden stop.

"Get in," Jack Jones, the county detective, said flatly. Jack was a middle-aged, bald, black man who had transferred in as detective from Kansas City, Missouri six years ago, and took his job seriously. He joined his brother, Christopher, and nephew, Marcus, as the only African American residents of Mattfield.

Carl unlatched the keys from his belt loop and handed them to Martha. "Have a good day, dear," he said, passing off the keys to his wife, a ton of guilt in his voice.

Martha, looking concerned, said encouragingly, "Just be safe. I'll see you later."

Sheriff Mills got into the passenger seat of the Tahoe.

As soon as his door shut, Jack let off the brake and shot out of the church parking lot.

Pulling the seat belt across his chest, Carl buckled himself in. "J. J., tell me what's going on," he said flatly.

"We're heading out to Coal Creek. I got the call from Erica. One deceased—apparently, it's pretty bad," Jack filled in the sheriff. "I called in the KBI to assist."

"The bureau? Did someone die in a work accident?" Mills quizzed. For his investigator to call in the Kansas Bureau of Investigation was cause for immediate concern.

"No, an employee noticed the gate open on their way to church. Saw that someone broke in last night. Erica and Keith responded first. All hands on deck after they found a nasty murder scene."

"Do we know who yet?"

"LaVern Stillman's truck is in the quarry. It's a safe assumption the remains belong to him. May need DNA to confirm that. Hopefully, the sermon was uplifting. I have a feeling the rest of the day is going to be hell," Jack said bluntly.

Mills thought about his interactions with Stillman over the years. They had never arrested LaVern that the sheriff knew of. Never got the impression he was a thief, either. Carl sighed, staring out his passenger window. Mills knew today was going to make him wish he'd already retired.

He grumpily commanded, "Have someone bring me coffee when we get there; I don't care who."

Lord, give me strength, he prayed.

Jack turned off County Road 10-99 onto Jackson Road and pulled into the drive of Coal Creek Rock Quarry.

"Stop," Mills said, opening his door.

Jack brought the vehicle to a halt.

Mills got out and surveyed the ground. Out of the corner of his eye, he spotted a padlock. The sheriff collected the lock, bringing it back to Jones. "Evidence. Used bolt cutters to get in here."

Jack inspected it, nodding in agreement.

The sheriff elected to walk to the next location from the gate: a white trailer building that handled gravel sales. Jack went ahead in the truck.

When Mills arrived, Jack was already there, waiting on him. Ascending the small ramp to the entrance, Mills observed that the door's window was busted out. He couldn't imagine much of value at the rock quarry besides heavy equipment. Good luck being able to hide a piece of machinery after stealing it. "Anything of value taken in here?" the sheriff inquired.

"Two boxes of dynamite. It's accounted for, though," J. J. answered. "Sir, we need to go down to the quarry for the crime scene."

"Just gathering an idea of events that took place. Looking for any reason he ended up dead. . . . No sign of a security system. It's possible the owner caught Stillman out here," Mills speculated, moving back down the ramp.

"Sir, this wasn't just some murder," Jack said uncomfortably. "Whatever happened in the quarry last night is going to take a while to piece together. Have a look over the edge, the aerial view. Can't unsee it. You'll understand," Jones asserted.

Carl picked up on his detective's emotions. Hesitantly, he looked away from Jack to the edge of the quarry. Slowly, he walked over to have a look. Each step revealed a view farther down into the quarry. When the Sheriff reached the rim, the crime scene came into view. His body jolted, taking a step backward. Mills's jaw hung open. His brain had instantly fallen into shock at the ghastly image. Taking a deep breath, he stepped forward to the quarry's rim once more. Jack quietly stepped up beside Mills after giving him a moment to process.

"J. J., why don't you get the KBI on the phone? I need to know what their ETA is," Mills said softly.

"Yes, sir," Jack responded. "I'll have to use the SUV's Wi-Fi. No service out here."

All Mills could do was nod in response. Jack walked away, leaving the sheriff alone with the bloody panorama. His eyes soaked in the details of the murder scene.

Dark maroon stains of dried blood painted the ground in a sphere around what remained of a human body. From the stain marks, the body had been drug across the ground a few feet before arriving at its current location. Mills thought he spotted an arm lying farther in front of the body toward the back of the brown-and-white two-toned truck parked near the ramp leading out of the quarry. Two of his officers were standing by the front of the rough-looking pickup.

Carl descended the steep path into the quarry.

Keith and Erica greeted him solemnly at the bottom. "I've not seen anything like this, Sheriff," Keith stated.

"We don't even know where to start on this," Erica followed up. "Trying not to contaminate the crime scene. What in the hell happened out here?"

Sheriff Mills poised himself before responding. "In all my years, I've never even heard of anything like this," Mills told his officers. "This is out of our league. I want you to shut down 10-99 at the next intersections—east, west, and south. Don't talk to anyone about what you've seen here."

"We had some theories, just looking at a distance. Maybe dynamite, or possibly heavy machinery," Keith put forth.

"I'm going to have a look around down here. Gather what visual evidence I can. We're going to need the KBI on this. After you get the perimeter set, bring the owner and employees of Coal Creek in to the station for questioning. Reach out to Stillman's family and find out if he was with anyone last night. Send J. J. down here. Get moving," Mills commanded.

"Yes, sir," Erica and Keith said in unison.

Carl watched as they hiked up the road out of the quarry. Jack would be down to help investigate shortly, he knew.

Turning his attention to the sprawling scene strewn across the quarry floor, Mills approached the Ford pickup. He estimated it to be a mid-'80s model. At first glance, he saw glass strewn around on the ground surrounding the truck from shattered windows. The windshield was webbed with cracks, but was still intact.

He shifted from the front to the passenger side of the pickup. His attention was drawn to the caved-in passenger door from an impact. The mirror dangled from the door, barely attached. Seeing blood on the ground below the door, Mills knelt down. There was more underneath the truck. Bloody shreds of a red-and-black flannel laid scattered.

Being careful where he stepped, Carl approached the truck's rear. An opened box that read "Danger Explosives" on the lid was in the bed. On the laid-down tailgate was another opened box. Dynamite from the opened box was scattered on the ground. Reaching over the bedside, he picked up a chunk of rock. Looking about, the sheriff noticed an abundance of small chunks of limestone. His gaze turned to the severed arm about twenty feet away.

Jones arrived as Carl inspected the chunk of rock. "What do you have?" Jack asked.

"Limestone, it's all over the place," the sheriff said, focusing in on what appeared to be a cavern opening on the quarry wall. "Look there on the face, some kind of cavity in the limestone. Large chunks of rock piled up, too. I'd say he used the dynamite. Caused all this shrapnel rock to be thrown around. At least two people. Maybe that's how someone ended up dead here."

Carl could see Jack absorbing the environment. "I say that's a fair assumption; dynamite played some sort of role here. You say at least two people?" Jack asked.

"Blood under the truck. Torn flannel shirt, too. From what I saw up above, our victim wasn't wearing flannel," Mills filled in his investigator.

Jack knelt down and peered at the evidence under the F-150. "They were alive to set off dynamite. Might've used too much of a payload. Got maimed. Whoever was still alive tried to drag the body before giving up and leaving," J. J. proposed.

Sheriff Mills believed that was a solid place to start. Maybe this scene was all just a sad accident.

Jack honed in on the passenger door of the truck. "There's glass scattered inside the cab. This door damage happened here. It's likely someone got propelled by the blast."

Carl nodded. Trajectory from the rubble lined up perfectly with the passenger door. "Let's inspect our victim," Sheriff Mills said, apprehension in his voice. He approached the detached arm in between the truck and mutilated body. Studying the appendage raised more questions. "That's interesting. If you look where it detached from the body, the damage isn't consistent with being blown off. More like *torn* off," Mills theorized.

"Tried to commandeer a piece of heavy machinery down here, perhaps. Got his arm ripped off," Jones added.

"Perhaps so. How far out is the KBI?" Mills inquired while he inspected the arm.

"They're sending the Kansas City team down. Should be here within the hour," J. J. assured.

Mills shifted his attention to the one-armed body next. He covered his mouth with a handkerchief, attempting not to gag. Giving a wide berth, the men had to make observations outside the radius of dried blood. Carl struggled to make sense of the crime scene they were witnessing. He felt all their theorizing was valid, but ever changing with each new piece of evidence analyzed. None of their conclusions added up.

The mangled body already had swarms of flies buzzing about. Lying face down, the head was disfigured, partially crushed. Still attached, the left arm sprawled out, lying palm up. Deep lacerations covered the back. Animalistic injuries in nature.

"We know for sure it's a white male—build looks a lot like Stillman. Seen him around enough. You can make out a peach-colored shirt in the shreds, unstained by blood. Flannel almost guarantees another person was here," Jones said. "I pride myself on being good at my job, sir. That said, I'm drawing a blank on what took place here. This body looks mauled."

Jones looked nauseous. Neither of them had dealt with a murder before. People did not get murdered in this county. They strolled a distance from the body to discuss further.

"Truth be told," Carl began, "we're out of our depth here. I'm seeing what you are. A few thoughts come to mind. None that really make sense to say out loud, but I'll do it, anyway.

"Clearly a larger animal. Hard to imagine coyotes coming down into the quarry. Injuries on the body—coyotes couldn't've done that. People have reported seeing mountain lions occasionally, so that's not out of the realm of possibility." Ideas poured from the sheriff's mouth. Carl just needed to get all his thoughts out for discussion.

J. J.'s head bobbed up and down slightly. Carl could tell how deeply frustrating this was for him. "Dynamite, multiple people, mauled body, heavy equipment," Jack shared in confusion. "We have an unfocused image. Each portion we zoom in on makes the event blurrier."

Attention shifted to the cave opening in the limestone rock. Sheriff Mills pointed at a flashlight he had missed before on the ground halfway between the pickup and the cavern. The mouth of the cave was shaped like a claw mark set into the rock bluff, sitting level with the quarry's floor. Carl scrambled over sizable chunks of rock to peer inside. He grabbed his cell phone and used the flashlight feature to shine into the dark abyss. No hint of light came from inside. The smell drifting out of the cool damp chamber was putrid.

Caves were not uncommon in this area of Kansas, he knew. Mills had heard old-timers talk of filling in crevasses on their properties to protect cattle from breaking legs. Not to mention prairie and timber rattlesnakes used them to nest during the harsh winters. Caves here didn't inspire awe, just liability.

Carl was content not to venture inside. Unsure of the bluff's stability after being hit with dynamite, he backed away. "It's a cave, alright. Couldn't see light coming in from anywhere else. I'm too old to risk trying to go in and investigate any further. Add it to the list of things that don't add up. Did Stillman and company know it was there, or is this just another coincidence?" Sheriff Mills asked tiredly. He ran a hand up through his gray hair, massaging his scalp, attempting to ease the budding frustration.

"Let's have a look around the machinery, then get out of this hellhole, " Jack said, pointing toward the machinery and then to the pickup. "Just observing the body and its position: body is face down, heading toward the truck. Drawing a straight line, you end up at the bulldozer."

Carl saw what was being proposed, adding it to the collected data swirling in his head. Jones's skills never failed to impress, an investigator with an intelligence far exceeding a position in rural Kansas. "Our deceased made a run for the truck, didn't make it. We'll see if the bureau can solve this mess," Mills said.

A sequence of events was not coming to fruition. Scattered pieces of a jigsaw puzzle. Carl couldn't force them into a cohesive picture.

Following Jack's intuition, the men walked over to the outside track of the bulldozer. The heavy machinery sat in a triangle formation. The bulldozer sat next to an excavator, and behind them, a mining drill used for coring blast holes.

Staying in line with the cadaver yielded immediate success, finding a Zippo lighter with a brightly colored Mexican Day of the Dead skull emblazoned on its case. An unlit stick of dynamite was at the lighter's side, along with specks of dried blood. More evidence leading to more questions.

What happened? Mills used his handkerchief to dab away sweat from his forehead.

"Sheriff, come have a look back here," Jones called from behind the bulldozer.

Dried blood covered the ground under the bulldozer's rear. Lying on top was a worn and bloody brown leather belt. Details of the event etched into the stains. Someone had crawled through the spilled blood or had a struggle before it dried.

Battling anxiety and fear welling up inside, the sheriff bent down to see under the machine. Once again, using his cell phone as a light, he brightened the bulldozer's shaded underbelly. Bloody prints where hands had gripped on the machine were visible. To the front of the dozer, more blood sat coagulated in a pool on the ground. "Someone was dragged or hid under here. Clear signs of a struggle. Probably used their belt as a tourniquet of sorts. Hard to believe someone lost this much blood and walked out of here. Maybe this is where the arm injury occurred?" Mills theorized.

"My best guess from the amount of blood here compared to where that body is lying would be—" Jack paused for a moment in thought, "—we're looking at someone else's blood here. Feeling confident that the body out there is Stillman, he still had his belt on, as well."

"Let's get back up top," Mills instructed. "We can fill in the agents with what we've uncovered so far. They'll analyze the crime scene with resources we just don't have. Get us answers. In the meantime, we can question people on the periphery of Stillman and Coal Creek. We'll turn up the missing pieces that bring this thing full circle."

Carl and Jack were both winded by the time they reached the rim of the quarry. Three black Chevrolet Suburbans with tinted windows lined up side by side to greet them. Men and women, all wearing matching black suits and sunglasses, were unloading containers of equipment from the vehicles. Mills counted eleven agents in total.

The passenger door of the middle suburban swung open. A short man with deep brown hair and beard, both flecked with gray, got out and approached them. Sporting the same black suit and sunglasses as his colleagues, his face and hands were tan and without a wrinkle. The watch on his left wrist looked to be a high-end Garmin. He extended a hand to greet them. "Sheriff Carl Mills, I presume. It's nice to meet you, sir. I'm Zachery Grant, lead detective on this for the Kansas Bureau." Grant turned to Jones. "Jack, we spoke on the phone earlier. What's the situation on the ground here?"

Mills extended his hand as an invitation toward the rim of the quarry. Together, the three men looked down at the crime scene. After spending over an hour viewing the situation from all angles close and far, it still sent shivers down the sheriff's spine. He watched the expression change on Grant's face.

Pulling off his sunglasses, Grant slowly folded them. Opening his jacket, he slid them into a pocket. Never taking his attention off the bottom of the quarry, he said, "Gentlemen, this is unexpected."

"Gets a lot worse up close," Mills shared.

"Any theories on what happened here?" Grant followed up.

Together, Carl and Jack gave him a quick rundown of their fact-finding mission in the quarry. Zachery remained quiet, nodding his head as they pointed to different locations, describing what they saw.

"This man we presume dead, LaVern Stillman, any known connection to the cartel?" Zachery asked.

Involvement of a drug cartel in his county hadn't crossed Mills's mind. "Jack will handle the questioning and follow up on leads at the station. Hopefully, he can uncover information to assist your team. Is there any reason you suspect the cartel?"

"The nature of the crime in question. Seems barbaric—evil, even. That's not something most Kansans are capable of. Most people in these parts would shoot someone, not have a dog rip their arm off. This is my preliminary theory, is all. Maybe he got in hot water with the wrong crowd. They brought him down in a hole in the ground and murdered him. We'll have a lot more to go on soon," Grant replied. "Speaking honestly, the cave is a bit of a curveball. Weirder things have happened, but someone by random chance blowing open a cave?"

Sheriff Mills pondered this theory. It was a better idea than anything he'd been able to come up with so far. Cartels running around the United States doing as they pleased was a known fact at this point. The county jail housed plenty of them—almost all transfers from Kansas City where they had run out of room to house the inmates. Mattfield always had room in its jail. Housing other counties' overflow inmates had turned into a primary revenue source.

"Trust me, this case gets stranger down there," Mills said. "We had better let you get to it. I'd appreciate timely updates. Mattfield is a small town; word travels fast. I'm going to need answers soon to keep the peace. This is going to shake our community. Jack has your number. Anything he turns up, you'll be the first to know."

"Understood. I'll have an update for you later today. Coroner will arrive shortly. We'll be expeditious with the deceased. Send someone out from your morgue to collect the remains."

"I'll let the morgue know," Mills confirmed. "Thank you." He walked away, leaving the agents to the task at hand.

His head throbbed, preoccupied with the quarry. And no one had delivered his morning coffee as requested.

Sunday was usually a day of rest in rural areas. His county was the type of place that came to people's minds when hearing the phrase "God's Country." The devil came to play where he did not belong.

Carl reflected on his long service in law enforcement. A murder had never taken place in his entire career. Martha tried her best to push him to retire last year. Stubborn as usual, he just wasn't ready to turn in the badge. A mistake that was exacting its toll. This was a new world now, he knew. Darkness was casting its shadow across the earth. Had he been a fool for believing the God-fearing would be spared. Today Mills realized he had grown weary. Serving justice in a world that was plummeting headlong into injustice.

He sent up a prayer for a swift resolution. The end of this chapter in his life was now blemished with blood.

Arriving back at the police station, another chaotic scene was unfolding. In the lobby, which doubled as the station's waiting area, Levi Douglas, the owner of Coal Creek Rock Quarry, angrily awaited the sheriff's arrival. "Someone breaks into my business to rob me and you bring me in for questioning?" Levi chastised the sheriff as he was heading for the safety of his office.

Carl paused and made eye contact with the man. "Repeat what you just said in your head, see if it makes sense. You aren't here to report a robbery. A dead man turned up at the business you own. So yes, we brought you in for questioning. You are not a suspect, but we need to gather all the relevant information. Jack will be with you in a few minutes. Thank you for your cooperation."

Levi attempted to get another word in, but the sheriff reached his office and shut the door. A disposable cup with a plastic lid sat on the desk in front of the computer. He picked the cup up. The cold coffee touched his lips. Carl hated cold coffee with a passion. He let out a loud sigh of dissatisfaction.

Sitting in his office chair, he saw a list of messages filling the computer screen. Snatching up the desk's phone, Carl requested to speak with Keith.

Within minutes, Keith snuck in through the door, shutting it behind him, handing a hot cup of coffee to Carl. "Erica and Patrick are maintaining the blockades out on 10-99. Since Jack stole you from church, I thought you might need some coffee," Keith said, taking a seat in a chair facing Mills.

"Good man," Mills replied. Relieved to have his caffeine, he took a long sip while gathering his thoughts. "We talked a while back about me stepping down. I will not be finishing out my term until reelection," Carl told Keith solemnly.

This news shook Deputy Sparts; Mills taking early retirement was unexpected. "Sir, are you sure? Because of what happened at the rock quarry?" Keith tried to make sense of the news.

"I decided before today. Viewing the quarry reinforced my decision. I'm tired, Keith. In years past, I would have been more proactive in preventing crimes of this nature in our county and communities. My best days in law enforcement are behind me now."

Trying to maintain his stoic exterior, Keith asked, "Where do we go from here?"

"I'll phase myself out over the next few months. In February, I'll ride off into the sunset. Martha and I plan to spend time with our grandkids in Florida. She wants to travel and sightsee. I feel she's owed that after sacrificing so much for my career."

"Have you informed Jack? Not finishing out until the election cycle changes the scenario we discussed before," Keith said hesitantly.

"I talked with Jack last week to get his thoughts. My goal is to transition out of here peacefully. He is content with being the county investigator. Doesn't care much for the politics that come with being sheriff." Mills paused for a moment, deciding how best to deliver the next part. "Effective immediately, I'm naming you as my choice to serve as interim sheriff when I'm gone. When elections come next fall, you have my endorsement," Mills declared.

Keith leaned back in his seat, surprised. "Thank you. I expected J. J. to be interested, too. I'm grateful, sir, truly," Sparts replied.

"This community respects you, Coach, and having that respect from the people you serve is important in this position. A concern I've always had inside was turning the law enforcement of Linn County over to the next generation. Until you started here. When I look at you, that worry is gone. I know you'll do the job well. You made moving on possible, so thank you."

Cracks were showing on Keith's face. The emotional wall he put up when conducting his job had fractured. Getting his feelings under control, Sparts pivoted to the investigation. "What do you need me to do in this case?"

"I need you to break the news to Stillman's family. We need to bring them in for questioning sooner rather than later."

"Yes, sir," Keith said, then rose and headed out the door, leaving the sheriff sitting alone again in his office.

That was a taxing conversation. He'd ripped the Band-Aid off by naming Keith interim sheriff. A weight had lifted off of his chest. These last six months would be the last pages written in this chapter of his life. For the first time, what came after was coming into focus. That next chapter transformed into a beacon of light in these dark times.

Pages filled with family and adventure were awaiting him on the other side.

Lead Investigator Grant called to give him the update he had anxiously awaited. The victim's wallet contained a Kansas driver's license identifying him as LaVern Stillman. His body was now in possession of the county morgue. The coroner established a time of death of around midnight. Stillman's body had been there less than twelve hours before being discovered. Wounds on the body suggested an animal attack. They collected DNA for analysis. Investigators took blood samples from all areas it was present: around the machinery, the F-150, the cadaver, and a few trails of blood leading between these objects.

The KBI would try to identify, or at least establish, other suspects. A spelunking expert would come to inspect the stability of the cave, and to see if anything of interest was inside.

Five sticks of dynamite in total were missing from the open box—only one accounted for, found with the Zippo lighter. Grant felt it was safe to assume the other four missing sticks caused the blast. The team lifted fingerprints from the truck and underneath the bulldozer. One major problem the agents ran into was the amount of blood under the bulldozer and suggested a second victim should be near death if not already deceased. His team was currently checking with area hospitals to see if anyone had turned up—although no blood trail led away from the bulldozer, leaving them puzzled. A search team and cadaver dogs to canvas the surrounding areas would arrive in the morning.

All the information the agents collected made Carl hopeful this case would have a speedy conclusion. Lab analysis could help pinpoint who, what, when, and where. A crime this bad, the sheriff assumed fingerprints should identify at least one suspect.

Martha picked up Carl from the police station after the update from Grant came in. Jack could not glean any new information from interviewing Levi Douglas, other than confirming they stored equipment in the quarry to be out of sight from thieves who may pass by. An ironic gesture after today's events.

Stillman's ex-wife hadn't talked to LaVern about anything but their son since their divorce a few months back, which left the case wide open with little else to go on, but only so much could get accomplished in a single day.

Carl learned a long time ago not to bring work home with him, but his phone was always on, in case new information came to light. Other than emergencies, he believed in a work life balance. That extended to all of his officers. If only for their sanity's sake.

Following his not-so-restful Sunday, Carl went to bed early, struggling to put off the images in his head from the quarry. Sleep did not come easy. When it came, his repose was not peaceful. Tossing and turning, nightmares plagued him throughout: a man being ripped apart by a large canine while shadowy men stood around laughing; wandering into the mouth of the cave, only to have the entrance collapse, leaving him trapped in the subterranean darkness; approaching the edge of the quarry to see it filled to the brim with mangled corpses, their dead faces staring at him.

This jolted Carl from his slumber. Light from the sunrise streamed through the bedroom window blinds.

Moving quietly to not disturb Martha, he went to the kitchen. Part of Carl's morning ritual was brewing a pot of coffee.

With a hot cup in hand, he sat at the kitchen table with a view of the television in the living room. Using the remote, he turned on the news. To his dismay, Coal Creek Rock Quarry was the leading story.

Typical, Carl thought. *The news stations wanted nothing to do with rural communities unless a tragedy occurred.*

Anchor Lily Roth was at the scene, reporting from the roadblock.

"Here outside the quiet town of Mattfield, a body mysteriously turned up at the locally owned Coal Creek Rock Quarry Sunday morning. The KBI is here to investigate the incident. A truck passed a few minutes ago with a team of cadaver dogs to search the surrounding area. We have not been told why. This rural community is reeling from yesterday's events. The same question is on everyone's minds: What happened on Jackson Road? We'll provide updates as we receive them."

Carl turned the television off. He'd rather enjoy his coffee in silence than listen to news speculation. Today would be tedious if the KBI wasn't able to produce answers.

His work cell phone rang.

Here we go, Mills thought.

The caller ID read "Keith Sparts."

"Sheriff Mills," he said.

"Good morning, sir. Nat Fuller just called dispatch—something about a dead cow. I reached out to go have a look. She threw a fit and said not to come unless it was you," Keith relayed.

Nat Fuller was a crabby old woman who lived alone on her farm. She was stuck in her ways and difficult to deal with.

"You assume lead at the station. I'll get around and go see what Batty Natty is on about this morning," Mills said.

"At least she sort of likes you. If we get any updates, I'll let you know. Bye." Keith ended the call.

As if Mills didn't have enough problems.

He headed to the bedroom closet and dressed himself in his uniform. He fastened the heavy police belt around his waist. "I made coffee. Nat Fuller called. I have to go check on her before heading to the station. I'll be home late," Carl said to Martha, still lying in bed.

Nat lived on a gravel road a few miles west of the Coal Creek Rock Quarry. In her eighties, she probably shouldn't be living alone in the middle of nowhere. Good luck to anyone who dared telling her that, though. She vowed to die on her farm, a sentiment Carl respected.

He took only gravel roads to get to Nat's house, with the windows down, enjoying the fresh air along the way. He enjoyed the quaint countryside drive. True beauty not enough people appreciated.

Folks from the city were dead set on scarring the farm land and prairies with windmills and solar panels to make themselves feel righteous. Anyone who actually cared about the environment wouldn't trade the natural world for man-made eyesores that served little actual benefit. Mills knew it was all about making themselves feel clean-handed. What happened to the places that had to deal with so called "clean" energy projects was out of sight, out of mind. How much electricity could get generated if every house in a city was required to have solar panels on their roof? That would directly affect the people living in the man-made cities producing the most pollution. Carl believed wholeheartedly that climate change was a manipulative movement based on scare tactics, emotions, and money laundering. Thankfully, the county commissioners had so far kept the foreign interests of faux clean energy at bay.

Ms. Fuller's home sat in the middle of an eighty-acre pasture. Barbed wire fenced the perimeter of the land. Carl turned into the long driveway stretching to Nat's residence. The police truck rolled across the bumpy cattle guards at the driveway's entrance. Rough to drive over but effective at keeping cattle contained.

Her house was a red and black brick home with a freshly shingled roof. Nat was standing on her wraparound porch, waiting for him.

Mills stopped the truck and got out. "Nat, how are you doing?" he asked. "Keith told me you needed help with a cow. New shingles look good."

Nat was frowning. "Had some Mexicans redo the roof in July. They did the whole thing in one day. Wish I could say I was doing well, Carl. My nephew comes over and does chores before school. Found one of my cows all torn up. It's real nasty, mountain lion, perhaps. FBI is on the way, I guess. I thought you might be them. They've been monitoring cows or something."

Mills felt a tinge of anxiety welling up inside. Flashes of LaVern Stillman's mauled body came rushing to mind. Nat's property was a mile from the quarry. Perhaps a coincidence, but eerily familiar.

Why would the FBI be interested in a dead cow? Maybe Grant had heard about the incident and wanted to examine the cow. "Let's go have a look at the cow. You say the KBI is coming by, as well?" Mills asked.

"These people weren't with the state; they were federal agents. Called me on my phone after I had talked to dispatch this morning. Been a few hours now. Anyway, follow me. Cow's not too far out behind the house," Nat said.

Mills followed her through a gate in the backyard, leading out into the pasture. Fifty yards from the gate, what remained of a cow laid eviscerated. Grass surrounding the animal's carcass was tinted dark red with dried blood. The cow's eyes were wide open in panic, and its tongue hung out from the side of its mouth. Portions of the rib cage were visible, having been ripped away. Behind the ribs looked as if the animal exploded. Entrails scattered out on both sides. The spinal cord hung on by a thread to the livestock's back legs.

"This was one of my good heifers, Sheriff. Had a bull out here. She was supposed to calf. I'm out a lot of money, losing a cow-calf pair like this. We aren't supposed to have predators that can kill a cow in these parts," Nat lamented.

Something large had most certainly killed this thousand-plus-pound animal. Seeing the break in the cow's spine had Carl perplexed. The amount of force needed was immense. Not even a mountain lion could do this type of damage. Nat was right. A predator capable of destroying a cow didn't belong here. "Nat, do you mind if we set up trap cameras around your property? I'm also going to reach out to the KBI working on Coal Creek. The body found over at the quarry, just a mile away, is similar—head crushed, arm pulled off. There's a chance the same thing happened here. Did you hear anything last night? More importantly, do you have a gun?" Mills inquired.

"Got lots of guns, Carl. Who do you think you're talking to?" Nat scoffed. "Slept right through this. I'm getting old, you know. Get your cameras out here. If whatever did this comes back for my herd, I'll mount it on my wall as a trophy," Fuller proclaimed.

"Animal that did this will take up a lot of wall," Mills fired back.

"I've got plenty of room," Nat replied, and cackled.

Doors slammed shut in Nat's driveway. Three people entered the pasture through the gate, joining them at the carcass. Two men carrying equipment cases followed behind a woman.

"Khloe Barton, Special Agent with the FBI. This man here is Aaron Lew, FBI. And that man is Simon Webster. He's been assisting us," Khloe introduced her rag-tag group.

She was youthful, but carried herself with confidence. Her brunette hair hung down to the middle of her back. She had soft features, green eyes, and was stunningly beautiful. It was hard to make any assumptions, but she appeared to have a mixed-race heritage. Dressed in a red T-shirt, jeans, and Keen hiking shoes. Everyone shook hands.

"What brings you out here to see a dead cow?" Sheriff Mills asked.

"That's a long story, Sheriff. I've been tasked with researching the phenomenon of cattle mutilations across the United States. We were actually a few counties west when our AI software picked up Ms. Fuller's report to your police station this morning. Which brings us to why we're here," Barton explained.

"This is nothing like what we've been seeing. This cow is ground up like hamburger," Aaron Lew addressed his team as if Carl and Nat weren't present.

Lew was a white man of average height. His blond hair was unkempt, with a thin mustache above his lip. He looked ragged in his black suit. The black tie hung loosely around his white shirt.

Simon Webster set his equipment case down and rummaged through it. Snapping on rubber gloves from inside the case, he pulled out sample jars and a scalpel. Lew did the same, putting on rubber gloves and slinging a camera around his neck.

"Very dissimilar, indeed. This bovine mute seems to've been torn apart by animals," Simon pondered aloud.

Simon's way of talking bewildered the sheriff. What an odd way to discuss a dead cow. Simon had short, thin brown hair with a deep widow's peak. His face was clean-shaven with round cheeks and horn-rimmed glasses. Wearing a tucked-in blue polo shirt, black belt with matching black dress shoes, and blue jeans. A socially awkward man from his word choice.

Webster seemed enthralled by the cow's carcass.

"Bovine mute?" Carl asked.

"Yes, bovine as in cow. Mute as in mutilated. That's how we refer to the phenomenon," Simon stated.

This pissed the sheriff off a bit. "Don't patronize me. I know what bovine means. That's a funny way of saying it," Carl countered.

Nat jumped in next. "If this man isn't with the FBI, then why the hell are you bringing him onto my property?"

Khloe looked embarrassed, stepping in to defend Simon. "We picked Simon up recently. He's a scientist we crossed paths with at the first couple of mutes Aaron and I investigated. Quirky, as you may have noticed, but well-informed. He's been documenting these types of cases for a decade now. There are tens of thousands of cattle mutilation reports spanning this country's history. Imagine how many have gone unreported. To gain access to the data Simon has collected, I had to agree to include him in our investigation."

"If he annoys *you*, imagine how *we* feel," Lew tacked on.

"I see you call this butchered animal a mute, as well," Carl pressed. "So explain to Nat and me exactly what it is you have been seeing and how it relates to this cow here."

"This cow, in particular, is an outlier," Khloe replied. "Maybe coyotes or something chewed it up last night. Usually, what we find is an intact cow with missing parts. The missing parts get cleanly removed with surgical precision, highly intentional. From what we've seen, scavengers won't touch the animal remains. Simon's records showed some cows even drained of their blood."

"What parts would be missing?" Nat asked.

"It seems to vary," Khloe replied. "Tongue, eyes, heart, and reproductive organs are happening at high frequency in our cases—which, from seeing your cow, Nat, doesn't line up with what we're researching. Allow us to grab a few samples and photograph the scene, and we'll be out of your hair."

"Yes, yes. This animal lacks all the typical identifiers of a mute," Simon mumbled to the group. "Too messy. The ritualistic organs appear either intact or eaten. No sign of precision, or advanced technology."

"Hey, Webster, how about you do your job and shut your mouth?" Lew berated him. "Don't start with your UFO bullshit. This is official FBI business. Bringing your freak show along is a privilege. I won't lose any sleep leaving you stranded somewhere."

"Guys, professionalism, please," Khloe chimed in. "Look, I know this is strange, to say the least. I'm taking the job seriously because it's an epidemic plaguing a lot of farmers and ranchers across the nation."

"I'm not surprised this is how our government spends our tax dollars," Mills said. "Finish up and get out of here. We have an investigation happening in this county."

Aaron methodically photographed the carcass and surrounding grass. Simon collected samples from the "mute." Khloe apologized for the inconvenience, and her team departed.

"Pardon my French, Carl, but that was fucking strange. They never showed us a badge. Probably weren't even feds," Nat said.

No amount of coffee could cure the headache that just kept getting worse for

Mills. An entire career of normal had rapidly collapsed into madness. Federal agents investigating cattle mutilations? What on earth was transpiring? "I don't know what that was. I also don't have time to think about it. Keith is going to come by with our newest officer, Patrick; they'll canvas your property and position trap cameras. Get used to Keith—he's going to be your sheriff come February. I'm going to give Zachery Grant with the KBI a call now. I'll give him your phone number, expect to hear from him."

"Oh my, Carl, are you retiring?" Nat asked.

"One year too late, it seems," Mills said.

Carl and Nat parted ways in front of her house. The sheriff called Grant from the comfort of his police truck.

Grant answered the phone. "Sheriff, I was just prepping to call you."

"Been a busy morning for me. I'm out west of Coal Creek in the countryside. Have a cow that was mutilated last night. Your team may want to come have a look at this. I can't shake the similarities I'm seeing to Stillman's remains."

"I'll send a few of my agents over there to check it out. We have a situation involving evidence collected from Coal Creek. Fingerprints got a hit rather quickly from Linn County. Thomas E. Morro. Man has a hell of a rap sheet for stealing and drugs," Grant revealed.

"Tom Morro has frequented our arrest records the past few years. Known trafficker and user of meth. Makes his money stealing and selling to junkyards. We'll track him down and bring him in." Knowing Morro was involved with breaking into the quarry was the least surprising thing the sheriff had heard today. Stillman mixed up with Morro seemed out of character, but everyone has their secrets.

"I suspect Morro was an accomplice at the quarry. We got his prints from the F-150 truck's passenger side," Grant explained. "We're still working on the prints lifted under the bulldozer. Full DNA profile from the blood samples and LaVern Stillman is going to take two weeks. Obviously, we started with the cuts on Stillman's body. Our intent was to identify an animal from those wounds. Sheriff, none of that DNA collected from the body registered as an animal. I sent agents to the morgue to try again. What's strange is DNA from the wounds seem to be from a human."

"Cross contamination from Morro or another party, perhaps," Mills said. "We'll get a warrant to search Tom's home over in Red Hill. I'll have a DNA sample for you to build a profile for matching today. Getting Morro into custody is our top priority. We'll need his testimony. Without him, this case is at a standstill until DNA can further tell us what happened."

Carl felt his heart sink. This case was about to drag on for weeks, possibly even months. Scientific evidence takes time to produce results. His worst fear of not being able to bring this case to a swift conclusion had manifested. Sheriff Mills felt compelled to provide an answer to the question everyone was asking. He heard Lily Roth's voice repeating in his head: "What happened on Jackson Road?"

6

MAN-EATER

Midnight was fast approaching in the village of Bandipur, Nepal. Liam Gable slept soundly in bed as a steady rain fell outside. August was the tail end of a rainy season for the country. The screen from a satellite phone cast a green light into the dark room as it started to ring. Liam was stirred awake by the phone's commotion. Answering the phone grumpily, he said, "Hello? Do you have any idea what time it is?"

"It's the afternoon here in Kansas. Are you traveling? I'm sorry to disturb you," the voice replied.

"I'm abroad, in Nepal. Almost an eleven-hour time difference between here and back home. Who are you and what do you need?"

"This is Sheriff Carl Mills. My station is in Mattfield, a few hours east of Wichita."

"Yes, I know where Mattfield is. Sheriff, why are you calling me?"

"Being away from home, you probably haven't heard. We had a man killed outside Mattfield in a rock quarry. Appears to have been mauled by a large predator, but we don't have DNA evidence to corroborate anything. Day after, just a few miles away, a thousand-pound Black Angus was torn to shreds the same. I don't know what to make of it. A friend got me your information. You have a reputation as a world-renowned hunter and tracker. Seeing as you live in Wichita, I was hoping to have you out to give us your expert opinion."

This was enough to at least quell Liam's anger over being woken up in the middle of the night. "I see. Rednecks are a dime a dozen where you're at, Sheriff. A big game predator stalking about won't survive a week before someone shoots it."

"I truly hope so. So far, no one has seen anything at all, but people are keeping an eye out now. Whatever it is tore the man's arm clean off. Damn near separated a cow's spine. Contacting you was a shot in the dark, but the county could pay you for your assistance."

Liam appreciated the gesture. "I do like being paid for my services. Fact is, I was hired here to hunt a tiger. Been on the trail for two weeks now. Every few days, another victim's remains turn up. Thirteen victims so far, Sheriff. My expertise will save lives here. I seriously doubt anyone else gets killed in your county. I would be a bitter man if I travel half away around the world and it's resolved before I get there."

"I understand that. No need to make a special trip for this. Like I said before, if you were in Wichita, or were heading home soon, the offer would be available."

"I'll text you my email address. Why don't you forward me pictures collected from the deceased man and cow. Maybe I can help give an idea of what you're looking for, at least.

"I worked a case in Texas years back. A man was keeping a tiger as a pet down there. Tiger escaped and killed a woman. Keeping exotic pets isn't legal in Kansas, but when does the law stop people from doing what they want? My recommendation to you: Ask around and be absolutely certain no one has been keeping a large predator. Specifically, lion, tiger, bear, or leopard. Another thing: Most bears in Missouri and Oklahoma are tagged and tracked. Check with those states' Fish and Game services. See if any black bear has been recorded even remotely close to the Kansas borders."

"I'll send over what we have. Thank you for your advice. Those are good ideas to further investigate. Well, I'd better let you get back to sleep. Good luck with your tiger hunt over there," Mills said sincerely.

"Thank you. I'll reach out after viewing the images," Liam said, hanging up the phone. Then, "Good luck," he mumbled, chuckling.

Using the satellite phone, he texted the sheriff his email before putting his head back back on the pillow. There was no luck in hunting a man-eating tiger; sheer determination and skill decided the victor. Many hunters fell victim to the animals they pursued. Especially a full-grown tiger. The animal could easily turn the tables on its stalker. No matter how experienced the hunter was, the tiger's instincts were unmatched. If just any regular hunter could take down a man-eater, he would be out of business.

A white Catholic family in Wichita, Kansas had adopted Liam Gable, an orphan in Vietnam when he was four years old. His adoptive family couldn't have children of their own. Raised in a loving home, he grew close to his game-hunting surrogate father. Together, the two traversed the world, hunting all sorts of big and small game animals. Over the years, they hunted white-tailed deer in Kansas, elk in the Rocky Mountains, moose and brown bear in Alaska, coues deer in Mexico, as well as the assortment of big game animals in South Africa.

Traveling to new locales became commonplace for Liam. Canoeing and fishing lakes for two weeks in Manitoba, eating only what they caught. Using dogs to hunt black bear in Wisconsin. They even hunted alligators in Louisiana one year. By the time Liam graduated from high school, he had become a lethal hunter with the compound bow and many calibers of firearms, an avid outdoorsman who felt more at peace sleeping on the ground than in a bed. He was a survival and backcountry navigation expert, armed with a skill set most outdoorsmen could only dream of.

Conservation was always a top priority for his adoptive father. That trait was instilled in Liam from a young age. Hunt only to eat, or donate the meat to those in need. Predator hunting was always about balance in an ecosystem. Tags for predators were generally limited and had stipulations attached. In order to take a brown bear in Alaska, you had to first take a moose, for example, creating a delicate incentive to protect populations. Liam never hunted for trophies of any species.

Before using his skills to protect innocent lives, he would've never dreamed of hunting any of the big cats. Tigers were apex predators, more fierce than the "king of the jungle." He despised poachers of any animal. Killing a beautiful tiger would bring him no joy. Saving lives was his justification. Even that was a hard sell some days. Did humans have a superior right to survive more than anything else? These days, a contingent of people would argue no. Those people lived in the first world and were never in any actual danger. Most of them would support communism, too, if it meant not taking any real responsibility in their lives. Liam learned long ago to focus on the people his hunting actually benefited. Animal rights groups were white noise, crying over something they never could truly understand half a world away from those affected.

Turning eighteen provided him freedom, yet restriction. His passion and expertise weren't going to transfer into a traditional career path. Becoming a businessman in a suit wasn't what he envisioned for his life. Although his adoptive father was highly successful in working in Wichita's aviation hub, Liam wanted to take the road less traveled. There was money to be made as a hunting guide, so he started his own business.

Living in Anchorage, Alaska for a decade, taking people out to the surrounding remote islands to bag a moose or brown bear, Liam was content for a time. He started to lose the feel of thrill and adrenaline from the dangerous terrain and hunts. That was a feeling he craved. His drug of choice. So, he moved on from Anchorage.

Keeping his business, he threw the door wide open for hunting propositions. That was when he got his first opportunity to hunt a man-eater. Hired by the Indian government to pursue a leopard that had killed thirty-seven people in a single year. A number of hunters from around the world were hired, as well. Liam came in and brought the leopard's spree to an end in nine days.

Overnight, he became a highly sought-after hunter for governments and rich customers alike. Deciding to plant his roots where he'd grown up, Liam bought a house and property outside of Wichita. Not that he was there very often. For the next twenty years, he spent most of his life in foreign countries. Some nights he got a bed, some nights a hammock, but most nights were spent sleeping on the hard earth.

At forty-eight, Liam decided to slow down. More honestly, his body decided for him, requiring back and knee surgery to ease ever present pain. A life full of adventure came at a heavy price.

For the next three years, Liam found happiness in the simplicity of living on his farm, raising barn animals. Now the only hunting calls he took were for dire-need emergencies, averaging a manageable one hunt a year.

Now fifty-one years old, his driving force was returning home instead of thrill seeking. Because of the way he chose to live his life, he had missed out on getting married and having a family of his own. That was by far his biggest regret—not having a son of his own to share in those experiences his adoptive father shared with him, fearing all the knowledge garnered from his long career would be lost to the sands of time.

When Liam awoke in the morning, the rain was still falling. Another wet, dreary day of stalking the ultimate predator was upon him. The room he was staying in was small but considered a luxury when on the hunt. Walking into the bathroom, Liam ran water in the sink until it warmed. Splashing his face, he looked at himself in the mirror.

For a fifty-one-year-old who had lived in the dirt all his adult life, Liam looked youthful. Not a strand of gray among his onyx-black hair. He guessed his hair was at least three inches long by now. When given the time, he preferred it much shorter. His face had been unshaven since leaving home. Black hair covered his features. Liam's skin made him appear much younger than he felt inside, having a darker tan from the summer sun in Kansas. Standing at 5'6", Liam's body was muscular. Probably more from starving some days in the backcountry than actual brute strength.

Back in the bedroom, Liam slid the laptop from his electronics bag and situated himself on the edge of the bed. He wanted to see if this Sheriff Mills had actually sent the files he requested. Sure enough, the files were waiting in his inbox. Normally, a random American problem wouldn't bother Liam. The richest country on earth had endless tools at its disposal to solve a problem. But this case hit close to home. Liam was proud to be a Kansan. He felt a sense of duty to help, if possible.

Liam downloaded the files sent to him by Sheriff Mills. Using a Starlink connection for the internet was a lifesaver during overseas hunts in the last few years. When the file opened, his screen filled with gory images. A rather unfortunate reality of his line of work, seeing dead bodies was standard, already seeing one on this trip alone.

Trying to size up the animal responsible, he zoomed in on the lacerations on the dead man's back, moving from image to image, studying the injuries. One arm was torn completely off at the shoulder. From where the arm was lying, it looked almost tossed. Discarded after it became detached. There were also bloody bite wounds with apparent partial crushing of the skull. Liam was gaining an appreciation for the sheriff's worry.

Picture evidence alone pointed to a large predator. Mountain lion was almost certainly ruled out in his mind. Black bear wasn't off the table—Liam had his doubts, but could not rule it out. Black bears generally weren't sport killers. If a black bear killed, it was for food. This man was mauled to death. It was much more common for a grizzly bear to commit a mauling.

He cycled pictures until finally arriving at the mutilated cow. The cow's disemboweled, shredded body painted a patch of prairie grass. These images strengthened his bear hypothesis. Trying to be objective with the data, Liam honestly couldn't think of another animal. Sure, one of the big cats was a possibility, but the odds of a lion or tiger being loose in rural Kansas didn't add up.

Exiting out of the collection of images, Liam saw a typed memo included, giving a basic rundown of evidence and events. He scanned through it for highlights that stood out. Dynamite was used, opening up a cave.

A cave, Liam thought. *This poor soul blasted open a cave with dynamite. A typical place for a bear's den. Chaos and confusion from the event could have sent a bear into a frenzy.*

Liam was confident in his analysis of the information provided. Finding it easier to lay out his conclusions via text message, he carefully detailed his findings, typing out his bear theory and what could have led to the sheriff's dead man. He specifically noted the animal as a black bear, but couldn't rule out a brown bear, however unlikely.

Satisfied with his response, Liam sent the message.

A knock at his door let Liam know breakfast was ready. He shut the laptop and tucked it back into his electronic gear bag. Time to focus back on the task at hand: There was a tiger killing innocent farmers.

After spending a few weeks following in the beasts' footsteps, Liam was focusing on the area south of Bandipur. Tigers ranged great distances between kills—at least confirmed human kills. A number of small villages had been this tiger's primary targets, ambushing unsuspecting citizens on the perimeters of their villages. Humans were easy pickings. Once a predator got the taste of a human, there was no going back to more difficult prey. Learning the ease of hunting humans was the cause of every man-eater. Tigers were silent stalkers who blended into the shadows, waiting for the opportune moment to present themselves.

Liam dressed in a pebble gray, waterproof, soft-shell jacket, tan hiking pants, and a pair of waterproof Keen hiking boots. He laced his belt on with a leather sheath holding a Damascus steel hunting knife. Strapping on the weight of his sixty-five-liter tan hiking backpack. He carried only essentials in the pack when stalking an animal — protein bars, water, fresh clothes, ammunition, and the satellite phone. Liam's rifle of choice for this trip was a scoped Browning bolt action .338 Winchester Magnum. The gun was effective in bringing down big game animals with ease.

Liam enjoyed a light breakfast that had been prepared by the family who graciously offered him a room in their home. They also stored any of his equipment not required on the hunt. He thanked them for their generosity.

Exiting the house, he was thankful to see the rain had subsided to a slight drizzle. Fog hung above the houses of Bandipur, obscuring his view of the towering Himalayas. On a sunny day, the extraordinary beauty of Nepal was otherworldly. Bandipur's view of Annapurna's snowcapped peak was breathtaking.

Standing as the tenth highest mountain on earth at 26,545 feet, it was known as one of the most difficult mountain climbs in the world. Holding the highest fatality-to-summit ratio for a number of years. Annapurna only inspires awe from a distance.

Liam stood on the cobbled street in the rain, water running down his soft-shell jacket.

Abhinav, the assistant and translator he had hired upon arriving in the region, was late. Every second of daylight for tracking was valuable. Gable spotted Abhinav jogging down the hill, wearing his rain jacket and hiking backpack.

"You're late," Liam said, irritated.

Abhinav was a nineteen-year-old man. He had a dark complexion and short, black hair. He'd worked as a Sherpa the last few summers, carrying gear for foreign hikers coming to Nepal, attempting to summit one of the many Himalayan peaks. Extremely strong and in shape, Abhinav was always pushing Liam to go faster. This morning, Abhinav was different. His breathing was stressed.

"Sorry, sir, I have news. Tiger attack at a girls' school. To the south," Abhinav muttered, winded.

"Was anyone killed?" Liam asked, concerned.

"I do not know. We can cut through the jungle. Two-hour hike," Abhinav answered.

"This attack falls right in the area. I suspected the tiger could appear next. We're lucky today. This animal could have traveled thirty miles in a different direction before attacking again. Let's get going. This is as close as we've managed since I started this pursuit. Remember, silence during the hike. Ears open and study your surroundings. There's always a small chance of crossing paths on our way," Liam instructed.

Setting off from Bandipur was a perilous expedition. The village sat on the saddle of a mountain, steep staircases etched into the rocky cliff sides. A wall of fog sat on top of the tropical evergreen forest below them. Although difficult to appreciate the view when worried one might plummet to one's death, Nepal's landscape was deeply mystical. No wonder people here primarily practiced Hinduism. Liam could not imagine any of the biblical religions capturing the essence of this country. Life, death, resurrection, karma, and the soul. You could feel that balance in the land. Liam was a non-practicing Catholic at this stage of his life. From his years of travels, he'd grown to understand all the world's major religions.

Halfway down, Abhinav's foot slipped on some loose scree. His hands shot out onto the mountain's rock face to steady himself.

"Careful now, I need you," Liam said.

"Sorry, I get moving too quickly," Abhinav said, embarrassed.

The harrowing descent came to an end as they crossed a shallow, crystal-clear stream at the base of the mountain. On the other side, the two men plunged straight into the dense jungle.

Abhinav was also a skilled navigator. This made Liam's job less stressful. Liam swung the Browning rifle from his shoulder, chambering a round using the bolt action.

This was the tiger's domain. Being prepared was crucial.

To his dismay, the hike was uneventful as they scrambled over fallen trees, creeks, and rocks. Besides birds, there were no signs of wildlife under the gloomy canopy. Covered in mud from the waist down due to the freshly watered earth, when the forest relented, they walked out into a fertile valley. Fields planted with green wheat stretched out before them.

"How far?" Liam asked.

"Close. Two kilometers," Abhinav answered softly.

Attempting to not trudge through farmers' planted crops, Abhinav located a walking trail. This helped speed up the last portion of the hike.

The all-girls' school came into view at last. A bright yellow, two-story building sat along a muddy road. The school house compared to a well-maintained cheap motel back home.

"This trip would have taken four hours by road," Abhinav declared proudly.

"Good work. I need you to communicate and find out what happened here," Liam ordered.

Liam stopped at the mud road. Being armed with a rifle, he thought it was best for Abhinav to talk with them alone. All the doors were shut, and the building was eerily quiet. Abhinav knocked on a classroom door before being let into the room.

After a few minutes, Abhinav reappeared, flagging his arm for Liam to approach. A female teacher wearing a sky-blue dress with yellow flowers came outside, shutting the door behind her.

"This is Ehani," Abhinav reported, "a teacher here at the school. The girls were outside this morning. One of them was taken by a tiger. They are all scared to death, have locked down the building."

"Can she show us where this happened?" Liam asked.

Abhinav asked her the question. Sheepishly, she guided them to the back corner of the building. Traces of blood were on the ground, leading off toward more jungle. Liam had a moment of silence for the little girl. He knew there was no happy ending to this story. Nothing affected him quiet like children being hurt.

"What was her name and how old?" Liam asked, disheartened.

Abhinav translated the answer for him: "Nirupama. She was ten years old."

Liam fought back the urge to cry. "Thank you. You can return to the children now," he told Ehani.

She left the two men standing alone with the blood trail.

"Are you okay, sir?" Abhinav whispered.

"I feel guilt. You wouldn't understand. I have been here two weeks hunting this bastard tiger. Now an innocent child has died. Because I haven't killed it," Liam lamented.

Abhinav remained silent after hearing Liam struggle with his grief.

"That makes fourteen lives gone," Liam continued. "This ends today. I'm not coming out of that jungle until the beast is dead. You should stay here and watch over the school until help arrives."

Startled, Abhinav said, "No, sir, I will not be protecting anyone as long as this tiger is still out there."

"Listen to me, please. I can't ask you to risk your life for this. I am going to do whatever it takes. This tiger is capable of stacking dozens of bodies within a year. If you go, you will die."

"I am a Sherpa. I carry rich assholes' gear up mountains for them. I risk my life for a lot less every day, sir. This saves lives. I choose that."

"Very well," Liam agreed reluctantly. He knew what it was going to take to bring an end to this predator—a tactic he had only deployed twice in his pursuit of man-eaters. At his age, he knew catching this tiger by stalking was out of the question.

The tiger had to come to him.

Liam prepared himself for what needed to be done. For the greater good.

Pushing back into the dense forest, this time he followed Nirupama's blood trail. Liam tracked the tigers' footsteps on the muddy ground. Stalking in rainy conditions gave them that advantage. Droplets of blood were on the shrubbery as they went. Coming to a creek in the forest, he lost track of the animal for a few minutes as he searched diligently for where the tiger had continued on.

"Here," Gable whispered, finding the predator's footsteps exiting thirty yards downstream, then following the animal step by step farther under the shadowy trees for what felt like an eternity. Each minute built anticipation for what awaited.

Liam passed the gun off to Abhinav before scrambling up a rocky hill. "Toss it to me; I put it on safety," Liam called out softly.

With a strong heave, the rifle went airborne, landing in Liam's outstretched hands. Abhinav climbed nimbly up the rock slope. Locating the tiger's tracks, they continued on.

Then something happened Liam did not expect. A soft whimpering came from a fallen tree as they stalked closer. Kneeling down, Liam clicked the rifle's safety off. Staying low, the men snuck toward the tree. The trunk had bark hanging off from being shredded by claws. Peering inside the hollowed-out trunk, Liam saw a little girl stuffed back inside.

"Nirupama?" he whispered.

Frightened and injured, the little girl nodded in reply.

"Abhinav, she's here, alive. I need you to dress her wounds while I stand guard. The tiger knows she's hiding. It's close by," Liam instructed. Unbuckling his backpack, he offloaded it to the ground. Abhinav dug the med kit out.

After a few minutes, Abhinav coaxed the little girl to come to the end of the tree trunk. Her leg was badly mangled from being in the tiger's jaws. She was scraped all over from being dragged such a great distance. Blood ran from cuts on her arms and face. Abhinav cleaned and bandaged Nirupama's wounds. Using a strap from his backpack, he used a tourniquet on the girl's leg. Liam doubted there was any hope of saving her leg, but she was alive.

Using the satellite phone, he marked the location of the fallen tree using GPS. "Tell her to remain hidden here until we return," Liam ordered, placing the phone in his front pants pocket.

"We can't leave her here, sir. She is badly wounded," Abhinav protested.

"We'll never make it out of this forest carrying an injured girl. Not while the tiger is still alive. She'll be safer tucked into the tree. I need your help, can't have you playing babysitter."

Abhinav relented, telling the girl to stay tucked away.

Liam could now put his plan into action. "Stay close. It's most likely circling this area."

Leaving the safety of the fallen tree and Nirupama behind, the men quietly moved on. Liam was looking for the right terrain for his plan to work. A low enough tree to tuck himself away in. A large enough rock to position on top of.

Leaving the tiger's tracks behind, he led on. There was little doubt in his mind the tiger was already surveilling them. Traveling a quarter of a mile, he spotted a tree with low branches spread out in a nest down in a gulley. It was perfect for positioning himself to take a clean shot. The ground was flat, the foliage thin enough for visibility. This was the place.

Standing quietly, Liam scanned the area for any signs of the tiger, slinging the rifle back over his shoulder when he was satisfied. "Are you religious?" Liam asked Abhinav.

"Hindu, sir," Abhinav said.

Liam put his left hand on Abhinav's shoulder. "That's good. You are a good man. You are going to save countless lives. Thirteen victims already. Luckily, Nirupama will survive. This is where luck ends. There is only one for sure way to get this done," Liam confided.

"We are heroes—" Abhinav's eyes grew wide in shock.

Liam held the handle of the hunting knife, the blade buried in Abhinav's stomach.

"Sir, sir. Why . . ." Abhinav whimpered.

"You are number fourteen. I know, I'm sorry. I have only killed two tigers before. Both came down to moments just like this. A choice: kill one to save many. You are saving Nirupama. She can't leave here while the tiger is alive. In your next life, I hope you understand," Liam explained, distraught.

"Please, you don't have to do this. Sir, please," Abhinav pleaded.

Liam pulled the knife out before plunging it back into his companion's abdomen. Apologetically: "This is the only way." Withdrawing the knife once again, he shoved Abhinav to the ground. He slid the bloody knife into its leather sheath. Scaling the nearby tree, he positioned himself facing where Abhinav laid. Rifle at the ready.

Liam felt vile for using Abhinav as bait, a feeling Gable didn't have from his previous tiger hunts. The young man deserved better. He moaned in agony as he laid in the fetal position on the wet ground.

Liam sat patiently in the branches, waiting. It was eerily quiet, highlighting the sounds of his dying companion.

Liam was slowly losing the battle with his conscience.

The first time Liam used a man for bait was in India, having successfully brought down numerous man-eaters to that point. Still young and spry at age thirty-six, he had never been requested to hunt the largest of the cats before. This one was an especially deadly predator, killing at a rate of almost one person per day. The lengthy tiger hunt had gone on nearly forty days after his arrival. The body count was sixty-eight individuals by the time he delivered the killing blow.

Liam had come across a poacher camped out deep in the forest. With a burning passion, his surrogate father instilled in him a hatred for poachers. They had pushed a number of the most majestic animals on earth to the point of extinction. So Liam acted as a vigilante, subduing the man, securely tying him to a tree before bleeding him for bait. From the man's pleading, Liam gathered he was French. That was all he ever learned of the poacher.

Sitting in wait for seven hours, the tiger finally showed. Screams from the Frenchman haunted him for a long time after that. Liam saw his first non-captive Bengal tiger prowling in the wilds of India that day. A mesmerizing experience ruined by the bloody end of the French poacher. Within seconds, his screams of terror were over. The hulking cat had gone straight for the restrained man's jugular. Blood ran from the tiger's mouth as it turned its head and stared straight into Liam's soul—piercing yellow eyes he would never forget.

Squeezing the trigger, the rifle went off. A clean shot through the lungs. Dropping that man-eater forever. A black-market hunter became victim number sixty-eight, the last. Killings in the surrounding villages ceased. Liam returned home being heralded as a hero, bearing the weight of what he had done alone.

Five years later, at forty-one, Liam received the strangest job of his storied career. A leader of the Jalisco cartel requested assistance with an escaped tiger. Under the impression that there wasn't much of a choice, he traveled to the Jalisco territory in Mexico where he was treated as an honored guest.

The cartel detailed the situation at hand: A massive Bengal tiger that had been fed a diet of rival gang members had escaped its enclosure. It proceeded to stalk the outskirts of their compound for weeks, picking off guards one by one. A man-eater created out of sick enjoyment was now killing its creators. Liam welcomed every death the tiger exacted against the group. He knew his life was in imminent danger from the cartel members if he failed to kill the tiger in a timely manner.

Liam instructed the cartel's leader how to bait the tiger, which only had a taste for human flesh. Unrestrained in a lawless region, the hunt lasted only five days.

He was provided with three rival cartel members to use. He felt no remorse for the situation they now found themselves in.

He directed for the men to be wounded with knives and chained to the steel fence along the compound's perimeter. Members of the cartel happily obliged. Liam positioned himself on the roof of a stone building, utilizing an umbrella for shade, with a clear shooting lane over the fence.

One of the men hung dead on the fence after a few hours of blood loss in the baking Mexico sun. At sunset, the tiger came for the dead and dying prisoners. With a shot from 130 meters, Gable put an end to the tiger's reign. He was celebrated that night, showered in tequila shots. Holding up their end of the deal, he was given a bag containing $50,000, a fee of $10,000 a day. Leaving the compound, all three men now hung dead on the fence.

They returned him to a remote airfield via armed escort, then provided a small plane to Mexico City, where he caught a commercial flight back home. Liam feared the day the cartel might request his services again.

Four hours had passed without the tiger showing itself. Abhinav was still alive, but would succumb to his wounds soon enough. Liam couldn't bear the thought of sacrificing the young man in vain.

Foliage rustled behind him. Holding his breath, Liam glanced over his shoulder. The Bengal tiger crashed into his perched position, its front paws stretched out. Liam dove forward, narrowly escaping the animal's grasp. Sloshing onto the muddy ground. Rolling over, the tiger was fighting to get loose from the nest of branches above. Branches cracked as the predator struggled to break free, inching closer to him. Jaws wide, the striped cat hissed.

Liam had lost the rifle in the attack. Scrambling to find his firearm, he looked up to see the Browning hanging above his head. The sling had caught on a branch. Jumping up, he snatched it, breaking its sling. Walking backward, Gable brought the gun to his shoulder, taking aim at the hulking tiger. He needed a kill shot. With the animal this close, there would be no chance to cycle in the next round. The tiger's eyes stayed locked onto Liam as it brought its front paws down onto the ground, wriggling free from the tree's embrace. As the shot lined up, Liam started to put pressure on the trigger. Then, as he continued stepping backward, he lost his balance, falling onto his back. He lifted the rifle as the tiger lunged. A thundering boom from the rifle echoed through the forest. The tiger collapsed to the ground mere feet away.

Stumbling to his feet, covered in mud, Liam saw he had tripped over Abhinav's motionless body. Kneeling beside his companion, he checked his pulse. Abhinav had passed away. Taking a few moments to gather himself, Liam withdrew the satellite phone. His fall from the tree had left the screen cracked. Using the GPS, rifle in hand, he backtracked to where they had left Nirupama concealed.

No one else would have to die now, Liam reasoned.

His mind wasn't allowing a revisionist history of events to take hold. Liam had committed the murder of a kindhearted, innocent young man. A tiger and the cartel had done the dirty work of his previous human baits; this time, he was solely responsible.

When the fallen tree came into sight, Liam was filled with dread. Broken pieces of bark and wood debris scattered across the ground. The tree's hollowed trunk was ripped open from the outside. He ran to where they left the girl concealed. Blood covered the inside of the log. Gable slumped down onto the ground, sobbing in grief. There was no need to search for Nirupama's remains. Anything left would be nearby. While enacting his plan to bait the predator, it had returned for the girl. His plan of trading Abhinav's life for the girl had failed. Liam's symbolism of virtue crumbled down around him. Murdering Abhinav to be a hero had failed.

Rain began to pour down through the canopy. Sitting drenched in the mud, pools of rainwater forming on top of the surrounding ground, he buried his face in his knees. Scenes of the dishonorable deaths he was responsible for flashed in his mind. Abhinav's pleading in shock, the knife's handle protruding from his abdomen. How did he arrive at a point where killing an innocent man was a sacrifice for the greater good? Would they have all made it out of the forest alive if Liam had listened to Abhinav's plea to rescue the girl? How many more would've died to the tiger?

Streaks of Nirupama's blood seeped into the puddle beside him. The earth would drink the blood of the innocent lives lost. Looking at the rifle, he thought about taking his own life. That would be too easy. Gable felt he deserved a far worse fate. Night came and the rainfall never relented. Shivering alone in the pitch-black, Liam cradled himself for warmth.

Daylight illuminated the forest when he awoke, so he hadn't just dreamed of finally falling asleep. Hunger and thirst occupied his mind. He felt undeserving of both.

Gable stood and stumbled off into the forest, leaving the rifle and hiking backpack filled with his survival supplies behind. Flashbacks of his Catholic upbringing plagued him. Maybe the curse handed down to Cain for committing murder would be his punishment. A fugitive and wanderer of the earth.

Liam realized his state of mind was deteriorating.

Two more nights came and went. Liam fell, crawled, and ambled, lost among the ancient trees. Mud had become his bed. Dehydration was setting in, yet he refused to drink. In a clearing, rays of sun shone down on the forest floor. He couldn't remember how many days it had been since last feeling the sun's warmth.

Standing in the clearing, Liam got goosebumps from the sunlight warming his skin. Eyes closed, he turned his head to the sky, soaking up the rays. The sensation of being watched came over him. Snapping his eyes open, he saw a Bengal tiger standing broadside, looking at him across the clearing. This was the fate he had earned.

For a few moments, they remained still, eyes locked on each other. Unexpectedly, the tiger turned away, continuing on. Soon the animal faded from view into the forest's shaded underbelly. Liam was convinced now he bore the curse of a murderer. Divine protection from a premature death.

Delirious, he decided to resume his journey amongst the trees. Night came again. Any idea of how much time had passed was gone now. Falling down in the dark became his place of rest until the light returned.

On the fourth day, Liam struggled to return to his feet, using a branch to hoist himself up. His strength had faded. His mind was shrouded in confusion. It took all he could muster to walk on. The forest gave way to short green grass. A yellow, two-story schoolhouse stood in front of him. Falling to his hands and knees, Liam crawled toward the building. Girls' screams and voices echoed in his mind. Dizziness became overwhelming. Collapsing face-first into the bright green grass, his vision faded to black.

Liam awoke in a bed. "What's going on?" he muttered.

"Sir, you are in the hospital in Kathmandu. You showed up at an all-girls school in bad condition. A teacher said you were there days before. Tiger hunter, yes?" a woman answered him.

"Yes," Liam said. He had no recollection of the school.

"A Sherpa traveled with you, and a little girl was taken from the school. Do you know where they are?" she asked.

"Dead. So is the tiger. I don't know where," Gable told her.

"Okay, sir. I'm with the government. Is there anything I can get you? We are grateful you took care of the tiger. You were out there for four days and have spent another two here in the hospital. The attacks have stopped. You did it," she stated.

Gathering his thoughts, Liam requested the only thing that kept him going these last few years. "I need you to get me on the next flight home. My work here is finished." He had promised to do whatever it took to kill the man-eater. His soul paid a heavy price to achieve that promise.

If karma existed in these lands, Gable was in fear of what came next.

7

BLACK DOG

Mattfield High was abuzz with gossip of a murder at the Coal Creek Rock Quarry. Dalton was having anxiety, thinking about how close in proximity he had been on Saturday night. Even worse, Marcus and Bradley abandoned his brother in a stupid prank on the road to the quarry. All the guys present huddled together Monday morning to discuss the incident.

As much as Dalton preferred not to keep it secret, they convinced him otherwise. If any of them came forward, the whole group would wind up being implicated. Nothing good would come from telling the authorities. Besides, none of them had witnessed anything. The last thing Dalton needed was the entire school branding himself, along with the others, as murderers. His mother was already angry they'd returned home late. When news of the suspicious death came out on Sunday, it only compounded her anger. Staying silent on the matter was, in fact, a virtue in this case.

Surprisingly, Brett didn't want to discuss anything about it. Dalton knew his brother's ego took a hit after Marcus pinned him to the ground. Leaving Saturday night's events behind was best for everyone. The quarry actually brought the group of guys together. All of them were now keepers of forbidden knowledge. What would have easily turned into school-wide gossip about Brett getting ditched, snipe hunting, then choked by Marcus stayed quiet. That helped soften the growing tensions between Brett and Marcus. Dalton was glad his brother's honor wouldn't suffer further.

His brother promised to help with research into the blog post when the weekend rolled around. Football was Brett's chief priority until then. The Mattfield Hawks were preparing for their season opener Friday night. Dalton wondered if the blog would need a new update on strange occurrences after the events of Saturday night.

Each day came and went with tidbits of new information reaching the public. County police were conducting an active manhunt for Thomas Morro of neighboring town, Red Hill. Dalton searched Morro's picture. He had never seen the wanted man before. From what he gathered from Henry, Tom Morro wasn't a guy worth knowing. A real "piece of shit," Henry had emphasized.

Red Hill was ten minutes west on Highway 32, which ran in front of Mattfield High. Dalton had not visited Red Hill. Being much smaller than Mattfield, the town didn't seem to have much going for it. All he knew about it was that Red Hill was a part of Mattfield High's school district.

Dalton got into a groove at his new high school. He had acclimated to his new environment rather quickly. In Kansas history class, he volunteered to go first with his presentation. Mr. Kincaid seemed pleased enough with the five-minute project. All his teachers were personable. They were actually taking the time to get to know more about him. For the first time in school, Dalton felt more human and less like a number.

Midweek, the police confirmed the deceased man's name: LaVern Stillman. The name had already been circulating around. Yet another person Dalton knew nothing about. LaVern had a son named Franklin in the sixth grade at Mattfield Elementary. He felt sad for the kid. It made Dalton contemplate his own father, no longer involved in his life except through phone calls. His father was alive and well, though, so it was hard to compare situations. Dalton looked forward to a day where things could go back to how they were.

Stillman's death opened his eyes to how small towns handled tragedy. Everyone felt the effects. This community was more like an extended family than merely a collection of people. His desk partner in biology class, Sara, particularly made him realize this.

"I babysat Franklin a few times this summer for Ms. Stillman," Sara excitedly gossiped to him. "So crazy to think about. She divorced LaVern earlier this year. They're saying he broke into the rock quarry with Tom Morro. Everyone knows Tom is a druggy and a thief. If that's who LaVern was running around with, it's no wonder."

Dalton knew people here weren't intentionally malicious about their gossip. They just couldn't help themselves. People really knew everything about everyone in Mattfield. You had to live with that here. It worked as a societal fail-safe in a way. Your mistakes instantly became highlighted to your neighbors—an extra layer of pressure to be an upstanding citizen. The circumstance of Stillman's death would be his legacy now. Memorized around Mattfield forever.

Something about that scared Dalton. What if you only made one mistake? Franklin deserved better than his dad being treated that way. How was this going to affect the boy's life going forward?

Those thoughts made him wonder about a man like Tom Morro. A universally maligned figure in the communities. How does one get that far gone? Dalton figured the man had to be a true sociopath. To know he was roaming around the area, sought after by the police, was frightening. Did a man of that caliber have limits on what he would do in service of himself?

Thursday rolled around, and with it another notice from the police department. This time it was a warning to be on the lookout for a wild animal. Anything not native to Kansas was to be reported, giving permission to shoot on sight. The notice suggested the animal was a black bear, but left room for some other large predator.

Once again, the high school came to life with whispers and rumors. What a strange request from the police. Mattfield had fallen into a craze. Gossip about a sophomore boy named Kyle telling everyone a mutilated cow was found on his great aunt's farm had been spreading. Told not to share the news by law enforcement, Dalton thought it amusing anyone thought that could actually stay a secret.

Grandpa Walt picked him up after school let out.

"Seen any bears running around?" Walt joked.

"I don't think anyone at school has seen a bear outside of the zoo," Dalton replied.

"I wouldn't imagine so. Sheriff Mills probably has good reason to put people on the lookout. Word is Batty Natty had a cow killed the day after LaVern Stillman turned up dead. You know, things were quiet around here before you and your brother moved in," Walt said, raising an eyebrow.

Dalton felt a fresh dose of anxiety. He couldn't figure out why. They were never even at the rock quarry. "Do you mind dropping me off at the library today? I can have Mom give me a ride home when she gets off work," Dalton said, changing the subject.

"I suppose I can do that," Walt agreed.

Today would be a good chance to get a jump on the blog post research. Brett wouldn't want to make a trip to the library, anyway. Dalton would determine if there was any evidence of missing newspapers. If that part checked out, Brett would be all onboard for a trip to the cemetery on Saturday.

Mattfield Public Library was on Main Street, only a few minutes from the school. Dalton had been working up the courage to pick his grandpa's brain about the strange occurrences. "Have any other strange things like the rock quarry happened around here, Grandpa?" Dalton asked hesitantly.

"Oh, many things over the years. People talk of ghosts at some of the old Civil War locations around. Then you have the Indian House. Never could figure out why they call the place that. Osage camped out on that bluff for a number of years out there after being relocated, but the house got built fifty years after they moved them farther south into Oklahoma.

"I suppose because of the weird things people say they've seen around that area—lights and such—people think the Natives cursed the ground. Didn't help that an author moved his wife and young son into the place and proceeded to vanish. Far as I know, no one has ever found them. That's probably been close to twenty-five years ago."

So, the blog was spot-on with the Indian House portion. That event was recent enough that people in the area could testify to it happening. Dalton felt little enthusiasm to do any digging into things involving the Indian House. The eerie rock home had haunted his dreams ever since laying eyes on the place in person. Something about that property was foreboding. Even without a scary story, the Indian House would have caused Dalton unease.

"My grandpa told me one of the strangest stories when I was a kid," Walt continued. "Granted, he was probably trying to scare me—and it worked. A man arrived in town and, shortly after, folks started dying. Everyone grew suspicious of him, but it took about two months before they arrested him. Spent another month trying to kill him for the crimes. Then a group took him by horse. He was never seen again after that. Been a long time. I can't remember all the details."

Dalton's brain lit up. His grandpa knew everything the blog post shared. The story of an undying man had real potential. Was it possibly just a story used to scare youngsters into behaving? "Our family has been around Mattfield for a long time. Can you remember anything else about this man not being able to die?" Dalton pressed.

"It's been too long. I believe they tried to hang the man, at least. I haven't thought about that story in many years. Our family *has* been a part of this community for a very long time. Means a great deal to have your mom move back here. Eventually, everyone gets back to their roots," Walt reminisced, pulling his pickup into a parking spot in front of the library.

"Thanks for the ride, Grandpa; I appreciate it," Dalton said.

"Not a problem. I'll see you tomorrow for the football game," Walt said with a wave.

Entering the library, Dalton gained a new appreciation for the blog. Whoever recorded the stories on there was onto something. His grandpa had made him a firm believer. He had to try corroborating the other facts. "Hi, my name is

Dalton. I'm here to look at archived newspapers," Dalton said to the librarian.

The small, plump woman behind the desk had kind eyes. "I can get them for you. What dates can I help you with?"

"April, May, and June 1869?" Dalton replied. Trying to hide any ulterior motives from his face.

Her smile dissipated a bit. "Those records I know for a fact we don't have. Lost in a fire back around that time, I'm afraid. Believe it or not, this isn't the first time someone came looking for those. No one has ever told me what it is they are looking for. Can I ask? Truly, I'd like to know."

Of course no one ever told her; they didn't want to sound like a complete nutcase. Dalton wasn't interested in that, either.

She confirmed those records were gone, but also gave a probable cause that wasn't out of the ordinary for that time period. "School project, post–Civil War. Fascinating stuff. How much of Mattfield's historical record burnt in the fire?" Dalton asked.

She seemed content with that answer. "School project, that makes sense. I believe most other records from before and after those months we have."

That math wasn't checking out for Dalton. "Wait, how would only three months' worth of newspapers get destroyed by a fire? And at a library, no less?"

With a laugh, the librarian answered, "That happened so long ago, the how or why is not answerable. We don't even have a record of the fire. That's just the story."

Because there was *no fire,* Dalton told himself.

Deaths that made the local newspapers in those three months got covered up shortly after the fact. They destroyed any evidence of the events. Something must have happened back then. A secret that left nothing to investigate—just a legend people would scare their children with in the generations that followed.

"Thank you; that's all I was looking for," Dalton ended the chat.

Walking back outside, he sat on a bench in front of the building. Going to the cemetery could confirm who died in that time frame, but then what? So much time had passed, there was just no evidence to be found. His grandpa told the same ending as the blog. Men took the suspect away on horseback and came back without him. This investigation Dalton convinced his brother to help with was speeding toward a dead end. If the guy supposedly couldn't die, what would they have done with him?

Friday night, the Mattfield Hawks opened their season with a narrow loss at home. Dalton and his mother knew better than trying to talk to Brett afterward.

There wasn't anything to be ashamed of. Brett played well with four receptions and a touchdown on offense. The team primarily ran the football through Marcus. On defense, his brother only gave up one big play for fourteen yards. The team lost as the game came down to a last-second field goal.

It seemed like everyone in Mattfield showed up for the game, the bleachers packed with fans. Those who showed up late stood along the fence that wrapped the field. Football was a place for the community to convene and forget about their worries.

Then the day Dalton had been waiting for all week arrived. Brett had to get up early to watch the previous night's game film with the team. His mom left for work around the same time. Dalton elected to be useful and mowed the yard. He parked the mower back in the garage when he finished. As he rolled the manual door shut, the sound of tires hitting the gravel driveway came to him.

Perfect timing, Dalton thought, mentally preparing himself to test the waters and see what Brett's mood was like today.

Brett pulled up to him, rolling down his window. "We doing this or not?" Brett asked impatiently.

Feeling relieved, Dalton hopped into the passenger seat. "We are. Just a heads-up, I went to the library Thursday after school already."

"And? Is it bullshit?" Brett asked, pulling the truck back out onto the road.

"I think the story is true. Grandpa even knew about it. The newspapers for April, May, and June 1869 are missing from the archives. The librarian said they burnt in a fire, but only those three months. It just doesn't add up. Then you add in the fact this story about the immortal guy also exists. Grandpa confirmed hearing it from our great-great-grandfather when he was a kid."

"Whoa, that's crazy. I get the feeling there's a catch you're not telling me."

"Look, of the little things we have to go on, we can confirm the story is true. That's it, though. I haven't been able to think where to go next. The blog has no other information because there isn't any," Dalton admitted.

"Oh, well, that kind of sucks." Brett sighed.

"Men took the suspect out on horses and returned without him. What do you think they would've done with him?" Dalton asked, hoping for fresh insight.

Brett pondered for a moment before responding. "Do we even *want* to know what they did with him? Maybe all the stuff about him being immortal isn't real. Took the guy out and buried him somewhere. What if they found out he was innocent and turned him loose somewhere for his protection? There are endless possibilities when we have nothing else to go on."

Brett was right; there was nothing else they could do. Dalton thought about burying a man who couldn't die. That was actually a smart idea. Assuming the man *actually* couldn't die. Historically speaking, nearly everyone dies. For the Christians, a few people rose from the dead. Those books in the Bible were two thousand plus years old, though. Nothing recorded after those events suggested people came back from the dead, or weren't able to die. Only death made up the historical record after Jesus' resurrection.

Using GPS, the brothers located the cemetery on the north edge of Mattfield, tucked away off the beaten path on a hillside. An arched metal sign hung above the entrance that read "Sunny Slope." Dalton didn't understand what was so sunny about a cemetery, but to each their own.

"Where do we look?" Brett said.

Dalton scanned the hillside, littered with headstones. In the far corner of the cemetery stood a large, stone monument next to a grove of tall, eastern red cedar trees. Pointing to the monument, Dalton reasoned, "Over there. That must be the Civil War memorial, which would make that where this cemetery most likely started. The Civil War ended in 1865; we're looking for 1869."

Brett looked at the monument. "Why do you even know that? If you're right, you need a girlfriend. I'll help find you one," Brett teased.

"I literally just did a project on Mattfield. That's why we're here in the first place," Dalton replied. He ignored the comment about needing a girlfriend. He had a crush on Sara, anyway. She wasn't exactly his type, but it was slim pickings in Mattfield.

Each taking different rows of headstones, the brothers canvased the area. Walking amongst the tombstones was making Dalton nervous. Seeing the dates on the headstones before the 1900s brought into perspective just how many people died young. More than a handful died at his age. Nothing freaked him out more than that.

Finally, he located what they were searching for. "Over here!" Dalton called to his brother. Four small, oval-shaped headstones sat next to each other, each marked with the date of death on April 18, 1869.

Brett hustled to see for himself. "Good find. Jeez, man, this kid was your age." Brett pointed at a headstone. "Solomon Guthrie, born February 22, 1853."

"Oh, thanks, I noticed. There's a lot of them out here who died young," Dalton replied.

The world was a different place before modern medicine. He had read somewhere online the average lifespan in the Civil War years was just thirty-five. No wonder people were more God-fearing in those days. They were off to meet their judge sooner rather than later.

"I think this is all of them," Brett said, walking down the line of small headstones. "Seven more all died a month after. May 18, 1869."

Dalton had now witnessed firsthand the blog's evidence. It was exciting to feel as if he'd discovered a secret. Also frightening to know the story bore weight. "These people were all murdered. An old-time serial killer. The story checks out," Dalton exclaimed.

"All but the weirdest part. What happened to the killer?" Brett asked.

"We'll never know. Let's get out of here. Seeing all these dead young people gives me the creeps."

"Don't be a chicken. . . . Speaking of chicken, I'm hungry. We can go get lunch," Brett joked. Brett's pearl white truck sat off in the distance. "Damn, dude, I didn't realize how far we walked."

Strolling back to the truck, Dalton came across a headstone with a familiar last name. "This one here is an Adams. Think we're related? Died 1904."

Brett had a look for himself. "Who knows? Our family has probably been here that long. Adams is a pretty common name, though."

The two stood admiring the headstone. Dalton couldn't imagine what his ancestors had endured back then.

A low growl cut off his train of thought. He felt the hair on the back of his neck stand up. Their eyes darted toward the grove of cedar trees. A large, solid, black canine stood at the edge of the cemetery, returning their gaze. It was difficult to gauge the animal from this distance. The canine had a wolflike appearance and build.

"Brett, what is that?" Dalton asked. His body trembled.

"German Shepard, maybe, I think. That thing is massive, like a wolf or something. It's not happy. Dalton, we need to run. Together, okay?" Brett said worriedly.

A low growl continued to rumble from the enormous canine. Dalton tried not to panic.

Surely someone's pet, he told himself.

"Okay, I'm ready. Is the truck unlocked?" Dalton asked.

"Didn't lock it. Do not fall down, you hear me? Ready? RUN!" Brett shouted. Together, they bolted down the rows of headstones. Dalton glanced back to see the canine charging in pursuit.

Oh, shit, oh, no, he kept repeating in his mind.

Heart racing, he was staying neck and neck with his brother's stride. He had never run for his life before, achieving a level of speed he didn't know was in him.

Brett slammed into the driver's door. Swinging it open, he dove in, hitting his head on the top of the cab, then slamming his door shut. Dalton went for the back driver's side door simultaneously, yanking on the door handle repeatedly.

Locked.

Without hesitation, Dalton threw himself over the bedside. With a snap, the canine's jaw barely missed his heel as he tumbled into the truck bed. Slapping the truck's back glass window, Dalton screamed out, "GO, GO, GO!" The truck roared to life. Large front paws perched on the tailgate as pointed black ears and bloodred eyes looked in at Dalton. This was no dog. Dalton slid backward as Brett put the truck into drive, accelerating.

Scrambling, the wolf tried to climb into the bed, mouth ajar. Dalton, now in the wolf's range, drew his leg back and kicked, connecting with the wolf's snout, knocking it loose from the truck. He sat up to watch the wolf roll across the ground. The beast climbed back to its feet, watching as they sped away.

Dalton laid back into the truck bed, trying to calm his heart rate. That was all the encouragement he required to never investigate the supernatural again. Some blood-eyed hell hound just tried to kill him.

Brett drove to Main Street before letting Dalton get into the cab. Brett was breathing heavily still. "Dude, what the fuck just happened? Do you think that was a coincidence? I mean, we go to look into some strange story, and get attacked by a black dog? Make it make sense."

"Let's talk about my door being locked. I almost died, dude. Thanks to you, I got to see that thing up close. That was no dog. It was way too big. It had scary-ass red eyes! Only albino animals have red eyes, not solid black."

"I'm sorry. I didn't know about the door. You think that was a wolf? There are no wolves in Kansas, especially not on this side. Are you sure it had red eyes?"

"Unfortunately, I'm sure. I kicked the damn thing in the face, man. Now that I'm thinking about the story again, it mentioned a black dog. Just a few days ago, the police told everyone to be on the lookout for a black bear, but that wolf has to be what they're looking for, right? They just misidentified it as a bear?" Dalton speculated. Dots connected in his mind.

"What do you mean, the story mentioned a black dog? You think it attacked us because we were looking into this stuff? I'm done, man, no more. Wolf or dog or whatever it was. They can't live a hundred and fifty years. I don't want to talk to the police about it. Let's forget it ever happened," Brett replied.

"There wasn't much written about it—just a line that said a black dog was spotted in the area back when the killing happened. They don't have red eyes, either. That wolf, if that is what it is, seemed unnatural. Maybe it exists to protect the secret. I don't know, I don't know. Trying to clear my mind. What if we don't tell the police and that monster kills someone?"

"Look, I need to tell you something. About Saturday night, but it stays between us. You got it?" Brett said, waiting to see Dalton's nod of agreement before continuing. "When I got left out there, I almost got hit by a truck. I saw a photo of that truck in the newspaper; it was at the crime scene. Then, after that, while walking, I heard an explosion like a bomb went off. Not long after that—and this is going to sound like bullshit, I know—there was a howl. I told myself then it was a wolf. I panicked, started sprinting. That's why I tried to fight Marcus. It scared the hell out of me."

Dalton was stunned by Brett's confession. "So that thing killed LaVern Stillman? That's reassuring, seeing how it almost got me. How can we not tell the police?" Dalton asked.

"And what do we tell them, huh? 'Hey, just so you know, we were out by the rock quarry where some guy died. Also, we got attacked by a wolf while investigating some local legend at the cemetery.' Do you hear yourself? Even though it's all true, nobody would believe us. They'd think we're crazy, or liars. Better yet, we would climb right to the top of their suspect list."

Dalton understood the point Brett was making. He felt guilty for not telling someone. Being treated as guilty of some crime seemed much worse, though. "So what do we do?" Dalton asked.

"We can talk about it later, brainstorm some more about what's happening when our minds settle down. Let's just keep to ourselves. The police are going to take care of all this without our help, I promise," Brett reassured.

Dalton agreed to the plan. If that wolf killed LaVern Stillman, that meant he came close to death today. This was the first time he ever had to think like that. He'd almost died. Thankfully, he'd made it out of the cemetery without joining its occupants.

Seeing other graves of teens his age was, indeed, humbling. Dalton hoped to avoid a repeat of anything resembling today for the rest of his life. Finding the eleven victims' graves gave him closure to the blog's story, free to leave secrets hidden in the past where he now knew they belonged—mostly out of fear.

He never wanted to cross paths with that wolf again. His mind kept picturing the bloodred eyes. He didn't know how to describe how it felt staring into them. One word came to mind: hell.

That glowing red stare earned a place in his nightmares forever.

8

CHILD OF THE
MID-WATERS

"I am adjourning court. We will resume in the morning," announced Judge Thomas.

Lucas Dream Walker grabbed his briefcase. There was no sense in arguing, but he saw no reason a simple DUI case would extend into a second day. Lucas exited the Osage Tribal Court on the way to his Toyota Tundra.

At a towering 6'4", Lucas intimidated most people. He had medium-brown complected skin, black hair cut short. No facial hair post–military service. Broad shoulders topped his bulky frame.

The defense attorney, John Proctor, caught up to him. "Lucas, make a deal with my client," John requested. He was a weaselly man with a reputation for corruption.

"What deal?" Dream Walker asked.

"A lesser charge. Community service. Anything, really. A DUI will cost the man his job. You don't want to do that," John pleaded.

Lucas stopped to engage. "There is no deal to be made. I would honestly consider it if this was his first offense, but this is Sam's second offense in two years. Men don't learn lessons without repercussions."

"A sobriety program, a probation officer. He stays clean," John offered.

"We tried that. Your client did not stay clean. Say I let him off easy, then I find myself back here because he drove drunk again. Killed someone. I won't have blood on my hands," Lucas said.

"He is your people. How does one become so callous toward their own kin?" John replied.

"I prosecute crime to protect our people. We each have our roles. I am not the guilty one," Dream Walker stated in frustration.

"What you are doing makes you a guilty man. A shame on our people. You should've never come back home," John lashed out.

Seething, Dream Walker raised his voice. "See you in the morning, John. You did your client no favor here today."

"Wait, I'm sorry. Sam's employers want this to disappear." Proctor defiantly refused to give in.

"I pay attention to detail, John. A minute ago, you wanted to make a deal to protect your client's job. Which is it?"

"They can't have Sam going to jail. Name your price. Let's make it go away," John said.

A bribe? Right in front of the courthouse? This actually surprised Lucas, which was rare.

"If a man can be bought, he has no worth," Dream Walker said.

Proctor grew callus. "So be it," he replied, recognizing he'd done his best to avoid trouble.

Dream Walker did not take kindly to threats. He would allow no one to question his character. Being a prosecutor in a small community made you quick enemies, but this was his first encounter with a bribe.

Opening the driver's door of his Tundra, Lucas drew his concealed Glock G43X from his waist, transferring it to the holster beside the driver's seat. He exercised his right to carry a firearm every day without fail—both for his protection and in undying support for the Second Amendment in the Bill of Rights.

Having spent eleven years serving in the US Army, Lucas firmly believed in justice and protecting the innocent. Seven of those years were as a Special Forces operator, fighting terrorism abroad. While deployed in Syria, he realized it was time to retire. An honorable discharge closed that chapter of his life.

Immediately upon retiring, and having honed his skills in discipline during his decade service to the Army, Dream Walker applied and got accepted into law school at Washburn University in Topeka, Kansas. While working toward the degree, he tried to decide what to do with his future. He had a feeling that kept growing inside. A longing to return home. Lucas got a Bachelor's of History Degree in just two years, sacrificing any personal life to accomplish the feat. Three years later, he graduated with his Juris Doctor.

Shortly after graduation, he returned to his hometown, Pawhuska, Oklahoma. With the bar exam passed, it was time to embark on a new career. The stars seemed to align for Dream Walker. He gained the endorsement of the retiring district attorney and got elected to fill the office. He was now just shy of a full year into his new role.

He enjoyed a day's work, but looked forward to returning home. Lucas endured years without a place to call his own. A sanctuary to hang his hat and unwind. He never imagined living a middle-class lifestyle. Perks of being a lawyer. The money easily supported his minimalist lifestyle. A place to sleep, food to eat, and his German Shepherd were all he needed. Nobody was happier to see him each day than his dog, Caesar.

Caesar kept guard of the house while Lucas toiled at his career. They had a daily routine together. Lucas got home and changed into running gear. Then he took Caesar for a three-mile jog in the countryside. At four years old, the young German Shepherd was bursting with energy. Lucas used the jog to decompress from his day in court.

Immediately after their jog, the two shared dinner together. He would cook either chicken or steak, paired with a vegetable. A couple nights a week, Lucas trained Caesar on commands. He spent an hour or two watching TV, then showered and they were off to bed. Caesar took up more than half of the king mattress most nights. Lucas gave up on that part of Caesar's training.

A simple life. The one thing he needed was a wife, but he'd patiently wait for the right woman.

Lucas stood at the sink, cleaning the plates from their meal. His cell phone buzzed in his pocket. Quickly drying his hands, he pulled it out. The caller ID read "Dad."

"Hey, Dad, everything alright?"

"I want you to come over in one hour," Paul said.

"It's late. Can it wait until tomorrow?" Lucas felt anxious at the thought of leaving home.

"No waiting. Come." Paul hung up the phone.

Caesar cocked his head at Lucas.

"Sorry, boy, change of plans tonight," Lucas explained to his furry companion.

His father lived on the edge of Pawhuska. A fifteen-minute drive from Lucas's home in the countryside. For most of his adult life, their relationship was strained. Nothing disappointed his father more than Lucas assuming the role as prosecutor upon his return. Like Proctor, his father believed it to be a betrayal of their people. But someone must do the job. Would it be better if a white man were prosecuting their people? Law and order were the stitches holding the fabric of polite society together.

When Lucas arrived at his father's home, he saw three other vehicles parked in front. The two-story home was a faded white, paint flaking off from age. The front porch light lit the approach in yellow from a vintage lightbulb. Lucas tapped on the frame of the screen door before letting himself in.

In his father's living room, three other men sat on rustic furniture. Lucas recognized Judge Thomas. "What is this about?" Lucas said.

"Sit." His father gestured to a wooden chair. "You know Judge Thomas. These two men are James Gray Eyes and Nicolas Brings Plenty."

Lucas was suspicious. What could be the motive behind this?

"Nicolas, please continue," Paul said.

"I am not saying it is anything, but it may be. My grandfather told the story he got from his father. Our people cursed a white man to kill his own, and he did. The man vanished from history, as if he never existed. A strange thing has taken place outside of Mattfield, Kansas recently. I suspect it may be connected," Nicolas told the gathered men.

This is what his father brought him here for? Story time? Lucas respected his elders, but resentment was building inside. "Dad, what am I doing here?"

"You are a student of history, son. It is your passion. Listen and you may learn," Paul said in his monotone voice.

"I have heard the story. It is bold to assume. Why do you think this way?" Gray Eyes asked.

"From what I have read, a cave was blown open. Under the light of a full moon. A dead man. Could be the work of a shape-shifter. Lost to time," Nicolas explained.

"Oh, for fuck's sake." Lucas couldn't believe what he was hearing.

"Son, I will not warn you again," Paul said.

"And why exactly am I here? I have asked, I have listened. All I am hearing are tall tales. If I wanted fiction, I'd much rather be at home reading a book. This has nothing to do with history."

Grown men gathered for this?

"But it *is* history. Our peoples. I expected more from you," Judge Thomas said.

"I have traveled the world. Served in actual battles with evil. Guess what? Evil is always human. It comes from the heart of man. *We're* the monsters," Lucas replied.

"I don't know where I went wrong. My son, do you remember how you got the name Dream Walker?" his father asked him rhetorically. "You couldn't wait to talk about the things that came to your dreams."

"In the modern world, it is called an imagination. Then I grew up." Lucas knew this wasn't entirely true.

"This is not much to go on. Right location, but how will we know?" Judge Thomas steered the conversation back.

"He reveals his true form during the full moon," Nicolas said. "With it, his bloodlust. I suspect we will get answers in a few weeks. If more die."

"Thank you all for coming. We shall reconvene if the need arises," Paul said, ending the meeting.

They all rose simultaneously. Nicolas and James exited without further discussion.

"A word of wisdom, if you have ears to hear it. Proctor and his client, Sam, are in bed with dangerous people out of Tulsa. I do not know of their trade. A minor infraction is not worth watering the ground with blood. You have already made them your enemy. Tread carefully," Judge Thomas shared, patting Lucas on the shoulder as he departed.

Likewise, Lucas turned to leave.

"Can we speak?" Paul asked.

"Not tonight."

Lucas left his father standing alone.

His patience was worn thin from the meeting, but the night was still young.

Arriving back at home, a black car sat in his driveway. Lucas drew his gun from beside his seat, sliding it into his belt holster, then covering it with his shirt. Barks from Caesar came from inside.

Four men rounded from behind his house.

"You are trespassing!" Lucas yelled to them, getting out of his vehicle.

The men got closer, all of them in black ski masks.

Here we go, he thought, and sighed.

He reached over the bedside of his truck, grabbing his trusty wooden baseball bat.

One man rushed forward.

Wielding the bat one-handed, Lucas jabbed it into the man's stomach. With a second jab, he hit him in the nose. The man dropped to the ground, writhing in pain.

"You fellas picked a bad night," Lucas called to the others.

All together, they charged him.

Two-handing the bat, he raised it above his head. A loud crack rang out as he connected with the first to get to him. There was no time to recover. Dream Walker got lifted off the ground by the next person. His back slammed against the door of his Tundra. The wind got knocked out of him as he dropped the bat. That man still clenched him. Another attacker aimed for a head strike. Lucas shifted his head at the last second. Perp number three connected with the driver's-side window. Cracks slivered across the glass where his fist landed.

Lucas hit the man holding his waist with two consecutive elbows in the back. The third man landed his punch this time. Force from the punch bounced Dream Walker's head off the glass. The blow left him in a daze. The first two attackers clambered back to their feet.

"We came here to teach you a lesson. Consider yourself lucky if we let you live," one of the masked men said.

The meeting Lucas attended had saved his life. He let out a loud whistle, which shocked all four men.

"Way to give yourselves up, boys. Now I know you're my kin," Lucas taunted.

"You know not to whistle after dark!" one of them shouted angrily.

Lucas chuckled at this. "I have had enough shape-shifter superstition for one night." He let out another whistle.

One of the masked men bent to go for the bat. Glass shattered as Caesar leapt through a window in the front of his house, barreling toward the men, snarling. The men panicked. Caesar took flight, tackling one to the ground. Lucas used the opportunity to break free, throwing three knees into the man who'd wrapped him up. Dream Walker received another blow to the face. It left a cut above his eye. In response, he gave two punches and an uppercut.

Caesar dragged his victim around on the ground, the man crying in pain. Lucas squared up to fistfight the last masked man. They went blow for blow, exchanging brutal head hits.

The man he kneed got hold of his concealed gun from behind. "NO!" Lucas shouted. He began a tug of war over the gun on his waist. A severe blow struck his head. Spun around, he tried to use the truck mirror to catch himself, to no avail. Lucas fell to his knees. One man pulled the gun from Lucas's belt. He received a pistol whip from his own weapon, planting him face down in the dirt. A thundering boom rang out in the night air. Caesar let out a whimper as he fell over, dead.

A masked man knelt down beside Dream Walker. He racked the slide of the gun. Catching the ejected bullet out of the air. He planted it beside Dream Walker's head in the dirt. "I could have killed you with that bullet. In a way, it contains your life. Don't forget this gift. Drop charges against Sam tomorrow. And from now on, do as you're told, without hesitation."

The four injured attackers made their way to their vehicle. Lucas saw the taillights leave his driveway.

Dream Walker held the bullet meant for him in his palm, then crawled to where his companion laid. He ran his hand through Caesar's thick fur coat. "I failed you. Thank you for protecting me." John Dream Walker made a last promise to Caesar:

"You will have justice."

9

HOMECOMING

Losing the first game of the season devastated the Mattfield Hawks. Coach lit a fire under his team captains to strive for greatness. Brett felt inspired to not only do better, but to elevate his teammates around him. Their next two games were on the road in hostile territory. The Hawks came away victorious in both games, neither of which were close affairs. The team was firing on all cylinders heading into homecoming week.

September had finally rolled around. Heat from the Kansas summer was phasing out to prepare for fall. Playing in full football gear was becoming a lot more bearable. Practicing and playing in August had been nothing short of torment. However, Brett felt the endurance he gained from the strenuous conditions. Weather in the low seventies was a breeze. His play on the field was elevating with the enjoyable weather.

Coach delivered his end of practice speech:

"Homecoming week is here, boys. We have done good things, but we have to continue putting in the work to get better. I'll be honest, since I have been coaching the Hawks, we haven't won the homecoming game. Four years running, so this next one is huge. There are a lot of distractions this week. Mattfield goes all in on us. There will be fun and games at school and the parade. We need to stay focused through all the noise. At season's end, we'll see where the chips fall.

"I know this team can make a run in the state playoffs. A win this week will keep all of Mattfield invested in your success. Temptation to slack off is going to be everywhere. That homecoming dance after the game won't be much fun if you're the losers. Hold each other accountable.

"Mattfield celebrates this team all week. In return, let's give them a victory. I'm not saying don't have fun. You can enjoy the festivities. Just be smart. All eyes are on you guys. Bring it in."

Then Coach added, "Brett, you lead today. Hawks on three."

Brett was relishing the leadership role. His teammates huddled around him tightly. "ONE, TWO, THREE, HAWKS!" he led as they shouted in unison. Breaking the huddle, everyone trickled back to the locker room.

Marcus and Bradley approached Brett as he got dressed into his street clothes. "You coming to float-building tonight at my parents' house?" Bradley asked.

"Yeah, I'll be there," Brett responded shortly. They had never apologized to him for what happened. He could tell they had both moved on from the incident. Brett couldn't let it go, but he knew more than they did. That night, he'd had a near-death experience with a truck. A man in that truck died a mile away from the scene. There was the wolf's howl in the distance. Then a wolf attacked Brett and his brother at the cemetery. He wasn't about to forgive Marcus and Bradley for what they'd done.

"We can tell you're still pissed off. It was just a prank, dude. Weeks ago," Marcus said. "Happened to us, too, when we were freshmen. I know the guy dying at the quarry made it seem bad. First time something like that has ever happened. We couldn't have known that was going to happen."

Brett wasn't about to hear them try to justify taking him snipe hunting. "You want the truth? I'll give you the truth. Stillman almost ran me over out there. I had to dive out of the road. It was that close. Left alone in the middle of the night, I thought it was you guys at first. I didn't have cell phone signal and almost died. That's not to mention all the shit that happened at the quarry. Oh, and to top it all off, I was supposed to be home by midnight. I had to deal with *that* when I got home, too," Brett fumed.

Marcus and Bradley exchanged a look of surprise.

"Wait, it was Stillman?" Marcus said. "We didn't know that. I feel terrible. It was an initiation. Welcoming you to our group, you know?"

"Can't change it now, can we? Let's just move on. Why didn't you say anything before?" Bradley added.

"I recall you guys making sure we didn't talk about it again. Not like you give a shit, anyway. You want to move on? That's fine by me," Brett said harshly, slamming his locker shut.

"Alright, man, I'm sorry. I'll text you my parents' address. People will show up soon. We better get going," Bradley said.

"Thanks for not talking. Coach would be up our asses if he knew," Marcus acknowledged.

Something inside Brett was different after his forced relocation to Mattfield. He would have never stood up for himself like this before. Some days, his anger was completely non-existent. Others, his rage was boiling inside. Cassie would be at float-building tonight, so he needed to get his emotions in check. She made Brett want to be better.

A class vote had selected Marcus and Cassie as the homecoming king and queen nominees during school earlier in the day. Brett felt jealousy toward Marcus, which didn't help during the locker room confrontation. Being honest with himself, deep down, he knew they both deserved the honor. He wished for himself to be paired with Cassie, but Marcus was a staple in the community. Brett was still on the outside, looking in on lifelong relationships. Nothing he could do in one school year would ever change that fact. His friends from the city were slow to respond to texts from him these days, as well.

He was separated from where he belonged, in a place he would never belong.

Bradley's home was in the middle of Mattfield. A surprisingly pleasant two-story home with a Sherwood tan stucco exterior. The yard was lush green, a difficult feat for mid-August in Kansas. Brett parked his truck out front, along the street, finding a spot among the mess of his classmates' vehicles.

He had never built a float before. Growing up, his family had been to lots of different parades, but Brett had never actually been in one. His favorite parade moments were for the Kansas City Royals 2015 World Series and the Super Bowl 54 parade for the Kansas City Chiefs. The Chiefs have had two more parades since then, for their Super Bowl 57 and 58 victories. Brett's father was out of town for work, so he missed getting to attend the most recent two.

As he stepped onto the grass, Brett heard loud chattering from behind the home. Leaving crossed his mind. That meant returning home. Nothing about that excited him, either. Instead, he joined up with his peers in Bradley's backyard. They were all bickering around a gooseneck trailer.

"Hey, Brett!" Cassie said, coming over to give him a hug. "We're trying to decide on what our float will be."

Brett saw snickers from some others. Their judgement did not faze him. Cassie was the only person in the school who had truly been accepting of his presence. "What have you guys come up with so far?" Brett inquired.

"As the senior class, we get to pick the theme," Marcus answered. "We decided on movies from the nineties. Other classes can't have the same movie. Each has to be submitted for approval. They won't get to start on theirs until we tell them the theme tomorrow. Now we just have to agree on a damn movie. I wanted *Remember the Titans*, but of course it came out in 2000."

Brett pondered the theme. There were a ton of all-time great movies from the '90s to pick from.

"How about we narrow it down to five movies, then go from there?" Bethany proposed.

Brett thought that sounded reasonable.

"Alright, as your king, I'm picking a movie," Marcus said. "Cassie as queen, picks a movie. Bradley and Brett are football captains. They each pick a movie. The rest of you pick one together."

People murmured amongst themselves, but there was no pushback to the idea. Brett was just glad they'd reached some sort of resolution. Brett already had a good idea of his top five, so he would just throw out a movie no one else picked.

"Everybody ready? My pick is *Shawshank Redemption*," Marcus stated.

"*The Lion King*," Bethany threw out on behalf of the group.

"*The Waterboy*," Bradley nominated.

"*Braveheart*," Brett proposed.

"*Jurassic Park*," Cassie said confidently.

Chatter among the group erupted again. They immediately passed on *Shawshank Redemption* and *Jurassic Park* on difficulty alone. Brett would have loved to see a *Jurassic Park* float.

Narrowing down the last three took a lot more debate. Few had even seen *Braveheart*, so it was the next to be eliminated from contention. *What a shame*, Brett thought. Turns out the only movie everyone was an actual fan of was *The Lion King*.

"It's settled, then, *The Lion King*. Start coming up with plans of how to make that work with the float and homecoming," Marcus ordered.

A new debate was born, but Brett had no plans to get involved. Whatever the senior class decided, he was ready to help build. He got the idea of the Hawks playing the role of Scar and dropping their opponent, the Bulldogs, off a cliff. Apparently, the proposition wasn't as dark as he thought. That was exactly what Bethany came up with, too, met with no disagreement.

"How would a *Jurassic Park* float work?" Brett asked Cassie.

"Oh, well, my idea was silly. I was going to have the Hawks in place of the T-Rex. The Bulldogs would be the lawyer on the toilet," Cassie said with a laugh.

Brett envisioned the scene in his mind, laughing with her. "I wish we'd gone with that," Brett replied.

"By the way, my mom dropped me off at school this morning. I hitched a ride to float-building with Stephanie, but her parents can be weird about her taking me home after dark. Do you mind giving me a ride? If not, that's okay," Cassie asked.

Without hesitation, Brett responded, "I can do that, for sure. I'll just shoot my mom a text. No big deal." No matter how much anger he felt any day, Cassie had a way of erasing it. She brought out the best in him. Brett never wanted to let her down. He saw that Cassie was blushing.

They were so focused on each other, neither saw Bradley approach. "Hey, love birds, we have a float to build," he said, giving Brett a wink.

Embarrassed by the exchange, the three of them joined their classmates. In the next hour, they made a list of everything needed to pull off the float, delegating jobs for everyone to help bring it to fruition. Most of the girls assumed creative control together. Brett got appointed to the simple task of spray-painting. Seemed easy enough to him, so he accepted. The senior class agreed to meet up the following two nights to assemble their float. Bradley's dad had already agreed to pull it through the parade for them on Friday afternoon.

Everyone migrated to their respective vehicles to head home. Brett sent his mom a text letting her know what he was doing. He didn't know if she would be fine with it or not, but giving her a heads-up was better than nothing, he thought. If his mom got mad about giving Cassie a ride home, Brett would deal with the consequences later. Her feelings were the last thing on his mind.

"This is a nice truck," Cassie said from the passenger seat.

"Thanks. This was my dad's truck. He passed it down to me after getting a new one. Family has always driven Chevys," Brett replied.

"That's awesome! I drive my mom's car most days. I'm hoping to get a vehicle in the next couple of months. The car I was driving died. Parents thought it would be a good idea to get me something more reliable before college," Cassie said. "Do you know how to get to my house?"

Brett didn't know where anyone lived around here. He knew her home was in the country, but that was all. "Not a clue," Brett admitted.

"Not a good stalker, are you? I live the opposite direction from your house. You'll get on the highway and head out of town, past the Ag Co-Op," Cassie instructed.

"Wait, you know where I live?" Brett teased.

"Don't get too excited. Everyone here knows where you live," Cassie replied with a smile.

Following her directions, Brett headed out of town. Admiring the two seventy-foot-tall metal grain elevators as they cruised out of Mattfield. Brett had seen plenty of silos from the road, but never this close. "Those things are enormous," Brett muttered.

"Don't have those in the city, huh? That place is going to be packed with semi-trucks hauling grain for the next few months. Harvest is a busy time of year around Mattfield."

"Your parents are alright with me taking you home?"

"You are on their radar, don't worry. Saves them a trip to town, so they don't mind."

Country girls are something else, Brett thought.

Whatever there was between Cassie and him, it was smooth to navigate. Flirting felt natural. Believing in destiny sounded silly to him, yet here he was, in a place he loathed, smitten with a girl he'd met on the first day. Life takes away, but also gives in return.

"Would you, um, would you be my date to the homecoming dance?" Brett asked, trying to appear confident.

"Yes," Cassie answered. They sat in an awkward silence for a moment. The sound of his truck tires on the pavement was awkwardly noisy in Brett's mind. Looking out across the fields around them he spotted lights from a combine harvesting grain into the night.

"I have been meaning to ask about your dad," Cassie said, breaking the silence. "You always mention your mom. He's never been to any of your games, has he?"

After hesitating, Brett opened up. "My dad is still in the city. Half the time he's traveling the country for work. I haven't talked to him since we moved here. Honestly, I don't really care to. A big reason I never liked sports at my last school was because he just didn't show up for me. My parents are still married for now. Mom moved us to Mattfield to get away from him. He was having an affair,"

Brett explained.

Cassie's face shifted to looking sad. He wondered if she regretted asking about his father.

The sun was setting on the horizon out her window, painting a moody purple backdrop behind her. Fitting for the conversation. Having to think about his dad brought Brett pain and regret.

"I'm sorry to hear that. I don't know if this makes sense, but I believe everything happens for a reason. Time helps you see the bigger picture. For whatever reason, you are supposed to be here in Mattfield. I'm happy you are."

She terrified him in the best ways. Sharing in some weird connection, they were on the same wavelength. Cassie didn't use the word destiny, but she'd just described it.

"You've made being here worth it," Brett responded.

She directed him to turn onto a different highway heading west toward the fleeting sun. Brett couldn't be certain, but he thought they crossed this highway while country cruising. There was a lot more maneuvering on this road as it wound through hills. Coming up to a sharp curve, Brett slowed way down as it turned ninety degrees back to the south.

"These roads out here are a lot of fun to drive," Brett said.

"That's the last curve before my house. We're almost there. You wouldn't believe how many people have wrecked going around that."

Brett was not having trouble seeing why. The ditches were deep on both sides of the road. Missing the turn heading toward Cassie's house would send you down a hill into a pond. Heading the other way, if you missed the turn, you'd run straight into a grove of trees on the north side of the road.

Unfastening her seat belt, Cassie leaned over the center console to him. Brett was trying to keep his eyes on the road. His heart was fluttering. "Kiss me," she said.

So much for safe driving. He wasn't about to pass up at this moment. Brett braked to slow the truck down some. The two locked lips for a brief moment, sharing their first kiss.

Out of the corner of his eye, something brown streaked in front of his truck. With a loud thud, they snapped back to reality.

"Oh, shit, what was that?" Brett asked, bringing the truck to a halt.

"I'm sorry. I had my eyes closed. This is my fault," Cassie replied.

"No, no, it's okay," Brett said. "Good thing we were only going forty miles per hour. I'm going to check the truck for damage." He didn't want to ruin what just flourished by overreacting. Cassie got out with him to inspect the front of the truck. Brett didn't see any dents at first. Scanning the front end, all he noticed was a crack in the truck's plastic grill with a few strands of brown hair lodged in the split.

"Deer," Cassie said. "They are thick around this area. Dad says they're overpopulated."

"Do you think it's dead? I've never hit an animal before," Brett asked, concerned.

"Not gonna lie. All that matters is your truck being okay. When I told you my car died, it was from a deer. Demolished my poor vehicle," Cassie admitted.

"Jeez, hitting deer happens that often?" Brett inquired.

"All the time. I don't think you can say you live in the country if you haven't hit one. Welcome to the club," Cassie joked.

Hitting and killing an animal isn't a big deal here. Noted, Brett thought.

The differences between city and rural life just kept growing. There was a fresh surprise and something to learn every day in these parts.

Frustratingly, Cassie's driveway was only fifty yards away.

Why did I have to hit a deer right at our destination?

He turned left and drove along a tree row up to her house. She lived in a single-story white home on the edge of a forty-acre clearing edged by tree lines.

"This is home. Parents own the ground, too. We've been here my whole life," Cassie said before adding, "In case you didn't know, almost all accidents happen close to home. That's what everyone says, anyway."

"Well, good to know. The kiss more than makes up for it," Brett replied, flirting. Since it was just an accident and the truck was unharmed, he was ready to forget about the deer.

"I thought you'd like that. Thanks for giving me a ride home. Sorry again about your truck," Cassie said, getting out.

Her dad opened the side door of the house and waved to Brett. Waving back, he said goodbye to Cassie. "Anytime. I enjoy being with you. I'll see you tomorrow."

"See you tomorrow. Have a safe trip home," Cassie said, shutting the door.

Brett flipped his truck around in the driveway and headed home. Still a little startled by the deer accident, he decided it was best to take his time. The sun had fully set now as the night sky took its place.

Once again, he slowed way down for the ninety-degree curve. It felt like turning at an intersection with no stop sign. He cruised through the countryside with his brights on. Sure enough, he saw more deer as he went. "Bastards," Brett said to himself. As he neared the turn to head north back through Mattfield, his headlights shone upon a man standing in the intersection.

"What the hell?" Brett muttered.

The man had a hand up to cover the light from shining in his eyes. Puzzled by the occurrence, Brett couldn't help but think about all the weird shit constantly taking place. Why did people actively choose to live in the middle of nowhere? That notion was bound to draw some oddballs.

Brett dimmed his lights, bringing the truck to a stop at the intersection.

Despite his rough appearance, the man did not appear to be injured. He looked familiar.

Brett felt nervous, actively deciding to leave the truck in gear with his foot on the brake. Rolling his window down halfway, he shouted, "You okay, man? Can you move? I'm trying to get home."

Engaging might not have been the best idea as the man strolled toward his window. Brett rolled it up a touch higher as a precaution.

"I need a ride toward town," the man said. His country accent was thick. He had long hair and a scraggly beard. Not someone you want to come upon alone at night in the countryside.

"What are you doing out here?" Brett pressed.

"Listen, kid, I said I need a ride." The man sounded angry now.

Brett had a shocking revelation in that instant. "Shit, you're Thomas Morro," he declared.

Without warning, the man lunged his hand inside across the top of the steering column. With a twist of the keys, the truck shut off. Morro turned his attention to Brett next.

As Brett crawled over the center console to get away, Morro grabbed his shirt, yanking his back against the driver's door. Tom's arm squirmed around Brett's neck, locking him into a choke hold.

"Should have just given me a damn ride," Morro said menacingly.

Brett panicked as his airway was being cut off. Reaching out, he grasped the keys and turned them to start the truck. Nothing. It was still in gear.

He immediately grabbed onto the door handle under his back, pulling twice, unlocking it. Pushing off his seat, he forced the door open until he was outside the truck. Brett dropped his body as dead weight. Morro cried out in pain as his arm pulled down against the driver's window. After a few seconds, Tom had no choice but to let go of the choke hold.

Time to fight, Brett coached himself. As Morro grabbed at his injured arm, Brett swept his feet with the door still between them. Tom thudded onto the pavement.

"You're a dead boy," Tom snarled, whipping around, grabbing onto Brett's right leg under the door.

Brett had a sudden revelation amidst the struggle. He felt he was much stronger than the man attacking him. It was time to let his pent-up anger out. Brett used the door and cab to stay balanced, lifting and stomping down with his left leg, once again freeing himself from Tom's grip. Leaving the safety of the door, Brett rounded to Morro's side, planting a stomp squarely between the downed man's shoulder blades.

"You know what I was thinking? For a piece of shit, you sure don't know how to fight," Brett taunted.

Tom tried quickly getting to his feet. Brett punched him in the back of the neck before latching onto the bottom of Morro's shirt, yanking it up over his head. Tom was bound up in an awkward position. Brett used the opportunity to throw a couple of upper cuts straight into the man's face. Using all of Morro's body weight, Brett bounced him off the front tire.

Satisfied with the beating, Brett tossed Tom, who rolled into the ditch.

Tom laid in the grass, moaning in pain. His movements were much slower than before. "You signed your death warrant. Hell, I may kill your family and friends while I'm at it. This ain't over, boy," Morro announced through gritted teeth.

Brett started getting back into his truck, but he had a question to ask Tom before he left. "Tough guy. One more thing before I go. Were you in the truck with Stillman that night of the quarry?"

Tom wiped at the blood coming from his mouth. "I was there. Go run and tell the cops. Won't make you a hero. They already think they know what happened."

"That's funny, but not why I asked. See, I was out there walking that night. You almost ran me over. So how about you cut all the 'I'm going to murder you' crap? Consider us even."

Morro chuckled. "You don't know what's coming."

"Whatever, man." Brett shut his truck door, then shifted the truck into park and started it. "If you want to get in the truck bed, I can give you a ride to the police station." Brett laughed at his beaten attacker one last time as he pulled away.

No longer concerned about deer, Brett sped all the way back to Mattfield. He *had* to contact the police this time. Tom was a wanted man, and that changed things. Plus, he'd threatened to murder Brett. Sure, Brett had kicked Morro's ass, but the threat of harming his family and friends was where Tom crossed the line.

Brett wanted nothing more than to see that psychopath behind bars.

1 0

REASONABLE DOUBT

The sheriff's truck pulled into Julia Adams's driveway. She was standing out front with her eldest son. Sheriff Mills got out to meet with them. "Good evening, Julia. This must be your son, Brett." Carl greeted the young man with a handshake. "I need you to walk me through what happened and when it happened."

"I gave a friend a ride to her home after my senior class's float-building," Brett started. "On the way back, there was a man standing in the intersection to go back toward Mattfield."

"Slow down. I have to know precisely where this took place. You aren't in any trouble," Mills reassured.

"On the highway that runs north and south through town. Highway 7 and I'm not sure what the other highway was. It was smaller, less traveled. We drove north on 7 for a few miles before turning right," Brett explained.

"Who did you give a ride home?" Mills inquired.

"Cassie Page."

"Thank you, that helps. You took 300 Road across to the Page residence. So, the intersection of 7 Highway and 300 Road," Sheriff Mills clarified.

"Yes, sir, I believe so."

Mills spoke into the radio on his shoulder: "Dispatch 10-5. Intersection of Highway 7 and 300 Road., verified sighting of Thomas Morro. Need all units canvasing the area. I want him brought in."

"Approximately what time?" Mills continued, turning back to Brett.

"Mom called you as soon as I got back home. It's probably been close to half an hour by now."

Carl relayed the time frame to dispatch. "Are you alright?" Mills asked.

"Scared me a bit. I thought the guy needed help. He attacked me." Brett held up his hand for the sheriff, revealing cuts. "I fought back, gave him a pretty good beating. Tom repeatedly threatened to kill me. Then my friends and family, as well."

"Coach tells me you have a football game to prepare for Friday night. We'll take care of Morro. Your family has nothing to worry about. I have to get going. Thank you for calling, Julia. I hope to see you under better circumstances next time."

"Thank you, Sheriff. Be safe out there. We'll be seeing you," Julia said.

She and Brett headed into their home. As sheriff, Carl couldn't openly admit that he was happy the young man had given Tom a beating. Morro was a lot of things, but had never been a violent criminal in the past. Maybe being a hunted man, or whatever took place at the rock quarry, broke him. Tom was acting reckless. Tired of looking over his shoulder, or living in isolation, Mills assumed. These types of mistakes were going to help bring him to justice. They direly needed Tom's testimony.

They conducted a grid search with spotlights, canvassing miles of roads surrounding where Brett got assaulted. Four hours later, the search for Morro was called off. Tom had either hunkered down somewhere or successfully got a ride out of the area. Yet another frustrating setback for the investigation. Almost a month out from the rock quarry incident, and still no answers.

DNA matching LaVern Stillman, Thomas Morro, and a third unidentified man was lifted from the quarry. Current efforts were underway to match the

DNA to a relative. The mysterious third individual's DNA was collected from the animal-like wounds on Stillman's body. To make matters worse, the KBI had produced no evidence of animal DNA. Not a single report had come in of an animal sighting. There had been no signs or livestock deaths since the cattle mutilation at Nat Fuller's place. The trail had run cold.

Mills had reached out to an expert hunter, trying to garner some direction: Liam Gable, a world-renowned master in his trade. By some miracle, the man still lived in Kansas when not away on work. Gable was of the opinion a black bear from one of Kansas's neighbors could be in the area. Mills checked with Missouri's and Oklahoma's Departments of Conservation. None of the tagged bears were near the border. In their expert opinions, both departments found the idea absurd.

Arriving home late, Carl went straight to bed. This case was always on his mind, keeping him from a restful night's sleep, replaying all the evidence and details over and over in his mind, but still drawing a blank. With the amount of evidence collected, they should have definitive answers. Instead, there were only more questions. Not bringing his community resolution was eating away at Mills. Professionals from the bureau looked into it, and even they were coming up empty-handed.

The way this case was going, Carl felt like he needed a miracle.

Then, back at the station the following day, a lead finally presented itself. Mary Stafle, a resident of Mattfield, requested to speak to Mills about her sister, Annie. Ask and you shall receive. A break in the case had arrived.

"Sheriff, I have been holding out. Annie was seeing Tom before all this went down. I wanted to tell you at church multiple times. I felt like I was looking out for my sister by not saying anything. Truth be told, I believe the opposite in my heart. She's lonely. Got mixed up with that man somehow. I'm not saying Morro is definitely holed up at Annie's place, but he could be. Maybe dropping in for a wellness check would be the thing to do. Our relationship is strained lately. I'm worried about my sister's safety. No one else knows about them seeing each other. A hard secret to keep around these parts. I'm sorry," Mary said.

"We could've used this information a lot sooner, Mary. Truly. A high school boy was attacked out that way last night. That said, thank you for coming forward. This could be the piece we've been missing to bring Tom in. I won't waste any more time. I'm leaving right now to go speak with your sister. Does she keep any weapons in the house?" Mills inquired.

"Oh, Sheriff, I don't know. Be safe to assume so. Most everyone has some type of firearm. Annie was never a fan of guns, but she might for protection. Annie is a lot of things, but she wouldn't hurt no one."

"I'm more concerned about Morro being present and armed. He's gotten desperate. Look, I'll go alone to speak with Annie. Try not to raise too much suspicion, or spook her. Thanks for stopping by. I'd better get moving," Mills said, standing up from behind his desk.

Carl tried not to get his hopes up. This investigation had been nothing but hurdles. Bringing Morro in on the eve of homecoming would bring some peace of mind to the community. To himself, at the very least.

Annie lived out in that area. Morro was close by in the last fifteen hours. It all aligned perfectly.

Mills ran into Mattfield's Mayor, Lloyd Glass, on his way out of the police station.

"Sheriff! Just the man I was looking for," Mayor Glass said.

"Lloyd, how are you?" Mills replied. He had a feeling there was an ulterior motive behind their run-in.

"Town is all ready for the big game tomorrow night. I heard you were retiring. Is that right?"

"Soon. The Coal Creek case was the last nudge out the door I needed."

"That's a real shame. You served this community well. Speaking of homecoming and all, that's the reason I came to chat."

Here we go, Mills thought. "How can I help you?"

"Look, I don't want to step on any toes here. How is it the police haven't brought in Morro? The man is a petty thief and an addict. I heard he attacked a high school boy, even. And yet the man is still out there, endangering our community. Now, I have made excuses for you, but patience is running thin. Getting him locked up before the big game tomorrow would put everyone's minds at ease."

"You're welcome to go look for the man yourself, Lloyd," Mills answered, annoyed.

"I don't mean offense, Sheriff," Mayor Glass replied.

"If you knew there was an attack, then you also know that we conducted an active manhunt last night. We have never had trouble catching up with Tom in the past. He could always argue with reasonable doubt and get out of pretty much anything we brought him in for. But we have evidence that puts him at the scene of a murder this time. Hunting a man that doesn't want to be found in this county is no simple task, given the terrain. It's only a matter of time until we catch him. I'm focusing all our resources solely on bringing this to an end," Sheriff Mills said.

"Maybe it's time to bring in outside help to wrap this up."

"Don't come to my place of work and tell me how to do my job," Mills snarled.

"I'm up for reelection this year, Carl. Some of us still have a stake in the game. God forbid someone else gets hurt on our watch."

"I'm going to stop you right there. How many DUIs have I covered up for you, Mayor? Two? I can end your career any day I want, Lloyd. If you come around here again, I will," Carl stated bluntly. He walked away, ending the conversation.

Mayor Glass stood silent, his face red with shame.

Carl fumed for a few minutes as he drove south out of Mattfield, making a conscious choice to push the conversation from his mind. The nerve of some people. Biting the hand that feeds.

Tensions were running high in Mattfield. He had never felt this much pressure. Annie Stafle was the best lead he had to go on.

The police truck came to a stop in the half-moon driveway of Annie Stafle's residence, a single-wide trailer with tan siding. On the west side sat a propane tank. Natural gas pumped straight to your home was a luxury city life provided. Out here, propane provided your heat in the winter.

Mills stepped out onto the gravel driveway. He pulled his handgun from its holster, using the truck door to shield his actions from sight, then pulled back on the handgun's slide to confirm it had a round chambered. He holstered the weapon once more before shutting the truck door.

Grabbing the shoddy wood railing, he walked up the three steps to the front door. Carl gave three thumps on the door. He heard movement coming from inside the trailer. He laid his hand lightly on the grip of his firearm. The door squeaked open.

"Sheriff?" Annie said. Her brunette hair was shoulder length and messy. Annie's skin was ghostly pale with freckles. She had clearly spent little time outdoors over the summer.

"Annie, good to see you. I'm not here to waste time. I've gotten word that you may be able to help us find Thomas Morro."

Stepping outside, Annie pulled the door shut behind her. "I thought someone would show up looking for him sooner."

"Before today, we didn't know you were involved with Tom."

"My sister, I suppose."

"Listen, you aren't in any trouble, but you very well could be. Harboring a fugitive is a serious crime, Annie. I have a hard time believing you weren't aware."

"Thomas didn't kill anyone, Sheriff. You know Tom; he has his problems, but he ain't a murderer."

"I agree it's out of character for Tom. Most criminals have their niche. But, Annie, he was at the scene of a crime where a man got violently murdered. Regardless of his involvement, we need his testimony on what happened at Coal Creek," Mills explained. "We're looking for answers—not to pin a crime on him."

"Tom knows you won't believe him. What happened out there has him scared to death," Annie said mournfully.

"I need to know what he told you," Mills pressed.

"I don't think you're ready to hear it. What Tom described shouldn't exist, but I believe him. If you could see the fear in his eyes, you would, too."

Carl was growing increasingly annoyed. "I can't see the fear in the eyes of a man who is evading capture—who you have given shelter to. Look, there are a couple of options here, Annie. You can refuse to talk, or help bring Morro in. Chose not to help, and I'll arrest you for aiding and abetting," Mills said bluntly.

Annie was growing nervous from the threat. "If you leave me be, I'll tell you what I was told. Just know it's not much," Annie offered.

"That's going to depend on the quality of information." He saw the hesitation written on her face.

"Fine. Arrest me if you want to. Tom said a monster attacked them. A wolf man. Said he barely survived. Ripped into his leg. That's all I know."

Mills stood puzzled. "Did you see these wounds on his leg?"

"No, Thomas didn't have any wounds when I saw him, but his jeans were bloody and shredded like what he said did happen."

"So, you are telling me Tom relayed that a monster attacked him, and he suffered a leg wound, yet you believe his story when he turns up with no injuries?"

"I am. He said the wounds healed," Annie added.

"Cut the bullshit, Annie. You're describing the rantings of a man high on meth. You didn't second-guess his story at all? Especially when the facts don't line up with the story? Dare I ask, are you hooked on that poison, too?"

"I ain't on meth, or any other drugs. Never have been and never will be. I didn't believe Thomas just because he told me—I saw it in his eyes. He saw something, Sheriff. It changed him. He has not been the same."

"Did it cross your mind that maybe Tom killed someone for the first time? Do you have any idea what the repercussions of that are on someone? How could you reach any other conclusion than the logical one, Annie?" Sheriff Mills pushed back.

"I tried to tell you. You're not ready to hear the truth. Tom is innocent," Annie declared.

"Innocent? You mean like being at Coal Creek in the middle of the night, robbing the place? The authorities found his dead accomplice at the scene. We have DNA from another unidentified male, as well. Do you know who that was, Annie? Better yet, where is Thomas at? Is he here? Why on earth would an innocent man try to carjack a high school student last night? Seems to me he's getting desperate. If that high schooler would've suffered any injury at all, I would have charges brought against you. I still might after this nonsense. Where was he trying to go last night?"

The threat of arrest got to Annie. "He never mentioned a third person being at the quarry. Lately, Tom has been going on about getting evidence to prove he's innocent. He left here on foot last night. Said he's in contact with some man. Refused to take my car. Thought the police were already aware of our relationship. He's been paranoid, but clean. Sober. He hasn't come back here. Doesn't have a phone, so I don't know where he could be. I'm sorry, Sheriff," Annie finished, looking at the ground.

Mills had finally broken her resolve. "Listen carefully. You need to heed my warning about everything I told you. Tom's story does not add up. How's he in contact with someone if the man doesn't have a phone? I don't care what your perception of it is; I've seen the evidence. Enough so that, at the very least, Tom's testimony needs to be on record. Him staying here puts your life in danger. What I need from you is, if or when Tom shows up again, you notify the police immediately. If you hear from him in another fashion, I need to know. We can keep you safe."

"I don't know if I can do that."

"You're out of options. If I hear anything at all that you do not report, I will have you charged with accessory to murder. Do you understand?"

"I understand," Annie said meekly.

"Good. You deserve better than being entangled with someone like Thomas Morro. That type of man will ruin your life. I'm sure you're beginning to notice. I expect I'll hear from you soon." Mills handed her a card with his information.

Annie went back inside the home, sulking.

Playing bad cop wasn't a tool Carl liked to use, but he was in a desperate situation with this case, forcing his hand to produce results. He harbored no ill will against Annie. She was a decent citizen. It was a head-scratcher how she could so easily believe a story like Morro had spun for her.

Back at the station, Jack Jones flagged Mills down. "Annie Stafle have anything?"

"Morro has been hiding out there. We'll have to bring charges against her if word gets out. She's our best chance right now of catching up to him."

"Understood. I had a phone call from Grant while you were gone. We should talk in your office," Jones suggested.

Carl felt eager to find out what new update the KBI had provided. Leading Jack into his office, he swung the door shut.

"I'll just come out and say it," Jones said hesitantly. "So, they finally finished DNA analysis on our deceased cow out at Nat's place. There was human DNA. Thomas Morro's DNA."

A sudden urge came over Carl. Striding over, he slid down into his chair. None of this made any sense. "No other DNA came up?" Mills asked.

"None," Jack replied.

Mills was at a complete loss. "Thoughts? Ideas? Anything that makes sense for what we're looking at?"

"Um, as far as the bureau goes, they'll assist us in the capture of Morro. That's our best lead on all of this. Evidence points to him going on a mutilation spree. There's one other development that came up," Jones added, "which is going to make even less sense. One of the premiere DNA heritage websites ran the profile, as well as the third, unidentified individual."

"What could make less sense at this point?" Mills replied.

"A match came back. Sort of distant relations. This man's relatives live in Iowa," Jones revealed.

"Iowa's not that far away. Why would it be so unbelievable to have criminals link up across state lines?"

"Well, the person who the profile matched with belongs to their great-great-great uncle."

"Three greats? Even if this family breeds like rabbits, this man would have to be a hundred years old. The KBI made some kind of mistake. We can't catch a break in this case. This investigation has repeatedly been cut off at the knees."

"That was my first thought, as well. They scolded me and assured me that DNA does not make mistakes. The KBI is going to dig into genealogical records for the family to see if we can't get a name," Jack said.

"I have no words, Jack. Not one thing that comes to mind. Have we lost our damn minds? Thomas Morro out mutilating men and livestock, accompanied by someone who should be long dead. That's where we are on this after a month?"

"I'm sorry. I wish I had more to offer. We're living in strange times. I'll give you any updates that come my way," Jack said, leaving the room.

DNA doesn't make mistakes—until it does, apparently. The state's finest investigators must have come back with a faulty DNA analysis. Retiring early was looking like a viable option. Let this be someone else's problem. He was rapidly becoming disinterested in a resolution. Maybe the KBI should lead the hunt for Morro and his geriatric sidekick. Being sheriff was better suited for a younger person, anyway.

Another day, yet another layer of mystery. Tomorrow, he'll put on a pretend smile and wave, driving in the homecoming parade. Maybe even throw out candy to the grade school kids along the route. This would be his last time in the parade. There were a lot of last times coming in the next few months. Carl wondered if he would recognize those moments. More than likely, he won't even realize. Only upon reflection will he recall those last times.

Last times made bittersweet by this confounding case.

11

BASTION

"The United States government has passed on a notice of suspicious activity out of rural Kansas. It's probably nothing. They've given us direct access to all files from the Kansas Bureau of Investigation, the local sheriff's department for the county headquartered in Mattfield, and historical documents. I'm assigning this case for you to monitor," Phillip Hawes told his subordinate. Hawes was an older man with a bald head and a gray beard.

"I've never been to Kansas. Thank you, sir. If their situation rises to our level, I'll take care of it," Elliot Verdun assured his boss.

"If this rises to our level, the United States has granted you full authority. They'll want a cover-up and plausible deniability. Include as few people there as possible. It's a tough country to keep things under wraps in. It's much easier to paint a few citizens as lunatics than an entire community. I trust your judgement, Elliot. That's why I chose you if this becomes Bastion's problem," Hawes said.

"Honestly, I hope it's nothing but incompetent law enforcement. I haven't yet returned to my home country since joining Bastion," Elliot replied.

"Yes, well, Bastion has fulfilled its duty. We've relegated the work we do to third-world countries where people still toy with forces better off forgotten. I had dreamed of becoming unemployed in my lifetime. Instead, I became the oldest surviving member of this organization. A burden, truly. Everyone I've served with over the years is gone. You're on the same trajectory as me. We're too good at our craft. So we bury those less fortunate around us until there's no one left to bury," Hawes lamented.

"My generation has done well. Three of us remain," Elliot reminded Hawes.

"A miracle, I assure you. You're the first generation to have three still alive in their forties. Recruiting eight every twenty years has worked out for us. It's a laborious task of finding all the right attributes, then getting the lifelong commitment Bastion requires. A thankless job. It sounds dramatic, but without us, evil would take hold of this world. Imagine what that would look like for humanity. That's what has propelled me over the years."

"I've grown numb to it," Elliot remarked bitterly. "There was a struggle early on. I realized what would happen if we didn't intervene. That thought drives me, as well. The vast majority of people live their entire lives doing meaningless tasks. Just existing. Because we provide that security for them. It's for the best. If they knew what was out there, their self-absorbed facades would crumble, along with their will to live."

"Vast difference between our lives and those we swore to defend, it's true. Besides, we receive fair compensation for the sacrifices we make. Governments would love to have our library and the information it contains. We see behind the veil. Centuries' worth of records pertaining to every unnatural thing that walked on this earth. It'd be equivalent to an army possessing the Ark of the Covenant, only malevolent. So, in a way, they all agree to let us exist, as well. Eradicating evil is more important to us because it's our sworn duty."

Verdun acknowledged that sentiment as a fair argument. Making sure a shipping container arrived on time still doesn't feel equivalent to having a monster try to rip you to pieces, but Elliot understood all the same. It was a matter of perspective.

"From what I'm reading, the common folk of the United States are less religious than ever, which means less belief in the supernatural. One would think being less inclined to the supernatural could benefit Bastion, but studies have shown the opposite. Demons are taking root. Their influence is becoming quite the battle for the religious institutions. What are your thoughts?" Elliot inquired.

"People are not less religious in the United States. There are those who compromise the drive in all of us to seek understanding. A large population has taken up worship of money, climate, gender, material, and celebrity—the bastardization of religious teachings. Too many have become susceptible to feeling guilty about things over which they have no control—ironically leading them to be a wicked scourge, compromised by charismatic leaders who are sociopathic fools. They have created a breeding ground for evil spirits to frolic. It stands contained in major population centers for now. As with all things, time will tell."

Hawes's intellect and discernment were unmatched. He perceived the world differently than Verdun. "Thank you for the chat, sir. I still have a lot to learn. Sometimes I question the point of it all. The people we swear an oath to protect have a tendency to throw themselves headlong into desolation. If I'm half the man you are someday, I'll consider my life a success." Elliot turned to leave the room.

"We all feel aggrieved at some point in our life journey. The work we do on this earth matters. Stay true to the cause. Always remember, no matter how many times you have been on assignment, be vigilant. Twenty years of experience is not replaceable at Bastion. Take meticulous notes. Our journals are the training books for the future recruits here to save countless lives," Hawes added in closing.

Elliot found it difficult to remain embittered after talking with Hawes. He got a lecture about taking notes every time an assignment arose—to remember, even in the thick of things taking place. Previous members of Bastion had, in fact, saved his life multiple times with the journals they'd left behind for the library.

Being selected as a recruit by Bastion was an exhilarating achievement for Verdun. Post high school, he planned to study physics at the Massachusetts Institute of Technology. His country had other plans. The United States made it seem as if he was being recruited into the CIA. After extensive mental and physical evaluation, he received an offer. In exchange for a life of service, Elliot would gain access to knowledge and secrets far beyond the material world. Initially, he envisioned alien crafts and biological lifeforms not of this world. Elliot imagined what it would be like to be at the forefront of otherworldly technology.

There was a heavy cost involved in accepting that offer. His United States citizenship was revoked, and contact with family and friends had ceased forever. To this day, an active missing person's case remained for him. Haphazardly, Elliot didn't take into full consideration what all of this meant. Desperate to be on the cutting edge, he'd blindly accepted. Any assumptions made about the offer couldn't have been further from the truth.

Elliot had surrendered his life over to a global organization called Bastion, headquartered in Greece for over two-thousand years. The rising and falling of civilizations saw periods where the group dwindled down to as little as two members.

In the modern world, they stood well above top secret, the group virtually unknown. Technology was forbidden among the members. Almost all technological devices— from cell phones to televisions—were compromised with a form of spyware. The only way to prevent hostile actors in this realm was to not partake. A few privileged agents in countries around the world served to monitor the strange cases that sprouted in their jurisdictions. Messages and relevant documents come to Bastion handwritten by couriers. Whatever the military and churches couldn't handle fell in their wheelhouse.

Skeptical at first, the veil lifted, revealing another layer of reality in the universe. Journals from their library alone made Verdun believe this was a thought experiment being run on him. That idea was short-lived. Bastion was an order founded in ancient times, etched into stories the public only knew as mere myth and legend, making war with supernatural forces wherever they appeared, creating the stories the next generations would tell their children to impart wisdom or fear.

On his first assignment, Elliot came to terms with the truth. Evil could manifest in this world. Whatever regrets he harbored became distant memories. Pledging his life to Bastion was the greatest thing Elliot could do for humanity. Over twenty years of service to a world that didn't even know he existed, acting selflessly, with the aim of holding back the floodgates of darkness. This ate at his ego the most. Bastion saved billions of lives, but eight new members every twenty years would be the only ones to know the truth of their sacrifice.

Returning to his office, he found all the case files for the assignment stacked upon his desk. Elliot dedicated most of his free time to poring over documents. Information was the key to success. It was a rare occurrence that a notice of suspicion led to an active assignment. Usually, there was some rather normal explanation for strange occurrences. Misinterpreted reality was the root cause of most unbelievable accounts. All it took was investigators overlooking a single piece of evidence.

Opening a fresh notebook to record events and evidence, he began to read through the material. It wasn't always easy, but Elliot attempted to keep his notes in chronological order. Naturally, he started with the historical records.

Mattfield was an old place for the Midwest region. A town coming up on two hundred years. he made quick notes of any relative information. Native American history in the area was always important to record. In their day, Indians had a special attunement to the spiritual world. That was before the settlers came, removing them from their ancestral lands, tainting all aspects of their way of life. The material new world subjugated their ways of old.

Yet there was nothing that stuck out until the early 2000s. An author and his wife filed multiple police reports about strange things happening on their property. The police responded a few times, but found nothing. Law enforcement soon labeled them insane. Then, their son vanished. A large search party failed to locate the boy. The parents were questioned relentlessly. Nothing came of it. Not long after, they vanished, as well. Federal agents have the case now. All these years later, still no answers. Verdun found that story worth recording. Maybe he could wrap up multiple cases if he traveled to Mattfield.

Elliot dug into the case that had landed the files on his desk. It became obvious why the case reached this level. Scanning the lines of information grasped his full attention. He sat up in his chair, enthralled. For a case to become valid in Bastion, it had to pass certain benchmarks.

The first step was suspicion. Suspicion was usually but not always brought to their attention by the agents on the periphery of the organization—an unexplained occurrence taking place somewhere in the world.

The second benchmark was an investigation—what Elliot was in the early stages of. Did the suspicion pass the eye test? Was there ample evidence present to press the issue further? Bastion's agents were of a limited number, so these first two steps were important so as not to waste valuable resources.

During the investigation, if there was ample evidence, it would lead straight into confirmation. Boots on the ground. This was to confirm, or put to rest, whether the case was, indeed, Bastion's forte. When a case was confirmed, the agent remained until it was taken care of, which is the final benchmark for the job: resolution. These four steps guided their work.

Elliot jotted down pages of notes poring over the Mattfield documents. A murdered man. A mutilated cow. The presence of a freshly opened cavern. Human DNA evidence. All intriguing. Opening his desk, Elliot revealed a calendar, matching up the dates of the recorded information—the nights of a full moon. This added another layer of curiosity.

There was a knock at the doorway. Felix Rifkind, a German-born member of Bastion, entered the room. Elliot and Felix joined the organization in the same class. They had become close friends over the years of service.

"What are you working on?" Felix inquired.

"Suspicion, out of Kansas of all places. Rural town. Not a large population," Elliot replied.

"Kansas? The United States doesn't need our help. I'm off to the Congo later today," Felix said.

"Seen enough to convince you?" Elliot asked.

"Plenty. A witch doctor is sacrificing children to an unidentified demon. Gathering quite the following. It's necessary to snuff that out promptly. People become so selfish and superstitious, they slay their own offspring for a chance at a better life. I can't think of anything more counterintuitive, yet murdering innocents rears its ugly head repeatedly. Since the dawn of man, I suppose. No one ever stops to ask themselves why. What forces drive you to believe your life will be better off with the killing of the most innocent? Demons have put on a masterclass in manipulation. Especially in the developed world. Humanity is so gullible, they delve into wickedness with open arms," Felix said, voicing his frustrations.

"Well, take pleasure when you bring those responsible to heel."

"For the witch doctor and those deemed to be in concert with him, their punishment will be slow and just," Felix confirmed. "What do you have on this suspicion from Kansas?"

"Some details jump at me. Early 2000s, a family complained about unnatural phenomenon. Their son vanishes, then soon after, *they* vanish. That house stands unoccupied to this day," Elliot said.

"Mm, and what do you think?" Felix asked.

"Well, the phenomenon gives me pause from completely dismissing it. Lights, apparitions, and something the father reported as a red storm. It's all strange. That said, the man was an author. Could be made up, or he lost his grip on reality. No one has found a trace of them since the disappearance. At our organization, I would say evidence points to a Drift."

"A Drift? It seems far-fetched to believe a Drift has gone unidentified in Kansas," Felix scoffed.

"No, I agree, but there was a Native American presence in the area before relocation, so I can't outright dismiss it entirely," Elliot explained.

"This is the case you're working on?" Felix asked, confused.

"No, it's not. Just something that caught my attention, is all. I have a murdered man and cow. Both in a mangled state. Apparently, a blasted-open cavern, coinciding with a full moon," Elliot said, giving the shortened version.

"You don't think? Those beasts are only on one continent these days. Is there enough evidence?" Felix asked.

"I think it's possible. Do I have enough facts to travel to Kansas? Not yet. I suspect the full moon this month will play a deciding factor in whether this case goes forward," Elliot stated.

"My great-grandfather swore he fought werewolves during the first World War. It's what got me interested in this line of work. You have fun with that if it, indeed, is true. Care to tag along to Africa?"

"I believe you can handle that situation on your own."

"Suit yourself. I think I'll roast the guilty alive over a bonfire. Have some witnesses present. Get the point across that iniquity has no place in this world." Felix smiled.

Elliot envisioned this scene in his mind. Felix gave a half bow before strolling out of the office. The penalty fits the crime committed. They reserved a certain level for those who would harm children. Evil begets righteous retribution.

After shutting the files, Elliot maintained a reserved demeanor as he waited for more information out of Mattfield. Within a few short days, there would be a full moon, which would answer his remaining questions.

In preparation, he would need to visit Bastion's armory. Arrangements should be set in place, his mind focused sharply on the tools and weaponry for the task.

Silver was vitally important. The precious metal would be the way to resolution if his suspicions became reality.

12

MEND

Homecoming in Mattfield brought back memories for Julia. The celebration and traditions had remained unchanged after all these years. To have her sons experiencing what was now a distant memory for her was wonderful. Each high school class competing through lively events. Even though it was an unstated rule, the king and queen would almost certainly be the seniors.

Julia wasn't sure if she could call Brett's love interest his girlfriend yet. Nonetheless, it was exciting to have some stakes involved. Julia had little doubt Cassie would win homecoming queen. In Julia's day, she got nominated for queen. Unfortunately, it was during her junior year. An honor to be nominated. She, of course, won runner-up to the senior who won. Tradition never failed.

This week had already presented challenges. Julia haphazardly accepted the night shift from Debra. She'd had to rush home one day this week to meet with Sheriff Mills. A dangerous criminal had attacked Brett. The challenges of being a single mother and pulling the night shift were impossible. And Julia's father was too old to keep up with his grandsons.

Today was the big game. Julia felt the need to be there for her son. She was still unsure whether that was a possibility. As a loving parent, she swallowed her pride, extending an olive branch to her estranged husband. Julia explained her situation to Michael over the phone. If, in fact, she wouldn't be able to attend the game, at the very least he could. It was the first time she had spoken with

Michael without a hint of animosity. She owed that to Brett.

Michael was appreciative, kindly accepting the gesture. Brett had refused to speak with him since the move. Maybe their broken family unit could use this homecoming as a launching point to heal. Julia prayed Debra would cover a few hours of extra time.

The day of the homecoming game was an awful time to ask—Julia had been so embarrassed by this blunder. Putting it off this long only intensified the feelings. Overwhelming regret gnawed at her.

The parade would get underway shortly. Julia exited her car and entered the hospital.

Receptionist Kari Sears sat behind the greeting desk. "Julia? You're in early. You should rest before the overnight shift," Kari said, perplexed.

"I'm actually here to chat with Debra. I won't be long. Brett's in the parade. I don't want to miss that," Julia answered.

The reception desk sat at the crux of a T intersection of the hospital. Staff entrance and offices were down the hallway left of the receptionist's desk. The waiting room and patient entrance were just opposite. Straight in front of reception sat the patient rooms. Some were for overnight stays, but most were for outpatient visits.

Debra came out of an out-patient room, holding an open laptop in her left hand. She was intently studying the screen—prepping for the next patient, Julia surmised.

"Debra, do you have a few minutes?" Julia called out.

Looking up from the screen, Debra said, "Oh, hey! This is a surprise to see you in so early," Debra said, befuddled.

Julia gathered herself. This had to be done. "Yeah, I know. So, I want to be completely honest with you. When I accepted the night shift this week, Brett hadn't told me he was going out for football. Because of how things have played out, I've put myself in a terrible position. I was afraid to ask this of you, but homecoming is a big deal for everyone in the community. My and my eldest son's relationship has been strained since the move. The last thing I want to do is be a no-show to the biggest football game he may ever play in. Senior year homecoming."

Debra was surprised. "You need me to stay late, so you can be there for your son? Julia, why didn't you come to me sooner?"

"I'm ashamed. Frankly, you deserve better treatment than this last-minute. My estranged husband will be in attendance, as well. There's no excusing this. It has all just overwhelmed me," Julia confided.

"Look, I get it. We're colleagues here. When you need a favor, just ask. I won't hesitate to do the same. Don't waste your time worrying about work. We're here together to manage patient care. More importantly, to care for each other. I know an opportunity will arise for you to return the favor," Debra said.

"I know, I know. Thanks for being understanding with me. Life has been difficult to navigate lately," Julia shared.

"As soon as the game is over, come relieve me, is all I ask. A hotdog and some chips would be good, too. Work a few extra hours in the morning. Deal?" Debra said.

"Yes, and thank you so much." Julia felt like crying in joy.

"Better get a move on. Parade will get underway soon. You should be proud of the job you're doing as a mom. Don't let your pride impede that," Debra encouraged. Turning, she walked to the next patient's room.

"See? Not so bad," Kari said with a smile.

Julia raced out of the building, overjoyed. All the worrying she'd put herself through was for nothing. Deep down inside, she knew this was the case. It was wrong to put Debra in that position. She couldn't turn Julia down without looking like a bad person. Hopefully, the opportunity would arise to make it up to her.

By the time Julia reached Main Street, the crowd had packed the area. Kids of all ages lined the roadside. The owners stood out front as businesses shuttered.

Parents, teachers, and other fans of the team gathered in wait. Mattfield High's band belted out "Welcome to the Jungle" as they began their march. A final celebration of homecoming for the community was now underway. One final boost to the Mattfield Hawks' egos before doing battle that evening on the gridiron.

Following behind the marching band were the first responders. Sheriff Mills sat in his truck as it crawled along. Red and blue lights strobed. He even threw candy for the grade schoolers to great fanfare. Fire trucks honked their horns as they rolled by. Cheers and whistles roared from the crowd.

All the hype gave way for the student-built floats. First up were the freshmen, having built their float based on the movie *Twister*. Nothing was more relatable in Kansas than a film about tornados. On the float was a mock tornado fashioned out of cotton rolls spray-painted gray. The mock tornado was emblazoned with a Bulldog face, the homecoming opponent. In a shout-out to the movie, the tornado had crushed tin cans hung in it as a tribute to Dorothy. Two freshmen dressed as Helen Hunt and Bill Paxton had a lasso around the tornado. When the float reached the heart of Main Street, they pulled the rope, toppling it over. Applause from the gathered crowd echoed between the buildings.

Two boys in black suits stood on the sophomores' float. Silence fell over the crowd. In between them was a cardboard box folded shut. The building of this float lacked ingenuity. One boy began yelling out, "What's in the box?!" He grew more obnoxiously frantic each time he hollered. At the center point, it was time for the big reveal. Kneeling down, the other boy slowly opened the box. Reaching in, he yanked out a bulldog mask and held it high in the air.

Not a bad ode to the film Seven, Julia thought. The crowd roared to life once more.

The junior class went above and beyond with the creation of their float. Blue tarps lined the edge and bottom of their trailer, filled with water, sloshing about, sending splashes of water onto the street. A girl kneeled on a wooden platform in the makeshift pool. Hanging on the edge was a Bulldog scarecrow. She shoved the scarecrow off the platform. Balancing on the board, she stood up, throwing her hands in the air. Quite a sight as the Bulldog floated face down on top of the water. This float was going to be hard to beat.

"That's Sara, my date to the dance tonight," Dalton said, sneaking up on his mom.

"Hey! I was wondering if I'd see you here. Your class did a great job on this," Julia said, hugging her son with one arm.

"Lot of duct tape. Went better than I imagined. It was Sara's idea to stand up at the end. We thought for sure she would end up getting hurt," Dalton smirked.

Brett's class had gone above and beyond building their float, as well. Rolling down the street was a paper-mache cliff. Kneeling on top was a senior boy. Below him, clinging to the side, was a boy in a Bulldog mask and jersey. The boy on top of the cliff grabbed the Bulldog as if to pull him up.

"Hard to beat *The Lion King*," Dalton said, and sighed.

"Why did they make themselves the bad guys?" Julia wondered aloud.

With a pushing motion, the senior on the cliff released the Bulldog, who fell a few feet onto the trailer. Standing atop, he beat his chest, then gave a loud rallying cry: "ARE YOU NOT ENTERTAINED!?"

"*The Lion King* and *Gladiator*, damn. Pretty sure *Gladiator* wasn't a nineties movie. That is kind of cheating," Dalton pointed out.

"Seniors make the rules," Julia reminded.

A gooseneck trailer brought up the end of the parade. Lined up back-to-back sat the entire football team, dressed in khaki pants, each sporting their red and gold jerseys. A chant of, "HAWKS! HAWKS! HAWKS!" broke out. In the center of the Main Street buildings, it echoed. This must've been what gladiators heard entering the Colosseum. Coming to a halt in the center of Main Street, the football players off-loaded.

"You better get in there and support your brother. I'll see you at the game tonight. Your father is coming. He's excited to see you boys," Julia said.

"I know, he texted me. Brett will not be happy about that," Dalton replied.

"Your brother will live."

"And what about you?"

"The first part to healing from a betrayal is forgiveness," said Julia. Inside, she felt nothing but anxiety. Slightly pushing Dalton forward, she turned and departed.

She'd moved to Mattfield with every intention to heal. She hadn't confided in her sons about the process. Michael had reached out to her about having dinner before the evening's game. After a lot of consideration, Julia accepted. It was time to have that face-to-face conversation, going in with an open mind and a sincere need to let go of the hurt.

Unfortunately, Mattfield was a relatively small town. There were only a few sit-down restaurants. Like it or not, people were going to see them. Gossip would follow. Being from here, it was nothing new. Having lived in the city for so many years, becoming the subject of whispers would be a throwback.

Consciously choosing to stay away from the horde downtown, Julia picked the Mattfield Inn for dinner—a misleading name, as it wasn't a place to stay. The inn was nothing more than a hole-in-the-wall diner.

She entered the front door, stepping into the brightly lit dining room. There were six booths and four tables in total. All the seating was open, having arrived early enough to beat the dinner rush. Michael sat facing the door in the farthest booth against the back wall. They looked at each other for the first time in almost two months. Emotions boiled inside Julia. Tears welled up inside her.

Michael stood as she slowly approached. "Julia, thank you for doing this," he said, coming in for a hug. Youthful in his appearance, Michael was handsome as ever, with a fresh haircut and shaped stubble beard.

She allowed her husband to hug her. Julia did not reciprocate.

They sat across from each other. An awkward silence fell between them. She could tell he was searching for the words to start.

"I took all we built together for granted," Michael began. "Our boys. Our marriage. You have listened to me apologize over the phone. At first, I was apologizing because I got caught. You were leaving and my life was spiraling out of control. Everything around me changed drastically. My knee-jerk reaction was, what do I say to make this go away? That was wrong of me. It is not about undoing the pain I caused our family. I cannot take back what I did; our family cannot forget what I did. My actions eroded twenty years of trust. Of unconditional love you provided. Support of my career, even though it kept me away from home far too much, where I lost sight of what matters to me the most: you. I'm inadequate and undeserving of forgiveness as a father and a husband. Yet, I'm here to ask for it. I'm sorry, Julia." Michael began sobbing.

Julia hung on every word. Tears flowed down her cheeks. No matter how much she tried, nothing could've prepared her for this conversation.

"I—" Julia started after a minute. "Leaving you behind was important for me. So I ran home to Mattfield. Pulled our boys away from what was familiar to them, with little thought for the consequences. Raising two teenage boys alone is difficult. Albeit, nothing new. Michael, you were not home. Not enough. But I knew how important your work was to you. And I supported you, even though I couldn't fathom how any job could take priority over your family.

"When the affair came to light, devastated doesn't describe it. For almost two months, I've been bludgeoned by hatred from Brett. Tortured inside by a thousand different emotions. For a short period, I even blamed myself, but you caused all that suffering. The road we're on now is long. There are no shortcuts back. That said, this journey has to start with me. As your wife, I will take that first step for you, Michael. I choose to honor the vows we made in front of God. I forgive you."

Michael broke down as those words left Julia's lips. He cried uncontrollably. Julia glanced behind her to see the people in the kitchen staring. Reaching out, she took her husband's hand.

"If you truly want to be part of this family, everything has to change, Michael. We may get into this process of reconciliation and decide this isn't right for us. I don't know what's going to happen, what new grievances may spring up between us. Life for the foreseeable future will be arduous, but I'll give you the opportunity to prove to our family that you can rise to the occasion," Julia added.

A weight lifted from her shoulders. She had committed to forgiving Michael and reaped the reward. Her tears were no longer of a broken heart, but of repair.

Julia had verbalized it, taking the first step. What she felt inside was more like a leap of faith. Faith in the man she married.

"I do not deserve that from you," Michael choked out.

"Forgiveness isn't something anyone deserves. It is a gift. What you do after you receive it is all that matters," Julia answered.

They made small talk over their burgers, even sharing a few laughs. No matter what came between them, they had still been each other's best friend for decades. A lot of hard conversations remained in their path, but those could wait for another day. Today, they would reconnect and celebrate Brett's homecoming game.

Dalton glowed with joy at seeing his parents together. Walt joined the three of them as they packed into the bleachers. Julia sat on the end, listening to her son chat up a storm with his father. Watching them, she beamed with pride.

A family reunited under the Friday night lights.

13

DEAD END

The crowd for the homecoming game was electric. The entire county's population packed into the stands in celebration. Brett stood on the sideline with his helmet in his left hand, his right hand held over his heart as "The Star-Spangled Banner" was being sung. He sang along to his nation's anthem in his head. Anticipation was building for the game. "And the home of the brave" brought the song to a close.

Brett already felt some anxiety outside of the game. He glimpsed his father in attendance, sitting with his mom and brother, feeling anger just at the sight of his dad. They hadn't spoken in over a month. He knew this was his mom's doing. Brett couldn't comprehend why she would invite him here. His father was the whole reason the family was in Mattfield. As far as Brett was concerned, his dad made his choice. That choice was to abandon his family. He wasn't around much before the affair, anyway.

Following the anthem, the emcee introduced all the homecoming candidates in pairs, positioning them in the center of the crowd on the fifty-yard line. Cassie wore a stunning black gown, walking arm-in-arm with Marcus in his football gear. Brett was happy for her, but part of him longed to be the candidate opposite of her.

"Ladies and gentlemen, it is my honor to present to you today your homecoming king and queen. Selected by a school-wide vote, give it up for Marcus

Jones and Cassie Meeks!"

A raucous roar erupted from the crowd. Brett clapped his hands along with the football team. What happened next crushed him. Marcus dipped Cassie as if they had just finished a dance and planted a kiss on her lips. Again, the crowd erupted in celebration. The king and queen from last year presented Cassie with flowers and her crown.

Brett felt a rush of emotions. Having to watch Marcus kiss her felt like taking a dagger to the heart. To hell with tradition. Marcus had it out for Brett ever since he got to Mattfield. Brett was sure he reveled in the chance to kiss Cassie in front of him.

All the candidates marched off the field. Brett seethed as the game got underway. Tonight, fresh betrayals fueled him on every front. The Bulldogs would be the recipient of his aggression.

Kickoff ensued, with the Bulldogs receiving the ball first. A quick three and out as the Hawks swarmed on defense, stopping two run plays and a pass attempt. There was no return on the Bulldogs' punt.

It was time for the Hawks' offense to get to work. Brett was playing as a slot receiver, working the middle of the field. They led with a run play where Marcus picked up eleven yards and a first down. The Bulldog's secondary defense didn't impress Brett. On the second play, the ball came sailing through the air to him, snatching it out of the air as he streaked across the center of the field. All that stood between him and scoring was the safety. Brett didn't avoid the defender. Barreling straight toward him, lowering his shoulder, a loud pop rang out as Brett collided with the safety, laying him out. Stumbling through the contact, Brett had nothing but green grass in front of him, trucking down the field, full speed to the end zone.

"Touchdown, Hawks!" the announcer roared over the intercom.

Cheers from the crowd rocked the night air. Brett couldn't believe how easily he had just scored. His anger had him so detached, it felt like an out-of-body experience. Heading back to the sideline, he saw the Bulldog coaches out on the field. The player Brett had just trucked was being evaluated. The Bulldog coaches helped the defender off the field and he never returned to the game that evening.

The Hawks were in full control of their destiny, putting up two more touchdowns before halftime while holding their opponents scoreless.

After the half, they kept their foot on the gas, finishing their challenger with a 31–7 homecoming victory. Brett led the team in scoring with two touchdowns. On defense, he didn't allow a single reception as cornerback on six targets.

Coach awarded him the game ball. It was a first for Brett. A little joy came to him in all the anger that raged inside.

"Hell of a game, boys, hell of a game. I'm proud of the work you put in. This results from that hard work. We have a long season ahead of us. Enjoy this one. Have a good time at the dance. Celebrate your victory. Wins are short-lived this time of year. Tomorrow, we look ahead to our next game. You represented your community well. Be smart tonight. We're back at it on Monday," Coach Sparts finished addressing the team.

Brett got cleaned up to prepare for the homecoming dance. The atmosphere in the locker room was abuzz with excitement. Swaths of teammates congratulated him on getting the game ball, making small talk about the plays he made. Brett appreciated the recognition. He solely fixated his mind on confronting his family, who were waiting to see him. Then there was Cassie and those emotions.

"Hell of a game, man," Marcus said, approaching him. "This may surprise you, but I'm glad you're on the team. You might have been the piece we were missing to make a run at the state championship."

Brett looked at Marcus in disbelief. He wondered if there was some ulterior motive. Was he trying to smooth things over after kissing Cassie right in front of him?

"Thanks," Brett said, tying the laces on his dress shoes.

"Come on, man. We just won the homecoming game. You're a hero now. We all see it. I need a little more than thanks," Marcus pressed.

Brett stood up to address Marcus further. "I just have a lot on my mind right now."

"Bro, what could be so bad that you can't enjoy what we did out there tonight?" Marcus asked.

Brett was finding it difficult to bottle up his annoyance. "Look, man, I am happy. As happy as I can be. Honestly didn't enjoy seeing you kiss Cassie, though. Maybe if you and I were cool with each other, it wouldn't bother me. But you've been a real dick ever since I got here. Makes me feel some type of way that you see I can play ball and now you want to be friends. Also, not that you care, but I have some family shit I'm dealing with," Brett replied, unloading.

Marcus looked taken aback. "Hey, man, we're the king and queen. The people demand that kiss; it's a tradition. It meant nothing. It was all for show. I'm truly sorry you still haven't got over the snipe hunting. That was me welcoming you into the fold. Like it or not, you are one of us now. You and I may be the best one-two punch offensively this school has ever seen on the field. I don't want bad blood between us anymore. I want people to remember what our football team is doing." Marcus paused, took a breath, then asked: "What's up with your family?"

And just like that, the feeling of hatred Brett felt toward Marcus eased. Marcus wasn't his enemy. Not like Brett had envisioned him. They'd gotten off on the wrong foot. "Alright, man. I forgive you. The whole reason Dalton and I are in Mattfield is because of my parents. My dad abandoned our family. He's here tonight. I saw him sitting with my mom and brother." Brett confided.

Marcus nodded, putting his hand on Brett's shoulder. "I'd give anything to have both my parents still. It's just been dad and me since I was a little kid. All I can say is, some things are worse than your parents being split up. I'd trade everything to still have my mom." With that, Marcus walked away, leaving Brett feeling remorseful.

Brett finished changing into his dress clothes. Black dress pants paired with a white button-up shirt and black tie. He slung the bag of football gear in need of a washing machine over his shoulder. Tucking the game ball under his arm, he exited the locker room.

Brett's hope that his father had already left was foolish. Outside the building, all the players' families stood huddled, waiting. When Brett emerged, the gathered parents cheered. He couldn't help but smile at that.

Grandpa Walt, Dalton, Cassie, and his father stood together waiting for him.

"You know, for someone who didn't want to go out for football, you sure make it look easy," Walt said.

"Thanks, Grandpa." Brett tossed Walt the football. "Got the game ball, too. Where's Mom?"

"Mom had to rush back to work. She was just happy to show up at all," Dalton explained.

"Proud of you, son," his father interjected.

Brett glared at his dad. "Yeah, nice of you to show up."

Guilt was plastered all over Michael's face. "I was hoping we could talk," his father said.

"Dalton and I have a dance to get to. I'd hate to keep the other guys waiting on us," Brett said sharply.

"Okay, of course. I'd better head back to the city, anyway. We'll catch up soon," Michael said.

"Sure," Brett said, ending the conversation between them.

"I'd better get home, too. You two stay out of trouble tonight," Walt said with a wave.

Cassie came over and embraced Brett. They locked eyes with one another as she came in and kissed him on the lips.

"Alright, enough of that shit," Dalton said, walking toward the gymnasium where the dance was being held.

That made Brett and Cassie giggle. "You guys really killed them out there tonight. Word is, you broke that guy's collarbone that tried to tackle you," Cassie relayed.

"Oh, wow. To be honest, that makes me feel kind of bad," Brett said in shock.

"Feel bad tomorrow. Tonight, we dance," Cassie said with a smile.

That brought a smile to his face. Locking fingers, they walked to the gymnasium.

School dances weren't Brett's cup of tea. He had never taken an actual date to one before. Cassie gave him hope that tonight would be different. Trying to put the kiss between Marcus and her out of his mind wasn't easy. Bringing it up to Marcus, who he cared little for, was one thing. He couldn't imagine addressing it with Cassie. Their relationship felt special. Bringing up the kiss wasn't worth ruining what they had.

The gymnasium was unrecognizable inside—from a brightly lit basketball court to a dimly lit dance floor. The DJ set up on the far side, taking song requests. The organizers arranged a few tables with chairs from the cafeteria around the outside. There was a station with drinks and finger foods. Mattfield High knew how to throw a party.

"Dancing with the queen tonight!" Bethany shouted at Brett over the music as they walked past her.

Brett laughed at that. He was on a date with the homecoming queen. What a weird turn of events.

"I'm going to go request us a song," Cassie told him as she scampered off.

Scanning the dark gym, Brett spotted Dalton visiting with Sara. He approached them, announcing his presence.

"What's up?" Brett inquired casually.

"Great game tonight!" Sara said.

"Thank you." As good as all the praise felt, he was prioritizing keeping a humble attitude.

"Cassie left you already?" Dalton jested.

"Left me for a DJ. Go figure. I'm not much of a dancer. I have a feeling she's going to fix that," Brett replied.

Bradley and Marcus showed up to join their growing huddle.

"This is just a warm-up. Who's ready for the after-party?" Bradley quipped.

"After the party?" Brett asked, confused.

"Country cruising, is all," Marcus added slyly.

"Yeah, remind me. Why go with you two again?" Dalton stated.

"Whoa, calm down, little bro. We're cool now. We'll bring along some girls this time. Sara, you can join if you want," said Marcus.

Before Dalton could prep a rebuttal, Sara answered, "I'm down for that. As long as I'm riding with Dalton."

Dalton shot a defeated look at Brett.

"Alright, then, we're in. I'm driving my truck, though," Brett said.

"Sounds like a plan." Marcus smiled.

The football seniors moved on.

"I'll be right back. I'm going to go say hello to some of my friends," Sara said, heading toward the refreshment table.

"Well, that's just great," Dalton lamented. "I wonder what they'll do to one of us this time."

"It's fine, man. Water under the bridge now. Marcus wants to move on and I agree," Brett explained.

"Mom also expects us to be home after the dance is over," Dalton said.

"She's working all night. As far as she knows, we *will* be home. Besides, I know she's the one who got Dad to come to the game tonight. What was she thinking?" Brett said, irritated.

"Oh, I don't know, that maybe our dad should be there to watch you play in your senior year homecoming game."

"If I wanted him there, I would've asked him myself. He abandoned us. I can't forgive that as easily as you can."

Dalton looked like he had a smart response ready when Cassie reappeared.

"Hey, boys. Sorry about that. Got caught talking with some girls. My song is coming up next. Shall we dance?" Cassie asked Brett.

"Let's do it," Brett agreed, exchanging a parting glare with his brother.

They walked out onto the dance floor as the DJ announced the requested song. "Next up, we have 'Demons' by Imagine Dragons," the DJ said enthusiastically.

"Wow, that's an old song," Brett remarked.

"Old? I think the right word is a 'classic,'" Cassie said smiling, "It's not exactly a slow dance song, but we're going to slow dance to it."

As the song began playing, Cassie wrapped her arms around Brett's shoulders, pulling herself close. He rested his hands on her hips. Butterflies took flight in his stomach. The room faded away, leaving only them.

The lyrics came blaring out of the speakers. Brett wanted this moment between them to last forever. Cassie made all his anger evaporate. As their bodies swayed to the rhythm, their eyes remained locked.

"I see your demons," Cassie whispered to him.

This shook Brett. All he could muster was a smirk. Part of him felt like crying. He suppressed the urge to avoid the awkwardness that would ensue.

"I'm not trying to hide them from you," Brett whispered back.

They were glued together on the dance floor for the next four songs in a row. Her arms wrapped around him brought comfort. After taking a brief break, they continued to share in a mix of slow and choreographed party dances throughout the night.

He had fallen head over heels in love with Cassie. Fear of rejection prevented Brett from saying it aloud. They hadn't known each other for long.

As the homecoming dance neared its end, Marcus approached them. "Hey, love birds. Cassie, we're country cruising after this. You in?"

Brett and Cassie shared a bashful look. "I can't tonight. My parents are waiting up on me to get home. Sorry," Cassie said with a reluctant frown.

"Damn, that's alright. I'll take care of lover boy here, don't you worry," Marcus said, annoyed.

"Like you did last time?" Cassie said, in Brett's defense.

Marcus put both hands up. "Jeez, *you're* holding a grudge over that, too? Nothing like last time, I promise."

"Good, do nothing stupid," Cassie said sternly.

She made both of them promise. It was a hollow promise, Brett thought. He was truly clueless about what he was getting into.

As the dance let out, Brett walked Cassie to her car. She shared a long hug before she planted a kiss on his lips.

"Don't be an idiot tonight. I mean it. Trouble seems to find you. You got abandoned in the countryside. A crazy, wanted guy attacked you. Just be careful."

"I won't and I will. I'll text you," Brett assured.

With that, Cassie got in her car and headed for home.

What a night, Brett reflected. He thought his social life away from home couldn't be better: fitting in at a new school, excelling in football, and being blindsided by romance.

Dalton was waiting at the truck with Sara at his side.

"We still doing this?" Dalton asked.

"Yeah, we're going," Brett reiterated.

Marcus's and Bradley's trucks pulled up beside Brett's. The window rolled down on Marcus's truck. "Let's get it!" Marcus exclaimed.

"How many do we have tonight?" Brett inquired. He saw Bethany riding shotgun with Marcus.

"I've got Bethany. Bradley has Henry riding with him. Looks like we're the magnificent seven tonight," Marcus joked.

"What's the plan?" Dalton couldn't help but ask.

"We'll let you lead the way. Wherever you go, we shall follow," Marcus encouraged, giving a two-finger salute.

"I like that. Try to keep up," Brett said cockily. Dalton and Sara got into the back seat of his truck. Brett got behind the wheel. "I feel like a chaperon," Brett said to his backseat companions.

"Shut up. Where are we going?" Dalton asked.

"One thing comes to mind. Revenge. Let's take them out past the rock quarry. See if we can't freak them out," Brett said, looking over his shoulder.

"Now we're talking," Sara added.

"Great. Let's do that, I guess," Dalton said reluctantly.

Brett knew his brother wanted nothing to do with the plan, but because of Sara's presence, Brett wouldn't have to listen to Dalton whine about it. He knew his brother had feelings for Sara. That was something Brett was taking advantage of tonight.

Exiting the parking lot, they turned left and cruised down the highway for a few miles. Then they turned the truck onto the now infamous Jackson Road. Brett sped down the gravel, leaving plumes of dust in the rear-view mirror.

Being behind the wheel was a different experience for country cruising. Brett understood why the other guys enjoyed it so much. It felt dangerous, yet exhilarating. He had control but then he also didn't. The gravel road shifted the speeding truck atop its surface. Brett imagined this was a more extreme feeling than surfing on a wave in the ocean.

As Brett was driving, he immediately recognized the spot where LaVern Stillman's F-150 pickup had almost struck him—a close call he'd tried to keep repressed. Finally, they reached the stop sign at the county highway. Crossing the county highway, he stopped the truck in the center of the road, right in front of Coal Creek Rock Quarry's entrance.

"I can't believe Mr. Stillman died there a month ago," Sara blurted out.

That sentiment brought an uneasy feeling to Brett. The dark countryside was well lit tonight by the full moon hanging overhead. Stillman's death coincided with a full moon—a startling realization. His intentions were to scare Marcus and Bradley, but Brett was only scaring himself so far.

Two signs stood across from the quarry entrance: "Dead End" and "Low Maintenance Road" in black lettering on a yellow backdrop.

Marcus pulled his truck up on Brett's left side. Bradley's truck mirrored the action on the right. Brett rolled down both front windows to engage with them.

"We going down dead-end Jackson Road?" Marcus asked.

"That's the plan," Brett said nonchalantly, waiting for one of them to decline.

"You see that sign, says low maintenance road? Out here, that means no maintenance. It's a one-lane road down through there. That's being generous. It's just two tire tracks with grass growing between them. Hills and valley. Nowhere to turn around until the end. You sure you're up for that, city boy?" Bradley quizzed from the passenger side.

"If you guys aren't up for it, I understand," Brett said, hoping someone would take the bait.

"Nah, we're up for it. Carry on," Marcus called his bluff.

With the windows rolled back up, Brett sighed. "I guess we're doing this," Brett said hesitantly.

Dalton finally chimed in, "We should keep cruising. What's the point if it's a dead end?"

"Come on, guys, it'll be fun," Sara said, enthused.

Brett had no one to blame but himself for this one, he knew. It was his idea and now he must follow through. Despite Cassie's plea for him to avoid idiocy, he persisted in engaging in foolishness.

He checked his cell phone to confirm his suspicions. No service. Of course not. This entire area was a dead zone out here.

Starting the truck out at a crawl, they began the trek down the dead-end road. Marcus's truck fell in behind him. The road started out fine but became a rocky mess. Dropping into the first valley, he bounced them all out of their seats as the truck scrambled over rocks. Dalton bounced up high enough to smack his head on the truck roof. "What the hell," he complained.

There was no way to calm the ride down. Bradley wasn't joking when he said this road had no maintenance. Brett had never experienced a rougher ride. After slowly traversing along for twenty minutes, they dropped into another valley, even worse than the first one. Bouncing, the truck descended until it reached the bottom, where Brett crossed a shallow creek. Water splashed as his truck rolled through. A loud metal-on-metal crunching noise brought him to a halt.

"Great, now what?" Dalton said, shaking his head.

Brett got out of the truck, illuminated by Marcus's headlights. Initially, he presumed a truck breakdown, then Marcus exited his truck and began yelling.

"Hey, man, what the hell?"

Brett walked across the shallow creek. Water soaked into his dress shoes as he went. Marcus stood at the back of his truck. Brett saw what the noise had been. Bradley had smashed his front bumper into the back of Marcus's truck. Bradley got out, throwing his hands up in the air, clearly agitated.

"Something broke on my truck man. Couldn't stop it, just smashed into you," Bradley said in frustration.

"Bro, we are out here in the middle of fucking nowhere. Your truck better be drivable," Marcus's voice shook.

"Let's figure it out," Brett said.

They inspected Bradley's truck. Panic set in when they found the problem. The front passenger tire was leaning to one side excessively, nearly touching the ground.

"Damn it!" Marcus screamed.

"It's not my fault, man. We knew better than driving down this shithole of a road," Bradley said.

"Alright, alright. Calm down. Panicking won't help," Brett asserted, taking charge.

"Yeah, well, do you have a tow rope? We need to move Bradley's truck from here. Which, to be honest, being down in the bottom of a valley, we'll probably need a tractor," Marcus replied.

"I can't believe this," Bradley said, panicked.

Brett thought for a few seconds. "Look, I don't have a tow rope, so if it's going to take a tractor, then we best get a tractor."

"It's midnight, man," Marcus whined.

"Well, I'm not from around here, so one of you better know someone with a tractor," Brett pressed.

"Look," Marcus paused, running his hand through his hair, "I'll get us a tractor. It will take a few hours. First, I have to get somewhere with phone service. I mean, we're at least four miles down in here."

"It's the only way, man," Brett responded.

Marcus opened the door to his truck and pulled out a flashlight. He secured his knife onto his belt before shutting the truck door again.

"Want anyone to go with you?" Bradley asked meekly.

"I think it's best if I cool off alone. Besides, I don't need anyone slowing me down," Marcus stated bluntly.

"What do you need a knife for?" Brett asked.

"I don't. It's my grandfather's knife. I carry it everywhere I'm allowed to," Marcus said. "I'll be back as soon as I can."

The beams from Marcus's flashlight faded into the dark after he finished the climb out of the valley. Brett only hoped he could get them out of this predicament before his mom got home from work. A dream, but he was hoping.

Soon everyone else was out of the vehicles, huddled up. Panic spread among the newly informed. Sara was the most upset, fearing punishment at home. She went sulking off by herself. Dalton chased after her to console her.

"Remind me when I get ungrounded from this next year to never go anywhere with you guys again. My parents are going to freak," Bethany complained.

"Here's what I'm picturing: Our parents will discover we're absent and contact the authorities to search for us. We're in so much trouble, guys," Henry said. "Coach might kick us off the team after this."

"Coach may get mad and punish us. He sure as hell can't afford to kick us off the team," Bradley said with a raised eyebrow.

"I agree with Bradley on that, but this is a big mess-up," Brett added.

"Oh, screw football. Guys, we're stuck! I need to be home!" Bethany shouted.

"Don't we all? What do you want us to do?" Brett asked. She was getting on his nerves now.

"Honestly, walk me the hell out of here," Bethany said. "I can get a signal and have someone take me home. I don't know about any of you, but my parents are strict. I should've left with Marcus."

Brett couldn't help but feel guilt over how distraught she was. "Okay, let's go," Brett told her.

"Really?" Bethany asked, perking up.

"It's not like we're doing anything. I'll walk you out of here and come back with Marcus," Brett said.

"Thank you so much." Bethany lit up with relief.

"We'll hold down the fort," Bradley added.

Looking over, he saw his brother standing with Sara by the creek. "Dalton,

I'm walking Bethany to the highway. I'll be back soon, okay?" Brett yelled to him.

Dalton held his arm up in the air with a thumbs-up, never turning to look at him.

With only cell phones for flashlights, Brett led Bethany as they trudged up the hill, thankful for the real-world use of his football conditioning.

Brett knew his mom would discover what happened. This time, the punishment would be severe. Cassie would not be happy, either. Her one instruction not to be an idiot blew up in his face.

Stuck on a backcountry road yet again. At least he wasn't alone this time—the one positive thing about the predicament.

A blood-curdling howl carried through the night air, a familiarly haunting sound he had experienced once before. Only this time, it was much louder. Much closer. Brett froze in his tracks as fear washed over him. The howl lingered in his ears until finally fading away. He felt Bethany's stare before turning to her.

"Wh— Wha— What was that?" Bethany quivered.

Ignoring her question, Brett focused his attention behind them. Then the screams came. Brett's body trembled in terror.

"Oh my God, oh my God. What is happening? Please!" Bethany cried.

Dread was welling up inside of him. "I need to go get my brother," Brett managed to say.

"Are you crazy? You can't leave me alone! We have to get out of here!" Bethany cried. Tears streamed down her face.

Brett saw that she was too frightened to be left by herself. "Listen to me. You need to be quiet now. Look at my hand; it's shaking, too. I'm scared. I have to get my brother. If you can't stay here alone, then you need to come with me. No noise, okay?" Brett said to Bethany as he grabbed her shoulders with his shaking hands.

Bethany nodded.

They walked back down the road to the edge of the hilltop. Everything in the valley below was still and silent.

"Listen, shut off your light and kneel. Make yourself small. Hold your hand over your mouth if you have to. I'm going down there. I'll be right back, I promise," Brett told her.

Bethany did as he instructed. Brett turned his light off and carefully made his way back down into the valley below. Staying low, he moved alongside the drivers' sides of the trucks. The air was eerily quiet. Using Marcus's truck to steady himself, he moved alongside it, stalking toward his own vehicle.

"Dalton," Brett called out softly. There was no reply. No sound was coming from anything. Staying low, he crossed the creek to his truck. Peering through the windows, there was no one inside. He took a couple of deep breaths to steady his nerves. Moving back across the creek, he went down the trucks' passenger sides, again using the vehicles to steady himself as he crept along. His hand brushed along something wet. Something warm. With his other hand, he clicked his phone's light on to see his hand covered in fresh blood.

Falling to his knees, he hyperventilated. Shining the light on the ground, he saw that blood covered the surroundings. This prompted Brett to shut the light back off.

Please don't be Dalton, please don't be my brother, ran across his mind on an endless loop. He scrambled back up the hill to where Bethany sat, gripping her mouth tightly.

"Where are they?" Bethany whispered as her hand lowered.

"Bethany, we need to go get help," Brett whispered back.

"But where are they?" Bethany asked once more, squeaking.

Struggling to find words, Brett just shook his head to express his lack of answers. Looking at his bloody hand, he wiped it on his pant leg. Seeing his bloody hand, Bethany whimpered in distress.

He needed to get them to the highway. More importantly, he needed to get help for his brother and the others. Brett grabbed Bethany by the wrist and pulled her behind him. Together they tiptoed down the dead-end road, taking care not to use flashlights any longer, an attempt to bring as little attention to themselves as possible.

They stumbled along the rocky tracks of the road in the dark, using the radiating full moon as their only source of light.

14

ABANDONED

Dalton stood next to the shallow creek running across Jackson Road. The light trickling sound the moving water produced was calming, even in the face of their predicament. There were no words to console Sara. They stood with their backs turned to the rest of the group. They all knew trouble awaited each of them at home after tonight.

Why do I always agree to go along with Brett's stupid ideas? This is the last time.

Dalton felt guilt for not saying no. All to impress Sara. She had been eager for the dead-end road until now. Everyone was excited at the prospect until inconvenience struck them. Sara would probably never feel the same toward him once they were all home and punished by parents.

"For what it's worth, I'm sorry. I didn't want to do this. I should've put my foot down," Dalton said to Sara. "The only reason we're out here is because I was trying to impress you."

"Well, I probably would have judged you for it. I wanted to be scared. Actions and consequences, I guess," Sara lamented. "I mean, it was fun until it wasn't."

"Hopefully, Marcus can get us the hell out of here in a timely fashion," Dalton added.

"I won't hold my breath. We'll be lucky if he comes back at all tonight," Sara said, shrugging.

Dalton had never considered that possibility. He had to put the scenario of

Marcus abandoning them out of his mind before becoming even angrier. Maybe they should all leave together if Marcus isn't returning. They were most likely getting in trouble, anyway, so why not? In the background, he heard Bethany whining about being stranded. Luckily for him, Sara had accepted their fate. Bethany's problem was none of his concern.

Brett called out to him from the other group. He had capitulated to Bethany's sob story. Dalton held a thumbs-up above his head in acknowledgment. Most likely, within the hour, they'd all be following suit. Dalton pulled his phone out of his pocket. It read 12:18 a.m.

"Twenty twenty-five, and we still have places without cell service. Unreal," Dalton said.

"That's just the universe rubbing it in our faces. We're screwed," Sara said.

"What would you like to do? Do you want to leave, too?" Dalton asked.

"I don't know. Marcus will be furious if he returns and we're gone. Let's see what Henry and Brad think," Sara replied.

Dalton found it odd that she was concerned about upsetting Marcus. Just a few minutes ago, she wasn't confident he was even coming back for them.

"Damned if we do, damned if we don't, then." Dalton sighed.

They walked over to join Henry and Bradley, fidgeting about the predicament.

"This is my fault, guys. I can't believe my damn truck gave out like that," Bradley apologized.

"It is what it is. What do you guys want to do?" Sara asked them.

"Bethany was crying up a storm, so Brett's walking her to get a ride. Marcus will find someone with a tractor to rescue us. We can't all leave. These trucks need drivers," Henry said.

"*Is* Marcus coming back? Because if not, we're going to sit out here for hours, waiting on help that isn't coming," Dalton pressed.

"Hey, man, he's coming back," Bradley defended.

"Suppose we leave, and help arrives along the way. We'd have to walk back. That'd be nearly ten miles," Henry remarked.

"How about we give him a few hours? If no one shows up, then we head out,"

Sara proposed.

To his dismay, Dalton nodded in agreement with them. He felt on the edge of a mental breakdown.

"I don't know about you guys, but I'm going to go sit in the truck," Dalton said in defeat.

All this just to impress a girl.

"Show me what's wrong with your truck," Sara inquired of Bradley.

Dalton walked back across the creek. Having wet feet just made everything worse. Arriving back at his brother's truck, he reached to open the door. A harrowing scream erupted from Sara. The hair on the back of Dalton's neck stood up.

What now?

Swiftly, he moved back toward the group. Henry and Bradley also began screaming in terror, a frightened choir of blood-curdling screeches.

He couldn't believe what he saw. A large fur-covered bipedal creature lurked in the shadows on the edge of the trees. Dalton froze, fixated on the creature. Water flowed over his feet as he stood planted in the creek. His three companions huddled together against the side of Bradley's truck.

Whatever it was just stood, staring right back at them. The screams turned into whimpers. Dalton felt shivers pulsing through his body with every heartbeat. Survival instinct took over. He stood the farthest from the creature. His brain was telling him to abandon the others. Find some place safe to hide. Actively fighting against the thoughts, he focused on Sara. She came out here with him. He needed to protect her.

The creature seemed to grow taller as it arched its back, releasing an echoing howl. At that moment, Dalton felt his body go weak, catching himself on the front of Marcus's truck as he almost fainted. The howl lingered on. Dalton ran beside Marcus's truck. Reaching over Bradley's hood, he grabbed Sara's shoulder. Her face was deathly pale.

Sara clambered between Bradley's and Marcus's touching trucks to join Dalton.

Upon her crossing, the monster charged.

Henry dove between the trucks, thudding on the ground beneath their feet.

Bradley never moved.

The beast cleared the distance in the blink of an eye. Bradley raised his hands to shield his face. He let out a loud cry that turned to a drowning gargle. The monster rocked the trucks as it lunged on top of him.

Dalton's mind was spiraling. Taking Sara's hand, he led her into the creek. They ran against the small current heading west, both of them panting and stammering through the darkened wooded area.

Climbing up an embankment, he pulled Sara behind him. Free of the frigid creek, his goal was to make less noise than trampling through water.

Sara attempted to speak, but nothing came out.

"I saw it," Dalton whispered, shaking. "We have to head south toward the rock quarry. I'm hoping moving in the creek will throw it off tracking us."

"What about Henry? I didn't see where he went," Sara said, finally finding her voice.

"I don't know. Look, it's you and me. Let's make as little noise as possible and get the hell out of here alive," Dalton said quietly.

Sara nodded.

Traveling in the woods in the early morning hours proved difficult. Every noise they produced tromping in the underbrush made Dalton shudder. The monster might catch up any moment. He hoped it wasn't actively seeking them out.

His brain was still coming to terms with what they all witnessed. Clear as day, illuminated by the full moon, Dalton was certain the creature was a were-wolf. Something out of legend that wasn't supposed to exist. How was that even possible? Did it kill Bradley? No time to process. Focus was trained on each footstep, trying to maintain absolute silence.

Since parting from the creek, he was uncertain in which direction they were heading. Glimpses of the moon reassured him they weren't walking in circles. Dalton repeatedly walked into thistle bushes and locust trees, each one leaving fresh scratches on his arms.

Finally, they reached the edge of the woods. An old, two-story homestead with a rickety barn stood before them. Both dilapidated and gray, someone had abandoned the buildings long ago.

"If what we saw is a werewolf, we hide until sunrise. This place looks secure," Dalton whispered to Sara.

"Full moon, werewolf," Sara stuttered, looking up at the sky.

Dalton put his hand on her shoulder, shifting his attention back to the forgotten homestead. Mustering their strength, they left the concealment of the trees, tucking themselves away in the barn's shadow.

"I can't imagine how solid either of these buildings are structurally. I'm thinking about the loft of the barn," Dalton said.

"I've been in abandoned houses before. They're sturdy enough," Sara vouched.

He observed the old home missing its front door and windows. Dalton wanted more degrees of separation from the outside. Thankfully, the barn door was still intact. Sneaking to the end of the barn, he saw there was an old tractor and plow below the hayloft opening. The plow was red with rust, the sweeps for tilling earth pointed upward. A relic left behind with the farm. He saw the hayloft door lying in the dirt beside the plow. The hinges had likely failed from years of neglect. None of the hiding places here were what he envisioned.

A figure came sprinting out of the dark into the homestead's yard.

"Henry!" Sara called softly.

Henry was holding his left arm, gasping for air. Dalton felt a fresh surge of anxiety. He saw blood dripping from Henry's injured arm. The werewolf was going to have a fresh trail straight to their hiding place.

"You left me!" Henry cried out angrily between gasps.

"Sara, we don't have time. Hide! It's coming," Dalton said.

She gave him a bewildered look. Sara wasted no time before running into the abandoned home.

"Henry, you need to run!" Dalton called out to his friend.

"I can barely breathe, man. I'm bleeding. I need your help," Henry answered in pain.

Dalton wanted nothing more than to help his friend because during the truck attack, Dalton never considered Henry; in the heat of the moment, he chose to only help Sara and himself. That wasn't the type of person Dalton was. He didn't abandon people he cared about. Fear had revealed the part of Dalton he felt ashamed of. But there was no aid to render Henry. They were all being hunted.

Dalton felt overwhelmed in the moment. His eyes filled with tears as he glanced at Henry one last time. Henry dropped to his knees from fatigue. Out in the dark beyond the yard, Dalton thought he saw a shadowy figure streak by.

I'm sorry, ran through his mind. He couldn't make the sounds to say it aloud.

Climbing onto the rusty plow, he looked up at the hayloft entrance. Steadying himself on top of the sharp sweeps, he lunged upward, grabbing onto the hayloft ledge. If he fell now, the plow sweeps would impale him. Dalton slithered his body inside the hayloft to a semblance of safety.

"Dalton! Don't leave me!" Henry cried out from the yard.

More tears came streaming down Dalton's face. In his distress, he nearly stepped on an old two-by-four with nails protruding from it. Carefully position-ing himself, he could see through holes in the barn's exterior. Henry remained kneeling in place. His friend had given up. Dalton knew deep down there was nothing he could've done to help. Life didn't prepare him for such a situation. Dalton could only protect his own life. Self-preservation had taken control.

The werewolf finally came into sight. It moved methodically in its approach. It didn't appear that the creature was in a hurry. A low, rumbling growl came from the monster.

Dalton gripped his chest. His heartbeat was so thunderous, he feared being discovered.

Each step of the werewolf's unique gait brought it closer to Henry. Dalton noticed the lengthy arms the werewolf possessed, matched by long, blade-tipped fingers attached to its large hands. Lethal tools in the creature's arsenal. But nothing was more frightening than its set of jaws embedded in the elongated snout of the werewolf's massive head.

Time seemed to stand still. Henry looked behind him before screaming in agony. He began crawling toward the house, using his one good arm and his knees.

Dalton peered through another hole, toward the house. Looking into the second story of the house, he saw Sara's outline sheltered inside. Turning his attention back to Henry, the werewolf stood over him, jaws agape, still producing its menacing snarl.

It lifted one of its large, clawed feet off the ground and planting it square in Henry's back, preventing farther crawling. Henry let out a scream, but began struggling for air under the weight. The werewolf's right hand reached down and ran its clawed fingers through Henry's hair. Dalton watched in confusion. What was he witnessing? Was this monster taunting its prey?

With snake-like speed, its jaws came down onto Henry's head. Dalton pulled his face away from the hole and bit his arm to smother the need to scream.

The sounds of Henry's last moments would forever haunt him.

Silence overtook the abandoned farm as Dalton wished to wake from this nightmare.

Gathering the courage against his better judgment, Dalton looked through the hole once more. Standing tall with its snout to the sky, the werewolf seemed to take deep sniffs of air.

Oh, shit, Dalton thought.

The pointed, furry ears twitched as if listening. Lowering its snout, the werewolf's attention was pointed straight toward the open door of the abandoned home. The low growl began again.

Lurching forward, the monster walked to the open doorway and maneuvered its large body into the house.

I have to do something.

Dalton's mind raced. He stared through the hole at Sara, who was standing by the second-story window. She was looking at him for help. Taking deep breaths, Dalton devised a plan. He moved back to the entrance of the hayloft. There was no easy way down. The old plow guarded below.

"SARA, THE ROOF! CLIMB UP ONTO THE ROOF!" Dalton yelled to her.

She went to climb out as instructed, then an explosion of splintering wood rang out. Sara seemed to drop straight down, her hands grabbing the windowsill. The last thing Dalton saw was her fingers lose their grip. Screams of terror lasted but a few seconds. Silence returned.

Dalton stood in stunned disbelief. The beast had pulled her down through the floorboards.

And he had just given away his position to save her. In a twist of cruel fate, he was now all alone. On an abandoned farm. With a werewolf. No one was coming to help. Fleeing was not an option.

An idea dawned on him. Maybe he could kill this thing.

The werewolf shone with blood in the moonlight as it reemerged through the open front door. It cocked its head. Their eyes met. Dalton saw nothing but death in the predator's yellow eyes.

His plan had to succeed.

"I don't have all night, bitch!" Dalton taunted. "You *are* a bitch, right?"

Whether the werewolf understood, the taunting worked. Moving out of the opening, Dalton grabbed the two-by-four with nails. Pressing himself up against the barn wall, he saw the hands grab onto the ledge as the werewolf climbed up inside. He waited until it stood up before swinging the board full force. Rusty nails from the old piece of barn wood sank into the werewolf's face as it flailed its arms. The creature leaned too far backward, tumbling out of the hayloft opening. Dalton nervously looked out. The werewolf laid motionless, impaled on the sweeps of the old plow.

"That's for my friends," Dalton said, spitting on the werewolf. Using his phone as a light, he made his way down to the dirt floor of the barn. With a few kicks, he knocked a board loose. Once outside, he wouldn't allow himself to look at Henry's dead body. He was also afraid of what had become of Sara.

Catching his breath, he followed the old homestead's driveway, which brought him back to the gravel road this nightmare began on. To save time, he jogged toward the quarry. Tears streamed over the loss of his friends. Then a strange thought came to mind. Dalton wondered if he was the first person to kill a werewolf.

If it was, in fact, dead.

15

THE PIT

Paranoia ravaged Brett's mind with every unexplained noise in the dark. Bethany had been sobbing for an hour straight. He couldn't bring himself to ask for her silence again. After an hour, they were still walking. Brett was plotting what to do after getting Bethany to safety. Finding Dalton was his key priority. Where had the others disappeared to? Most importantly, whose blood did Brett have on his hand?

Silhouettes of gravel piles became visible. Coal Creek Rock Quarry was now in their sight.

"We did it," Bethany's voice cracked. "We're getting out of here."

"*You* are getting out of here. I have to find my brother," Brett corrected.

"Brett, you can't leave me! We have to get help for the others," Bethany replied.

"No! I won't leave my brother. I did earlier. Dalton's out there somewhere," Brett said, pointing back the way they came. "I have gotten you to safety. The highway is close. That's as far as I go."

She didn't insist on discussing it more. Brett's tone made his point clear.

Something on the ground reflected the moonlight. Brett bent down and picked up a cell phone with a cracked screen.

"That's Marcus's phone," Bethany said, becoming more distraught.

The safety of reaching the highway faded for Brett. Even now, they remained in grave danger. Fear and desperation fueled his determination to find a solution. Studying the surroundings, he worked on formulating a new plan. His gut instinct reminded him of LaVern Stillman's death a month ago. Their circumstances left little choice.

"Change of plans. We need to hide. Coal Creek is our best option," Brett said.

"No, no. We should get out of here. Marcus's phone. This place isn't safe," Bethany responded in disbelief.

"I know. Moving about in the open makes us easy targets. Tom Morro. He threatened to kill my family and friends. The lunatic must be here with us. This is the same place he killed LaVern Stillman. Look, I kicked his ass once, but if he's armed, I can't protect us," Brett said.

Bethany contemplated his theory. "There was blood at the trucks, Brett. Morro can't be in two places at once. What happened to Marcus? And that howl? What was that?"

Brett thought about it. He remained perplexed.

"Morro has help. He's evaded capture for a month. No one does that without help." Brett struggled to find the right words. "I've heard that howl once before. I was close by when Stillman got murdered."

Surprise washed over Bethany's face. "What do you mean? You were here?" She took a step, backing away from Brett.

"No, not here, but close. I heard the howl that night. Dalton and I were told by the guys to keep quiet. None of the information we have changes the investigation at all," Brett asserted.

"I've read everything that's come out about Mr. Stillman's death, Brett. None of it mentions anything about wolves," Bethany said.

"Fair enough," Brett answered, not wanting to waste time arguing, "I'm going to Coal Creek's office building. Maybe we can find Marcus."

He could tell Bethany wasn't sure if she trusted him any longer. "I got you this far," Brett said, reminding her.

He climbed over a barbed wire fence protecting the property. After a momentary delay, Bethany joined him, slapping his hand away when he tried to assist her over the fence.

They passed by two mountains of different-sized crushed rock. Stillman's death transformed a work site into a harrowing environment, intensified by the darkness of night. Since leaving the trucks, Brett had kept his eyes scouring for any sign of danger. To his relief, nothing had threatened them outside his own imagination.

"Thank God," Brett said, relieved to grip the railing outside the white office trailer, then walking up the ramp to look inside. They had boarded up the door's window. Morro's previous break-in damage, Brett assumed.

"I should be able to get in, but I'll need something to pry the board off." Brett thought a screwdriver would suffice.

"Well, that's illegal," Bethany said, taken aback.

Brett glowered at her.

"Brett?" a voice called out. "Brett, is that you?"

He recognized the voice. "Marcus?" Brett called back, swiftly moving back down the office's ramp. Using the light from his cell phone, he searched under the wooden ramp, finding Marcus tucked underneath. Marcus had his silver-bladed knife held out in front of him in a shaking hand, shirt stained red with blood from his left shoulder down. The blade of his knife was also wet with blood.

"Marcus, what happened? Are you alright?" Brett asked, afraid he already knew the answer.

"I've been better. Fucking thing bit into me, man. Got a few stabs in, though." Marcus said. His voice broke from the throbbing pain.

"Bit you? Like an animal?" Bethany questioned.

"Nah, a werewolf," Marcus replied.

Brett was in disbelief, but how could he mock the situation? "Come on, man. What the hell happened?" Brett pressed.

Marcus reiterated, "Guys, no joke. A werewolf attacked me. Or at least— I mean, that's the truth. Maybe it's something else. I don't know what else to call it."

Concern was growing inside Brett for Marcus's health. "Werewolves aren't real. You need medical attention as soon as possible," Brett said.

Marcus chuckled at that. "Werewolves aren't real? Tell that to my shoulder, man. It's a miracle I'm even alive."

"You think that's a miracle? The actual miracle is you carrying a knife. Not just any knife. Just so happens your knife has a silver blade. Those odds aren't likely to begin with, but here we are. Wouldn't you know, the one kid carrying a silver-bladed knife gets attacked by a werewolf? A fabled creature that doesn't exist and can only get hurt by—you guessed it—silver. That's what you're telling us?" Brett asked. "You have better odds of being struck by lightning."

"Don't forget to factor in me being black. That's more like destiny than just a coincidence," Marcus said as the odds became even less likely.

"I can't." Brett threw his hands up.

"What about the howl? We both heard it earlier. From what you told me, you've heard the howl once before. The same night Mr. Stillman died at this quarry," Bethany said, pointing upward. "That's a full moon, Brett. So, if you're going to talk odds, factor in all the data."

"Thank you," Marcus said.

Marcus could be delirious from the wound. There was enough evidence to force Brett to at least entertain the idea. Attacked by a werewolf? That could gain you confinement in a psychiatric facility. And yet, ironically, it made a lot more sense than Brett wanted to admit.

"What do we do, then?" Brett asked.

"With your help, I can manage walking. Let's get the hell out of here," Marcus whispered, his voice filled with a trembling urgency, as if they were being watched.

"We can't leave the others behind," Brett pushed back.

"No, we can't stay. You didn't see it, man. We're as good as dead if it comes back. Do you have a better idea?" Marcus had never projected fear to Brett before.

"I have a plan," Brett said. "I'm going to find my brother."

"That's not a plan. That's suicide," Marcus said.

"Maybe so. You didn't let me finish. Bethany will scale the closest gravel pile. She'll be the same height as the area's tree tops. Hope to God she can make a phone call. Oh, and I need to borrow your grandfather's knife. I'll find the others."

"You'll never make it," Marcus said.

"I have to try," Brett replied.

"I can climb the gravel, no problem," Bethany said. "Attempt to call 911. I can do that. Marcus, you're in no shape to be moving. Besides, if there is a monster waiting for us, we for sure won't stand a chance in the open. Being up high will make me feel safer."

Marcus's eyes told a different story than his words. "Alright, then. I— I love you both. Good luck out there," Marcus stuttered as he sheathed the knife before handing it over to Brett.

The sentiment was awkward for Brett. Marcus was afraid they were going to their doom. "We got this," Brett said, then fashioned the sheath onto his belt.

Bethany jogged alongside him, back toward the closest mountain of gravel, stopping at the base to catch their breath.

"Watch your footing. It's going to give out as you climb. Try not to get buried," Brett said.

"Not my first rodeo, city boy. I got this. Be careful out there. I hope you find the others," Bethany replied. With that, she began scaling the mound of gravel. Each step higher brought the sound of cascading rocks sliding down behind her. Within a minute, she was secure on top of the pile.

A wave of exhaustion came over Brett. This had become one of the longest days of his life.

Just push for a little longer, he told himself. *Your brother needs you.*

Without Bethany, he ran at an even faster pace back toward the road, vaulting over the barbed wire fence with ease. Fear of the unknown had unleashed a rush of adrenaline, making him feel almost superhuman. Stepping back into the tracks of Jackson Road, he stared ahead in the darkness.

Brett had promised Cassie not to do anything stupid tonight. So much for that.

Taking a few steps before halting, he heard the pitter-patter of feet. Standing in silence, the noise continued, growing louder. Someone was sprinting toward him. Brett watched as Dalton became distinguishable from the night. Winded, Dalton paused.

Brett ran to him instead. "Oh, thank God, man. I went back to the trucks. All of you had disappeared. There was blood. I'm just glad you're okay." The words poured out of Brett.

Hunching over, Dalton breathed heavily. "That was, uh, Bradley's blood. I think he died there." Dalton got words out with each exhale.

"Died? I didn't see him. What about Sara and Henry?" Brett asked.

"They're gone. You wouldn't believe me if I told you," Dalton continued.

"Werewolf?" Brett tossed out.

Dalton's demeanor changed. "Did you see it, too?"

"Well, no. Marcus swore a werewolf attacked him by the quarry."

Dalton looked puzzled. "I think I killed the one that attacked us. Can't be for sure. I didn't stick around. Werewolves aren't supposed to be real, but they are. So it's hard to say how much is based on truth, you know? Maybe they can die other ways. I hope it's not just silver."

Brett unsheathed the knife to show his brother. "Borrowed Marcus's silver knife."

"Trust me. You don't want to be close enough to use a knife," Dalton said.

That wasn't reassuring. Marcus got torn up in the process of using the knife. "Bethany is trying to call for help, and Marcus needs a hospital. We should get back," Brett said.

Dalton held his hand up. "We need to be careful, Brett. If an attack occurred on Marcus here, it implies multiple werewolves."

The thought had crossed Brett's mind, but it was hard enough to convince himself there was even a *single* werewolf.

A howl carried to them from down Jackson Road. This was really happening.

Brett led the way as they sprinted. All that stood in their way of Coal Creek was the barbed wire fence.

Up and over, just like before. Hearing the howl compounded the stress. They needed to hurry. Grabbing a fence post, Brett used it to lunge over the top wire, but his right quad caught on a barb this time. A sting of pain went down his leg as it ripped open, leaving a long rip in the pant.

"Aw! Damn it!" Brett yelled.

Dalton saw what happened and tried to climb between the middle wires instead.

"Up and over, man! Come on!" Brett yelled.

His brother became ensnared by the barbs of the wires.

"I'm stuck! Help! It's cutting me!" Dalton cried in pain.

Brett, wide-eyed, watched as a hulking werewolf, its fur shimmering in the moonlight, erupted from the pitch-black abyss. The air filled with the bone-chilling growls and snarls of the beast. A pungent aroma of rotten meat choked Brett. Fear seized every fiber of his being.

Turning to look, Dalton recognized his expression. "Brett! Hurry!" Dalton screamed.

Springing into action, Brett started prying loose the barbs buried in his brother's flesh. The werewolf closed the gap within seconds as it ran at full speed toward them. Brett shook in fear, trying to free his little brother. There just wasn't enough time.

Brett's breath caught in his throat as the towering figure of the werewolf loomed over the fence. The moonlight cast eerie shadows on its massive, seven-foot-tall frame, accentuating the creature's terrifying presence. Engulfed in a thick coat of ashen gray fur, it had an otherworldly appearance. The stench of death permeated the air. Brett's heart pounded, his skin prickling with a mixture of fear and anticipation. Blood spewed from punctures in the beast's abdomen. It was definitely the werewolf that attacked Marcus.

Acting quickly, Brett stood up, ripping the knife from its sheath.

"Run, Brett! Go!" Dalton cried.

"I'm not leaving you again," Brett said, teary-eyed.

With its clawed hand, the werewolf reached for Dalton. Brett lunged, swinging across the top wire and slashing the knife downward. A howl of pain came from the werewolf as the knife gashed its arm. Its eyes narrowed in on the knife, letting a low growl rumble out from its throat.

Dalton freed himself from the fence, tumbling onto the ground on Brett's side of the fence.

Eyes glowing with intensity, the werewolf lunged with its left arm, maneuvering under the fence's rusted bottom wire, grabbing Dalton. Its razor claws dug into Dalton's trembling back. He let out a scream of excruciating agony.

Brett twirled the knife in his sweaty palm, facing the sharp blade toward the ground. His arm windmilled high into the air, unleashing a powerful swing. The impact reverberated through his body as he felt the monster's free arm block his punishing blow. In shock, his grip on the knife came loose. He watched his only means of offense soar into the night sky.

A swift pull dragged Dalton under the bottom wire of the fence, his cries echoing.

The tables twisted with alarming speed, causing a disorienting whirl in Brett's senses. An incessant ringing filled his ears, drowning out the shrieks coming from his brother.

"Please!" Brett's voice erupted in a desperate plea. The monster's gaze fixed upon him, burrowing into the deepest recesses of his soul. Yellow eyes like molten sulfur seemed to reflect the very abyss of Hell. His brother was now held in the clutches of death itself.

The werewolf, palming his head, lifted Dalton off the ground with ease, the boy writhing in torment as his toes kicked just above the earth. The werewolf extended its right arm out as if goading Brett.

"Take care of mom," Dalton breathed out, his voice barely audible. He felt the weight of his impending demise.

The werewolf's claws intertwined, creating a crude blade in the moonlight. Slashing its arm across Dalton's neck, his lifeless body dropped free. His head remained clenched in the werewolf's hand.

Brett turned away, his steps faltering as he reached out with his hands to steady himself before finding his footing again. He fought to stay conscious, his mind reeling. He tripped and crashed onto the ground, using his elbows to drag himself forward. Determination surged through him as he kicked up dirt, propelling himself into a desperate sprint. Brett knew he had to flee, feeling like prey being hunted by a merciless predator.

At full speed, Brett leapt into the air, colliding with the mountain of gravel as he bear-crawled toward its peak.

"Brett? What's the matter?" Bethany asked at his frantic appearance.

Brett's breathing was erratic. He was in stunned disbelief. Ignoring Bethany, he scanned below them.

"You look rabid, man," Bethany expressed concern.

"Dead. They're all dead," Brett whimpered.

Bethany shuddered at the revelation. She pulled her phone out.

"I've had no luck. I'll keep trying," Bethany declared. "Wait, Brett! It's ringing! The phone!" she shouted with joy. Bethany put the call on speakerphone.

They listened with anticipation as the phone rang. On the second ring, someone answered.

"Nine-one-one, what is your emergency?" the voice inquired.

"We're at Coal Creek Rock Quarry. Mattfield, Kansas. I don't know how to explain." Bethany's voice cracked. "Please, we need help."

"Hang on, ma'am. Help is on the way. Are you injured?" the 911 operator continued.

Bethany dropped the phone, her voice quivering, "Brett, Brett. It's here."

"Ma'am?" the 911 operator said.

Brett reached down to scoop up the phone, but the loose rock gave way sliding it down the side of the gravel pile.

Bethany let out a scream of terror.

The werewolf started climbing.

"Bethany, quick!" Brett shouted, dropping his feet on the side the werewolf was scaling. "Did you learn the mountain climber exercise, like in grade school?

If we pump our feet, we can slide the gravel down. Maybe it won't be able to get to us."

She joined in, dropping beside him. Their legs moved in synchronized motion, creating a rhythmic sound as the gravel beneath them slid away. The werewolf's menacing growls came from below as it desperately reached out for them. Ignoring the fear, they pumped their legs faster. Gravel let loose beneath the monster. Brett felt the swipe of claws brush against his foot just before the werewolf tumbled backward, crashing to the ground.

"We did it!" Bethany cheered.

"We lost a lot of ground, though," Brett observed.

The werewolf violently flailed its arms, digging into the gravel mound beneath them. The air filled with dust.

"What's it doing?" Bethany asked, bewildered.

Brett felt the gravel giving way. They were now on the receiving end of the sliding rocks. "Bethany, it's trying to cause us to fall. We have to slide down the other side," Brett said.

"We can't go down there!" Bethany yelled.

"I'll distract it. I'll give you as much time as possible," Brett assured. "Help is on its way."

This would be his last stand.

With no alternatives left, they set their plan in motion, aware of the dire circumstances. Side by side, they descended, the rough surface scraping against their palms, the suffocating dust filling their nostrils. Their feet contacted the ground, sending a jolt of adrenaline through their bodies.

As they rose to flee, the gravel erupted with a cacophony of clattering stones. The werewolf, navigating through the loose rock, emerged right behind them. Its razor-sharp claws swung through the air, grazing Brett's chest, tearing his shirt apart, exposing his vulnerable skin. Blood cascaded from the fresh wounds.

The werewolf swung its arm back, catching Brett square in the chest with a powerful wallop. The impact was so strong, it launched Brett into the air, his body bouncing off the stone ground as it crashed back down. As he rolled to a stop on his belly, the hard earth pressed against his skin. With his right side dangling precariously over the edge of the rock quarry, Brett's heart raced, his senses heightened as he assessed his dangerous position.

Gathering his senses, Brett twisted onto his back, away from the shadowy pit below.

As he sat up, he saw Bethany frozen in place between the werewolf and where he now laid. She turned around to look at Brett. Her body convulsed, contorting in pain. The skin on her front was gone. Dropping to her knees, a gut-wrenching sight unfolded before his eyes. Bethany's insides were visible to the world. Rhythmic spurts of blood pumped from her chest, splattering the rocky earth with crimson stains. The metallic smell of blood filled the air. Where once her kind face radiated warmth, only a grotesque display of muscle and bone remained. Overwhelmed by agony, Bethany's body gave way, collapsing forward with a sickening, squishy plop.

Brett's last ounce of fight dissolved as the putrid scent of the werewolf filled the air. Its massive, four-toed paws loomed above Bethany's lifeless form, while Brett's gaze met the creature's towering figure. The silence hung heavy, broken only by the distant echo of a howl. Beset with despair, Brett yearned for a quick and merciful end.

The fingers from the monstrous creature gently brushed through Brett's hair, sending shivers down his spine. The werewolf's mouth stretched wide open, revealing sharp, glistening fangs, while strands of drool spewed out. Its eyes darted from Brett to the side, filled with an unsettling intensity.

Determination in his eyes, Marcus lowered his shoulder and charged toward the ferocious beast. The impact of Marcus's tackle resonated with a bone-cracking sound, toppling the werewolf over the precipice. Brett's gaze fixed on the terrifying sight as Marcus and the creature plummeted into the yawning darkness of the quarry. The deafening thud of their bodies colliding against the unforgiving rock below reverberated through the air.

Exhausted by the chaos that had unfolded before him, Brett's eyelids grew heavy, surrendering him to unconsciousness.

PART II

16

BAD MOON RISING

Thomas sat on his couch, watching the evening news on television.

All a bunch of bullshit, he thought.

The news covered a wide range of the adjacent counties surrounding Kansas City, but one would never know that. Unless something catastrophic happened, like a tornado or a drug bust, the news stayed focused on stuff around the metro.

Tom saw the lights from a vehicle paint across the living room wall. He looked out the window to see it pull into his driveway. "It's about damn time," Tom said aloud. Digging in the couch he pulled out the remote. After jamming the power button a few times, the TV finally shut off.

Morro was a rough-looking white man. He wore a red and black flannel shirt unbuttoned too far with a white wife beater underneath, and the same dirty blue jeans for the third day in a row. He had dark brown hair down to his shoulders. A scraggly goatee in need of a trim rimmed his mouth. Tom suffered from years of alcohol abuse and methamphetamine addiction. Turning forty in December, he looked easily a decade older.

Wrinkles covered his forehead. Remarkably, he still had most of his teeth. He incessantly brushed them every day. Tom loved the high from meth, but hated the thought of his teeth rotting out. Morro self-identified as "trailer trash" and no one would argue that fact. Whatever grace people in the community had once shown him over the years had evaporated. No one would hire him because of his reputation. Like any good tweaker, Tom now made a living stealing other people's belongings.

Morro grabbed his faded black trucker hat, cigarettes, a Zippo lighter, and keys off the counter. The front door to his trailer house swung open with a screech as he exited. He immediately lit up a cigarette outside and approached the brown and white two-toned truck. It was a dented up regular cab 1986 Ford F-150.

"Where the hell have you been?" Tom barked. "You were supposed to be here an hour ago."

"Just get in the damn truck," LaVern Stillman yelled throwing his hands up.

Tom took a drag off his cigarette as he walked around the front of the pickup. The passenger door squealed upon opening. Tom made sure to slam the door shut when he clambered in.

"Well, where are we going tonight?" Morro was still irritated LaVern was late.

LaVern Stillman was forty-four years old. A short, stocky man with a bald head and face. His barrel chest and belly were level with each other. Tanned from working as an oil field hand during the day, Stillman was a lot newer to the game. His life would spiral out of control after he put in the time Tom had. He had oil-splotched jeans on a dirty, peach-colored sleeveless shirt.

LaVern's wife had recently left him for Mattfield's pawn shop owner. Years of hard labor and it got him nowhere. Tom saw an easy target at the bar one night drinking alone. LaVern had been helping him steal ever since.

"You usually tell me where we're going. I'm not good at picking places," LaVern replied nervously.

"Well, the place I cased out had a strict time table, so it's off-limits now. You ruined the whole night," Morro said.

"I'm sorry I was late, okay? My son needed a ride home. I wasn't going to leave him stranded," LaVern said in his own defense.

Tom decided to let him off the hook. "Alright, fair enough. That job will be there another day." He checked his watch. "Look, it's almost eleven now. I've had a place noodling around upstairs for a couple of months. I think it could be a big pay day for both of us," Morro said.

LaVern appeared to be deep in thought. "You know I need the money. The divorce broke me financially. If you think we can pull off a big one, I'm in. Where?"

Tom was happy to see LaVern willing to take bigger risks. "Drive. Head out of town toward Mattfield," Morro instructed.

LaVern backed the truck out of the driveway and left the town of Red Hill behind.

Rolling down the highway at night, they never met a single vehicle. "Know where the Coal Creek Rock Quarry is at?" Morro asked.

"Yeah, right off the county road, 10-99, I think," LaVern confirmed.

"Yep, 10-99 and Jackson Road. We'll take Jackson in eight miles, cruise north all the way to the quarry. Stay on gravel. Hopefully not get seen. Who knows what kind of stuff they got out there? Job is riskier being so close to a paved road, but seems like a slow night for traffic. We'll load up what we can and take gravel roads back. I have a place we can stash whatever we get our hands on until things cool down," Tom explained.

Ten minutes later, LaVern turned the F-150 north onto Jackson Road. Odds of seeing any sort of law enforcement were slim to none on dirt roads.

Tom lit another cigarette and rolled down his window.

"What do you think they got out here?" LaVern quizzed him.

"Hard to say, really," Morro tossed out. "Been curious. That's why we're going. A lot of heavy machinery, of course. As much as I'd like to, we probably can't get away with stealing any. We can strip some parts and wires off if we think we have enough time. Tools and smaller stuff will be our best bet."

Tom slept through most of the daylight anymore, effectively shunned from the world of light. Morro took ownership of his actions. These days, he embraced the cycle of chaos his life had become. Steal and sell items to get money. Use money to get drugs. Enjoy the high while it lasts. Occasional overnight stay in the county jail. Repeat. The lifestyle had turned him into a creature of the night.

Staring out the passenger window, enjoying his cigarette, Tom admired the full moon. "Uh-oh, full moon tonight. All the crazies will be out," Morro quipped. He made himself chuckle.

"You still seeing Annie?" LaVern asked in an attempt at small talk.

Morro didn't care much for small talk with Stillman. He knew LaVern was only here to reap the benefits of working with an experienced thief. Likewise, Tom viewed him more as a pawn in his enterprise. Stillman sure as hell made loading heavier, more valuable items easier. Tom knew they weren't friends. If the two of them ever caught heat for their crimes, they'd both rush to sell the other down the river.

"On occasion," Tom answered shortly.

"She's better than you deserve, you know that?" LaVern challenged.

"Why, gee, thanks," Morro said throwing him a glare of contempt. Tom thought about strangling Stillman in that moment. He flicked his cigarette butt out the window. Sparks showered as the outside air caught it. Morro laid his head back against the seat and closed his eyes. Wind sailed in, soothing his face.

"What are you doing? It's August. You're bound to start a grass fire throwing cigarettes out like that," LaVern laid into him.

Tom was growing more annoyed by the second. "That's not a bad idea. Imagine the score we could get if we started a fire. Draw all the law enforcement to one area. I wish I would've thought of that," Morro proudly stated.

"Do you hear yourself? Arson? What is— OH, SHIT!"

Morro opened his eyes just in time to see someone diving out of the road into the ditch. He looked through the back glass to try and get a glimpse. Everything behind them was a void of dust in the air. "Who the hell was that?" Morro asked, surprised.

Stillman was shaken up. "We almost hit a kid, man. What the hell is a kid doing out here on a Saturday night, walking around? Should we go back?" LaVern said, panicking.

Morro collected himself. "First thing, *you* almost hit a kid, not *we*. Why the fuck would I know what he's doing out here? No need to go back if you missed him. All I care about is if he is able to identify your truck a mile from the damn rock quarry," Morro said, raising his voice in frustration.

"Let's just call tonight off, then," LaVern reasoned.

"Listen, you were late. We missed out on a golden opportunity. Now that we're basically to the rock quarry, you want to quit? I don't think so. Do you need money or not?" Morro lashed out. It wasn't *his* truck that would be identified. If the rest of the night went off as planned, nothing would tie him to the events at all.

"I do. You win. We drove all the way over here, so let's just get this done. I'm sorry. It just freaked me out," Stillman apologized.

"We can kill the kid if that makes you feel better," Morro tossed out half-jokingly.

Shaking his head, LaVern told him, "You are one demented piece of shit in need of serious help."

"Don't you forget it."

Crossing over 10-99, LaVern turned off the truck's headlights and coasted to the gate for the Coal Creek Rock Quarry, telling Tom, "Bolt cutters are in the bed."

Tom hopped out and retrieved the bolt cutters. Pulling the handles apart as he moved to the locked gate, he slid the cutters' steel head around the padlock shackle, which secured the gate. Morro gritted his teeth, pushing the handles together. A loud clink rang out as the bolt cutters severed the shackle.

With his free hand, he slid the broken lock out and tossed it aside. Then he unlatched the gate and gave it a kick with enough force that it swung wide open. Tom tossed the bolt cutters back into the truck bed and resumed his place in the cab.

LaVern drove to the only building on the property. It was a refurbished semi-trailer converted for office space. A ramp led up to a windowed door. The building had two long windows with shades inside covering them. Morro surveilled the landscape. Mountains of different sizes of crushed rock surrounded the top rim of the quarry. There was a single, massive rock crusher and a scale for weighing trucks.

"Let's search the building, see if they keep anything worth our time," Morro told his accomplice. Tom walked up the building's ramp to the door. He tapped his knuckles against the door's window. "Real glass. We can get in here easy," Tom said, relieved.

LaVern brought him a crowbar from the back of the truck. Gripping the crowbar like a baseball bat, he swung. The window shattered on impact. Morro used the crowbar to sweep the bottom edge of the window, knocking all the jagged pieces out. Reaching inside, he unlocked the dead bolt and door handle.

They were in.

Tom opened the door and flipped on the lights. Nothing of interest caught his eye. File cabinets, desk, computer, and papers. Walking farther into the trailer, he found a door with a padlock. "Get me the bolt cutters again," Tom ordered.

LaVern was back in an instant, cutters in hand.

Morro took them and repeated the process he'd used on the gate. Inside the room were two flattop wooden boxes. Using the crowbar again, he pried the lid. His eyes lit up. "Dynamite," Tom muttered. They each grabbed a box and loaded them in the truck bed. LaVern shut off the building's lights on his way out.

"How are we going to sell dynamite? As soon as this stuff is reported missing, it'll be the feds who come looking for it," said LaVern.

"I can sell dynamite. These two boxes here are more money than we could ever make stealing whatever fits in the bed of your truck," Morro stated. "We're done with the building. Drive us to the bottom of the quarry so we can look around before we get out of here."

LaVern maneuvered the truck down the path carved for equipment going in and out of the quarry. It was a sharp decline down. Tom had never been inside a rock quarry. It was over a hundred yards wide and three hundred yards long. It was dark, but he guessed the quarry was over thirty feet deep. The headlights shone on a few pieces of equipment hidden in the bottom.

"Alright, get the truck facing the exit to this hellhole. Take anything not tied down and let's get," Morro instructed.

LaVern turned the truck into position as told. The two split up as Morro hunted around the bottom of the quarry. He inspected an excavator, bulldozer, and mining drill. It was the mining drill that got him thinking about the dynamite again. The quarry drilled blast holes with the machine. Setting off charges of dynamite in the blast holes broke away the rock face. Tom had heard blasts coming from rock quarries countless times before. He'd always wanted to witness the dynamite go off—to see a limestone cliff face give way as thousands of tons of rock came crumbling down. Today was going to be that day.

Morro returned to the truck, determined. LaVern was loading up a trash pump the quarry used to keep rain and ground water from flooding their man-made crater.

"This thing is brand-new. Not a bad find," Lavern said as he opened the tailgate on his Ford.

Morro helped him load it into the bed. He slid a box of dynamite onto the tailgate, using the crowbar to pry open the wooden container. he produced four sticks of dynamite, long fuses sprouting from their tops.

"Are you insane? Put that shit away. You're liable to spark one with a cigarette," LaVern scolded.

Tom spun the fuses tightly, weaving them together, ignoring Stillman's concern. "Got any duct tape? Need to fasten these together," Morro said, focused on the task at hand. He felt LaVern starring at him. "Don't make me ask again," Tom threatened.

LaVern went to the cab and got duct tape from behind the seat. Handing it over, he said, "Are you going to blow up a piece of equipment? An explosion like that is going to get us caught."

"Calm down. I need to make sure this dynamite is worth trying to sell. I'm just going to blast some rock," Morro replied. He wrapped the four sticks of dynamite snuggly with the duct tape. Tom was satisfied with the bomb he had created. Holding the explosives in one hand, he reached into his pocket and revealed the Zippo. With the flick of his thumb, the lid flipped open and he hammered down on the flint wheel. A flame hovered from the top of the lighter.

"Please don't do that," LaVern pleaded.

Morro shrugged his shoulders as he brought the flame and fuses together. Sparks showered, lighting up the night around them. Cocking back his arm, he heaved the dynamite. It smacked against the rock face thirty yards from the truck and dropped straight down to the ground.

They sheltered on the far side of the truck bed, covering their ears. Time seemed to slow down, anticipating the blast. The sky lit up with a blinding flash. Morro was knocked out of his kneeling stance onto the ground. Shrapnel of rock shot through the air, pelting the truck and shattering the back window. Morro saw LaVern flat on the ground next to him as bits of rock rained down. The men struggled to get to their feet. Tom pulled LaVern up off the ground. He starred at the plume of dust rising high into the air.

"Happy now, jackass? You fucked up my truck worse than it already was!" LaVern yelled.

Tom was shaken up from the explosion.

Will have to be farther away next time, he thought.

"I'll pay for the damage," Morro said, putting his hand on Stillman's shoulder. The power of the dynamite frightened and exhilarated him at the same time. Most of life didn't register excitement for him anymore, but Tom felt alive again for the first time in years after the thundering blast.

"I'm leaving with or without you right now," LaVern said.

Morro was still amused with his own handiwork, fascinated by how much rock was blown off the side of the quarry.

A large pile of limestone had formed. Tom noticed what looked like a black rip where the rock face suffered the blast. He wondered what he was seeing in the dark. "Do you have a flashlight?" Tom asked.

"What did I just say!?" LaVern yelled.

"I think we might have opened a cave. I need a flashlight," Tom reiterated.

LaVern must have been somewhat interested because instead of leaving Tom behind, he put a flashlight in his hand. Together, the two men approached the opening in the limestone. Morro clicked on the flashlight, aiming it at the freshly opened tear. He was stunned to see it was, indeed, a cavern of some kind.

"We should go get you a lottery ticket after this," Stillman said in disbelief.

Standing only ten feet away, they marveled at the uncovered cavity. "I want to look inside," Morro said to his partner, who lacked conviction.

"Go for it. I'm not getting any closer to a rock wall you just blasted with dynamite. It'll make a nice tomb for you if it caves in," LaVern replied.

Even though Stillman whined about every little thing, Tom knew the man was right on this one. Morro questioned the stability of the rock himself—especially seeing a cave running back into the rock face.

Unexpectedly, two glowing eyes appeared in the light his flashlight cast into the opening. Both men took a few steps backward, startled. Whatever the eyes belonged to was a massive animal, Morro judged by the distance between the shining eyes.

"What the fuck is that?" Stillman sputtered, fear in his voice.

"That is our cue to leave," Morro responded. But both men were fixated on the cave, neither one of them brave enough to turn their backs on the entrance. They both froze as large, dark, fur-covered hands reached out, grabbing both sides of the cave's mouth. The furry gray hands had fingers tipped with pointed claws.

Morro felt himself get woozy, but snapped out of it before he fainted.

LaVern's breathing was audible and labored.

A snout protruded from the opening as the eyes inched closer to the outside world. The beast's jaw hung open, showing off its jagged teeth. "It— It— It's a bear," LaVern managed.

Tom was thinking along the same route. "Bears don't have fingers," he whispered in response.

A low, rumbling growl emanated from the creature. Tom felt absolute terror. His eyes began to water from sheer fright. As the monster's head fully emerged from the cave, it let out a blood-curdling howl. The creature's enormous head looked like that of a wolf. Morro was finally able to say the quiet part out loud: "Werewolf."

"Werewolves aren't real," LaVern cried in fear.

"Sure as hell looks real. On the count of three, we run for the truck," Morro said.

His eyes darted to Stillman, who was nodding in agreement.

Just then, the monster pulled its hulking, gray-fur body out of the cave. It had to be every bit seven feet tall, looming large on gigantic, pawed feet. Tom imagined the reach of its long arms.

There was no counting. Both men bolted for the truck.

Morro's door was the closest. The mirror on the door was bent around toward the windshield from the dynamite blast. In the reflection, he saw the fast-approaching monster behind him. Tom knocked the wind out of himself diving to the ground. He rolled underneath the F-150 just as the beast slammed into the passenger door. The Ford rocked as broken glass rained down around it.

Scared for his life, Morro had to devise a plan in seconds. He looked toward the rear end to see the box of opened dynamite spilled on the ground. Reaching out, he couldn't get his fingers on a stick. A long gray hand lunged under the truck, trying to grasp him. Claws dug into his side. Crying out in pain, he rolled out from under the truck on the driver's side, ripping away part of his shirt. He felt warm blood running from the exposed skin of his torso. Taking off at a full sprint, Tom scooped up a stick of dynamite by the tailgate, angling for a hiding place among the heavy machinery.

Morro zigzagged in an attempt to lose the monster. He knelt down in front of the excavator, fumbling to get the lighter out of his pocket. His adrenaline kept him from feeling the wound as blood dribbled onto the ground. Tom pulled the lighter out in his vibrating hand and mashed the flint wheel. The flint shot sparked, but his Zippo wouldn't produce a flame. "COME ON!" Morro screamed. He heard the thuds of the monster coming up behind him. Stealthily, he shifted positions over to the bulldozer.

LaVern was sheltering behind the machine's large track in shock. "Help me get this lit," Morro whispered desperately.

LaVern appeared to be barely conscious. Tom continued to strike at the Zippo, to no avail. They heard the low growl from the beast as it approached their hiding spot. Morro gave up, dropping the lighter and dynamite. He knew it was every man for himself now. Tom truly felt sorry for what had to be done. "Alright, we have to make it to the truck. It's our only chance," Tom coaxed Stillman. "Can you run?"

LaVern gave him a slight nod. "Ready? Go, go, go!" Morro shouted, giving him a push on the back. Tom pretended to take off, but stopped. He watched as Stillman sprinted from behind cover, making a beeline for the truck. For a big man, LaVern moved with surprising speed. An enormous gray streak came flying from between the machinery on LaVern's heels, overtaking him. Tom couldn't watch the rest, turning away to focus on finding some place to conceal himself.

Stillman's agonizing screams echoed around the quarry. Then a quiet stillness returned to the night.

Tom peered under the bulldozer.

This is perfect, he thought.

If Morro could tuck himself away far enough beneath the machine, he'd be safe. Getting on his hands and knees, he crawled under the bulldozer. A clawed hand wrapped around his ankle. The force of the grip felt like his bones were turning to dust. Screaming out in terror, he writhed, digging his fingers into the solid rock ground as he was dragged backward.

Turning his head to see behind him, the jaws of the werewolf came down on his leg. Teeth raked through his flesh as if it was paper. Flipping over, he used his hands to grab onto the under carriage of the bulldozer. Using his free leg, he thrust kicks at the beast's head with all the force he had. Over and over, he struck his boot against the monster's face. Out of pure luck, he connected a blow to the werewolf's nose. His bloody leg dropped from its mouth.

Scrambling quickly, he wormed himself all the way under the front of the bulldozer. The beast's long arms stretched out toward him, trying to get ahold. The werewolf snarled as it tried to reach his hiding place, but since he was lying on solid rock, the creature couldn't dig its way to him.

Sacrificing LaVern paid off for Morro. For the moment, he was safe. He turned his attention to the wounds he had suffered. Tom pulled off his belt and tightened it around his mangled leg as a tourniquet. Wincing, he touched the claw marks in his side. They would need stitches, but weren't life threatening at the moment.

Tom wondered how long the werewolf would wait around. He was desperate to get to a hospital.

No one would ever believe his story of what took place. Tom knew his reputation was too damaged for that. As his adrenaline wore off, waves of burning pain started to creep into his body. He longed for alcohol or drugs to numb his wounds. Finally, he succumbed to exhaustion and fell unconscious entrenched under the bulldozer.

17

COUNTING BODIES LIKE SHEEP

A distress call went out to 911 around four in the morning. Sheriff Mills was promptly woken from a restless sleep by dispatch. There hadn't been a single night of good sleep for him in the last month. One more surely wasn't going to hurt.

Dispatch relayed a phone call from a girl in distress at Coal Creek Rock Quarry. Carl's stomach sank when he double-checked the location. The phone number was registered to the Cook family. Within minutes, dispatch confirmed with the Cook family that the number in question was their daughter's. She had not returned home after the school dance.

There was a faint hope in Mills' heart that some high schoolers were pulling a prank. Wouldn't be the first time. What better opportunity than the location of an unsolved murder? Or maybe someone had just broken down.

Dispatch said Bethany sounded genuinely in need. Leave it to high school–age kids to be in a place like that. Carl remembered being young and dumb all those years ago.

No matter the case, the call was made to 911. Thus, this was to be considered an active emergency. Carl called in aide from Keith, Jack, and Erica, filling each of them in. No one was enthused by the rude awakening.

Arriving on the scene first, Mills parked in front of the gate into Coal Creek. It was locked this time. There were no other vehicles in sight. He wondered if anyone was here at all. The deputies and his detective funneled onto Jackson Road one by one, parking behind him. They exited their respective vehicles.

"Sheriff, what's going on?" Erica asked.

"I don't know. Bethany Cook made a 911 call. Gave them Coal Creek Rock Quarry as her location. Said she abruptly stopped talking, but there was background noise. They didn't know if there was a struggle. We need to get in there and have a look around," Mills commanded.

The first rays of sunrise danced across the sky, painting the morning clouds with shades of pink and gold.

Keith went to his truck and reappeared with bolt cutters. Putting them around the padlock, he gave a squeeze, slicing through the shackle. "Two cut locks in a month. Mr. Douglas is going to have a fit," Keith joked.

Jack had his flashlight out, scanning the area, then fixing the light on something down the road. "Guns drawn. Everyone on me. There's something down here."

Pulling his handgun from its holster, Mills positioned his hands on the grip. "Spread out at the ready, follow Jack's lead."

Moving tactically, they jogged down the road together. Mills realized what Jack had spotted was a body.

"Alright, everyone." Mills halted the group. "This is a crime scene. Watch your step. Stay ready." He gave everyone a hand signal, and they pushed forward slowly.

"Sir. Oh. Oh my. There's a head here. I— I recognize him. That's a high school boy," Keith said woozily. He was looking in the ditch across the road from the body.

"Who is it, Keith?" Mills asked, bewildered.

"Dalton Adams, youngest son of Julia Adams. Morro tried to carjack his brother," Keith replied.

This is really happening, Carl thought.

He knew he had to take charge of the situation and leave the emotions for later. "Alright, Keith, you're involved with the high school. You're done out here. I want you to get 10-99 shut down now. I don't want to see you near this crime scene. Jack, you get Zachery Grant on the phone and tell him to get his team down here. Bring as many extra agents as he can get. Better check on your nephew while you're at it. Erica, I need you to get EMS, the fire department and the coroner on their way. No one with a high school–aged kid is allowed to respond. Get dispatch to identify anyone who didn't come home last night. Have them gather the families at the Baptist church. Jack and Erica, I'll need you two assisting me as soon as possible."

The sky steadily grew lighter as they hustled back to their vehicles. Mills separated from the others, kicking open the gate to the quarry. He decided to check the office building first. The door remained sealed shut. Under the ramp, he noticed what appeared to be dried blood.

He shifted his attention to the quarry itself. Moving around a gravel pile, two bodies came into view. Gravel was showered about on the ground all around. A female body laid face down in a pool of blood. He got close enough to see she had been mutilated.

Carl had gotten out of bed and walked straight into a living nightmare.

Moving to the edge of the quarry, he bent down next to a boy. Immediately, he recognized this to be Brett Adams. With a shaking hand, he checked for a pulse. The boy was cold and clammy to the touch, but alive. He used the radio on his shoulder to call it in. "Get those trucks moved from the entrance. I have a survivor. I need an ambulance yesterday. Victim appears to be in shock."

Unwilling to leave the boy, Mills sat next to him and held his hand. "Brett, this is Sheriff Mills. You're going to be okay," Carl kept repeating.

A little over ten minutes went by before the ambulance pulled in.

"Here, he's over here! Get a stretcher!" Mills ordered.

The two EMS personnel unloaded the stretcher, running it toward them. "We'll take it from here, Sheriff," one of them promised.

"Don't let anything happen to him. We need him," Mills asserted.

"He's going to be fine," the other EMS assured.

With Brett taken care of, Mills scanned around with his eyes. He didn't see any more bodies. He started to walk away when it came to him. Why was the boy lying on the edge? Turning around, Mills went back to survey the quarry's bottom. Nothing. Mills lowered his head to leave. That's when he saw another person lying straight down below.

Squeezing the button on his radio once more, he said, "I need another ambulance!"

Déjà vu washed over the sheriff as he descended the road into the quarry. This place had become his personal hell. On approach, Mills recognized this boy. It was Marcus Jones, lying on his stomach on the rock floor. Just as before, he bent down to check vitals. He was alive. Giving a gaze upward, then back to Marcus, Mills imagined he had some serious internal injuries from a fall that high.

"I'm in the bottom of the quarry along the east wall. Get a stretcher down here!" Mills shouted.

There were already hundreds of shifting ideas flowing in his head. Did Thomas Morro really carry through on the threats he made to Brett? One man couldn't have managed this much barbarism. A beheading and another mutilation. Why was Brett on the edge of the quarry and Marcus straight below him?

Turning, he saw two more EMS workers bringing a stretcher into the quarry.

"Pick it up!" Mills barked.

Mills stepped out of their way to let them work. Using a backboard, they carefully shifted Marcus's body onto it, then grabbing the board, they lifted Marcus onto the stretcher. After hastily buckling him down, they rushed back to the surface.

Mills made a quick pass around the bottom of the quarry. No one else was down here. Nothing appeared to be part of the crime scene up top.

On his ascent, he was met by Erica and Jack.

"Ambulances made good time," Erica stated. "Fire department should be out here any minute. Dispatch is identifying missing teens."

"KBI will be here in less than an hour," Jack added. "Feds will take this away from us. This is national news–type shit."

"Erica, call your father and have him bring his UTV out. I want to drive this road," Mills said. "We have a bunch of kids and no vehicles. How the hell did they get here?"

"Yes, sir," Erica said, parting ways again.

"Jack, that's your nephew in that second ambulance. If you need to go, I understand. If you stay, I don't want news or reporters within a mile of here. I will fire anyone who talks to the press. Those vultures love to exploit tragedies and I'll have none of it," Mills said.

"I'm going to do my job," Jack replied. "County highway and all other property accesses are shut off. There's no controlling a narrative on this. We have dead teenagers, Carl. This is worse than bad. Whatever façade existed about the safety of life in this county is gone. For this to happen to a community like Mattfield . . . Everything changes now."

"Two deceased so far. At least two survivors. If they both make it, we might finally get answers to what's going on. I'm afraid the price we paid to get those answers will be more than this community can handle. More than I can bear," said Mills. His heart was breaking with every beat.

"Doesn't matter. Whatever has happened here is over. You couldn't've prevented it. What we *can* do is bring the wrath of justice down on whoever is responsible," Jack replied. "Those families are going to look to us for that. I will kill whoever laid a hand on Marcus."

Erica pulled up in a sunburst yellow Can-Am Commander. "I'm heading out," she told them.

"I'm going with you. Better to have two guns in case of an attack," Mills said, climbing into the passenger seat.

"Coroner is going to be here any minute. I'll assist him. Radio if you need help," Jack said, giving a halfhearted wave.

Erica stepped on the gas, whipping the UTV onto the dead-end road. "This thing runs. Are you alright with hauling ass?" Erica asked her superior.

"Drive. Let's see if we spot anything," Mills directed.

Erica stepped on the gas as the Commander accelerated. Carl had never been in one. The power was surprising. The utility vehicle set him back in his seat.

The sun was now now up,, casting rays of blinding light in his eyes. He listened to the roar of the engine as they raced toward the unknown. Mills couldn't remember the last time he had been down Jackson Road.

Dropping down into a valley, Erica slammed on the brakes as three pickup trucks sat lined up in front of them. The sheriff sprung agilely from the UTV. Taking a defensive stance, he moved with his weapon at the ready.

"These trucks look familiar," Erica said quietly from his left shoulder.

"Yes, the far Chevrolet belongs to Brett Adams. That is the one Morro tried to carjack. Middle truck is Marcus Jones's Dodge Ram. This F-150 belongs to Bradley Higgins," Mills replied, identifying the vehicles.

Erica moved down the driver's side of the trucks, Carl down the passenger's. A smattering of dried blood was painted on the F-150's bedside. It appeared a hand had been dragged through the blood when it was still fresh.

"Erica, I have blood on the bedside," Mills called out.

She circled around Marcus's Ram truck. "What's with the truck's wheel?" she noted, looking at the ford.

"Ball joint or something must've given out," Carl theorized. His attention had been focused on the blood.

"There's a lot of blood," Erica said, stating the obvious.

"Scour the area," Mills ordered.

Flanking the roads was underbrush. Groves of trees populated this valley along the creek.

"Sir." Erica's voice shook. "I have a body."

The sheriff looked to the sky. How can this be? The teens' killer officially reached serial status with this many victims. He joined Erica at the edge of the trees. He recognized the boy as Bradley Higgins. At the base of an old oak, his body laid mangled. Dried blood was painted up the tree's bark to the first branch.

"He was trying to climb to get away. You really think Thomas Morro is capable of all of this?" Erica whispered.

"All the evidence we have points to him," Mills declared.

"What is he using to mutilate bodies like this?" Erica asked herself aloud.

Mills turned away. He couldn't bear to look upon the scene any longer.

"Jack, we have another deceased," Carl radioed in. "The vehicles are a few miles down from Coal Creek. I'm going to leave Erica at the scene. I'd better go check out the old Carpenter homestead. Those're the only structures out on this road. We need a team of dogs combing these woods."

"Keep your guard up until help arrives. I'll cut through the woods. Come pick me up when you can," Mills requested.

Crossing to the other side of the road, the sheriff ventured off, walking along the creek's bank. Pushing, he struggled through the thick underbrush. Low-hanging tree limbs and thorn bushes grabbed at him as he went. It was claustrophobic. Stressful, even. Pressure from the external world reflecting his internal soul.

Breaching into the clearing of the old homestead brought a sense of relief. A small reprieve for a fleeting second. In the homestead's yard laid another body. He hurried to render aid, but the boy's remains were a bloody mess. The head had been crushed. He diverted his eyes from the gruesome image. Fear that he was going to suffer a heart attack started to set in.

Checking the barn doors, Mills wasn't able to gain access. At the front of the barn, there was blood covering the spade sweeps of a rusty old plow. A two-by-four laid on the ground with old nails protruding from it. Upon further inspection, he determined they were covered in dried blood. A possible weapon used to attack these teenagers.

His attention fixed on the old Carpenter home. The front door was gone. Common for old abandoned homes. Thieves and even teens had a knack for ransacking abandoned places. Readying his firearm, Mills crept toward the dark entrance. He saw blood pooled on the floor inside. As he stepped in the home, something rubbery touched his face. Alarmed, he jolted backward. Sticking his head back in the doorway, he looked upward.

Erica came flying down the drive to the Carpenter residence. She rushed to Mills's aid. He sat planted on the ground in the yard, his firearm lying in the lengthy brown grass.

"Sheriff. Sheriff, are you alright?" Erica asked in a panic.

"Stay away from the house," Mills said quietly.

"What's in the house?" Erica asked. "You have blood on your face. Are you bleeding?" Her eyes darted to the entrance.

Mills remained silent for a moment. He didn't recall how he got to where he now sat. "There is half a body hanging through the ceiling just inside. Intestines. The legs are off in the corner of the room. Torn in half. I think a girl," Carl murmured.

"At least two more bodies at the old Carpenter place," Erica broadcast across the radio.

"Let's get you out of here. This is beyond us. You can better serve the community elsewhere," Erica encouraged.

After an internal fight, the sheriff allowed himself to be helped up. Erica guided him back to the UTV. Firing up the engine, she sped back toward the quarry, driving in the ditch for a stretch to allow dozens of black SUVs by.

Carl remained silent. Images of the teenager's lifeless bodies having been killed in the most horrific fashion were branded into his mind.

Jack is right. Everything changes now.

The FBI and KBI would supersede his authority in short order. He needed to formulate a plan of action for his constituents.

What appeared to be hundreds of red and blue flashing lights awaited them back at the quarry. The entire area was being swarmed by first responders and investigators. Mills stepped out of the UTV into the chaos. No sooner had his feet hit the ground than Jack and Zachery Grant arrived.

"You're a good man," Grant said. "That's why you're hearing it from me first. I'm assuming control of this investigation effective immediately. As bad as this shit is, I won't be surprised if the feds want to bring charges against your department."

"God help us all," Carl answered. "Jack will be the only one staying as a point of contact. I have families needing to know where their children are. My priority will lie with the people of Mattfield."

"I'm hesitant to pass judgment here. Your department never captured Thomas Morro. Why our assistance wasn't requested is beyond my understanding. That's a high level of incompetence," Grant added, clearly angling for a confrontation.

Mills turned around to walk away before changing his mind. He spun back, grabbing Grant by the shirt collar. "Incompetence? You think Morro is committing atrocities alone? What's the best your team provided, Zachery? Don't forget the only help you rendered was some shit DNA analysis!"

"Tread carefully, Sheriff," Grant said.

Having made his point, the sheriff let the agent go. Back in his truck, Carl gave himself a few minutes to cry, overwhelmed from holding back all the despair, and confronted with his own shortcomings—a failure that had left a trail of bodies. He thought of the poor, distraught families. Praying, waiting for word of their children.

Mills knew the time had come. He would head to the Baptist church to deliver the news no parent ever wanted to hear. Their kids were never coming home.

Solemnly, he addressed those gathered in the sanctuary. There were few facts to present at this early time. Out of the seven reported missing, there were five confirmed deceased. He had no answers to give. No promises to make. The case was in the hands of state and federal agents. The families' reactions to the news were visceral. Lives forever changed. Families forever broken.

"I am truly sorry for each of your losses. Your anguish can never be extinguished. Your lives can never be made whole again. The loss to this community—and the loss this world suffers without your sons and daughters—is immense," Sheriff Mills finished. Bowing his head, he walked down the aisle.

Screams and wails echoed throughout the room. Reverberating sounds Carl would never forget. Upon exiting the church, he went straight to the police station.

Mayor Glass was out front, pacing. When he saw Carl, his hands flung up into the air. "Carl, what the fuck? Please tell me the rumors aren't true," Glass bemoaned.

"By all accounts, it appears we have five deceased teenagers at and around Coal Creek. All appear to be high school students at Mattfield," Mills regrettably informed him.

"How? Oh my lord. How can this be? Carl, this is Mattfield. We have a serial killer in rural Kansas? Is it Thomas Morro?" Glass asked, trying to come to terms with the situation.

"We don't know that. I just spoke with the families. Here's what you can do for me. I need a curfew put into place indefinitely: 10 p.m. You will be arrested after that time. No exceptions. Get a hold of the Mattfield school district's superintendent. Have him cancel two weeks of school. Counselors need to be in place when it resumes. Football and volleyball seasons are over. All after-school activities are done. Do not equivocate. Understood?"

"I am not an authoritarian, sir," Glass pushed back.

The sheriff shot Mayor Glass a stern look. "This conversation ended when I told you what will be done. If it is not taken care of *today*, I will personally end your career."

"Alright. I'll take care of it," Glass agreed.

Mills entered the police station. Keith was chatting with dispatch.

"Keith, we have an arrest to make. You're driving," Mills directed.

"Yes, sir. Where are we going?"

"I left Annie Stafle skating on thin ice a few days ago. I have lost my sympathy," Carl stated.

On the way to Keith's police cruiser, Mills grabbed the AR-15 from his truck, slamming a thirty-round magazine in the rifle. He pulled back on the charging handle, chambering a round. Making sure the gun was on safety, he climbed into the passenger seat of Keith's car.

"Think you're going to need that?" Keith asked.

"No more pulling punches," Carl said.

"Thank you for not keeping me out there. It was more than I can handle. Those kids look up to me," Keith said.

They cruised along, heading south.

"I'd retire today if I could. Move away from here and never come back," Carl shared.

"No offense, but why don't you? Why put yourself through any of this?" Keith asked, concerned.

"I refuse to run out on my hometown in its darkest hour. For better or worse, I couldn't live with myself if I did. Which is a bit ironic because sticking around just might be the death of me. Besides, retiring now would set your career up for failure. If you stepped in as interim sheriff in the middle of this, you'd be run out of town. You may not want my endorsement when this is all said and done. Mattfield is going to blame someone in charge. Best it be me. At least I'm at retirement age. My years of service will be overshadowed with what took place last night. A damn shame."

Keith swung the car into Annie's driveway. "I appreciate that. For what it's worth, I don't want the job if I can't have your endorsement. The responsibility for this lies solely with the murderer."

"I wish that's how the world worked," Mills told his deputy.

Keith popped the trunk of the police car. Together, they exited the vehicle. Mills armed himself with the AR-15, putting the weapons sling around his shoulder. Keith shut the trunk and chambered a round into his identical rifle.

The front door of the trailer burst open. Morro stood there, using Annie as a human shield, a handgun pressed against her right temple.

Carl and Keith pointed their weapons at Tom. Sheriff Mills clicked the safety off.

"Put down the gun!" Mills yelled.

"Drop your weapons, or she dies," Morro snarled.

"This ends with you going to jail or to the morgue. Your choice, Tom," Mills replied.

"You and what army? Whole damn county is busy today, Sheriff. I ain't going down for murder. I haven't killed anyone!" Morro said.

"Coming from the man with a gun pressed against his girlfriend's head," Carl said.

"I caught her trying to turn me in. Betrayal is a real bitch. I'm not be going to jail," Morro snapped.

"Option B is forever, Tom. People get out of jail. Nobody gets out of the grave," Carl asserted.

Unexpectedly, Morro flung Annie forward off the front steps, then immediately opened fire while their shooting lane was obstructed.

Keith rushed to scoop Annie off the ground.

"AHH!" Keith cried out, one of Morro's bullets catching him as he dragged Annie to shelter behind the police car.

Morro retreated inside the trailer house for cover.

Mills squeezed the trigger, sending multiple rounds into the house before taking shelter with the others.

"Are you hit?" Mills asked, frantic.

Keith reached around, touching his back. "He got me in the vest. I'm good," he said, relieved. Taking up his gun, he fired multiple rounds, shattering two front windows.

More shots came from the trailer house. Glass rained down around them as the windows of the car were shot out.

"He has a lot of ammo inside, Sheriff. A few more guns, too. He won't be running out anytime soon," Annie said.

Weighing their options, Mills eyed the propane tank.

"Annie, how much propane do you have?" Carl asked.

"Tank is about thirty-five percent. Why?"

"Keith, I'm going to give you cover. I need you to get a road flare from the trunk," Mills instructed.

Keith gave him a bewildered look, but using the key fob in his pocket, Keith popped the trunk.

Shots continued penetrating the car body. A tire was hit, screaming as it deflated. Propping up onto the hood, the sheriff unleashed a volley of rounds into the house. Brass casings bounced off the hood with each pull of the trigger. Morro ceased firing at them. Keith lunged his hand into the trunk, producing a flare, then reconvening behind the safety of the car.

"Did you get him?" Keith asked. As soon as the words left his mouth, bullets began peppering the car once more.

"Light that flare and throw it beside the propane tank. Then give me cover fire," Mills said.

Red flames ignited from the road flare. Keith tossed it end over end like an axe. The flare landed underneath the propane tank. Grabbing his rifle, he popped up and began shooting into Annie's house. Taking a deep breath, Mills stood up and shot across the roof of the police car. No sooner had the shot rang out than the propane tank exploded.

Half of Annie's house was blown away in a fireball. Black smoke rolled from the rubble. Pieces from the house fluttered from the sky all around them. The shooting from inside stopped.

"Think I got him," Mills said confidently.

"You blew up my house!" Annie shouted.

"We saved your life," Keith corrected.

"What about Tom?" Annie snapped.

"Tom's dead. I don't hear any gunshots, do you?" Keith said sarcastically.

Annie laughed out loud at this. "Tom ain't dead. I'm not even sure that man can be killed."

It was hard to believe anyone could survive an explosion of that magnitude, but Carl wasn't about to take any chances. The sheriff stood, training the rifle on the half-demolished trailer. Keith followed right behind him. There wasn't anything left standing to hide behind inside the ruined home.

"I don't see him," Mills said, confused.

Exiting the destroyed trailer, they rounded to the backyard. Morro was limping along at the edge of the yard. Carl put him in his crosshairs. "Tom! You stop right there. It's over!"

Tom turned to face them, handgun still clenched in his grip. His skin was burned off from his chest up to the left side of his face. "This is far from over," Morro remarked, lifting the handgun.

The sheriff sent a bullet down range. Keith popped off multiple rounds. All of the shots hit Tom as he staggered. The gun slipped from his grip as he toppled over.

They both ran to where he laid. Keith immediately secured the handgun. Carl checked for a pulse.

"He's gone," Mills pronounced.

"Good riddance," Keith said.

They checked on Annie as they radioed for assistance. No one was going to be happy about another dead body today, but at least their number one suspect was no longer a threat.

It took the first responders almost half an hour to arrive.

"Today of all days you guys choose to kill someone? Do you know what we have had to deal with?" the EMS driver said upon arrival.

"Do your job. He's out behind the house." Mills brushed off the attitude. Today, justice had been served. So it seemed.

The EMS worker reappeared from behind the house. "Hey, dumbasses, there's no body."

Letting out a sigh, Mills headed to the backside of the house. "You drive that ambulance? You should get your eyesight checked," the sheriff said defiantly. Rounding the house, his eyes grew wide. Tom's body was gone. "KEITH!" Mills yelled out.

Keith came running. He froze in his tracks when he saw. "Where the hell is the body?"

Drawing their handguns, they searched around the property, then pushing out into the field behind the house. There was no sign of Morro.

"Those gunshot wounds were fatal. Every one of them into his chest. The condition he was in before that, half burned. I don't understand," Keith said in shock.

"Dead men don't walk away. We need dogs out here to help find his body," Mills determined.

KBI agents arrived at what was left of Annie's house. Keith filled them in on the current situation. Once more, an active manhunt ensued for Thomas Morro.

Erica arrived as they handed over the reins of the investigation. "Keith, your car is shot to shit. Are you guys alright? Who blew up the house?"

"We'll talk later. Get us away from here," Mills said.

Annie was the only one to speak during the car ride to the station. "I tried to tell you," she asserted.

Protocol deemed Deputy Sparts and Sheriff Mills were to take time off after an active shooting incident. Keith was instructed to get checked out at the hospital.

Carl was ready to be at home, his body weary from the day. Mind exhausted. Martha was waiting anxiously. She would have all sorts of frantic questions, none of which he'd want to answer.

Entering his home, Carl set his keys down on the kitchen counter. Martha hadn't come to greet him. The television was audible in the other room. He sat at the kitchen table with line of sight to the living room. Martha sat forward on the edge of the couch. She was watching the news. Lily Roth was reporting from the police road block:

"I have gotten reports of at least five deceased. We aren't hearing ages just yet. Sources are saying all involved were juveniles. Identities may remain classified if that is truly the case. The plot thickens here outside of Mattfield. Just one month ago, a man was found brutally murdered in this same area. The county police assisted by the KBI have not produced any answers. I have been told the KBI has assumed complete control as of this morning. The FBI is on scene, as well. This has evolved into a national travesty, heralded as one of the worst events in Kansas's storied history."

Turning to someone off-screen, she continued, "We are now hearing the local sheriff's department tried to make an arrest of a suspect. Those events led to a shootout a few miles from here. A trailer house was blown up in the firefight. Suspect Thomas Morro allegedly sustained multiple gunshot wounds. As of right now, he has not been captured."

"Turn it off," Mills uttered, running his hands through his thinning gray hair.

Martha did as he asked. "Carl, what's going on? A shootout?"

"I don't know. What I saw around the quarry—Martha, it's worse than I have words to describe. If DNA results from LaVern Stillman didn't point to a person being responsible . . . I mean, the murders are animalistic in nature. Soulless.

"Annie Stafle, I paid her a visit Thursday. I should have arrested her then. She gave shelter to Thomas Morro. He is at least responsible in some fashion. When we went to arrest her today, Morro used her as a shield. Annie is safe. Keith and I put kill shots into Thomas's chest, but his body was gone when help arrived."

"What are you going to do? Oh, those children's families. What did Mattfield do to deserve this?" Martha began sobbing.

That was the question he'd been asking himself. "Honey, it's the nature of evil. It preys upon the least deserving. If this was happening to another small town, the fact would remain the same. Nobody deserves what I saw today. I instructed the mayor on safeguards I want put in place. This community needs to mourn our losses. Then we begin to pick up the pieces. I'm afraid it will never be the same. How could it be? My department is no longer involved. The state has assumed control. I can't help but feel responsible. Serve and protect. That's the oath. I have failed." Carl broke down.

For the remainder of the day, Mills was detached from reality. He picked at the supper his wife prepared. His body needed the nourishment, but he felt more sick than hungry. The sheriff sat up in bed for most of the night, nodding off occasionally, only to awaken in fright. The nightmares his intermittent naps presented he could live without—seeing the quarry filled with the dead. Was that how many lives Mattfield would lose before this ended?

Martha startled him awake. "Carl, you were breathing rapidly in your sleep. I wanted to let you rest, but Jack is here to see you." She spoke warmly, brushing her hand on his cheek.

"What time is it?" Carl answered groggily.

"It's just after nine."

"I overslept. No wonder Jack's here. Everyone's probably looking for me," Carl complained.

"Jack looks shaken. They might've found something."

Sheriff Mills got dressed in a hurry. Jack was waiting in the kitchen with a cup of coffee.

"Jack, I'm sorry. Didn't sleep much last night. I should have set an alarm," Carl apologized. He knew something else had happened by Jack's body language.

"You needed the rest. This is only getting worse. Sit down." Jack beckoned him to a chair.

"What happened?" Mills asked. Jack extended the cup of coffee. Taking it, Carl sat at the table.

"There's only bad news. Morro still has not been found. Investigators recovered a bloody slug, like he pulled it out of himself. They're starting to question the veracity of what Keith and you said happened," Jack said calmly.

"The man was dead, Jack. I checked myself," Mills reiterated.

"I'm not saying one way or another. Evidence says otherwise. But that's not why I'm here. Nat Fuller was murdered last night," J. J. announced, his voiced riddled with grief. "All five of the deceased from Jackson Road have been identified. Marcus has yet to wake up."

This news made Carl slump back in his chair. Nat Fuller, as well?

Jack described the scene. "Nat was armed during the attack. A spent 12-gauge shell was found on the back porch. She's all over the living room walls of her home." One by one, he listed the victims: "LaVern Stillman, Dalton Adams, Bethany Cooks, Sara Young, Bradley Higgins, Henry Sutton, and now Nat Fuller."

Each name listed was like receiving a lash. "We're counting bodies like sheep," Mills averred.

"I'm going to keep an eye on evidence collected. You'll be the first to know when anything's found," Jack said in parting.

There was a tone of lost respect in Jack's words to his superior. Someone was going to take the blame for all of this, just like Carl had predicted to Keith. Blame was starting to fall upon his shoulders—where he wanted it to be placed. Accepting the fault, he hoped, would shield the rest of his police force. Maybe one day they could realize that and be grateful.

A call came across his cell phone from dispatch.

"Sheriff Mills," he answered.

"Hey, Sheriff, it's Erica. I have a call for you. Number is out of Oklahoma. A man says he needs to talk to you about the case."

"Put him on. I'll deal with it," Carl instructed. A loud beep was heard through the speaker. "This is Sheriff Mills. Who am I speaking with?"

"A curse was placed upon your town long ago. The people back then found a way to contain it. I have sat in meetings. My elders believe the curse has returned," the man said with authority.

"I'm going to stop you right there. Do you have any idea what we are going through? The last thing we need is nut jobs bothering us!" Mills shouted in anger.

"I'm sorry. I won't keep you. Just know I speak the truth. You are looking for a man. Out of place. Out of time. You will know when you see him," the man replied before abruptly ending the call.

Mills sat alone in silence, angered by the phone call, yet oddly curious. Crazy people tended to rant and rave, enjoying the sound of their own voice. This man called to deliver a calm message. What did he mean by elders? That's not a term people used too often.

It was probably best to have the number traced. Another piece in an increasingly complex puzzle.

18

THE MOURNING AFTER

It had been around twenty-four hours since Julia got any sleep. A week of the night shift was difficult to navigate when accustomed to daytime work. Word started to circulate just after sunrise of a terrible incident at Coal Creek Rock Quarry. She tried to reach her sons by cell phone, to no avail. Part of her wanted to chalk it up to teenage boy behavior. It was expected from Brett, anyway. For Dalton, on the other hand, it was out of character. Julia couldn't shake the feeling of worry in the back of her mind. Was it mother's intuition? After a few more failed attempts at calling, it was time to act.

There hadn't been any action at the hospital all night. Deciding she wouldn't be missed for half an hour, without saying anything, Julia ran to her Trailblazer and sped home. Her breathing became erratic when Brett's truck was not parked out front of their home. Fumbling with her keys, she busted inside the house, bolting up the stairs to the boys' rooms.

Both beds empty.

Running down to the laundry room, she looked for Brett's football gear. Nothing. It registered that they hadn't returned home last night.

How had she known something was amiss?

Back in her vehicle, Julia dumped the contents of her purse onto the passenger seat. Picking up her cell phone with trembling hands, she called the police department.

"Linn County dispatch," a man answered.

"Hi, yeah. My name is Julia Adams. My sons didn't come home last night. Brett, seventeen, and his younger brother, Dalton, he's sixteen," Julia said.

There was a period of silence on the other end of the line.

"Okay, ma'am. I need you to report to the Baptist church. Do you know where that is?" the dispatcher replied calmly.

"I know where the church is. Why do I need to go to the church?" Julia asked, unable to hide her fear.

"Good. Ma'am, I need you to go to the church, okay? Your kids aren't the only ones who didn't come home. The other parents are gathering at the church. Stay there and someone will be by to address the situation," dispatch relayed.

"What the hell is going on?!" Julia yelled in frustration.

"Ma'am, please. Do as I ask. We will have more information for you soon," the dispatcher declared. There was a click as the phone call was ended.

Julia headed for the church, calling her husband to let him know what was happening.

"Julia?" Michael answered groggily.

"Michael, the boys. The boys didn't come home last night. I'm scared. I don't know what to do. I called the police station and they told me to go to the Baptist church. Something has happened," Julia cried.

This promptly woke Michael up. "Listen, honey. Do as they ask. Stay calm; we don't know anything. Let's not assume, okay? I'm heading out the door right now. I'll be there in less than an hour. Call your dad; he can be there faster than I can. I'm on my way."

Julia hung up the phone and dialed her father.

Walt answered the phone. "Good morning. You happen to know what's going on? Heard a whole lot of sirens off in the distance this morning."

"Brett and Dalton are missing. I've been told to go to the Baptist church.

Dad, I need you," Julia's voice quivered.

"Oh, good lord. I'll meet you there. Ten minutes. Just breathe, get off the phone, and focus on driving," Walt demanded, hanging up.

Whipping into the church parking lot, she saw a few other vehicles parked near the entrance. Inside the sanctuary, family units sat together, all of them distraught as they turned to see if Julia was bringing news. Solemnly, she found an empty area of seating alone and sunk down into a chair. Chatter filled the area as frightened mothers were being comforted. Julia noticed a black man seated alone in the corner of the room. His head hung as if in prayer.

I'm not in this alone. Everyone is feeling the same emotion: fear.

Walt arrived and came straight to her. He embraced Julia with a comforting hug. There were no answers as to what they are waiting for. The anticipation of bad news filled the void between everyone in the church.

"Have you heard anything?" Julia whispered to her father.

Walt shook his head. He took Julia's hand in his. "Listen up. This is a first for Mattfield. Never had missing kids. Never gathered the families at a church like this. Julia, it is a madhouse out there. Blockades on the highway. Ambulances, fire trucks, police, black SUVs. I wish I knew. I'm afraid something dreadful has happened," Walt bluntly acknowledged.

It was what Julia feared—as those sitting in wait all did. Julia felt she might faint. She rested her head on her father's shoulder. Time slowed to a crawl, waiting for word from the authorities. Anything to bring clarity to the situation.

The door to the sanctuary sprung open. Michael rushed to her side. "What's going on? Do we know anything? The sheriff is in the lobby." Michael's voice was shaky. He took Julia's other hand to hold.

"Our boys," Julia managed as she began to cry.

"No word yet," Walt added.

Sheriff Mills entered the sanctuary, head hung low. Carl went straight to the podium to address the gathered families. Deep in thought contemplating what he would say, it was a few minutes before he began to speak. "You are all here because your children did not come home last night. A 911 call was placed by one of the missing earlier this morning. I, along with my deputies, responded to that call. About twenty minutes was our response time. Upon arriving at Coal Creek Rock Quarry—" Mills paused. "Upon arriving at the scene, we quickly discovered a . . . deceased—" Mills struggled to deliver the news.

Gasps of shock and whimpering went up from the families. Julia sat frozen in place. Tunnel vision overcame her. Michael and Walt both squeezed her hands tighter.

Mills rubbed his neck. He took a deep breath, then continued, "I personally found five deceased. Two survivors were transported from the scene to the hospital. Marcus Jones and Brett Adams."

Wailing and screaming drowned out the Sheriff as he explained, "It's early in the investigation. I have nothing else for you at this time. The Kansas Bureau of Investigation has assumed control of the scene. Federal agents are now en route. Stay here as long as you need; the church has offered their resources."

Julia started to slip into unconsciousness. Michael caught her before she fell forward onto the floor.

Did I hear correctly? Brett is alive.

But if Brett was alive, that meant her youngest— She screamed out in agony. The sanctuary was filled with howls of agony.

Carl gave his condolences, then promptly left the church to allow them to mourn. After a few minutes, the black man in the back of the room stood up and ran out.

"We lost our baby boy," Julia cried.

Michael remained silent in disbelief. He looked pale. Tears soaked his shirt as they left his face. Walt stroked Julia's hair. They stayed seated in the sanctuary for over an hour. The chaotic distress wore off enough for her to think.

"Brett. I need to see my son," Julia said, muffled.

Michael and Walt helped her up and they left the building.

They made the two-minute drive to the hospital. Arriving back at her work felt surreal. This was Julia's place of employment. A sanctuary of healing. Julia found herself walking into the visitor's side instead of the staff entrance, being held up by her husband and father, her entire body numb.

They found themselves sitting in the waiting room, not allowed to be at her son's side. No information to go on. Not even confirmation that Dalton was deceased, but in her heart, Julia knew it to be true. She could no longer feel him in the world. Someone had taken her intelligent, loving, sarcastic boy from his family. A soul who illuminated the dark was consumed by it. For no rhyme or reason. The war raging between good and evil since the dawn of time took no prisoners. Leaving the brokenhearted to carry on in its wake.

A short man wearing a black suit entered the hospital waiting room. "Mr. and Mrs. Adams?" the man asked.

"Yes," Michael responded.

"I'm Zachery Grant with the Kansas Bureau of Investigations. Not that it's going to mean shit to you at this time, but I want to extend my deepest condolences. I know this is an awful event, so I'm going to keep this short. Your son and Marcus Jones are key witnesses in this case. Speaking with him as soon as we can is our number one priority. With his help, justice will be served," Grant stated.

Julia looked to her husband. She gave Grant a nod that she understood.

There's no justice for the dead, she thought. *Not in this life.*

Grant stepped forward and handed Michael a card. "I hope your son wakes soon. Both of the boys. You may get the idea to pack up and leave Mattfield. I'm going to ask that you refrain from doing that under penalty of arrest. A difficult request, but as of right now, this entire thing is running on empty. It's connected to the yet unresolved Stillman case. DNA takes time. Testimony gets us to where we need to be before this can happen to anyone else. You have my card. Thank you," Grant finished, then wandered back out of the hospital.

"I'm not strong enough. I can't do this," Julia sobbed.

"You don't have to be. I'm not going anywhere. Ever again," Michael reassured.

Julia looked up at him. Michael truly meant what he said.

"How do we survive this? How do any of these families? Burying our baby boy. It's not fair. Why us?" Julia shook in anguish.

"I haven't been able to process anything. I feel like I'm in a fog," Michael said, voice cracking. "I'm just so sorry, Julia. I wasn't here. This has nothing to do with fair. Our boys never deserved this."

Debra White came down the hallway to them. "Julia, I don't have words. I am so sorry. For you all. If you are ready, you can see your son now. We've gotten positive signs. Brett should wake up soon," she assured. Tears welled in her eyes.

"I'll stay here. You two should be with your son," Walt offered.

With her husband's help, they walked down the hallway. Julia scanned the white boards for Brett's name. Room 2 had Marcus Jones. Julia felt a fresh rush of grief. On the white board outside of Room 3, "Brett Adams" was scrawled. They entered the dark room silently. The quiet inside the hospital room was broken periodically from the beep of the EKG machine.

Her mind tried to comprehend seeing Brett this way. Unconscious in a hospital bed. Monitoring systems attached to his body. He had been so full of life, playing in the homecoming game half a day ago. Brett was a shadow of that lying here. His youthful spirit diminished. Did he know his brother was gone? Julia felt an overwhelming sense of failure. Mothers protected their children. What kind of failure did this make her?

Michael dragged a chair to the side of the bed for her to sit. Julia took her son's hand. Michael seated himself in the corner.

"It's the least of concerns right now," Michael whispered, "but considering everything, I'm quitting my job. I want to be here with you. For you both."

Julia refused to take her eyes off Brett until he awoke. "We need you now more than ever, Michael," Julia said, absent emotion. "I ran away from our problems. I brought our boys here. What have I done?"

Shuffling in his chair, Michael disagreed. "Julia, no. I don't ever want to hear you say anything of that nature again. This is not your fault. It's—"

Brett stirred in the bed, cutting his father's words off. Their attention turned fully to him. Sleepily, his eyes batted a few times as he regained consciousness. Julia felt him squeeze her hand.

"Brett, honey, you're okay," Julia comforted.

"M-mom? Where am I?" Brett asked, confused.

"You're in the hospital, sweetheart. Do you remember anything?" Julia asked gently.

Alarmed, Brett's breathing grew rapid. His heart beat increased on the EKG machine. "Was it all a nightmare, Mom?" Brett moaned.

"The police found you at the rock quarry," Julia said calmly.

Reflected in his vitals, Brett teetered on the edge of a panic attack.

"Breathe. You need to calm down. You are safe," Julia tried to comfort her son.

His heavy breathing subsided. Brett locked eyes with Julia. "Dalton. I tried to save him, Mom. I was so scared," Brett blubbered. "We are the furthest thing from safe."

Julia sensed immense fear coming from her son. Michael came over, putting his hands on her shoulders. She knew the question must be asked: "What happened to your brother?"

Brett's eyes were enlarged, unblinking. "It killed them all," he mumbled. Suddenly, he fell unconscious again.

Julia felt Michael squeezing her shoulders tighter now.

"It? Do you have any idea what he's talking about?" Michael asked.

She managed to shake her head no, befuddled by the exchange. Why did Brett use the word "it"? He was most likely suffering from PTSD at this point. Julia wondered if his recollection of events was reliable. The only other implication was the killer may not be human at all.

Answers would have to wait. Brett needed rest more than anything at the moment. Julia had a nagging concern for his mental and emotional health going forward. Would Brett ever be the same? An emerging fear was taking root.

She may have lost both of her sons.

19

SURVIVOR'S GUILT

Something about seeing a monster in the flesh made his brain repress the memories, a survival instinct to avoid sending his body into shock and mind spiraling into madness.

Monsters were real. Werewolves hunted in the full moon light. That was the new reality Brett found himself living in. He witnessed the brutal horror and awe of such a beast. Rendered helpless to stop it. Once his grip came loose on the silver knife, so did any hope of defense. Dalton and the others stood no chance.

Brett was told he spoke to his parents, a conversation he had no recollection of. Three days had passed confined to a hospital bed. Julia never left his side. Countless law enforcement—both federal and state—came to ask questions. It was too overwhelming. Words would not come to Brett. He sat silent for days, processing the traumatic experience. Nothing could have changed the outcome, except maybe the silver knife. Even then, the werewolf conveyed intelligence. The short knife ultimately had little deterrence.

Testimony of the events was of the utmost importance to investigators. They all wanted answers. Who could blame them? Brett knew what he had to say would fall on deaf ears. The truth was a one-way ticket to the insane asylum. How do you explain that a werewolf is responsible? Nobody would believe that. He wouldn't fault them, either. Everyone operated under the presumption that monsters were mere legend. Brett did, too, until proven gravely naive.

One other witness survived the assault: Marcus, who unfortunately still lay unconscious, his vitals pristine. There was hope he might wake at any time. Brett prayed for his recovery.

Inches from death, Brett had been ready to follow Dalton into the afterlife. Marcus acted selflessly to protect him. Brett desperately wanted to apologize. He had been ambivalent about Marcus's plea for forgiveness. Lost in anger. Life had a cruel way of making you regret assumptions.

Brett held out hope that the two of them together could convince others. For the next full moon was coming. When it rose, the embodiment of death would rove.

Under guidance from the medical staff and KBI, Brett was released to recover at home. Agents stood guard outside, day and night. A symbolic gesture. There was no viable threat for a few weeks. They would abandon duty by then. Not that their presence would make a bit of difference. If the werewolf came, they would die just the same.

At home, the air was thick with emotions. Julia was caught in the thralls of grief. Michael, as well, but he was busy playing caretaker. Walt came each morning and stayed with them all day. Brett became aware his dad wasn't going anywhere. Anger boiled inside. However indirect, Dalton was gone because of his affair. The audacity to show up for the family after that. Fathers protect their family. Michael was no father. Any chance of redemption in Brett's mind died with his brother.

Visitors came by to express their sympathies. The Adams family received gifts of food and even financial assistance. Coach came by to check in on Brett, a shell of the leader Brett had grown to know. That's when Brett realized the events didn't happen to just those on Jackson Road. It happened to the community. Part of Mattfield died with the teenagers. They were mourning the young lives brutally taken. From raucous celebration, straight to the darkest depths of despair. Football season rightfully cancelled, dreams of a playoff run were over.

Cassie made an appearance. She offered no words, just a hug. Brett held her tight as they both cried. He'd lost his brother. The others at Mattfield High had lost lifelong friends, family, and classmates. She stayed for an hour as they sat in silence. Nothing took the pain away, but Brett was appreciative Cassie thought to visit. It reaffirmed she really did care for him.

Due to the circumstances of death for the five teenagers, funerals were on hold. Law enforcement insisted on time to gather evidence—a difficult ask for families to postpone burying their loved ones. Funerals were essential in giving closure, but so were answers to what took place.

The lead investigator, Zachery Grant, came to question Brett after a week at home. They sat in the living room for the interview. Julia sat beside her son on the couch.

"Your mother says you haven't spoken. I won't pretend to know what you're going through. My agents and I worked the crime scene. Horrific doesn't begin to describe it. Your wellbeing is important to us, Brett. That's why agents are guarding the home. We want you to feel safe.

"Listen, Mattfield needs to know what you saw. I want to get justice for your brother and your friends. If you can't speak, how about I ask some questions? You just nod yes or no. Are you willing to do that?" Grant asked in a kind but assertive voice.

Brett composed himself. "I can do that."

"Good boy. Our DNA evidence keeps turning up two men. You had a run-in with Thomas Morro. Was he at the quarry?"

Brett shook his head.

"Did you see a different man?"

Again, Brett shook his head.

"What about an animal?"

Brett looked the investigator in the eyes. This time, he nodded his head. Zachery looked surprised.

What Brett saw was more animal than man.

Julia perked up at this. That was a new development for her.

"Can you tell me what animal it was?" Grant asked.

The words wouldn't form. Brett forced a single word from his mouth: "Wolf."

"A wolf? Son, I have a hard time believing that. Are you certain?" Grant asked.

The limit had been reached. Brett began to cry. Images of the werewolf loomed in his mind. Julia took him in her arms.

"Mr. Grant, we are a grieving family. Maybe we should try again at a later date. He told you it was a wolf. My son has no reason to lie," Julia said.

Grant took off his caring disguise. "I'm trying to do my job. Brett is the key to this whole thing. We need to know how Marcus Jones ended up in the quarry, directly below where your son was found. These are not answers to put off. Families deserve the truth."

"What are you getting at?" Julia asked.

"It has been brought to our attention your son and Marcus did not get along," Grant said.

"Get the hell out of my house. Take your agents with you. From here on out, you will not contact my family without a lawyer present."

Brett saw his mother seething with vitriol. "Marcus and I did not get along. There was bad blood between us. He left me in the countryside as a prank when we moved to town. The night Stillman died at the quarry. He was sorry, but I wouldn't listen. The only reason I'm alive is because he protected me." This was the most Brett had spoken in a week.

Grant left them with parting words. "Julia, you should get that lawyer. If your son was anywhere close to the quarry when Stillman died, that ties him to both crime scenes. The truth will come out."

Brett knew he was innocent. So why did he feel so guilty? It was *his* idea. He put the group out there. They all paid the ultimate price. Dalton died feet away. Bethany mutilated. Death stood towering above him. Now Brett remained all alone, being berated by people who didn't have the slightest clue.

This burden of knowing the truth . . . Life would be simpler had he gone out like the rest. What Marcus did was a blessing, and a curse.

"I want to see Marcus," Brett said to his mom.

"Honey, I don't know if that's a good idea," she said.

"Please?" Brett's lip quivered.

Julia obliged. She drove him to Mattfield Hospital. "I'm going to stay in the car. Don't speak to anyone. Mr. Grant made it clear our family is in legal jeopardy. Until we speak with a lawyer, it's in our best interest to keep to ourselves."

Brett nodded. Returning to the hospital produced an ache in his heart—a beacon of hope and healing, it also contained suffering and death. People turned their heads to look at him as he moved down the brightly lit white hallway. Infamy was attached to his name. Brett the survivor. Some of them assumed he might even be Brett the killer. Ignorance brought out the worst in society. Conspiracies lurked behind every event these days.

Nothing sounded more like a conspiracy theory than a werewolf.

Quietly, Brett let himself into Marcus's room. The lights were off as he maneuvered to his rival's bedside. Marcus slept in silence. From Brett's observation, he looked completely healthy. Why hadn't he woken up? Brett seated himself beside the bed. Tears ran down his cheeks. "Thank you," he whispered. Something shifted behind him, elevating his heart rate.

"What are you doing here?" a man's voice said. The lights flipped on. Although they hadn't met, Brett recognized Marcus's father.

"Mr. Jones, I— I wanted to come visit your son. Needed to," Brett said.

"Please, my name is Christopher. I dozed off. You startled me. You look like you're doing well," Christopher said.

Hands shaking, Brett told the truth. "I'm not."

"It's a real blessing you woke up, son. Don't take that for granted. They say my son is medically fine. Marcus has stalled on the edge of regaining consciousness. Nobody can tell me why."

"The only reason I'm sitting here is because your son saved my life. He's my hero." It was important to Brett that Mr. Jones knew that.

This made Christopher tear up, as well. "Have you spoken to the authorities? They implied to me you did this to Marcus. He was found at the bottom of the quarry, below where you were found. I can see why investigators would assume that. Do you want to share how Marcus ended up there?" Christopher asked.

"Sir, I, watched my brother die. Then Bethany." Brett quivered, recalling the events. "When it was my turn, Marcus defended me. I don't deserve to be alive. He's the reason I am."

Christopher rubbed his chin. "So there was a struggle? He fell?"

"Marcus delivered the best tackle I've ever seen. I remember the pop when he collided. Momentum sent them over the edge." This was cathartic to share. Brett stood fast in refusing to name the assailant.

"Who attacked you?" Christopher asked.

"You wouldn't believe me. The police sure as hell wouldn't. At least until Marcus recovers and can back me up."

"You're afraid to say that it wasn't a person."

"Yes," Brett mustered in response. "I should go. My mom will be upset that I talked to you. The KBI made it clear my family is in trouble."

"What was said here, I'll keep to myself. If it helps, I believe your story," Christopher said.

Relief welled up inside. Maybe people would believe what he had to say, after all. Brett headed to the door. "Thank you. I hope Marcus wakes up soon, and his shoulder doesn't cause him trouble."

Jones raised an eyebrow. "Shoulder? Marcus doesn't have any injuries. Take care of yourself, Brett. Talk to someone."

No injury?

Brett slowly walked back to his mother's car waiting outside. Was he remembering correctly? Marcus had been bitten. Shirt torn, soaked in blood. A host of ideas came to mind. If silver hurt the werewolf, maybe all of its mythology was rooted in fact. Brett saw the bite wound, brought up the fact Marcus needed medical attention. Did this mean Marcus was infected? Would he become a monster? Things were about to get worse if more werewolves could be created. Zachery Grant *did* let slip that human DNA was being recovered from the victims. That alluded to the fact that these creatures are, in fact, human.

There was too much information for one traumatized teenager to process. Mattfield was in dire need of help from someone who knew how to combat werewolves.

On the car ride home, Brett confessed to speaking to Mr. Jones. Thankfully, his mother wasn't upset with him. She could tell how much respect he had for Marcus.

The silver knife kept materializing in his mind. Had the authorities found it? He didn't think so. Grant would have mentioned it. He considered a special trip to the quarry to try and recover the weapon.

When Julia's Trailblazer turned into the drive, Brett saw his father carrying boxes toward the front door. "What is he doing?"

Julia let out a sigh. They had avoided this conversation for a week. "He wants to be here for us. Your father quit his job. I need you to patch things up. We have a lot of hardship ahead of us. We must stick together, as a family."

Brett was in disbelief. "Mom, no. Hell no. Are you serious? I don't even want to call him Dad. He can't stay. Look where that man got us."

"That is not going to be tolerated. Do you understand me? Dalton is gone. I need help. You need help. It doesn't mean we forget, but we do need to forgive him, and I have. None of us will ever be the same. Brett, you have been consumed with anger since we got to Mattfield. It's time to suck it up."

Life always found a way to get worse. "No, my brother is dead! I can't tell anyone what happened! People will think I'm insane! That's me sucking it up. I have to live while everyone else around me died. We are in danger if we don't leave this place. Instead of moving away, we're just going to add the person who got Dalton killed to our household? Make it make sense for me."

"Nobody knows what you went through! You haven't told us! Besides, your father didn't move us to Mattfield. I did! How do you think I feel? The cops have said we can't leave. You are a suspect. What's that going to look like if we run away?" Julia asked.

"Who cares how it looks if we get to survive! I don't want to be here with him. Let me go stay with Grandpa."

She looked ready to continue the argument, but relented. "Fine, pack a bag. Go stay the night. Think about what I've said."

Not having to be told twice, Brett went to his room. Dumping the contents of his backpack out onto the floor, he stuffed it full of clothes. Michael tried to engage him as he headed outside. Brett ignored the nicety. He was unwilling to partake.

Julia gave him the keys to her Trailblazer. Until the police released his truck from impound, Brett would have to borrow or get a ride.

Grandpa Walt's dog, Buck, came out to greet him upon arrival.

"Hey, boy," Brett said, petting the fat yellow lab.

"Spoke to your mom! She told me you needed a place to stay tonight!" Walt shouted from the back porch of his home.

Backpack slung on his shoulder, Brett went to greet his grandpa. "I hope that's okay?"

"You're more than welcome here whenever you want," Walt said.

"Thanks, Grandpa. I don't know what to do. This is the hardest thing I've ever been through," Brett said, tearing up.

"Brett, I hope this is the hardest time you ever go through. It will take years to comprehend what took place. We have some daylight left. My fishing poles are ready to go. What would you like to do?" Walt asked.

The idea of fishing didn't currently appeal to Brett. One thing had been on his mind. He needed to gain experience in self-defense. "I want to learn how to shoot. Will you teach me?"

"Yeah! Let's do that." Walt got excited at the proposition. They went inside to the gun safe. "Anything in particular you want to learn how to use?" His grandfather opened the safe door to reveal an arsenal of firearms.

Brett marveled at the array of guns. There must've been fifty or more. "What do *you* think, Grandpa, for self-defense?"

"Well, you're too young to carry. Have to be twenty-one in Kansas. Guns used for self-defense depends on setting. A shotgun works well for home defense, but it's mainly for birds. Hard to maneuver in a house. Whatever load you're using determines stopping power. Farther someone is away from you, lethality drops off significantly with the shotgun. Most everyone who conceal carries goes with a nine-millimeter for a host of reasons. More rounds, less recoil, they come in all sizes and, with practice, are accurate at a hundred yards. A few choose the forty-five ACP for stopping power alone. That size of round hampers the shot count and increases the weight exponentially. Fifteen rounds in a nine-millimeter versus seven in forty-five," Walt explained, gleefully imparting his knowledge.

That was a lot to absorb. Brett considered the options. Stopping power would be beneficial due to the size of a werewolf, but then it would have to be close quarters. Did he want to be that close to one ever again? "Okay, I want reliable and powerful. Where do I start?"

Walt scanned the gun safe. "Oh, how about a revolver? I have a Smith & Wesson Governor. Fun to shoot. Can fire two types of rounds — three-inch four-ten shotgun slugs, and forty-five Long Colt. That forty-five LC packs a wallop. Plus, I'm set up to reload it."

"Alright, that's the one. What do you use to reload?"

"I have everything. The dies for molding bullets with lead, gun powder, and a press."

"Do you have to use lead?" Brett asked, thinking about the silver knife.

"Not at all, just the cheapest. Ready? There's some targets set up out back. We'll see what you can do." Walt took the revolver out of the safe with a box of

Winchester .45 LC ammo.

Behind the house, Walt ran through gun safety with him. Treat each fire-arm as if it is loaded. Never point a gun at anything you don't want to shoot. Know your surroundings and what's behind what you're shooting at. "This gun is a revolver, so you push the cylinder release on the side to open the cylinder. That's how you load and unload the gun. Being a revolver, it has a hammer. The Governor is a double-action. You do not have to pull back on the hammer to fire it. The trigger is weighted differently if the hammer is cocked or not. For accuracy, it's better to pull the hammer back. Less time anticipating your shot."

The revolver was transferred into Brett's hand. "It's heavy," he said.

"That's unloaded, too. Something that has the power to take life should have weight to it so you understand the responsibility you have. No matter what you hear, guns do not kill people. Cain murdered his brother with a rock. It's the will to commit that evil, not the tool used. Kids grow up with them out here. They inherit respect for firearms from their families. We'll talk more about our Second Amendment rights over dinner. As Americans, we're one of the few nations with an armed citizenry. Without the inherent right to bear arms, all the other freedoms we enjoy are null and void."

Responsibility was evident in the gun. To bear the power of death made Brett uneasy. Everyone who loves firearms must feel this way. A sacred duty the founding fathers knew to implement. An ability to wield destiny.

Walt passed him six rounds to load the Governor. Brett slid each into the cylinder while Walt gave instruction on how to properly align the front and rear sights. Brett took aim at a paper target twenty yards away. With his right thumb, Brett cocked the hammer back. An explosion erupted from the barrel as he squeezed the trigger.

"Good shot, just left of center. With some practice you'll be a pro in no time."

Hope crept into Brett's mind for the first time since the quarry. If no one was coming to save Mattfield, then it would be up to him. "Grandpa, I want to shoot every day."

This made Walt chuckle. Their sorrows were grounded in a fleeting moment of joy. "Gets expensive real fast. Come over every afternoon, and we'll shoot."

Five more shots tore through the paper target. One for each person killed homecoming night. Brett imagined the bullets punching holes in the werewolf's chest. Vengeance for Dalton.

No longer did he feel weak. His wrath would end the monster that murdered his brother.

20

OMENS

Lucas held the brass 9mm round tightly. This bullet held his life. The men spared him in hopes he would comply. They were sorely mistaken. He dug a hole and buried Caesar in the backyard. Each scoop of the shovel inflamed his anger. A plot for revenge fixated in his mind. Dream Walker had taken care not to kill any of his attackers that night. That restraint was gone.

Judge Thomas allowed him to drop the DUI charge against Sam. Lucas couldn't get to the man if he went to prison. Proctor was delighted by the fact, chalking it up as a victory for his client. It was a funny thing when individuals committed crimes and then proclaimed themselves innocent.

For the next few weeks, Lucas worked on identifying his attackers to no avail. Sam would have to be interrogated to gain answers. Yet the man was nowhere to be found. Dream Walker did not possess the skills of a detective. A warrior through and through, he searched while attempting to keep his motives hidden. Then, out of the blue, Sam came to him. It had been a long day prosecuting a domestic abuse case. Sam caught him as he exited the Tribal Court.

"Long time, no see," Sam said, not realizing the grave mistake he'd made by showing up.

"Do you normally walk into the lion's den?" Lucas asked. He noticed a bruise protruding from the man's hairline. Sam must've taken the big hit from the bat.

"I'm sent here on business. There's a case on your docket. Charges need dropped. Peter Vos. Get it done," Sam had the audacity to say.

"That's not going to happen," Lucas said.

"Look, you are on the team. Don't make things difficult for yourself again." Sam did his best to be threatening, but Lucas couldn't help but laugh. "What's so funny?"

Lucas put his hand on Sam's throat and squeezed. Sam squirmed from the pressure. "I did drop the charge against you. For a single reason. You'd be safe from me in prison. I want the names of my attackers."

"Stop, I can't breathe. They will kill you!" Sam was a slow learner.

For a brief moment, Lucas considered where he was, and the repercussions for his career. Then he thought of Caesar. His free hand balled into a fist as he swung. Over and over. Blood fell from Sam's face onto the concrete. After delivering a barrage of punches, Lucas released his grip on Sam's throat. Then delivered a powerful kick to Sam's chest, sending him rolling down the concrete staircase. He laid beaten to a bloody pulp on the sidewalk.

"Tell me their names!" Lucas gave him another chance.

"You're a dead man!" Sam said defiantly.

Lucas saw red. He descended the stairs to deliver another round of punches. In the chaos, he had been unaware of his surroundings. Two officers caught him from behind as he lifted his leg to stomp Sam into the pavement. He did not resist as they cuffed him.

"This isn't over," Dream Walker promised Sam.

"Enjoy seeing how the other half lives," Sam said through bloody teeth.

The officers led him to a police car and placed him in the backseat.

At the police station, he was booked into custody. He sat in a cell alone for the rest of the day, unapologetic for his actions. A need for justice put Lucas behind bars, but maybe there was a better way than this—vengeance without sacrificing the moral high ground. The plan he devised weeks ago was already in motion.

His attackers would come for him again, which was what he intended.

A guard came to his cell door. "Bail's been posted. Time for you to go." The officer unlocked the door.

In the lobby, Lucas saw his father. When their eyes met, remorse set in. "Thank you," Lucas said.

Paul remained silent. Lucas followed him out of the station. Once they were in the vehicle, Paul spoke. "They say you beat a man on the steps of the courthouse. Why do such a thing? All those years you spent at school, just to come home and throw it away."

"I was prosecuting that man for DUI. He and three others came to my house. They beat me, and killed Caesar. Left me with a bullet, like I owed them my allegiance for not murdering me," Lucas replied.

"Why did you not go to the police?"

"I don't know who can be trusted. The man I beat came to make a demand. Judge Thomas said to be afraid of them. So my plan was to take care of it myself."

"You said evil is in the heart of man, yet you still chose to do evil instead of taking the appropriate avenue. Now they have defeated you. People will force you to resign over this."

"That just means I'm no longer beholden to the law."

"Vengeance is not justice."

Paul drove them to his home.

"Why are we at your house? Who is here?" Lucas felt tricked. He recognized the same vehicles from their last gathering.

"The time has come for us to reconvene. No comments from you if they do not add to the discussion."

"Please, Dad. I've had a long day." Lucas wished to still be in his cell.

"Today is different. You haven't heard what has happened. Come inside."

He owed his father for posting bail. Lucas would attend as repayment.

))))))) ● ● ● ● ● ● ●

The room was alive with murmurs. The four men assumed the seats they'd occupied previously.

"What you did today was reckless," Judge Thomas scolded.

"I am no one's puppet. Have you bent the knee to those thugs?" Lucas had a hunch Judge Thomas may be in on it. Why else put a delay in a DUI case?

"How do you expect to fight them? If I recall, you chose to drop charges. That doesn't fit your persona." Judge Thomas was equally as accusatory.

"My plan for handling them is underway," Lucas said.

"Did you like jail that much? Because if you go to war, that is where you will spend the rest of your days. I'll see to it," Thomas advised.

"Enough bickering. This is not why we are here," Paul said, butting in. "It is national news."

National news?

"What are you talking about?" Lucas asked.

"Same as last month. Only much worse. At least five high school kids were killed outside of Mattfield, Kansas." Nicolas delivered the news.

This was new information to Lucas. You miss a lot while locked up.

"Tell us what is known," Paul said.

"The murder last month has gone unsolved. Another full moon, and with it, more bodies. In the same location. Deaths so brutal, whispers of an animal attack continue. An animal that has so far gone unidentified. I was afraid of jumping to conclusions before, but this is the work of a shape-shifter. I am certain," Nicolas explained.

Gray Eyes opened a box he brought with him. Inside were knives and arrowheads. "These are pure silver. Old. To protect from an evil spirit. We may find ourselves in need of such weapons if the curse spreads."

Lucas received a silver arrowhead, admiring its shape.

"What are the chances this stays contained to Mattfield?" Paul asked.

"The attacks have been outside of the town. Once the shape-shifter lays siege to Mattfield, it could swallow this part of the country within a year. When the curse spreads, so will death," Nicolas replied.

"We can fortify, protect our people. Even forge modern ammunition with silver," Judge Thomas said.

His elders were true believers. Dream Walker found himself somewhat intrigued. How had the killer evaded law enforcement? Nicolas had predicted more deaths on a full moon. What were the odds of him being correct? Having strayed from his heritage since he'd left home, he was unsure, but maybe his elders' wisdom was more than just stories. Lucas began questioning what he believed, but he needed to see actual evidence.

"Alright, let's say this is real—that a shape-shifter got set loose." Lucas wrestled with his inner voice over how nonsensical that sounded. "Why should we wait?"

"What do you mean? All we can do is wait," Gray Eyes said.

"Those people have no idea what they are dealing with. You all say that we do. Not to mention we are all holding the tools to get the job done. I'm asking why fortify Pawhuska. How many innocent people will die before it gets here?"

"Tens of thousands," Nicolas said.

"What is it you suggest?" Thomas asked.

Dream Walker held the arrowhead up for the room. "This. The hunt."

"No," Paul said bluntly.

"Hunt a shape-shifter? Are you mad?" Thomas asked.

"I do not seek death," Gray Eyes added.

Lucas was in disbelief. "Your big plan, then, is to wait until things get so bad they've spread over a hundred miles to our doorstep. Will your fortifications even stand a chance at that point? While thousands of innocents die and we do nothing?"

"*Tens* of thousands. This meeting is to protect our community. Would those people come to help us?" Nicolas asked.

"Yeah, I imagine they would if a demon of their culture got loose and started killing our people." The subject of the conversation was irrelevant. Lucas couldn't stand by if innocent lives were at stake. He was angered his elders would allow that to happen.

"For someone who didn't want to be here, you sound convinced," his father rebuked. "Lucas, I just got you from jail. Your plans do not work. You cannot make war with this."

"Father, I am far from convinced. We should want to render aid on principle. Cowards wait until death arrives at their home. Evil must be met head-on."

"Dead men serve no purpose," Thomas said.

"I will not go," Gray Eyes added.

"Our plan is to gather silver while we have time. Prepare ourselves and hope that we are wrong," Nicolas said.

"I can be the eyes and ears on the ground in Mattfield," Lucas offered.

"No! You do not understand! That is final." Paul's voice quavered.

"Fine, I will do it your way." Lucas conceded. "Take me home. Most likely the men who want me dead will succeed long before a shape-shifter makes it to us."

"In one month, we gather again. If the threat persists, we go all in on preparation," Nicolas insisted as he stood to leave.

"I will leave this box of weapons here until we meet again," Gray Eyes said.

"To stand on the precipice. Who would have imagined?" Judge Thomas asked, in awe of the developments.

The men exited the house together, each going to their respective vehicles.

Lucas got into the passenger seat of his father's truck. "My vehicle is at the Tribal Court. Take me there," Lucas demanded of his father.

Paul did as his son asked, pulling the truck onto the road. "Dark days lie ahead. We must protect our own."

"If this is happening, we shouldn't see it as us versus them, Dad. It is good against evil. I refuse to sit idle."

His father changed the subject. "You have created problems here at home. What will you do about it?"

"Tomorrow I will resign. Take the opportunity away from them to publicly shame me. Our people can't have a criminal prosecuting crime. My enemies lose what they perceived as a puppet. When they come for me, it will be final." Dream Walker would invoke self-defense.

"When they come for you," Paul reiterated his son's statement, "will their deaths bring you peace? Is murder justice? I fear you want that. This is your plan. Does that not make you their equal?"

"They will try to kill me. Should I let them?" Not many alternatives came to Lucas's mind.

"Resist calls to step down as prosecutor. Make clear what took place. Defeat them with the law." Sage advice from his father.

Paul dropped Lucas off at his truck. In parting, his father said, "Remember who you are. Stay true to that."

Back at home, Lucas's brain raced. This had been the most eventful day since leaving military service. Did he really believe an evil spirit was killing people? Evidence suggested something was amiss, but a shape-shifter? That didn't mesh with his worldview. He had left his heritage behind. Lucas felt life pulling him back to his roots. The time had come to embrace his name, Dream Walker, to seek guidance from his visions while at rest. It was worth a shot to garner knowledge. Dream walking isn't any more far-fetched than the existence of a shape-shifter. Dream Walker consciously made the decision to open his mind to the possibilities.

Lucas missed the routine and companionship he shared with Caesar. The bed felt empty without his guardian. He laid there, focused on how to best handle his enemies. His father was not wrong. Dream Walker's intention was to provoke and then eliminate his enemies, to deliver justice for Caesar, but Paul's questions had made him reconsider. Handling it that way was evil begetting evil. Judge and jury comes before executioner. In his rage, he'd lost sight of his own ideals, but there was time to course correct, to bring them down without devolving to their level.

An idea came to Lucas as he drifted off to sleep. . . .

It was dark with the silvery full moon hanging in the sky. A statue of three marble men stood before him. Lucas recognized one of the figures as himself. An owl swooped down from the night sky, landing atop the monument. This struck fear in his heart. To his knowledge, Dream Walker had never seen the other men before. Owls were the harbinger of death. What did this mean?

Turning from the statue, a dim light caught his eye in the distance. Intrigued, he walked toward it. The light vanished as he approached. Brick buildings towered on both sides of him. The owl returned with a nose dive, causing him to duck. Then he saw the three bodies. One body sat hunched forward as if leaning against an object. A woman's body lay face-down with a hole punched clean through her chest. A third body sat crumpled in a pool of blood. Were these the attackers who would come for him?

Agonizing pain overtook him. Dream Walker fell to his knees. Blood flowed from wounds covering his body. He lifted his left arm to touch cuts across his chest. To Lucas's horror, a bloody stump remained just below his left elbow. A familiar sound came to his ears. The hammer of a gun being cocked back. Snapping his head up, a rifle's barrel sat inches in front of his face. A shadowy figure held the rifle at its shoulder. Wings spread, the owl descended, floating down in front of the assailant's face. Just as its feet touched the gun, a flash came from the barrel. . . .

Dream Walker sat up in bed, breathing heavily. He had dream walked. The great spirit granted a vision for the first time since his youth, an ominous nightmare of his own demise. Others would perish with him, as well. With the foreknowledge in his possession, could he change the outcome? Lucas wondered how much time was left. He had to find another way to deal with Sam.

Revenge left Lucas's heart.

Vengeance could be achieved without death.

21

ADVENT

The news was plastered across the entire world—especially in Wichita, Kansas: teenagers slain outside of Mattfield. In the same location, a man was found dead a month prior. One night after the teenagers got murdered, an elderly woman living alone on her farm met the same fate.

What Liam had brushed off as a black bear now appeared more serious. Still, a bear was not entirely impossible, just extremely unlikely. Reports said the wounds appear to be from an animal. This would have to come from something larger than a black bear. Highly aggressive and territorial.

A request for help had reached him in Nepal. Liam outright dismissed the case as nothing of significance. Now he felt a debt owed to the town. The toll exacted from the tiger hunt left him a broken man, his sleep interrupted by vicious nightmares. Abhinav haunted Liam throughout each night, a young man cut down in his prime for what turned out to be no reason at all.

Liam had to own up to reality: He was a murderer.

He had been back home for a month. On the farm, Liam went about menial tasks to occupy his mind, to no avail. Images of the five murdered teenagers were everywhere he looked. Soon, they joined Abhinav in his nightmares, unleashing torment night after night. "Why didn't you save us?" they cried out while Abhinav stood behind them silently. What more could he say? Abhinav pleaded for his life, but Liam took his life, anyway.

On two separate occasions, Liam executed his routine before a hunt, meticulously packing everything to travel to Mattfield. Clothes, traps, supplies, and firearms. Then he would talk himself out of the trip, unpack, and continue wallowing in isolation. What help would he be? It was only a matter of time before authorities in Nepal discovered what he had done. Maybe they already had. Any day, federal agents would arrive to extradite him for his crime. That day couldn't come soon enough. Abhinav's family deserved justice.

News coverage of the investigation prevented the deceased from being laid to rest, prolonging the families' suffering. Abhinav didn't receive a proper funeral. Liam left his body lying in the jungle to rot. Guilt burrowed its claws in.

Abhinav finally spoke to him in his dream one night: "Are you going to let them all die?" Then another boy from television joined in. Dalton Adams begged, "Please, don't let my family die!"

Liam awoke frantic, his path to Mattfield made clear.

He would not allow himself to harm another human being. Redemption wasn't on the table. Instead, an opportunity to save innocent lives, to turn his actions around, to do something right. Nightmares would drive Liam into madness if he stayed on the farm.

For a third time, he prepped the gear needed for a hunt. This time, Liam crossed the threshold. Piece by piece, he loaded bags into his Jeep Gladiator's bed. His guns went in the back seat of the cab.

He elected to bring three different rifles: a Marlin 30-30 for close quarters; a Browning X-Bolt .308 for putting down any big game predator; and lastly, a gun he didn't expect to use—his personal favorite, Shiloh Sharps 1874 Quigley 45-70. The gun traveled with Liam on every domestic hunt, but a chance had never presented itself for use.

The Gladiator loaded down with weeks' worth of gear, it was time. Liam placed a call to the neighbor who watched over his farm while he was away on business. He paid them well for their help. GPS on his phone pinned Mattfield at a two-and-a-half-hour drive. Arrival just past noon. There was no plan in place, or arrangements for somewhere to stay—a detail-oriented man heading out with no direction.

Nepal ignited the death of the old Liam. To be a changed man meant leaving that persona behind. He remained Liam Gable in name only. Layer by layer, he would peal back the man capable of murder until something new was crafted of him. Fear remained that whatever beast prowled around Mattfield would make his old ways essential.

God forbid the killer be a tiger.

Mattfield stood a solemn place. Few milled about on the town's main drag. Some shops sat empty. A shell of its former self, Liam imagined. Rural towns were usually vibrant with life. People supported small businesses within their communities, visiting with one another on the streets. That spirit was absent, drained of joy and peace.

Liam's jeep crawled slowly as he took in the surroundings. The residents had previously known nothing of tragedy—not of this magnitude. These deaths could very well be the town's downfall, joining the ranks of all the other ghost towns across the plains.

Red and blue lights flashed in his mirrors. Liam looked back to see a police truck behind him. He carefully parked the truck on the side of Main Street.

In town for less than ten minutes, and I'm already making a stir.

An older gentleman exited the police truck and approached. The cop took note of the gear in the truck bed.

"Good way to get robbed is not having a bed cover," the cop commented.

"A bed cover limits room. I need as much space as I can get for my gear." Liam noticed the name on the officer's shirt read "Sheriff Mills."

"Do you have firearms on you?" Mills asked.

"Yes, a few."

"Deer hunter?" The sheriff was fishing.

"No."

"I'll have you step out of the vehicle, sir. I didn't get your name." The sheriff opened the door of the Gladiator.

"That's because you didn't ask. I'm here to offer my expertise to you. Lucky me, here you are." They were going to meet one way or another. Liam supposed this was fate getting straight to the point.

This gave Mills pause.

Liam saw the dots connecting in the sheriff's mind. "Liam Gable, big game hunter. Did you get your tiger?" Mills asked, but his tone was misleading. It came across almost sarcastically.

"I did. The tiger claimed fourteen victims before it was over. I heard things have gotten worse here. So I came to help," Liam said.

"Too late for that, don't you think? Besides, I'm not in charge of the investigation. I respect your decision not to come before, but showing up now is salt in the wound."

Liam knew the sheriff's pride was injured, his standing in the community tainted. "If you have no obligation to investigate the case, then you and I can hunt whatever did this."

"And you want to do this out of the kindness of your heart, I assume?" Sheriff Mills asked.

"I can't tell you what finally brought me to town. That's something I'm still wrestling with myself. What I know is, this is where I'm supposed to be." Liam wasn't about to explain the recurring nightmare that brought him to Mattfield.

Mills studied him. The sheriff must have found the answers genuine. "All of our deceased appear to have been killed by an animal. DNA analysis says they were murdered by people. Nobody has a plausible theory for what we're seeing."

Human DNA? Mattfield was dealing with a crazed lunatic. "Put me in the vicinity. Man or beast, I can track it."

A proposition Mills couldn't resist. "Alright, we can try first thing in the morning."

"Also, I'm going to need a place to stay." Liam made sure to save that part for last.

With a puzzled expression, Mills extended an offer. "My wife and I have a camper, if you'd like."

"In my profession, a camper is considered luxury. I would be grateful." Beats sleeping on the ground.

Mills gave him a nod. "Follow me."

Liam followed the sheriff into the countryside northeast of Mattfield. No surprise to see he and the sheriff lived a similar lifestyle. A quaint farmhouse on a few acres, detached from the chaos of their professions, to rest from a day's work in peace.

The camper's accommodations were more than Gable could ask for. A queen-sized bed, kitchen, and bathroom with a shower. He transferred all the gear from the truck bed to his temporary residence. Mills got to work hooking up water and electricity. Within an hour, the camper was set for habitation.

"Thank you," Liam said, expressing his gratitude for the sheriff's kindness.

"I should be thanking you for coming to our aid. This is the least I can do." Mills's initial bitterness had vanished. "My wife, Martha, will insist you join us for dinner."

For a few hours, Liam settled in to his living quarters. To calm his mind, he studied maps of the area. It would be difficult to find a trail without starting at Coal Creek Rock Quarry. From there, the challenge would be the passage of time. A predator, or human, would have to conceal itself somewhere with resources. Mattfield Reservoir sat within two mile as the crow flies. The lake was narrow, but stretched a few miles in length. That was a logical place to search. Access was limited without a boat, or hiking. Not many people would walk through the brush just to fish, providing ample places to conceal one's presence.

At dinner time, Liam went to the Mills's home. Martha greeted him at the door. "Not every day a world-renowned hunter comes to supper. I hope you like spaghetti." She was jovial, but it didn't mask the pain—the same broken spirit he saw on Main Street.

Dinner plates were already prepared at the table. Liam sat straight across from the sheriff.

"This looks wonderful, I'm honored to be your guest." Liam hadn't eaten a proper meal since his return home.

"Don't be silly, and you can call him Carl. Sheriff Mills isn't allowed at home anymore," Martha said.

Carl shook his head at the comment. "I've brought too much baggage home lately. Martha advised to leave business at the door for my sanity's sake."

"Smart. We live in a dark world. It's good to revel in the little things, if only for a few hours each day." In the past, Liam had done the same.

"So, you didn't make plans for this trip. Do you have anything in mind for tomorrow?" Carl asked.

"I went over a few maps of the area. What caught my attention was the Mattfield Reservoir."

Martha sighed. "Do we have to talk about this at dinner?"

Carl brushed off her comment. "The reservoir and surrounding acreage are city-owned. Supplies the drinking water to most of the county."

Liam nodded. "Precisely. No homes or water sports. Besides recreational fishermen, nobody's out there. That's a good place to start. Someone could easily conceal themselves. The lake provides everything necessary for survival."

"Gives us a start without crossing paths with the feds. It could take a few days to search that entire area." It was clear the sheriff hadn't thought about it.

"I'm here to see this through. We'll branch out to secluded ponds if nothing turns up at the reservoir. I need to know what the directive is. Consequences between hunting an invasive species versus a man are vast." A question Liam feared he knew the answer to.

Reaching below the table, Carl presented a badge. He tossed it in front of Liam. "You will have the protection of the law. Our suspect's name is Thomas Morro. I suspect there to be an accomplice. Personally, I put kill shots into Morro's chest. That was almost two weeks ago. His body has not been found.

Any perceived threat is shoot on sight. We will bury the consequences."

Martha took her plate and went to the living room.

A shutter shot down Liam's spine. To have murder sanctioned to him. He swore never again. Now it was offered free of punishment. Out of everyone to have this conversation, why him? Liam wondered if this was where he would've ended up had he lived his life as a better man. "We've just met. How can you ask this of me?"

"You have the look of guilt. I see it when I look at myself in the mirror. We carry the dead with us. The ones we believe could have been saved. This is our chance to not add to that burden. You came here to see this through. More people will die if we don't. I'd rather carry the guilt of killing a thousand murderers than the guilt of a single person I failed to protect."

These words hung on Liam. If only the sheriff knew the man he spoke to. Did it take a murderer to stop another? He took the badge in his hand. "I'll help you do this."

That night, Gable fell asleep to the eerie cries of coyotes. Their sound diminished his hope of avoiding nightmares. Abhinav was awaiting him as Liam began to dream. He came alone this time. . . .

"A murderer given the opportunity to do what he is best at."

"Please, I will not kill again," Liam said, falling to his knees.

"Murder, murder, murder. Where does it end? Your intentions for killing me were selfish. A desire to save little Nirupama, how stoic. Remember when you tried to talk me out of going with you? Do you know what hurt worse than cold steel being shoved into my stomach? That a man I looked up to was capable of taking my life. Those are bad seeds. A man asked you to be okay with murder and you accepted." Abhinav paced back and forth. "Be honest. Are you going to kill again? Will you use the sheriff as bait? Someone else? I think you already know how this ends for you. Harvest time for your rotten fruit is coming. You will reap what you have sown. That is, death."

Abhinav felt real in his nightmares. His theft of the man's life had bound them to one another. . . .

Dense fog hung on the morning air as Liam made his way outside. Mills greeted him with a cup of coffee.

"I hope I haven't kept you waiting," Liam said.

"No, I soak up the fresh air in the morning. Helps prepare for the day," Mills replied.

"It *is* beautiful. Shall we head out?" Liam asked.

"Grab a rifle; you can ride with me."

Given the terrain, Liam chose his lever action 30-30 for today. An excellent brush gun for close-quarter shots. On gravel roads, it was only a few minutes to the reservoir. They devised a plan on the way. Mills would drop him off at the lesser-known back entrance. Liam would scout on the north side of the lake, heading east. Carl would drive to the public entrance, and they would meet in the middle, then repeat for the south side the following day.

When Liam exited the vehicle, the sheriff handed him a walkie-talkie. "Channel 4. Feel free to engage. Call if you need backup."

Tangles of thistles, poison ivy, and cedars were his obstacles for the day. He had little confidence in actually finding anything of value, but this was just the beginning. Bobbing and weaving, Liam went about his journey, serene nature on all sides. A cool breeze ruffled his hair. God's country. Liam kept eyes on the lookout for signs of life.

An hour in, he found the first peculiar sign. A canine paw print in damp earth. *Too large to be a dog,* he observed.

The only logical explanation was a wolf. In eastern Kansas? Highly unlikely proposition. Using his cell phone, he photographed the anomaly. Before moving on, he readied his rifle. There wouldn't be much warning if attacked in this foliage. A hundred yards later, Liam discovered a rudimentary camp. Old-school in nature. A deer hide was hung up to cure. A makeshift shelter was built, as well as a fire pit from loose stones. Not a setup for an average redneck. This camp belonged to a survivalist who knew what they were doing.

Inside the makeshift shelter, Liam found a half-burnt black T-shirt. Sticks cracked behind him. Gable raised his gun as he turned his attention. A man took off sprinting as they made eye contact. Liam led the man with the rifle, an amateur shot he could make any day. Liam lowered the firearm, consequences be damned. To squeeze the trigger meant to spiral further into oblivion. There had to be another way.

Using the walkie, he reported his find to Mills, leaving out the fact he saw a man.

Liam sat at the camp for an hour, waiting for the sheriff. Once again, sticks cracking alerted him. Standing, he said, "About time . . ."

An enormous black wolf stood twenty yards away. With catlike reflexes, Gable trained the gun on the predator. Time stood still. Red eyes beamed from the beast's head. A low growl rumbled from its jaws. Unafraid, Liam fired a shot directly into the wolf's chest. The wolf let out a loud yelp. Cycling the lever action, he put a fresh round into the chamber.

Another shot rang out, this time from Mills as he approached. Snarling, the wolf raced out of sight into the cedars.

"I hit him square with the thirty-thirty," Liam said. "I can't imagine he'll make it far."

"I did the same with my two-seventy. One of these guns should have dropped it where it stood," Mills replied in disbelief. He then examined the camp, immediately taking interest in the burnt shirt. "Thomas Morro's shirt."

"How do you know?" Liam asked.

"Those burns are from when I blew him up with a propane tank. Then my deputy and I shot him several times."

The man Liam had glimpsed looked completely uninjured. It couldn't be the same person. "How far away did that happen?"

"Quite a ways from here. On the other side of Mattfield. Look, it's not possible he could be alive. Not without a long stay at the hospital. I checked his pulse. Thomas Morro was dead," Mills explained.

"How can that be? People don't die from bullet wounds, then miraculously recover." Liam couldn't believe what he was hearing.

"His girlfriend laughed at us. Told us Thomas couldn't be killed. I've been in law enforcement my entire life. What we are dealing with, this is different. Nothing makes sense," Mills said.

"Are you telling me you believe this is supernatural?" Liam asked.

"I don't know what to believe anymore. I have faith in God, so in a way, I already believe in a higher supernatural order," Mills replied.

To hear Carl speak like this caused concern. By all accounts, the man didn't appear crazy. Almost as if sharing it out loud pained him. Things were becoming stranger. "What have I gotten myself into?" Liam murmured. Reflecting on his nightmares, Liam had new questions of his own: Why did the dead want him here? What part could he possibly play?

"I hope you'll stay. Mattfield's future hangs in the balance. People will move in droves if we don't bring this to an end," Mills said.

"I've been having nightmares. In them, the dead begged me to come." Liam put it out there. The sheriff was in no position to judge.

"The dead?" Mills asked confused.

"It seems I have a part to play," Liam said.

"My nightmares have been of the quarry. Stacked to the brim with bodies. If anyone heard this conversation, we'd be locked up. I don't know what our next move is," Carl said.

"I'm afraid we're going to need all the help we can get," Liam responded.

2 2

FAITH

Frigid water sloshed between Julia's hands. She splashed her face with it. In the mirror, Julia barely recognized her reflection. Unkempt hair, bags under her brown eyes, and sorrow written across her forehead.

I look like shit, she told herself.

A matriarch in mourning. Today she would lay Dalton to rest. Weeks of waiting on investigations, the day had finally come. His body, along with Brett's truck, were released to the family. Still no answers. Tax dollars well spent.

Inside her closet, she sifted through the extensive clothing options. Julia did this to calm her nerves. The black dress and heels she would wear today were selected a week ago, but it didn't hurt to have another tour.

Parents should never bury a child. A black hole forever in her heart. Nothing could fill that void. Brett's future forever in ruins by Dalton's untimely death. No, not just death. Being dishonest wasn't honoring his memory. Dalton's life was stolen. Her sons were the victims of a heinous crime. The audacity of an investigator to suggest Brett had anything to do with it. Julia knew her son to be aggrieved. To stretch Brett's disposition to the point of maniacal mass murderer was blasphemy. Angry teenage boys were a dime a dozen. Julia recognized that Brett's heart was pure, and that he had grounds for his disillusionment with the current family dynamic.

To show strength today was a choice.

Julia went to Michael, who waited in the living room. He was dressed in a black suit with matching shoes and tie. Nothing had to be said between them. Michael took her in his arms.

"Is Brett ready?" Julia asked.

"He's still upstairs. I don't want to rock the boat—not today," Michael said.

"Brett, sweetie. We need to get going," Julia called out for her son.

The rumble of footsteps heralded Brett's arrival as he came down the staircase. Julia could tell he had been crying.

Outside, Walt leaned against the front of his truck, waiting. Sunshine warmed their skin. A light breeze brought breaths of fresh air.

A beautiful day to lay my son to rest, Julia thought.

For the bleakest of occasions, in the absence of positivity, she would will it into existence.

"I'll drive us," Walt volunteered.

Julia sat up front with her father. A deafening silence as they each rode, absorbed in grief. Dalton would be laid to rest next to his grandmother at Sunny Slope Cemetery, a graveside ceremony for the immediate family members. Dalton's memory would be honored by those who loved him most. The funeral home would handle the rest.

They arrived at the cemetery. Then the hearse came into view, and she lost control. Three hands, one from each of the men rested on her in support.

They took a moment to compose themselves before exiting the truck. Brett came to her side and locked arms. "Dalton and I were here, just a few weeks ago," Brett said softly. "Some stupid stuff. He found a story and wanted to look into it, so we came to find answers."

Julia brushed his cheek with her free hand.

Another car pulled in behind Walt's truck. The homecoming queen got out of the driver's seat. Cassie came to Brett's side. She locked her arm with his, opposite Julia. This girl genuinely cared for her son. A high school romance was one thing; Julia found a deep respect for Cassie. It took real love to show up when life got arduous.

Brett stood speechless at her arrival.

"Thank you for coming," Julia said.

Cassie gave a nod in response.

Pressing forward, the five walked to Dalton's coffin. Julia saw her mother's headstone. Half the people buried here were gone too soon.

A preacher awaited them as they gathered around.

"On behalf of the community, I want to share with your family how profoundly sorry we are for your loss. Hollow words, I know. There is nothing worse than losing a child, a grandchild, a brother. Dalton Michael Adams joins his grandmother in the promise of Heaven. God tells us in Psalm 34:18, The Lord is close to the brokenhearted and saves those who are crushed in spirit. It is times like this when people lose their faith. Who can blame them? Suffering of this magnitude is grueling, life altering. It shakes the foundation of our world. The path forward is full of hardship before healing can take place.

"In the Sermon on the Mount, Jesus shared, 'Blessed are those who mourn, for they shall be comforted.' Jesus went forward to die for our sins. God gave His only begotten son for us. By doing that, He gave us hope. A reason to celebrate, and the promise of reuniting with our loved ones in the end. Now is your time for grief, but walk in the ways of the Lord, and Dalton will see you again. 'I have told you these things, so that in me you may have peace. In this world you will have trouble, but take heart. For I have overcome the world.' John chapter 16. I will leave you with a final piece of scripture from Revelation: 'He will wipe away every tear from their eyes, and death shall be no more, neither shall there be mourning, nor crying, nor pain anymore, for the former things have passed away.'

"Funerals mean the pain is fresh. The loved one was just here. You can still hear their laugh, feel their touch, and see their future. We stand here in celebration of Dalton's life, what he accomplished with the time he was given on Earth, lives and hearts forever impacted by his memory. Live each day in honor of him. Hold fast to your loved ones as none of us are guaranteed tomorrow. Know that God hears your cries, feels your pain, and above all, loves you. Forgive those who trespass against you, for our time here is but a little while. I'd like us to recite the 23 Psalm together."

Julia had strayed away from her Christian roots. Excuses of being too busy. The words spoken for her son brought comfort. She joined in the Psalm with her family.

"'The Lord is my shepherd; I shall not want. He maketh me to lie down in green pastures; He leadeth me beside the still waters. He restoreth my soul; He leadeth me in the paths of righteousness for his name's sake. Yea, though I walk through the valley of the shadow of death, I will fear no evil; for Thou art with me,'" their voices said in unison.

Julia felt the desire to get her family back into church. To honor Dalton. To make certain they would be reunited in the end.

Over the next few days, Julia returned to the cemetery to speak aloud with her inner voice. "Hi, Mom. I hope you're showing Dalton all the wonderful things to do up there. It's easy to get self-absorbed down here. My life has never meant less to me than now, losing my baby boy. I would trade the world for another minute with both of you. Death doesn't scare me anymore, as long as I get to be with the two of you again. When my time comes, I will be ready."

School reopened after Mattfield was given a two-week grace period to mourn. A good thing—Brett should be mourning the losses with the rest of the student body. There was a lot for Mattfield High to figure out.

Michael extended an olive branch to Brett at home, but he was yet to give his father a chance. A constant presence and time would hopefully heal the divide. Michael had chosen patience, hoping the father and son relationship was salvageable.

In the meantime, Julia encouraged Brett to meet with school counselors to talk. Brett still refused to open up about the events. Investigators circled like vultures, but the family effectively shut them out with a lawyer. Despite using modern technology, it was rather embarrassing the federal and state agents couldn't provide answers. They chose to go the path of threats and resistance, alienating their only witness.

Julia spent long hours contemplating what to do. Work made sure she was not required to return until ready, but would she ever truly be ready? Julia craved work to occupy her mind.

Start with half days and work up to a full schedule. Get back on the horse, she thought.

It was unhealthy being stuck inside her mind with the demons. Plus, the motherly instinct wanted to be there to help care for Marcus. The boy remained in an unconscious state. Brett was steadfast that Marcus saved his life. Julia desired to repay the favor, to help another family bring home a son. Mattfield had endured enough, and now offered an abundance of daily prayers and hope for his recovery. The miracle when he returned to them could be the inspiration Mattfield needed to carry on.

Plenty of time arose for Michael and Julia to work on their marriage. Michael held his fair share of guilt. As parents, they felt remorse. Michael was of the belief that he was the sole cause. He'd cheated on Julia, the action which led to her reactionary move. There was sound logic in the argument that Julia would not deny. Regardless of why the family ended up in Mattfield, she still found herself feeling guilty. She could have kicked Michael from their home in the city, forced him to get an apartment, but the transplant of her kids was how Julia handled the affair—an affair for which she later forgave her husband. Who knew the consequences of their disgruntled marriage would manifest this? Sins of the parents led to the death of their youngest son. Neither could change the outcome. To heal meant accepting that fact. Their journeys would be unique from each other, but they were determined to weather the storm as one.

"I want to renew my vows to you. Before God and everyone. You have shown unconditional love. Whatever I need to do from here on out is in service to you, to Brett, to this family," Michael said one day, sharing his heart.

"God's listening. You can tell us now," Julia said.

Michael was caught off guard. He sat up straight and took Julia's hands in his. "I vow to love, cherish, support, and protect you. There is no repentance for the debt I owe, but I promise to repay your heart with interest each time the sun rises. My eyes see only you, my heart beats for you, and my mind relishes you. Until the day I die. Nothing will ever come before this family." Michael delivered his new vows flawlessly.

"I accept. There's no one I want to go through this life with but you," Julia said. The past must be left where it belongs. She took Michael's words to heart. He was sincere. Julia knew her husband had a change of heart before tragedy struck. Michael stood to be the best version of himself going forward.

Marriages either fell apart or became unbreakable in catastrophe.

"Can I be honest with you? How does your faith remain? Julia, I'm struggling. Dalton, why was he punished for what I've done?" Michael's voice cracked as he held back tears.

"My faith is renewed from this. I have to believe someday I will see my boy and my mother in Heaven. Dalton was not punished. That's the worst way to view it. Our family put God on the back burner for years. I believed, but didn't make time for Him. Not even an hour on Sunday.

"You're asking the wrong questions. Sins compound over time. Where we are right now is the result. We have to break the cycle in order for this family to survive. Chaos is inevitable, but destruction of the soul is preventable. Faith is a test. The devil seeks to devour those who find themselves questioning. Show courage for Brett, and honor Dalton's memory, as the father you're capable of being," Julia said to encourage and strengthen her husband's resolve.

Michael took a moment to process what she'd told him. "Do you think the devil did this?"

That was a deep question. Julia found herself thinking theologically about the nature of the world. "That's too far down the rabbit hole for me. Especially since we have no answers. Brett saw something. It's written on his face. When Zachery Grant interviewed our son, he said 'wolf.' Does a wolf, or even a pack of wolves, make any sense? How has nobody stumbled across one? Our family is caught up in something I've not seen before. Did you know Brett's been learning to shoot with my dad? He's afraid. We need to find out of what. He has to tell the truth."

"Could be a false memory? His mind tricking him to protect against the trauma. Do you think he should be shooting?" Michael asked.

"Crossed my mind. Medically, it can happen. I'm going to go visit my dad, try to determine Brett's intentions. Grant alluded to Brett being a suspect. You and I know that's bullshit. I need Dad to let us know if anything else is going on. Also, I've decided to return to work. They need me, and I need to occupy my time."

"Are you sure?" Michael asked, concerned.

"There's no right time. I'm sure. You and I are struggling with the meaning of our lives. Some normalcy may help. Hard to tell until I try," she said.

This was one of many conversations the two of them shared. True love blossoming forth in disaster.

Concerned for Brett's safety, Julia drove to visit her father. An obsession with firearms was out of character. Why all of a sudden? He had never been interested in the past. Walt did have a way of projecting the sport onto people, though.

There was nothing inherently wrong with Brett gaining an appreciation for guns; Julia just needed to be reassured this was being done for the right reason. Her son would never want to hurt anyone—at least not that she was aware of. Threads dangled in her mind, unanswered. Why did Brett not tell anyone before about the night Stillman died? What were the chances Brett, of all people, would have a run-in with Morro? How did he survive the quarry? Everyone had given Brett space for weeks. However uncomfortable, people had to hear the truth.

Julia hoped Walt might provide information gleaned from their daily target practice.

The Trailblazer came to a stop in Walt's driveway. Buck came out to greet Julia, tail wagging with enthusiasm.

"Good boy," Julia said, giving the yellow Labrador an ear massage.

"Doesn't make a good guard dog. Buck would open the door for anyone if he had thumbs," Walt said as he approached.

"Hey, Dad. How are you?"

"Doing the best I can to keep hold of my faith. When my time comes, I'll have a lot of questions," Walt replied.

A recurring theme, Julia thought.

Everyone in the county must be facing the same examination. "I came to talk to you about Brett. He hasn't opened up with us—with *anyone* that I know of. The KBI forced our hand into getting a lawyer to protect him. His mental state is fragile. As a mother, I don't want to have Brett relive the trauma. We're running out of options. Law enforcement has yet to make an arrest. No answers. Which means Brett will not be able to remain silent for much longer. Maybe the school counselor can get him to open up. Has he said anything to you?"

"I don't press him for answers. Brett has lost control of his life. For the hour or two we spend together each day, I give him freedom. He's become quite the shot. Look, we both know he has issues with Michael. Don't expect that to go away overnight," Walt said.

"So, nothing?"

"Not a word about Jackson Road—what led to it, what took place. Brett's coming here to gain a sense of control again. A gun makes you feel safe and dangerous at the same time. I get the sense Brett is afraid."

"He is not hiding it well. Do you think training firearms is a good idea? There are so many questions. Investigators don't rule out that Brett played a bigger part in the deaths. I can't let myself believe it for a second; I don't think he would hurt anyone."

"Yet you're here, questioning his motives. Which means a part of you believes he's capable. Julia, Brett is not a killer. The guilt and fear he shows is from failure, not a fear of law enforcement. This conversation tells us all we need to know about why the boy won't talk." Walt understood Julia's heart was in the right place.

Her father was right. Julia spoke of her son's innocence, but inside, she had reservations. "Do you think the experience was so traumatic, he refuses to talk?"

"Traumatic is an understatement. He witnessed death firsthand. American kids don't contend with that in this day and age. It's a foreign concept that's rare here. I believe Brett fears no one will believe what he has to say, including you. A teenage boy can sense doubt."

"The information Brett shared with the investigator, it just doesn't make sense," Julia said.

"Sometimes the truth is stranger than fiction. Stories that are the most implausible are usually true. Ones you can wrap your mind around can be riddled with lies. Brett isn't out here trying to convince people of anything. Liars do that."

"I sat with him for the questions. He said a wolf was responsible. Dad, how can that be true?" Julia asked.

This was news to Walt. "I'll talk to Carl. Maybe he's heard something we haven't. Believe in your son, Julia. Give him trust. You might get the answers you're looking for. I have questions of my own, but not about Brett's innocence."

"What questions?"

"First off, are you okay with Brett coming here to shoot still?"

"Yes, until we have reason to be concerned. Promise me the guns stay here. The last thing I want is my son carrying a firearm." If Brett found target practice therapeutic, it was best he continued.

"Alright, then. Dalton had me take him to the library after school. About a month ago. He asked all sorts of questions about a local legend. I didn't think much of it. I've noticed a pattern. Everybody who has died, it's been in the two-day span when the moon is the fullest. Why is that? Seems to be modus operandi for a serial killer. Kansas is notorious for the sort. BTK, Slavemaster—hell, even the Bloody Benders. Unexplained things were in Mattfield's history, too. Dalton was on about the mysterious man from the 1800s. None of it makes sense, a picture out of focus."

"Teenage boys. Of course the first thing they pick up on in Mattfield is the story of the undying man, the Indian House, and all the nonsense. I don't see how that relates to this," Julia said.

"Those events are stranger than fiction. The truth lies somewhere in between. We're living through a modern version. We need to be open-minded to all possibilities. If Brett said a wolf, then I believe him."

Julia refused to believe without evidence. She was a medical professional, not a conspiracy theorist, living based on physical and material facts. Not once had she thought about the connection with the full moons. That was evidence, but of what? A full moon serial killer? Thomas Morro transitioned from petty thief into criminal mastermind? These were questions without logical answers, an absent catalyst to align the events. That is, if you didn't include Brett. Her son was tangled in the web of events.

Is he the spider?

23

INTO THE FRAY

Elliot stood at the window in his office. A gloomy afternoon—gray, overcast sky blocking the sun from providing its warmth. He would get no sunshine before his departure. Rain drops began splashing the window, trickling down the glass panes.

"Off to Kansas, then?" Hawes announced his presence in the doorway behind him.

Elliot turned to address his superior. "I've seen enough."

"How long do you think it will take to establish confirmation?" Hawes inquired.

"The next full moon. Sir, I expect to be gone until December at the latest," Elliot estimated.

"A full moon? December? You can't possibly think they're dealing with a werewolf in Mattfield, Kansas," Hawes scoffed.

"Probably more than one by this point," Elliot clarified. The curse'd had ample time to propagate.

Hawes stroked his beard in disbelief. "Are you certain? There hasn't been a werewolf incursion since Lithuania, 1917. All the way back during the First World War. Bastion eradicated them to folktales outside of—" Hawes was getting grandiose before Elliot cut him off.

"Trust me. I haven't set my eyes on one yet, but that's what I'm dealing with.

A remnant of the past, I surmise. Contained in a cavern underground. Someone knew to lock the cursed away. Details on that are lost to history. The curse of Lycaon has been set loose," Elliot stated.

Hawes paced back and forth. "I can travel with you. No living member of Bastion has dealt with these creatures. From the writings, those fiends killed a lot of our ranks over the centuries. If it truly is Lycaon's curse, God help us," Hawes said worriedly.

Elliot took notice. His superior was showing fear. Although Hawes would never admit to it, he was visibly shaken. Elliot began to feel he had underappreciated the werewolf. "You are of no use to me on this. I'm glad the case landed on my desk. Believe, I'll get this done. I have convinced myself a Drift is in play. Under that assumption, it solves a lot of unanswered questions."

"An extinct creature and an undiscovered Drift in Kansas, you say? You understand the absurd probabilities," Phillip said rhetorically.

"Extinct? You know that not to be the case," Elliot said, annoyed.

"At least the others seem to be halfway civilized," Hawes replied. "The curse comes from a Drift so I understand your reasoning. All of this is hard to imagine. Hopefully nothing else arises while you're away for such an extended period of time."

"Felix should be returning in a few days."

Anger spread across Hawes's face.

Elliot was prepared to apologize if he had given offense.

"Felix. Reports have reached me about the work he has done in the Congo," Hawes proclaimed. "The man is on thin ice, if true. I may be seen as soft in my age, but make no mistake: This job is a sacred duty we bear. It is not an excuse for barbarism. We fight the forces of darkness. If we commit wicked acts, then we are just a different form of evil. I will not allow the degradation of Bastion on my watch."

That sounded like Felix had held to his word about how he would handle those committing child sacrifices. Elliot knew he would have done the same.

"Sir, I'm sure Felix handled the situation appropriately. Child sacrifice can never be compared to the work we do here," Elliot said in defense.

"Then he should do the damn job the right way. Not roast men and women alive over a fire while an entire village watches. When we deal justice, it is to be certain and swift. Our punishment for dishonor has always been death. A foundational law that hasn't been enacted in a very long time. Maybe Bastion needs a reminder," Hawes fumed.

"Speak with him when he returns. Get the truth of it. Bastion can't afford to lose a member of his caliber, especially to an outdated law," Elliot said.

"Caliber, sure. His character, however, we can do without. I trust in you to be a better man. Do not disappoint me, Elliot. When I'm done here, you will sit in my place. Bastion must be protected just as *we* protect. I wish you well on the task you have been appointed. A fearsome foe lies before you," Hawes said. He gave a small bow before leaving the room.

Yet again, Hawes had reiterated the inherent danger. Elliot consumed all the recorded knowledge available over the previous month. The werewolf's weakness to silver. Injury by conventional means were only short-term. Their bodies could heal from every wound but those inflicted by the precious metal. Verdun spent many hours pondering on this. Silver and the full moon mirrored each other in ancient times. There was something to that. Another answer lost to the ages. The Dark Ages saw the destruction of Bastion's library. And with it all, the sacred knowledge that came before.

Lycaon's curse was the oldest story available to Bastion involving werewolves. A king turned into a wolf for attempting to feed human flesh to the god Zeus. A legendary tale which must be founded in some form of truth. Each story of werewolf encounters he read were accompanied by an eyewitness account of a large, black wolf. He felt it would be a reach to say that wolf is King Lycaon himself. Nonetheless, the curse that beast spreads bore his name. So the wolf has been called Lycaon through the ages.

Another curious fact was the mutation of the curse. Once Lycaon spread his curse to an individual, they themselves became a hybrid, transforming into a menacing half man, half beast in the light of the full moon. It was the assumption that Lycaon was either never actually human, or none of his humanity remained after he became cursed. With a bite from his jaws, the infected lost half their humanity. The created werewolf spread the curse just the same. That curse to this day was irreversible. Each transmission to a person ultimately ended with their death out of necessity.

Not many things born from darkness in the world can be undone.

A good deal was understood about Lycaon. He was not openly roaming the world. He inhabited another realm. Bastion was of the belief that the wolf was able to be summoned. When summoned, he could infect a person. Though the practice was thankfully forgotten. A German man in 1917 was believed to be the last to ever summon Lycaon. Those events led to a ceasefire while the warring armies of Germans and Russians fought side by side to eradicate the werewolves.

The wolf was known to hang around wherever his curse was active. That created problems when he inevitably infected more people. Once the curse was eradicated, sightings of Lycaon would cease. Being drawn back into a Drift to the realm he calls home—a cycle of events recorded multiple times over a few hundred years. For these events, Lycaon earned the nickname the Shadow of Death—named so for his black fur coat and the impending doom he ushered.

Elliot fully expected the wolf would play a role in his journey to Kansas.

Preparation only took you so far in the situations Bastion dealt with. Elliot felt he prepared accordingly. There were always unpredictable variables. Over his twenty-year career, he'd learned to take what was given. He had focused in on one individual in Mattfield. That assistance would be invaluable dealing with the community. An assortment of firearms, silver ammunition, and other tools crafted from silver were already loaded into trunks in his vehicle.

Elliot exited through Bastion's front door. A familiar dark thought crept in. Nothing was guaranteed in this line of work. It very well could be the last time he set foot in Bastion.

The headquarters was an enormous, four-story, stone mansion hidden among hills. Most everyone working the property had no inkling of what purpose the building or its residents served. They were paid well enough to not ask questions.

Elliot descended the stairs, briefcase in hand, to the asphalt drive below. A black Tahoe awaited him. The driver stood at the curb, dressed in an expensive black Italian suit, arms crossed. "Good day, sir. To the airfield?" the driver asked.

"Yes," Elliot replied.

The driver opened the rear door for him to climb in. There was a tinted barrier to prevent further interactions with the driver. Bastion possessed a private airfield and three jets donated to them from different countries. No preferential treatment was ever given, but gifts were always accepted.

In Elliot's briefcase were files pertaining to the case. He would refresh his memory on the flight to the United States. His first goal was to observe the community. The next full moon was fast approaching. Elliot would then need to convince his chosen assistant of the mission. Easier said than done when confronting the supernatural.

Sheriff Carl Mills was also long in the tooth. It would be a daunting task to convince him. Having the sheriff's aid was essential in achieving resolution. Although unaware, Carl Mills's entire understanding of the world around him was about to change.

Monsters were real. Werewolves would descend upon his hometown. They all drifted into our world from the same place.

A tear in the fabric of reality must be hidden somewhere outside Mattfield.

24

FORGE

Mattfield High's soul had died with the five teenagers. Hallways full of laughter were silent. Students dragged their feet like zombies milling from one classroom to the next. Each period saw students stream in and out as they took turns with the counselors, drained of their youth. At this age, everyone should believe they will live forever. Reality came for them like a thief in the night.

Brett found it a struggle to care about what was being taught. Why did any of this matter? The façade of learning had evaporated. Monsters were stalking the countryside. All his peers were in a state of imminent danger. Not a single one of them remotely aware. Brett existed in a place between the truth and a lie. A shepherd among a flock of sheep. Wolves already at the gates.

Brett's popularity cultivated on the football field vanished. Once again, he stepped into a hostile environment. His classmates avoided contact with him as if he carried the plague. Rumors that began with the investigation had taken root. It was safe to assume most of the school thought Brett was involved in the murders. He lacked the energy to argue. A single goal drove him forward: to obtain silver bullets. Only then could a semblance of safety be achieved—at least the ability to defend against creatures of the full moon. Brett had learned the hard way. Running was not an option. Bethany paid in blood.

Stress was eating away at Brett. Time was of the essence. Stuck at school for eight hours a day hindered progress. Marcus's silver knife had to be found.

Grandpa would need to be convinced. An entire plan rode on uncertainty. Mattfield found itself in a war the citizens were unequipped to fight. To believe in monsters meant to lay eyes on one. But by then, it was too late. Five out of seven had fallen easily on Jackson Road. He'd merely survived by a stroke of luck. An act of sacrifice spared his life. That gave Brett the motivation to fight. His friend's act of courage would not be in vain.

Gauged from overheard conversations and whispers in the hallway, belief in Marcus's recovery had begun to wane. If he was going to wake up, he would have by now. But Brett had a desire to hold out hope.

The situation grew bleaker with each passing day. Why had he not woken up? The bite wounds Marcus bore on his shoulder were unknown at the hospital, which meant they'd healed. It would make sense for him to also have recovered from the fall.

Police hadn't found another body in the quarry, so the werewolf had presumably fled the scene. No theory Brett came up with seemed plausible. When the federal government took over, it wasn't out of the realm of possibility they'd engaged in a cover-up. An impossible secret to keep in Mattfield.

"Brett, it's your turn to go see Mrs. Glass," Mr. Kincaid said. He had been Dalton's favorite teacher in school. "Brett?"

Reality came rushing back to Brett, tunneling his way back out of his train of thought. "Sir?"

"Would you like to speak with Mrs. Glass?" Kincaid asked.

Did he want to? Absolutely not, but his mother felt therapy may be beneficial. Low probability of that. Honing his skills with the revolver was the sole remedy that eased Brett's worry. But what harm could a visit with Mrs. Glass cause? He made the decision to go, on the off chance speaking with her presented a benefit. "Okay," Brett said.

The door to Mrs. Glass's closet-sized room stood ajar. "Brett, come on in. Have a seat." She shut the door behind him. "I cannot imagine what you have been through—what you're *going* through. I'm sorry for your loss."

"Thank you," Brett said. It was a sentiment he had grown numb to.

"I'll explain a little bit about what it is you feel. All the students I've met with so far are struggling with post-traumatic grief, which occurs when your life is impacted by a sudden, unexpected loss. My goal is to address the issues that arise with that. Preoccupying thoughts, trouble sleeping, anxiety, and loss of appetite. Are you experiencing any of these symptoms?" Mrs. Glass asked.

Yeah, all of the above, Brett thought. He nodded his head to confirm with Mrs. Glass. She mimicked his head movement.

"First things first, and it's important you understand: You are not crazy Brett. What you feel is completely normal. Grief of this magnitude can put your mind in a fog for upward of a year—sometimes less; it depends on the individual. You have to come to terms with the loss. Realize it's not your fault. Easier said than done, I know. What I would like to do is establish a routine to help regulate your emotions. Do not stay holed up inside; it's better to talk and share—with your family, friends, or me. Are you open to sharing?" Mrs. Glass asked.

Brett felt genuine care coming from the counselor. He dropped his guard. To hear someone say you aren't crazy. She had effectively gotten through the walls he put up for protection. "They all whisper about me because I'm the only one left to talk about. I think a lot of people believe it's my fault. They're not wrong. It was my decision to go out there past the quarry, to try and scare the others as payback. We ended up stranded. Bradley's truck. Our group split up. Then it—" Brett paused.

"This is a safe place, Brett, I promise," Mrs. Glass encouraged.

"My brother died in front of me. There was nothing I could do. Then Bethany. When it was my turn, Marcus took my place. None of them deserved to die. Why do I get to live?" Rivers of tears flowed from his eyes.

"Oh, Brett, I don't have an answer for that. Do you remember who did this?" Mrs. Glass asked.

"A monster," Brett said.

"Thomas Morro? Someone else?" Mrs. Glass asked more specifically.

Thomas Morro? Brett had a sudden realization. This interaction didn't have anything to do with grief. His counselor didn't care what he was going through. She'd disarmed him by pretending. Mrs. Glass was fishing for answers. "We're done here," Brett said, standing up.

"Wait, you just started to open up. Are you sure?" Mrs. Glass asked.

"I know what you're doing. To take advantage of me is messed up. You're a piece of shit." Brett swung the door open. It crashed against the wall.

"That kind of disrespect will not be tolerated. Go to the office!" she yelled.

"I'm going back to class. Give Grant a message for me." Brett held up his middle finger to her.

Back in the classroom, no one from the office came to punish him, a clear sign his hunch was correct. Hopefully this would be something his family's lawyer could handle.

At noon, the lunch bell rang. Brett got food in line and sat alone. Students packed into tables to avoid his.

This is the new normal, he thought.

Until Cassie came to sit beside him. For whatever reason, she never failed to show up.

"You should eat," Cassie said.

"I'm not hungry. Thanks for sticking by my side," Brett replied.

"I wasn't asking. Eat. Why wouldn't I sit with you?" Cassie asked.

No need to argue with her. Brett picked up the pizza boat on his tray and took a bite. "I don't know. Social suicide?" Brett said.

Cassie looked around at the other tables. "I don't care what they think, Brett. Most of my friends died with your brother. We need to be there for each other."

"I love you." Brett's heart thundered. There was no reason not to tell her the truth.

Cassie laid her head on his shoulder. "I love you, too. My parents keep harassing me. Are you okay with coming over for dinner?"

Meet the parents? This relationship is getting serious.

"Sure, when?"

"Next week sometime. My mom always cooks enough food for eight people. You don't need to give a heads-up. Just whenever," Cassie said.

"That works for me. Did you meet with Mrs. Glass?" Brett asked.

"No, my parents don't like her husband. He's the mayor of Mattfield. They say he's a drunk. Last thing I want is to be told how to feel, anyway."

Her husband's the mayor?

Of course. The investigators would use them as informants. "I did. You made the right choice. She's a snake."

"You can talk to me, you know? I trust you, Brett. If you want to talk about it," Cassie said.

"I do, more than anything. Trust me. Nobody's going to believe. That includes you," Brett said.

"Why would I not?" Cassie asked.

"Do you believe in monsters?" he asked in return.

"What do you mean, like ghosts? Vampires? Those are just stories," Cassie said.

"Exactly," Brett replied.

Cassie had a confused expression on her face. If she wouldn't believe what he had to say, no one would.

They made small talk for the rest of the lunch period.

It had been a big step to profess his love to Cassie. She deserved to hear that. But inside, worry for the coming full moon drove his intentions. Surviving a werewolf attack shifted his priorities. What if he didn't get another opportunity? Marcus had said it to them at the quarry. Brett thought it was odd at the time. In hindsight, he respected Marcus for saying I love you. Life was short. People needed to hear those words more often.

When school let out for the day, Brett took a breath of fresh air. So much sorrow trapped inside the building, it was suffocating. He walked Cassie to her car. They shared a kiss before heading their separate ways.

The joy of their relationship wasn't what it should be. Mrs. Glass's words came to him, preoccupying his thoughts. After school, he normally headed straight to his grandfather's house to train a skill he may have to rely on in the near future. Today, though, there was an extra stop to make.

Back to the scene of Dalton's demise. To hunt for the silver blade.

He was concerned about being discovered near the quarry. He could see the headline now: "Killer returns to the scene of the crime."

A perfect chance to arrest him. But silver was worth the risk.

Brett devised a cover story if he ran into trouble. He'd come to pay respects to his brother. Dalton would be cool with the excuse. If Dalton were alive, he would help search. Not without complaint, sure, but they were best friends.

Brett couldn't think of a reason to try and hide his truck. That might draw suspicion. Instead, he parked right out in front of the shuttered rock quarry. Yellow tape enveloped everything around the area.

He walked to the fence line where Dalton met his fate. Images of homecoming night came rushing back. He had replayed the events over and over for weeks, wondering if anything would have changed the outcome. A foolish loop to be trapped in. The past was fixed in time. No amount of thought could produce a different outcome. Yet he remembered the finest details. Nobody saw a werewolf coming. A bizarre killing machine out of pop culture and classic horror films, in the same place as a bunch of kids on an old, dead-end road. Marcus called it destiny—maybe he was right.

The barbed wire that caught Dalton in its grasp had been cut away—evidence collection, Brett presumed. He stood in the same place as the night of the attack, allowing his brain to relive the tragic moment, attempting to block out the noise of Dalton's screams. Brett had driven the knife downward. With its arm, the werewolf had knocked his grip free. A glint from the blade as the moonlight caught it sailing away into the air, across the road.

Brett walked forward, crossing over the road. On the other side, thick cedar trees grown up in the fence line shrouded his view. He fought his way under the branches to open pasture. Worry for the search alleviated:

The knife was there. Ten feet in front of him. The blade stuck in the ground with the handle to the sky.

Had investigators even been on this side? Lucky day, but this isn't how Brett wanted to cash in his luck. He strode forward and gripped the handle. A slight tug freed the knife from the dirt. He admired the intricate design. To melt down the mesmerizing weapon—passed down to Marcus as a family heirloom—felt criminal. But it was the price for a chance at survival.

Grandpa Walt sat outside waiting on Brett. "Sorry I'm late, Grandpa," Brett said.

"That's alright. Beautiful day to sit outside. You ready to shoot?" Walt asked, holding up the S&W Governor.

Hours of thought went into how to approach this conversation. It was obvious his grandfather wouldn't be duped. Being straight up was the only way. The worst he could be told was no. "I need your help," Brett said, revealing the knife from behind his back.

"What do you have there?" Walt asked.

"This is a knife, with a blade made of silver. It belongs to Marcus. His grandfather gave it to him. Pretty old, maybe French?" Brett handed the blade to his grandfather.

"I've not seen anything quite like this. How did you end up with it?" Walt asked.

"That's why I'm late. We used it to protect ourselves that night. I stopped at Jackson Road on the way to find it."

Open and honest, Brett kept telling himself.

Walt didn't know how to take in the information. "You went back there? Brett, how did you know where to find the knife?" Grandpa was at least curious.

"I had to go back. Silver is more valuable than gold in Mattfield. Dalton may still be alive if I hadn't lost my grip," Brett said.

"What are you saying?" Walt picked dried blood flakes from the blade.

Here goes nothing.

"More people are going to die. Next week during the full moon. I need silver bullets. If you get close enough to use a knife, odds are not in your favor. Grandpa, monsters are real. A werewolf killed Dalton and the others," Brett said.

"A werewolf? Brett, do you hear yourself?" Walt asked.

"Look at me. What do you think? Ask yourself why the investigators can't find answers. If you don't want to help me, that's fine. It feels good to be honest with someone. Why do you think I haven't told anyone? Because no one will believe what attacked us. Not you, not mom, not the police. But I chose to trust you."

Walt sat in quiet contemplation. "This knife injured the werewolf? Silver, just like the stories. And Marcus just so happened to have silver. Brett, why are you telling me this?"

"It killed your grandson. We need to turn that blade into bullets. I want forty-five LC for the power. To kill one." Brett's passion made his voice crack.

"Let's get one thing clear. This knife is an artifact. I'm not going to allow it to be melted down for ammunition. You should return this to Mr. Jones. I'm sure he would want it back," Walt said, handing the knife back to Brett.

Dream as he may, this is what Brett knew would happen. Deflated, he headed toward his truck.

"Where are you going?" Walt asked.

"Home, Grandpa. I have less than a week to figure out a way to protect myself," Brett said.

"I have a few silver coins in the safe. How about we use those instead? That old knife deserves better," Walt said.

Brett froze, perking up. "Really?"

"Look, I don't know what it is you're going through. Whether monsters are real or not. But if making a few silver bullets brings you peace of mind, we can do that. As long as you promise not to hurt anyone," Walt replied.

"You believe me?" Brett asked.

"What I believe doesn't matter. I can see that you do. Gun stays in the safe, understood?"

That request was not going to be possible but best to give his grandfather the reassurance he needed. "Yes, the gun stays."

"Good. I'll go grab the coins. Meet you in the shed." Walt went back inside the house.

Opening the shed door revealed his grandfather's reloading station. Tools and odd machines lined the counter of his work bench.

"What do you think?" Walt asked.

"Where do we start?" Brett had no idea what any of the tools did.

"Lucky for you, I've got a few brass casings ready. It's a process. Cleaned them, oiled, got a new primer in place, then poured gunpowder. All we have to do is melt the silver. Then we cast it to forty-five Long Colt. Put them in the press. Just like that, silver bullets."

Lucky, indeed, Brett knew. Today presented more personal wins than he'd anticipated. "Sounds easy."

"Easy, sure. Most of the time-consuming stuff is done." Walt walked to a bowl on the table. With the flip of a switch, the small machine turned on. He twisted the knob to the right. "This particular model can get hot enough to do the job. Ammo reloads generally stick to lead. Lead melts around six hundred degrees Fahrenheit."

"Six hundred! How is that safe?" Brett asked, astounded.

Walt chuckled at this. "Silver is a denser metal. That's why I turned the temperature up. Takes around seventeen-hundred degrees to melt."

"That's insane," Brett said, mouth agape.

Walt fished in his jacket pocket, producing a silver coin. "This here is five ounces of 99.9% pure silver. A Trump 2024 coin, worth about one hundred and eighty-five dollars, valued off the price of today's silver. Each bullet requires around an ounce. We'll see how many we get." He reached over and dropped the coin into the electric pot.

To learn this stuff was more exciting than any subject at school. Brett stood over the pot. Waves of heat caused sweat to form on his face. Slowly, the coin began to drip into liquid silver. "Can you believe they took a shot at Trump?" An attempt at small talk while they waited.

"Unfortunately, I can. You're young. It takes a number of years to form a worldview. In this country, the movers and shakers get shot. Never fails. Abraham Lincoln freed the slaves; Martin Luther King fought for equality; JFK wanted to institute change on some three-letter agencies. The powers that be fear change that takes away their ability to subjugate others. Those are the people that must be defeated."

Five ounces of liquid silver formed a hypnotic pool. Walt put on a pair of heavy leather gloves. "Stand back, don't want this on you. I'll pour the silver into the mold." With a ladle, Walt transferred the silver into the .45 LC mold. Using a pair of iron tongs, he took the mold outside, lowering the mold into a rusted metal bucket full of water beside the building. Steam billowed into the air. A loud hiss came from the meeting of hot metal and cold water. Back in the shed, Walt knocked free the freshly cast silver bullet. He repeated the process, forging four bullets in total.

They shifted their attention to the reloading press. "Alright, almost finished. This machine will seat the bullets we made into a brass casing. Then they're ready to shoot." Walt had been reloading the .45 LC rounds Brett ran through every afternoon. Four times he placed the bullet into the die. Brett pulled down on the lever to seat each of the four rounds into their brass case. "Hold out your hand."

Brett put his hand out as his grandfather dropped the freshly repurposed rounds into his palm. A sense of accomplishment overtook him. "Thank you,

Grandpa. You didn't have to do this. It means everything to me."

"Oh, it's no big deal. I rather enjoyed doing it. Those are the most expensive bullets I've ever made. Do you want to shoot them?" Walt asked.

"No, not today," Brett said. These bullets served a greater purpose than target practice.

"Silver being a denser metal, at close range those will do a hell of a lot of damage. Lead tends to break apart. Those are hole punchers." Walt beamed with pride over their creation.

A victory, to be certain. Brett took back control of his life today, secured the means necessary to slay a werewolf, his eyes fixed on the future. Part of him wanted to never cross paths with the creature again. Another sought revenge for Dalton. Soon, the full moon would return.

Unsure what lay ahead, he was ready for whatever may come.

25

OUTSIDER

Mills stood inside the entrance to city hall. Lloyd Glass came out of his office to greet him.

"Sheriff, what do you need?" Lloyd didn't appear enthusiastic after their last run-in.

"Quick question, Lloyd. Did Mindy try and coerce information from Brett Adams at school? I've been contacted by the family's lawyer, just gathering facts." Mills put him on the spot. Penny Little, the receptionist typing at the computer, began paying attention to them.

"Why don't you step into my office," Lloyd said.

"No, I'm good right here. Who's pulling your strings?" Mills asked.

Glass became red in the face. "Please, what is this about?"

"I'm sorry, were you not listening? Your wife infringed the fifth amendment rights of a minor. On behalf of Zachery Grant, I assume. I ought to arrest the two of you. Make a hell of a headline for the newspaper," Mills threatened.

"That is not necessary," Lloyd said.

Mills held a finger up. "This is your last warning. Cut the shit. I'm still the law in this county. Doesn't matter who's in charge of the investigation. You and your wife break the law more than the damn junkies. Next time, consequences are coming."

"Damn you, Carl, I'm not the bad guy. Mindy was asked to help get answers.

It seems like everyone but you wants to get justice for the families who lost their kids. I'm not going to get extorted for that." Lloyd tried his best to sound tough.

Lip curled, Mills snarled back. "Put your hands behind your back, Lloyd. I'll take you in. Two DUI charges. Maybe it's time you had to learn from your mistakes."

"Don't forget who covered them up," Lloyd said in defiance.

"I'm on my way out of office. I've got nothing to lose. What about you?" Mills asked.

"Alright, alright! I'll talk to Mindy. KBI threatened to dig into our lives if we didn't do what they asked," Lloyd said.

"Then you come to me! It's that simple. Show me the respect I've shown your undeserving ass!" Mills yelled.

"I said alright!" Lloyd shouted back. "What do you want to do about the curfew? It's been in place for almost a month."

"Keep it in place until people's safety has been assured. It's been enacted county wide—that'll be in the newspaper tomorrow," Mills said.

"County wide? Why?" Lloyd asked.

"There's a pattern to the crimes that's been brought to my attention. They coincide with the full moon." Mills exited the city hall building.

Liam sat in the passenger seat of the sheriff's truck. "How'd that go?" he asked as Mills got in.

"I'm really looking forward to arresting that man," Mills said.

"That well, huh? We don't have but a few days until the full moon. What do we do to prepare?" Liam asked.

"Brett Adams, the only witness there is. We start by questioning him," Mills said.

"I thought you came here to protect the boy," Liam replied.

"I did," Mills said. They would question Brett outside the confines of the law.

'Anything you say or do will be held against you' didn't invite honesty. To get answers, the boy had to feel safe. To save lives, the law must take a back seat.

Carl drove them out to the Adams' rental house. A man came out to greet them. Mills and Gable got out of the truck to talk.

"What's this about?" the man asked, a sign that previous run-ins with law enforcement had not gone well.

"I'm Sheriff Carl Mills. This here is Deputy Sheriff Liam Gable. You must be Michael. I've known your wife since she was a little girl. Then Brett from his run-in with Thomas Morro. I responded to the call at the quarry and found your son. Got him and Marcus to the hospital."

"Thank you for doing that. No offense, but we have a lawyer. Any questions need to go through him. We're sick of coming under assault by abusive behavior. Innocent until proven otherwise used to mean something in this country."

Michael was making his distrust known—who could blame him?

Mills presented his offer: "I just spoke with Mr. Glass about a report we received from your lawyer, Greg Norton. That situation is taken care of. He understands the consequences of a repeat offense. Let's cut to the chase. We came here to speak with Brett. Off the record. Not as police, but concerned citizens. Zachery Grant and I had a falling out over how he has decided to handle the investigation in my county. My goal is to protect Brett from further malpractice of the law. Anything your son tells us will be inadmissible in court. This provides me with information and him protection from future prosecution."

"Just like that, huh? You would openly commit dereliction of your duty as sheriff? What's the catch? You show up here in a police truck and in uniform. With this man who you say is a deputy in plain clothes. Liam Gable, right? I've heard that name before. Can't say where, but I don't think you're a cop. This feels like a conversation of half-truths." Michael discerned an ulterior motive, his intelligence a formidable asset to defending his wife and son.

"By trade, I'm a big game hunter. I'm well known. Sounds conceited but nonetheless true. Carl gave me a badge when I arrived to assist the county. The work we're doing is outside the law, with the benefit of bending the law to our advantage. There's no trick at play. Your son deserves to be heard and believed without playing gotcha."

Attention turned to the front door as Julia came outside. "Carl, what's this about?" she asked.

They caught her up to speed.

"What do you think? Should we consult Mr. Norman first?" Michael asked his wife.

"No, I trust Sheriff Mills. This community loves him. He's giving us a way to protect our son. Brett hasn't opened up to anyone. It's worth a shot," Julia said.

"Alright, we're in agreement. Do not take our blessing for granted. Our son has suffered enough. He's at his grandfather's house. Walt's been teaching him how to shoot. Target practice seems to bring Brett peace of mind," Michael said.

"Thank you, Julia. Michael, welcome home," Carl said.

With the Adams's blessing, they drove out to Walt's house. Sure enough, Brett stood rattling off shots from a revolver. Walt sat in a lawn chair observing his grandson. A yellow lab came out to meet them. "Down. Good boy," Mills said to the dog.

"Buck, leave the sheriff alone!" Walt hollered. "What brings you all the way out here?"

"This is Liam Gable. To be honest, Walt, we're doing our own investigation outside what the state and feds are working on. We just left Julia's place. She and Michael gave us the green light to ask Brett a few questions," Mills said.

"Don't think the big dogs can handle it?" Walt asked.

"Liam and I are taking a different angle. Thing is, there's a lot that can't be explained away. They seem to be taking the approach of pinning blame on Brett. I found all the bodies. No high school boy did that. If he'll speak with us, it ensures his due process is tainted," Mills said.

"Doesn't sound like something you'd normally do Carl. Why?" Walt asked.

"For Mattfield and all those who have died. Retirement is coming in the near future. I want to leave office knowing this county is safe. My record will always have these deaths attached. This is our chance to prevent others from that fate. We have reason to believe the killer strikes during a full moon. Just over forty-eight hours away."

"Oh my," Walt said. His eyes grew large as he turned to look at Brett as if he'd had a revelation. "You'll want to hear what my grandson has to say. I hope you brought an open mind."

Mills exchanged a look with Gable, wondering what Walt's been told to garner that kind of response.

Two grueling months without answers. The boy had the potential to blow this case wide open. Mutual trust had to be established.

"Brett, the sheriff would like to speak with you. It's in your best interest to tell him everything. Your parents gave permission," Walt signaled. With that, he left the three of them alone.

"Why should I trust you? My brother and friends died. People keep trying to pin me with the crime," Brett said.

"We're not with them," Carl began. "This man isn't even a cop; he's a hunter by trade. Talk to us so this can end. The three of us working together can save lives."

"A hunter? What do you hunt?" Brett asked Gable.

"Over the years, I've killed a little bit of everything," Liam said.

"Dangerous animals?" Brett asked.

"Animals that have taken hundreds of lives in total," Liam answered.

This fact captured Brett's intrigue. "What about monsters?"

"What about them?" Mills asked.

"If the man hasn't killed any monsters, he's not much help," Brett stated.

"The animals I'm hired to hunt are monsters. Anything that preys on human beings," Liam said.

"See, I don't think you want to hear what I have to say," Brett said.

They were losing the boy's willingness to speak. "What about a black wolf?"

Carl asked. "We ran into it at the reservoir. Have you seen the wolf before?"

"You saw it, too?" Brett asked. The hook was set. Mills had the boy's attention.

"We did. Even shot it. Never did find its body. Seems to be a lot of that going around. Coach and I shot Thomas Morro. He got up and walked away. Any idea how?" Mills asked.

"Well, yeah. I have a pretty good idea. My brother and I got attacked by the wolf in the cemetery. We went looking into the old Mattfield legend about the undying man. Sounds crazy, but that's the truth. Then we found out the rest of the story—the part that's lost to history," Brett confided, not exhibiting the behavior of telling a lie.

"What's the rest of the story?" Gable asked.

"It all comes across as too convenient," Mills said, hoping not to offend. "Don't you think? I'm not questioning your integrity, but Brett, you do see why the bureau assumes you are at the center of it all, right? All these things are revolving around you being there. Care to elaborate?"

"Trust me, I think about that a lot. Marcus said something to me at the quarry. Before, you know. He called it destiny. Hard to argue with that. How else does it make sense? Why me? 'Wrong place at the wrong time' doesn't quite cut it."

The investigator in Carl made it hard to rule Brett out as being a suspect. Sociopaths were often convincing of their innocence—exactly what Zachery Grant's instincts focused on.

Coincidences of this nature don't occur. Stay open-minded. Let the boy speak, Carl told himself.

"All DNA evidence points to humans being responsible for the killing. Can you confirm that?"

"I think that's accurate, outside of when the moon is full," Brett responded.

"Kid, are you saying what I think you're saying?" Liam was picking up on something Mills was unaware of.

"I am," Brett said.

"Which is?" Mills asked.

"Werewolf," Liam blurted out.

A sigh went out from the sheriff. This was a waste of time. Carl shot Liam a look of disbelief. He knew from the interaction that Brett believed this as true. "Have you been evaluated for psychological trauma, or a mental health disorder?"

Brett smirked at the question. "No, but I did meet with the school psychologist. You already know how that went. Sheriff, you have to wonder about the evidence. Why it doesn't make sense. I have no reason to lie to you."

You have every reason to lie, Mills thought. *Prime suspect as sole survivor of a massacre.*

"Fact of the matter is, you are the only witness."

"I'm not, actually. The other witness just hasn't woken up," Brett said.

"At the reservoir, you began to question what's possible," Liam said to Carl. "Why the sudden change of heart? Is what Brett's saying strange? Yes, but it's not entirely unreasonable from what you've experienced. I'm an outsider to the situation. Each of your testimonies on their own are absurd, but those experiences taken together paint a more compelling picture. Carl, why should I believe you over the kid? Or vice versa? We need to consider *all* the data. I told you my story, as well. Our lives are intersecting for a reason."

"Brett, you can go. Send Walt out for a word." Mills dismissed the boy. Then to Liam: "Why have we not heard of anything like this before? A werewolf?"

Walt rejoined them in the driveway. "Well?"

"Do you believe your grandson?" Mills asked.

"Let me share a piece of information. Under my guidance, I assisted Brett with the construction of four silver bullets. He was adamant about needing them for protection. I didn't do that because I believe him. When you look into his eyes, you can see that *he* does. The gun remains here. His attitude shifted after we made those bullets. It's real to him," Walt said.

"Do you not see the inherent danger? To give him that level of reassurance in his delusion?" Carl asked.

"I'm a see-it-to-believe-it type of guy, same as you. Your background is guiding what you think. We can't change our programming. I can't push away my only living grandson—not when everyone is turning against him." Walt became emotional sharing his opinion.

"Thank you for your time, Walt."

Mills drove back toward Mattfield.

Liam broke the awkward silence. "So, what do you think?"

"You know damn well what I think," Mills said.

"Consider the evidence. The kid provided the missing piece," Liam said.

"Add in a mythical creature, everything makes sense." Mills didn't want to have this conversation.

"Open mind, Carl. It sure explains the DNA problem, which has been the most unusual fact to contend with."

A war raged inside the sheriff's brain. Liam was correct about the DNA, but the leap to a werewolf was where he drew the line. "Do you think it odd that the rules for a werewolf in horror movies are what Brett is abiding by? Walt confessed to forging silver bullets at Brett's behest. That raises alarm bells for me."

"All fiction has its roots in the truth," Liam said.

"Yeah, maybe so. That's enough for today; I'll take us to the diner. We can grab supper before turning in for the night."

Mills felt a slight headache coming on. Too much stress today. He'd find himself on blood pressure medicine if things kept heading in this direction.

He parked the truck next to a new black Cadillac CT5-V Blackwing. Windows tinted darker than highway legal. Carl noticed the car lacked a license plate. "Must be government, above the law."

"Sharp car. More of a jeep guy myself," Liam said.

Entering the diner, no one greeted the sheriff—a change brought about by his failure to protect the community. Carl's heart ached. His reputation had been depleted. He scanned the room for a place to sit. An odd man caught his eye, seated alone in the back corner. Police instincts built a profile. A white middle-age male, brown hair, white shirt worn under a buttoned black jacket, black gloves, and wearing black sport sunglasses indoors. Attention naturally gravitated to the man. Mills would oblige.

"That your Cadillac outside?" Mills asked.

The man removed his sunglasses, revealing blue eyes. "Sheriff, the man I came here to meet. I am not disappointed."

The man spoke in an accent unknown to Mills. "When a cop asks you a question, you answer."

"Yes, that is my car," the man responded with a slight grin.

"Just because you're law enforcement doesn't give you the right to break the law. Car has no license plate. The people pay your salary. The government should treat the taxpayers with more respect," Mills said.

"You are mistaken. I'm not law enforcement," the man stated nonchalantly.

Mills got unnerved by the way the man spoke. He carried himself like a federal agent. Someone who felt themselves untouchable by the law. "Who are you? And what are you doing in Mattfield?"

Something about the man's grin inspired fear. "Who I am is for you to decide. I came to Mattfield to see the full moon. Rumor says it's to die for. Would you agree, Sheriff?"

Was that a threat? Mills remembered the phone call he'd received. *You are looking for a man. Out of place. Out of time. You will know when you see him.* This encounter fit the description. "Do you have ID on you?"

"No. You could say I'm not from around here," the man replied.

"Are you a reporter?" Mills pressed.

"In a sense, I do take notes, but not for the news," the man said.

"And you came here to meet me, why?" Mills's patience ran out. Making arrests was never a part of the job he enjoyed.

"I did. Have you seen one yet, Sheriff? This will be a whole lot easier if you have," the man asked.

"Alright, I'm placing you under arrest. Your car will be towed to the police station. We'll start there. Refusing to identify yourself makes holding you in detention a whole lot easier. Stand up," Mills commanded.

The man didn't resist, doing as instructed. Liam cuffed his hands. A pat down of the man only produced enough money for his meal. Carl read the man his rights as they loaded him into the backseat of the police truck.

"Sorry about dinner," the sheriff apologized to Liam. "We'll book this guy first and come back." They put the man through the booking process. Hopefully his fingerprints could identify him. Mills personally walked him back to a cell. "You brought this upon yourself."

"Don't worry about me. I have a feeling you'll want to talk after the full moon. That is, if you survive. Please do. I'm counting on your help," the man said.

"And why would I want to speak with a man who can't even tell me his name?" Mills asked.

"My name is Elliot Verdun. Like a moth to a flame, you were drawn to me. All it took was removing a license plate and a pair of sunglasses. Try as you might, nothing will turn up on my identity. Effectively, I do not exist. I'm sorry about the diner. That was not a conversation to have in front of others. The fewer people involved, the better. You are the person I selected to assist me."

"With what exactly?"

"That idea already noodling around in your head. When you see what you can't unsee, then you'll come to me for help. I look forward to that conversation."

"If you legally don't exist, loopholes in the law are going to keep you caged for the foreseeable future. Best get comfortable, Mr. Verdun."

Verdun let out a chuckle. "This attitude is the entire reason we can't have the conversation yet. You need humbling. I'm sorry for what's to come."

Fear of what could happen next hit the sheriff. "I'm ready to talk. What do you have to offer?"

"My job is impossible behind bars. Have you had a change of heart about that?" Elliot asked.

"Not a chance," Mills said.

"I prefer to speak free man to free man. Don't be too hard on yourself, Carl. The people about to die, you wouldn't have been able to save them," Elliot replied.

Those comments got under his skin. "You're sick, you know that?"

"I am the cure. Skeptics fall to their knees and grovel for my aid. A month ago, that was you, I imagine. But look at you, back on your feet. So proud. Two months of death and you still can't accept the truth. Pride comes before the fall, Sheriff. Some insist on being taught hard lessons."

"You've come to save lives, is that it?" Mills asked.

"A few must die. You can't have life without death. The majority will be delivered," Elliot replied.

"Out of the kindness of your own heart. Do you work for someone, Elliot?" Mills asked.

"We can't have that talk until you open the door," Verdun said.

Mills turned his back and exited the jail, anxiety crawling in his chest. Elliot Verdun had the characteristics of a cold-blooded killer. Contrast him with Brett—they couldn't be more different. Had he finally caught the murderer? Carl desperately wanted that to be the case—a sliver of hope to dangle from.

Dread hung in the air as the clock ticked closer to the full moon.

CHAPTER 26

WHEN THE SUN GOES DOWN

A cool breeze from the north rattled the leaves of the trees. Their green leaves had changed to burnt orange, red, and gold. Soon the leaves would scatter the ground as the mighty oaks, silver maples, and walnuts embraced the onset of winter. Typically, Brett looked forward to sweater weather. He found that joy replaced with terror. October 7th had arrived. Tonight, in a few short hours, the full moon would rise. His nightmare's reprieve was over. Creatures of legend would roam the dark, seeking those whom they may devour. Shadowy death would come for those unprepared.

Silver bullets safeguarded Brett's fate, serving as both sword and shield.

When school let out, Brett made his way to Walt's for target practice. "Hey, Grandpa!" he said.

"How has your Tuesday been?" Walt asked as he and Buck sat outside.

"Hanging out with you is the only thing I look forward to at school," Brett said.

"I'm flattered, but you do need to learn while you're there. Want to try a different gun today?" Walt asked.

"Let's stick with the Governor," Brett replied.

"Figures. I should've started you out on a gun that uses cheaper ammo," Walt said, half joking.

Three weeks of meticulous practice with the firearm had paid off. Brett could group all six shots within the three-inch center of the target while standing, kneeling, and lying prone. A living target was going to be a whole other scenario, though. On fundamentals, aim, and poise, he felt sufficiently primed. Against an actual werewolf, it would come down to courage under pressure.

An opportunity to steal away the firearm presented itself. Someone who lived on the same section of land pulled into Walt's drive. His grandpa referred to them as neighbors. The term was relative to one's living situation, apparently, whether next door or forty acres down the road.

"I better holler at Todd. You okay?" Walt asked.

"That's it for me today. I better get home," Brett said.

"Do you mind putting the gun back in the safe for me?" Walt asked.

Not at all, Grandpa.

"Yep, no problem," Brett lied.

He went inside the house, navigating to the mammoth safe. He tucked the Governor in the front of his jeans before covering the grip with his shirt. In the safe, he took the four silver bullets in hand. For a second, he felt the conflict of right and wrong. This was neither.

Life or death, Brett told himself.

Walt would be upset when he discovered the gun missing. Consequences worth the punishment. Brett's only regret was betraying the trust built between them. Being honest, their relationship was always heading to this moment.

I choose life.

He dumped the bullets into his pocket before shutting and securing the safe door.

To avoid further attention, Brett made a beeline for his truck. Walt, preoccupied in conversation with Todd, held up a hand to wave goodbye. Brett gave a wave back as he left the driveway.

At the first stop sign, Brett put the truck in park. He drew the Governor from his waistband. His hand shook. A successful heist. Using a thumb, Brett sprung open the cylinder by pressing the release. One by one, he transferred the four silver bullets from his pocket to the cylinder. Brett shut the cylinder and tucked the revolver under the driver's seat.

No turning back.

At home, his mother sat on the front porch, dressed in her medical scrubs. "How did shooting go?" Julia asked.

Had he already been caught? "Fine, just another day," Brett said casually.

"Good. Did school go okay?" Julia followed up.

Guilt became relief. She was just probing as usual. "Yeah, it was alright. Why are you in work clothes still?"

"Debra asked if I could take the night shift. She'll have her pager if I need help. Part of small-town life is doing things for others. Debra has done a lot for us the last few weeks. I owe her a lot," Julia said.

No. He had to convince his mother to stay home. This was not the night to be at the hospital. Just in case. "I want to hang out with you tonight, Mom. Call someone, tell them you can't work the shift. Please."

She gave him a puzzled look. "That's not how this works. I work in a hospital, taking care of people who need me, like Marcus. As much as I want to be at home with you."

Tears welled up in Brett's eyes. This was not part of the plan. "Mom, I need you at home."

"Honey, your father will be here. You two have room to grow."

His mind raced for the words to change her mind. "Do you want to know the last thing Dalton said to me?"

This made her choke up. "What? Brett, what are you saying?"

"Dalton told me to protect Mom. At the end, he thought about you. I can't do that if you're at the hospital." Brett shed tears.

"Why did you wait to tell me?" Julia whimpered.

"Because today it matters. Your work is not safe. Please." Brett gave his best effort.

Julia wiped tears from her cheek. "It's just for a few nights. I'm not going back on my word. I'm sorry."

Well, that didn't work like he hoped. Nothing he could say would convince her. Brett went to her on the porch. They shared a long hug. "Be careful. Call for help if you need anything. Promise?"

"I promise. I love you," Julia said.

"I love you, too," Brett said back.

"Your father will make dinner. I better get to work." Julia rubbed his hair.

Brett gave her another hug before they went their separate ways.

He ran upstairs to his bedroom window to watch his mom drive away. His plan for the night had imploded.

Marcus's silver knife was tucked neatly between his mattress and box spring. With the Governor stowed in the truck, there wouldn't be much use for the knife tonight. The last place he wanted to be was stuck at home with his father. That could be remedied. Time to meet the parents.

Brett sent Cassie a text. She replied within a minute, inviting him over for dinner.

In an attempt to avoid his father, Brett snuck to the front door. All for naught.

"Hey, Brett, what are you doing?" Michael asked from the kitchen.

"My girlfriend invited me over for dinner with her parents," Brett said.

"No, I don't think that's a good idea. For one, you didn't even ask permission," Michael said.

Brett's hand squeezed the door handle. "Mom's gone until tomorrow. I already told Cassie I'd be there for dinner."

"I'm right here, Brett. If you want to make plans, then you ask. Pretty straight forward. I'm making dinner for the both of us. Tell your girlfriend it will have to be another night."

"What makes you think I need to ask you to do anything?"

Michael raised his voice in irritation. "Excuse me? Do you want to try that again? This shit attitude you have toward me needs to end. I'm done tolerating it."

"You don't get to just show back up and demand respect. I learned on the football field you have to earn that. What have you earned, Dad? It took Dalton's death for you to come crawling back to us!" Brett yelled.

Those words cut threw Michael like daggers. "What have I done to you, Brett? I've been defending you. Why were you even out there at the quarry? You're quick to put blame on everyone else. We still don't have any answers."

Rage overtook Brett. "Are you blaming me!? You've never been around. Dalton forgave you for abandoning us. But I won't, ever. A father wouldn't trade his family for some whore. I hate you." Brett rushed out the front door, slamming it shut.

Michael made no further attempt to hinder him leaving.

Brett sped out of the drive toward Cassie's house. That gave him a fifteen-minute drive to bottle his anger back inside.

Brett slowed the truck down to go through the two tight curves—a landmark that he was almost there. Nerves set in as he pulled down the long driveway to Cassie's house. Caught up in his anger, not much thought went into how to impress her parents.

With a deep breath, Brett went to the door. An orange cat glided under his feet as he walked. As he went to knock, the door swung ajar.

"Hi, Brett. I'm Cassie's mom, Nora. It's nice to finally meet you. You have to watch out for Whiskers. He likes to walk under your feet. I've fallen down a few times. Please come in." A homely woman dressed in a green sweatshirt with sheep scattered across it, Nora's personality was warm and bubbly. It made Brett feel at peace.

"Thanks for having me; it's nice to meet you, too." Brett stepped inside his girlfriend's house for the first time. With a glance behind him, he saw the sun setting behind the trees in the yard. A knot formed in his stomach. Blinded by hatred, Brett found himself away from home on the night of the full moon—the last thing he'd wanted.

I'm far enough away from the quarry, he thought. *It's going to be okay.*

"This is Cassie's dad," Nora said, beckoning him toward the dining room table.

"Hey, Brett, thanks for coming." Paul shook his hand with a firm, calloused grip. Short but stocky, the man's physique told you he does hard labor for a living.

"Thanks for having me over," Brett said.

Cassie came bouncing down the hallway into the living room. "You made it!" she said with a smile. Her presence lit up the room.

"We're having tacos tonight. I hope that's okay," Nora said.

"Of course," Brett replied.

They all took a seat around the dining room table, each building ground beef tacos from the assortment of condiments spread out between them.

"I'll get the awkward out of the way. My wife and I are sorry for your family's loss. Cassie spoke highly of your brother. We understand you probably don't want to talk about it, but I'd feel some type of way not addressing that. She speaks highly of you, Brett. It's hard to impress our daughter."

Brett mustered a nod. "Cassie has been a blessing. I can't say enough about her. Everything about moving to Mattfield has been hard. I'm lucky to have met your daughter."

"You are sweet," Nora said.

"Damn good football player. We went to the homecoming game. Do you think you'll try college ball?" Paul asked.

Playing football at the next level wasn't an idea Brett had given thought to. "If I got an offer. Maybe a junior college would want me."

"I promise, he's not always this nervous," Cassie said.

That spurred a laugh from all of them. Leave it to Cassie to make light of the tension. He truly loved the girl.

They made small talk over tacos as Nora and Paul got a feel for their daughter's boyfriend. Brett grew more comfortable in conversation. Cassie's parents were great people. Hopefully that was a mutual feeling between them. Brett helped carry the dishes to the sink when they finished eating.

"Cassie, I forgot to get the mail. I renewed the tags on our vehicles. They should be in today. Do you mind running out to the mailbox?" Nora asked.

"Yeah, come on, Brett."

They stepped out into the night air.

"It's starting to get chilly," Cassie noted.

Brett hadn't noticed the cold. His attention was drawn to the full moon shining in the eastern sky. They walked out toward the driveway. Hyper-aware of the surroundings, his attention was drawn to the blinding floodlight on the side of the house. All was calm. *We're safe.* "Where's your mailbox?"

"Out on the road. I wish they delivered mail to the door. You should know. I'm sure it's the same at your house." Cassie took his hand and locked fingers. He felt her shiver.

"I have a hoodie in my truck. Do you want me to grab it for you?" Brett asked. A thoughtful reason to get him to the revolver. Being outside without it heightened his anxiety.

"No, that's alright. Takes two minutes to walk out there and back."

"Alright." He set the pace, leading in front. Sound from their shoes on the gravel drive crunched.

Let's get this over with. The less time out here, the better.

"You in a hurry?" Cassie tuned into his discomfort. The floodlight silhouetted her features.

"Oh, no. Just, the dark makes me uncomfortable. After—"

Cassie halted. "I'm sorry, Brett. We can go back. I wasn't thinking."

"No, it's okay, really. I have to face my fears and move on. Thank you for understanding," Brett said.

There was no more hesitation as they reached the mailbox. Out of the reach of the floodlight, they were shrouded in darkness. Cassie retrieved the mail, slamming the tin mailbox door shut as it let out a creak. She felt his face, then leaned in for a kiss. They made out for a minute. "See, I made it worth the trip," Cassie whispered to him.

Butterflies fluttered in his stomach, a feeling he had forgotten over the past month. They continued to hold hands on the short trip back to the house, this time walking straight into the beams of the floodlight. "Jeez, that thing is bright," Brett complained as he held his free hand up to shade his eyes.

"Daylight bulbs to keep critters away. Doesn't work. Possums still show up to eat Whiskers's food," Cassie said.

Just then, the light vanished. Whiskers let out a hiss and darted full speed between them, scurrying off toward the road. Brett lowered his hand to see the light wasn't off. Something stood between them and the house blocking its rays.

"Who's that?" Cassie asked in confusion.

"Oh, fuck," Brett said. He began to tremble uncontrollably. A low growl all too familiar rumbled from the werewolf.

"I'm scared," Cassie whimpered as the mail she had been carrying fluttered to the ground.

Afraid to take his eyes off the creature, he tried to formulate a thought of what to do. Just then, the door to the house sprung open. Two blasts rang out as fire erupted from the end of a shotgun. The werewolf screamed as it darted off into the dark.

"Kids! Get inside!" Paul yelled to them.

Hand in hand, they sprinted toward the front door. Brett thought about the revolver once more. When he tried to break away to retrieve the weapon, Cassie tightened her grip. "Inside, Brett!" she cried out.

This could be a fatal mistake, he knew, but he followed her lead. They burst into the house. Paul closed the door, locking the bolt. Panic ensued in the house. "What is that? I got a good look at it. It looked like a—" Paul got cut off.

"A werewolf," Brett said.

"A what?" Nora raised her voice in disbelief.

"I mean, that's what I saw, too. Those aren't real," Paul said.

Weak-kneed, Brett slid down the dining room wall to the floor. "They're not supposed to be."

"I'm calling the police." Nora got her cell phone out.

"Brett, was that thing at the quarry?" Cassie asked.

"We're going to defend this house. Brett, how are you with a gun?" Paul asked.

Words weren't registering in his mind. He was in shock.

Why is the werewolf all the way out here? Am I being hunted?

"Brett, look at me. Are you good with a gun?" Paul asked again.

This pulled him back to reality.

This is a different situation. They have phone service. Walls. Firearms. Maybe they stand a chance.

"With a revolver, yeah."

He heard Nora frantically on the phone with police dispatch.

Paul went into a back room and returned with a revolver. "It's loaded. Be careful not to shoot anyone on accident. I trust you to take care of Cassie, understood?" Paul extended the gun to him.

Brett accepted the weapon. "Yes, sir."

"That's a Colt Python three-fifty-seven Magnum. Six shots. Cassie, Nora, I want you to stay in the center of the room on the floor. Brett, there's a backdoor. Easy enough to cover. You can see it from the kitchen. We'll be in sight of each other. I'll guard the living room windows and front door," Paul instructed.

Doing as he was told, Brett positioned himself in the kitchen, gun trained on the backdoor.

"The police are sending someone out. They said there's another situation in town tying up resources," Nora said.

Attention split between the living room and the backdoor—kitchen counters to his back with a small window view to the front yard. Brett found comfort that an officer was en route. They only had to hold out for twenty minutes, tops.

His budding hope got a dose of reality: Suddenly the lit-up house went dark.

"Power's out. Hold tight," Paul said.

A thud rattled the backdoor. Brett backed up against the kitchen counter. "Here!" Brett shouted.

"Unload if that door comes open!" Paul called out.

Brett aligned the gun's sight in anticipation, all other sound drowned out by his own breathing. He took a deep breath to control it, but the sound continued. Looking over his shoulder, the face of the werewolf stared in at him through the kitchen window, its hot breath, leaving a fog with each exhale. Brett sprung backward, hitting the refrigerator. With a squeeze of the trigger a shot exploded from the revolver, shattering the window into the werewolf's face. Howls of pain came from outside.

"I hit it!" Brett said excitedly.

Paul opened the front door, unloading round after round into the beast writhing in pain on the grass. When his shotgun emptied, he began loading more shells, keeping his distance.

"Cassie, get him back in the house!" Brett yelled out.

Nora got to it first, running to the door. "Paul, get in the house!"

"Not until this thing is dead," Paul said.

Brett watched the scene unfold from the kitchen window. He shot three more times, slowly walking toward the werewolf. Then the beast's body went still. Quiet settled over the yard. He actually did it.

Cassie joined her mother at the front door. "Is it dead?"

"It's dead," Paul confirmed. "Tough bastard."

Paul's curiosity had him slowly getting closer to the motionless creature. Brett joined them at the front door. He gave a warning. "Sir, that is not a good idea."

Paul turned to look at them. "It's alright, I—" His final words.

The werewolf reanimated. It had played possum to lure in its prey. Rows of jagged teeth latched onto Paul's thigh. He screamed out as the razors dug into the bone.

Cassie and Nora screamed at the attack. Brett pulled the front door shut to shield the view of whatever came next. Twisting the bolt lock, he screamed, "Go hide!"

Glass from the living room window exploded. He sheltered his face. The werewolf had leapt into the room with them. Brett took Cassie by the wrist, dragging her into the kitchen.

"Mom!" she screamed.

Nora blocked the doorway between them and the werewolf. "The backdoor. Run!"

Say no more. Cassie struggled against his pull, but Brett dragged her along behind him as she broke down in frantic tears. When Brett got the door open, horrid screams came from the kitchen. Nora's bloody body slammed against the kitchen wall behind them, arm outstretched toward Cassie as she tried to crawl.

"Mom!" Cassie screamed again.

Mrs. Meeks made sure they could escape. Brett meant to capitalize on her sacrifice.

Brett led the way around the side of the house to his truck. He helped Cassie in the driver's side to slide across. The truck roared to life as he put it in gear and tore down the driveway.

Reaching under the seat, Brett placed the Governor beside him. He turned toward town, his goal to encounter the police response on the way.

To keep Cassie safe.

27

WAKE

Coming back to work the night shift presented unique challenges. A month ago, Julia came home to find her sons absent. Dalton gone forever. She had mixed emotions stepping back into the role. This was a choice made out of respect for Debra. They were meant to split the work load in the hospital. To not work nights was unfair to her counterpart. Julia knew the entire night she would stress over Brett. Being in charge of Marcus's care served as a constant reminder of what can happen. Tomorrow was never a guarantee.

Discussions were being had about Marcus's future, a plethora of differing opinions about how to address his situation going forward. There were no logical answers for why he hadn't awoken. They were in talks with Christopher Jones about transferring Marcus to a long-term care facility. Everything the hospital could provide had been exhausted.

Mattfield had lost hope in a hometown miracle. Reality set in on the boy's situation. No one could say with confidence Marcus would ever recover. Julia continued to pray. If he did, rehabilitation would take years. By now, his vocal and motor functions will have been set back to infancy.

Nights provide an opportunity to catch up on paperwork—an easy thing to fall behind on in a hospital. Julia had a tedious backlog to get through, to avoid corporate jumping down her throat. At some point, patience and understanding ran out. A cog in a money-making machine. Given an uneventful night in the emergency room, she could finish before shift's end.

Tucker volunteered to run admissions for the night. He preferred to work whenever Julia was on. They had built a strong rapport since her arrival. She knew Tucker had a bright future ahead of him in medicine.

On the desk, her cell phone began to buzz. "Hey, Michael, everything alright?"

"Brett went to Cassie's for dinner. I tried to convince him to stay home. I wanted to work on our unresolved issues. You were able to forgive me, but I don't know if he ever will. My son told me he hates me tonight. So, I let him go," Michael explained, on the verge of tears.

Of course. She couldn't leave the two of them together for just one night. "Cassie has been there for Brett. I guess if he's going to be out, I'd rather it be with her. Are you okay?"

"I will be. Hits different when you hear it. I assumed a lot about his anger toward me. Now I know," Michael said.

"Make sure he gets home safely. I'll speak with him tomorrow. You remember what it was like to be his age, and we didn't go through anything compared to what he has these last few months. I can't stress this enough: Give our son time. Show up, be present, and he'll come around."

"I will always show up, for both of you. I promise. Sorry to disturb you at work. Just thought you should know," Michael said.

"Thank you. Get some rest. Don't sit around and stress. We're going to be alright." Julia ended the call.

Teenagers ventured off all the time, she had to continuously remind herself. Before last month, she never second-guessed letting them. What happened was an anomaly. Fresh in her mind. Forever in her heart.

Brett is going to be fine. He's on a date with a lovely girl. Cassie would make sure to keep him out of trouble. Thoughts Julia manifested to ease her conscience.

Brett's safety would be a lingering worry until he safely returned home. She wandered from her office to check in with Tucker.

"Still nothing?" Julia asked.

Tucker rapped his knuckles against the wood desk. "Nope. Night is still young. We'll get someone with heartburn in a few hours. Don't you worry. Mr. Ulger is resting. No signs of infection from the gallbladder surgery. Most likely be going home tomorrow afternoon."

Leaving the desk, she decided to check in on Marcus. Quietly, Julia crept into his room. A lamp beside the bed cast a dim light in the corner. Vitals normal, as ever. For being confined to a hospital bed, the boy's muscles hadn't appeared to deteriorate from lack of use—an odd occurrence the doctors made sure to record. God works in mysterious ways.

She left the room and moved across the hall, this time giving a light knock.

"Come in," Mr. Ulger croaked.

"Just making the rounds. You need anything?"

"My bed, and a cold beer would be nice," Ulger said.

She smiled at the sly remark. "You and me both. I'll come check on you throughout the night. So, if you're okay with it, I'm going to leave the door cracked open, try to avoid waking you up when I do," Julia said.

"Fine by me," Ulger replied.

"Hit the call button if you need help. We're just down the hall." She pulled the door within an inch of being shut.

Julia walked back toward her office. "Don't fall asleep," she said to Tucker in jest.

He grabbed his coffee cup and held it up.

Out the staff entrance door, Julia saw the parking lot light come on. Twelve hours until sunrise. Nothing hits like that post-work shower before sleeping your day away. Just as she got comfortable at her desk, an alarm rang out.

At a jog, Julia rejoined Tucker. "What the hell is going on?"

"It's Marcus, his heart rate is spiking," Tucker said, bewildered.

"Let's go," Julia ordered.

The two ran down the hallway to the boy's room. Julia swung the door open to see Marcus's chest violently pumping, his rapid breathing audible. As she moved to get closer, his back arched unnaturally, held up by his head and heels. Marcus's fingers dug deep into the bed.

"I think he's having a seizure. Get me a vial of Midazolam, and syringes. Hurry!" Julia ordered.

Tucker sprinted from the room.

Julia hit the call button on her pager to signal Debra for help. The main priority was to make sure Marcus didn't bite off or swallow his tongue. Grabbing at his mouth to try and force it open, a hand jutted upward, wrapping around her throat. Julia began to panic under the death grip as she squirmed. "Marcus." His eyes shuttered open. Absent pupils, the eyes were white with blood, veins coursing through them. Julia clawed at his arm to break free. Unexpectedly, the grip loosened. She stumbled backward to the room door, choking for air.

Marcus let loose otherworldly screams as he writhed in agony.

Julia felt unqualified to handle this. In all her years, she had never experienced something of this nature. "Tucker!" she screamed down the hallway. Where the hell was he? Marcus rolled off the side of the bed, crashing onto the floor. Tucker came into sight.

"Put that shit on the desk and fill a syringe!" Julia shouted.

The contents in his arms scattered onto the reception desk. Tucker tore into the package of a fresh needle. "I got it!" he yelled, rejoining her.

Marcus stood up, head bowed forward, growling as if he had two voices rumbling inside him.

"It's not possible. He's been in a coma for a month. How can he stand?" Julia said in amazement.

"That noise. Is he possessed?" Tucker asked.

They were in uncharted territory. Marcus slowly lifted his head. Bloodshot white eyes had become yellow, coal-black pupils at their center. Wrinkles spread across his face.

"Let's back up and give him some room." Julia felt duty bound to Marcus's care. Deep down, though, she wanted to run away. By all appearances, this was supernatural. As a Christian, the concept of demon possession wasn't outside the realm of possibility. What else could this be?

Step by step, they backpedaled. Marcus took shaky steps toward them.

"Do you think we can sedate him?" Tucker asked.

"He's strong. We can't miss. He already choked me," Julia said.

Marcus stumbled across the hallway, slamming into the wall. "Help me," his two-toned voice called out. His teeth had grown into a jowl full of daggerlike fangs.

"Julia! What the fuck is going on!?" Tucker yelled in panic.

Julia teetered on that edge with him.

Marcus used the wall to brace himself as he continued moving toward them. He got to the slightly ajar door to Mr. Ulger's room. His body weight swung the door inward as Marcus vanished into the old man's room. "This is our chance." Julia ran back to the reception desk to load another syringe. "Look, this is the job. We have to sedate Marcus. For his safety and ours."

"But I'm scared," Tucker admitted.

"Trust me—me, too. Debra will be here soon. We can do this, Tucker," Julia encouraged.

Just then, the vitals for Mr. Ulger took off as the warning alarm rang.

"Stay here," Tucker said. "Be my back up if I don't get him sedated." A roar came from the room. "When this is over, I quit." Tucker went down the hallway to Mr. Ulger's room, syringe in hand, wielded like a knife.

Behind the reception desk, Ulger's vitals flatlined. "Oh my God," Julia gasped.

Tucker had paused outside the door to the room. "Tucker! Come back!" Julia yelled to him.

He turned to look at her. An immense black fur hand with claws reached out of the room. Tucker must've felt uneasy as he spun back to the doorway. The hand grabbed his torso. Like a rag doll, it jerked him into the room. Screams reverberated into the hallway.

Seconds later, silence fell over the building.

The computer's alarm from the code still blared. In shock, Julia moved to the keyboard and shut it down. Crouching, she peered over the top of the desk, not willing to turn her attention from the patient room. A loud crash came from inside Ulger's room. Tucker's body fell through the florescent hallway light. Sparks and debris scattered onto the floor. His foot caught on ventilation in the ceiling. His lifeless body dangled above the tile floor. The hospital lights went out at the same time. Emergency halogen lights kicked on along the walls. These provided minimal light, leaving swaths of hallway in the dark.

Julia typed out a message to Michael. Placing a phone call would give away her position. "Call 911, send police to the hospital. In danger. Hurry."

Within ten minutes, help should arrive.

On the desk sat the full syringe of Midazolam. Worst case, she could defend herself with the sedative.

There was the sound of blood dripping onto the tile floor as it pooled underneath Tucker's body.

Escape out the staff entrance would be the safest option.

A voice in the dark startled her. "Julia? Why are the lights out? What are you doing?" Debra asked, casually approaching.

Survival instincts sprang into action. Julia covered Debra's mouth and pulled her down behind the desk. "We have to be quiet," Julia whispered. She posted back up to look down the hallway. An immense shadowy figure stepped out from Ulger's room.

Debra had a look, as well. She covered her mouth to hold in a scream. Both women sat down on the floor together. "What is that? Is Tucker dead?"

"I don't know," Julia whispered. She had assumptions but couldn't be sure. Loud sniffs came from down the hall. A low growl rumbled to their ears. "We need to leave," Julia whispered even quieter.

"Can we make it?" Debra asked.

They both looked to the staff door. Easily forty yards away.

Uncertain, Julia replied, "We can't stay here."

Cautiously, Julia took a look toward the monster. To her horror, it had been slowly closing in on their shelter. A roar came from the creature. Chills coursed through her body. In shock, she hadn't felt the pinch. Julia turned to see Debra pull the needle from her shoulder. The plunger fully pressed. The Midazolam started to set in.

"Debra?" Julia tipped over onto the floor.

"Sorry," Debra said, positioning in a crouch. She took off at a full sprint toward the staff door.

Julia's head rested on the cold tile in a struggle to stay awake. The desk jolted sideways, hitting her. The creature bolted down the hallway in pursuit. Unable to move, Julia was resigned to watch.

Debra almost reached the exit. Outmatched in speed, the beast caught her. Julia heard and watched Debra being torn apart. Blood splattered and disconnected limbs painted the white hall. None of it emotionally registered. She had the sensation of peace brought on by the drug, as if floating down a river. Marcus had made quick work of Debra. For the first time, Julia got a good look at the monster in all its dreadful grandeur.

A werewolf.

Drowsily, she noticed they were both gazing at one another. Her eyes grew unbearably heavy. Julia shut them as she drifted off to sleep.

2 8

THE ROAD TO HELL

Cassie's cries made it difficult to focus on the road. Brett wanted nothing more than to comfort her, but there would be time when they got somewhere far away from here. They were both survivors now. A connection deeper than love. Something he wouldn't wish on his worst enemy.

To watch a person be killed changes you. Let alone your own family. Brett couldn't escape the guilt that this was his fault. The werewolf remembered. It came straight to him. By not staying home, others suffered the consequences. Cassie would never be able to forgive this, but as long as she was alive, Brett would live with the regret.

He had to slam on the brakes for the ninety-degree curve, navigating at a snail's pace around the sharp bend. One more curve, then it would be pedal to the metal. He reached over to brush Cassie's hair from her face. Coming out of the first curve, he looked at her, then past her out the passenger side window. His eyes couldn't register in the dark, but he swore something was heading toward them across open pasture.

"Shit!" Brett yelled, putting the gas pedal to the floor, accelerating to forty-five mph. A shadow took flight across the barbed wire fence, smashing into the passenger-side door. Glass shattered into the cab. Cassie's bloodcurdling screams rang in his ears. The truck rocked, causing Brett to lose control of the steering wheel. Both passenger side tires dropped off the edge toward the deep ditch.

He saw the werewolf's head in the cab, jaws clamped around Cassie's shoulder.

"No!" Brett went for the revolver at the same time he jerked the steering wheel. It was too much, overcorrecting the vehicle. The passenger-side tires skidded back onto the pavement, sliding the truck sideways. Gravity took over as the truck went into a barrel roll, its full weight crushing down on the werewolf. A squeal of pain went out from the monster as its jaws let go of Cassie. Brett's body ragdolled about in the chaos. His truck made one and a half rotations, coming to rest on its top.

He gathered his senses, supported upside down by the seat belt, his body numb and in shock. Cassie's arms hung limp against the roof of the cab. Blood ran from her finger tips. Using the steering wheel as leverage, Brett unfastened himself. To get free of the wreckage, he maneuvered out the driver's window. The crunch of glass shards beneath his hands and knees raked his skin. Outside in the dark, an eerie quiet. Using the truck for support, Brett clambered to his feet. In the moonlight, he saw debris scattered on the road from the accident.

Steadying himself, Brett hobbled to the passenger side of the truck. A commotion drew his attention back to the highway. The werewolf slithered across the road. Outstretched arms dragged its paralyzed legs as it crawled off into a grove of trees.

Safety, at least for the moment.

Brett bent down to check on Cassie.

Please God, he begged.

Lying on his back, he worked to free her. Mustering what strength he had left, he got the seat belt to release, gently lowering Cassie down to the roof. Weak limbs gave him little option. He was forced to drag her across glass, out into the night air, her body lifeless on the cool pavement. Brett let out a gasp. Cassie's eyes stared blankly to the sky. Mouth slightly agape. She had passed away.

"Cassie?" Brett sobbed in disbelief. "I'm so sorry."

The only person that made him feel at home in Mattfield was gone. Who stood by his side, no matter the repercussions. A girl he fell madly in love with. Brett had failed to protect her. Just as he'd failed to save Dalton.

Righteous anger boiled inside. Vengeance overtook what humanity he had left. It was time for this to end.

Brett plunged headfirst back into the wrecked cab, hands shifting about in search of the revolver—a jolt to his system when he felt the grip of the gun on the roof. Back in the moonlight, he held it up. The weapon appeared undamaged. Brett shuffled his feet through wincing pain down the road.

Red and blue lights came around the curve behind him. As Brett turned his attention to the police cruiser, he was engulfed by a blinding light, raising the hand that held the Governor to cover his eyes.

"Brett! Are you okay? Jesus, what the hell happened? You're covered in blood. Is that a gun?" Coach Sparts hurled a flurry of observations. He saw Cassie's body on the ground beside the wrecked Chevrolet. "Dispatch, I need an ambulance!" Keith rushed to her body.

Nothing was going to stop him from what needed to be done. Brett left the roadway, heading into the grove of trees. Shade of the canopy cut off the moonlight. In the dark, he relied on his other senses, hyper-aware of the danger at hand, but impossible to know if he was walking in circles. He heard the rustling of grass. Gun at the ready, Brett shuffled toward the noise, out of the trees into a grass pasture hidden from the road. Twenty yards away, the werewolf struggled upon the ground.

Grunts came from the beast, still employing its arms to elevate its torso off the ground. Its head was tilted high as the monster arched its back. Brett heard bones crack, as if snapping into place. Chills ran down his spine. Brett had a startling realization. The werewolf's body was regenerating, unaware it had an observer.

Soon he would possess no advantage.

"Hey!" Brett yelled out to draw the creature's attention.

Instantly, the werewolf fixed eyes on him, head cocked, remaining completely still. Brett had trained with the revolver at this distance. This was a shot he could land. Instincts told him to wait. A simple wound could cause it to flee. They stared each other down as if in a duel. Illuminated under the full moon, tension in the space between them was palpable. The ruse paid off.

Without warning, the werewolf charged. Brett aligned the sights. Sweat from his palms on the grip. For only using arms, the beast moved at an astounding speed, freakishly dragging its limp body. At ten yards, it lunged into the air, arms stretched out to snatch him. Fire burst from the end of the revolver as Brett pulled the trigger. At the last second, he contorted out of the way.

The werewolf rolled onto its back. Blood spurts came from a hole in its chest, arm twitching as it reached out for Brett, fingers wriggling in the thralls of death.

Brett squeezed off a second shot. Smoke drifted from the barrel into the sky, obscuring his vision. Echoes from the discharge bounced back from the surrounding hills. A direct shot to the head had ended the struggle.

The werewolf's arm dropped to the grass. Its lengthy pink tongue drooped from the side of the monster's hideous snout.

Brett, overcome with emotion, fell to the ground. A flick of the wrist let go of the revolver. He pounded his fist against the grass. Rivers of tears ran from his face.

I did it. For Dalton, Cassie, Marcus, and the others.

Minutes went by as joy and sorrow came pouring forth. Out of the corner of his eye, Brett glimpsed the werewolf's body. In panic, he sprung to his feet.

What now? he thought.

Rapidly, the body shrank, features of a horrific monster becoming human. Where claws had been resembled a human hand. A protruding snout melded into a man's face until the individual became recognizable. The bullet wounds to the forehead and chest had survived the transformation. The legendary creature morphed into someone Brett knew all too well. Thomas Morro.

This revelation left Brett reeling. Had his run-in with Morro caused a chain reaction of events? Was he, in fact, being hunted out of revenge? One thing was for certain: Morro made good on the promise to kill Brett's loved ones. He stood over Morro's naked body in awe. Clarity and closure to so many questions. Yet Brett found himself with new queries.

How did Tom become a monster of the full moon?

"Brett!" Sparts called out. He rushed out of the grove of trees with a flash-light. "I heard gunshots."

Telling the truth was difficult before, but now it was impossible. Self-preservation was the safest way. Brett would have to stay quiet about what had transpired.

Coach lit up Morro's dead body with the flashlight.

"Thomas Morro. You killed him?" Sparts said in amazement. After spotting the Governor, Keith retrieved the weapon.

"I did," Brett confirmed.

"You shot a naked and unarmed man? Why, Brett? At best, they'll charge you with second-degree murder for this," Keith said in complete disbelief that a kid on his team would do such a thing.

"At least no one else will die," Brett said.

"There's a situation at the hospital that needed my help. But here I am out in the boonies dealing with this shit. I'm at a loss for words." Keith had no reserva-tions about Brett's guilt.

"The hospital? Is my mom alright?" Brett had been in his own battle for life and death. He forgot about the potential Marcus problem. A new layer of panic formed.

"That's the least of your concerns. I need to know what happened to Cassie. You left her on the road to die. Who does that?" Keith asked.

"She was dead when I left. I made sure her killer would never hurt anyone again," Brett said.

"We'll sort all of this out at the station. To be clear, you are under arrest. I have half a mind to put you in cuffs. You look pretty beat up already. Any nonsense from you and I will not hesitate, got it?" Keith commanded.

"Yes, sir," Brett said.

They walked back to the road, a journey much easier with the aid of a flash-light. Stepping back onto the road, red and blue lights lit up the atmosphere. An ambulance on scene parked next to Coach's police cruiser. Two EMTs stood at the back with the doors open.

"I'll put you in the back seat," Keith said.

At the car, Coach opened the backdoor. Just as Brett ducked his head to get in, he caught a glimpse at the back of the ambulance. "Wait." He shuffled around to the open doors of the ambulance.

"No, get your ass—" Keith shut up before finishing the sentence.

Brett shared a look of confusion with Coach. Together, they both turned their attention to inside the box. Cassie sat upright on a stretcher.

"Nasty wreck. Girl seems to be fine, though," one of the EMTs said.

"Got pretty lucky," the other declared.

Brett's eyes met hers, their stares piercing into each other's soul. In his heart, he knew.

The nightmare was far from over.

29

DARKER STILL

Steam rolled from the sheriff's coffee cup. Liam and Keith sat across from him.

"So, the plan is to sit around all night? Shouldn't we be out on patrol?" Keith asked.

"Patience is a virtue," Liam said comfortably.

"We need to be ready to respond when a call comes in. Odds are fifty-fifty whether patrolling helps or hinders us," Mills said. Patrol the wrong direction, you may not be able to render aid soon enough. The young deputy still had a lot to learn, but that didn't make him unqualified to be the next sheriff. Every day was a new experience in law enforcement.

Erica gave a knock before letting herself in. "We're all set for tonight. Keith, can I holler at you for a minute?"

"Sure thing." Keith stepped out of the office.

Liam gave Mills a smirk. "Is love a conflict of interest?"

That got a chuckle out of Carl. "They do their jobs well. It's funny how people think they can hide a relationship. Your face can't hide what's in your heart. As long as it doesn't interfere with their professional lives, I pretend not to notice, like the rest of the department. You've never found love?"

Liam withdrew a flask from inside his jacket. "Travel too much. A younger me dreamed of having a family. I fear it has passed me by." Amber-brown alcohol poured into his coffee cup. He held the flask up as a gesture.

"Yeah, why not. Take the edge off. Don't make excuses. You're a man who gets things done. There's nothing to stop you from being happy." Mills extended his cup over for Liam to spice up his coffee.

The flask went back into its hiding spot. "And who says I'm not happy?"

They knew little about each other, but Mills had a talent for reading people. "Well, I'm not going to tell a man what he feels. Like Keith and Erica, people can't hide what's in their heart."

"Not from you," Liam said.

"Death is the opposite of life. Love and hate. Law and crime. Good and evil. There's a duality to everything. Spend too much time with one without the other and it corrupts your soul. That's what I believe," Mills shared.

This put Liam deep in thought. "I've spent most of my life dealing in death which, as you say, corrupts the soul."

"Are you living life between hunts, or merely existing until the next? Has a life of killing made you more inclined to participate in the negatives or the positives?" Mills asked.

"A hunt is both. It's killing and helping those in need."

"See, there's the duality. That's all I'm saying. It's what makes us human. Make sure to not tip the scales too far in one direction. That path always leads to death."

"And when someone always chooses the positives?" Liam asked.

"They nailed that guy to a cross," Mills said with a laugh.

"Fair enough," Liam said.

The door burst open. "A 911 call came in. We have a situation at the hospital," Keith announced.

Here we go, Mills thought.

The three men gathered in the lobby. Erica sat at the desk on dispatch duty. "Who placed the call?"

"Michael Adams. His wife, Julia, sent a text message that she's in trouble. Michael is en route to the hospital, as well," Erica reported.

The phone on the desk rang. They all fell silent. Erica answered the phone.

"Nine-one-one, what's your emergency?"

"Let's go," Mills said, but Erica held up a finger for them to wait.

"Yes, ma'am, help is on the way." Erica hung the phone up, bewildered.

"Was that Julia?" Mills asked.

"Nora Meeks. She claims their house in under attack," Erica said.

In a race against time, Carl formulated a plan. "Not an ideal situation. Keith, you're going solo to the Meeks'. Can you handle that?" Mills asked.

"Yes, but I've got a bad feeling about splitting up," Keith said.

"We don't have a choice. Let's get to it."

Liam joined Mills as they headed to the hospital.

"Feels coordinated, splitting up resources," Liam observed.

"We'll know soon enough." He drove the police truck onto the sidewalk outside an emergency exit door. "I've got a key to this door. Gives us an element of surprise." With the door unlocked, they prepared to breach. Liam chose to go in with his 30-30 rifle. A truck flew into the parking lot straight for them. It slid to a stop beside the sheriff's truck.

Michael got out with a shotgun. "I'm going with you."

"I don't think that's a good idea," Mills said.

"My wife is in there. I wasn't asking," Michael replied.

They didn't have time to argue. Mills drew his pistol. "Side by side. Pay attention to what's behind your shots if it comes to that." He quietly propped open the door. Guns raised, the three men tactically entered the patient wing of the hospital.

Right away, they knew something had gone wrong, the hallway dimly lit in sections by emergency lights. Down the hall, an object slumped from the ceiling. "Safeties off," Mills instructed.

Shoulder to shoulder, they walked in unison. Mills decided it best not to use the flashlight on his pistol. They cleared the first few rooms, which were unoccupied. It became clear what they saw hanging was a body.

"Julia," Michael called out softly.

"Be quiet," Liam said as he concentrated on the environment.

A white board mounted outside Room 2 read "Marcus Jones." The body hung suspended upside down directly in front of them. "Check the room across the hall." Mills clicked on his light to survey Marcus's room. Signs of a slight struggle, but empty.

"Sheriff, a deceased victim over here," Liam called out.

Mills shuffled across the hall. Room 4's sign read "S. Ulger." A man he knew well. Liam shut the door as Carl went to have a look. "You don't want to go in there. Bloody mess, that is. Body in the hallway entered the ceiling from that room."

Attention turned to the hanging body. Carl covered his mouth to get a closer look. Intestines dangled out onto the man's chest.

"Tucker Ross. He's just a kid. Damn it," Mills said. These last two months desensitized him to this level of graphic violence. When would it end?

"Do you hear that?" Michael asked.

A crunching noise came from behind the reception desk. Intermingled with snarls.

"That's the sound of a predator feasting on its kill," Liam muttered.

Whatever that creature was, it had no fear of them—a tell-tale sign of an apex predator. Mills let a warning shot rip into the wall behind the desk. A wolf's head popped up, startling the men. It grabbed the desk with a black fur hand.

Wolves don't have hands, Carl thought, panicked.

Flood gates opened in his mind. The case from hell finally made sense. Brett was telling the truth. Mattfield was dealing with a creature that wasn't supposed to exist.

Back hunched, the beast stood up. It loomed tall, dwarfing an average man, tethers of freshly torn flesh visible in its jaw. The werewolf tilted its menacing head backward to swallow the human meat. No signal was given. Gunfire erupted from all three firearms simultaneously. A hail of bullets filled the monster with lead. Smoke from the discharged gunpowder filled the air. Flailing about, helpless against the barrage, the werewolf jolted out of sight. Glass shattered as the beast made an escape outside.

"Stay here," Mills ordered Michael. Reluctantly he went to identify the victim. Checking around the corner, he saw the glass door busted out, remains of another victim strewn about the staff hall. His stomach sank. They arrived at the hospital within minutes, but still couldn't save a single life. A staff badge laid by the edge of the desk. He stooped down to grab it. As he feared, it read Julia Adams. Eyes watering, he faced Michael. Without a word, the message was delivered. Michael collapsed in a heap upon the tile floor.

How much could a man lose? Michael let out trembling yells of morbid frustration. "No! No!"

With Liam's help, they stood him up, carrying his body weight one on each side, exiting the hospital the same way they had entered, side by side. It took some convincing, but Michael relented, getting into the backseat of the sheriff's truck.

"We all saw the same thing?" Mills questioned his own rationale.

"I think we did. I find myself questioning everything I thought I knew," Liam said.

At least Carl wasn't alone in that sentiment.

Back at the station, they got Michael inside.

"Erica, have you heard from Keith?" Carl asked his deputy.

"There's been a car wreck. An ambulance should be on scene out there. What's wrong?" Erica observed the state Michael was in.

"Call Zachery Grant, the FBI, the army. Whoever will answer. All hands on deck. Get them here tonight. I need to go speak with our prisoner," Mills said.

"What do I tell them, sir?" Erica asked.

"To save our town." Mills went down the hall that connected to their holding cells. Buzzing himself in, he walked straight to Verdun's cell.

"That didn't take long." Elliot sat on his bed as if expecting this moment.

Mills ignored the mysterious man, thumbing through the keys on his belt. At last, he unlocked the cell door. "Let's go."

"What was it like?" Verdun said.

"No more games. I want you to tell me everything you know."

"I'm glad you survived. Mattfield may yet have a chance. Though the hour is late. Get me access to my car. We need to properly defend ourselves. No one is safe until dawn," Elliot said.

"And how do we do that?" Mills asked.

Verdun smirked. "Silver, Mr. Mills. Just as the stories tell us. Poison for those cursed under the full moon."

PART III

30

DRIFT

Verdun stayed up throughout the night, getting his chosen companion up to speed.

"Why silver? Why is silver the only metal that can kill them?" Mills asked.

"A lot of truth is in the dustbin of history. Many of the caches of records are lost. The Library of Alexandria burned. So, too, did our earliest records in a different incident. We know a great deal, and yet not near enough. It is safe to assume the Vatican possesses some information we don't. Until their veil of secrecy is lifted, I guess we won't know. I have my theories, of course, but they're just that—theories," Verdun said.

"Let's hear them," Mills said.

"Well, the curse is ancient in nature. Safe to assume prediluvian, before the waters reshaped the world. When the ancient humans saw the full moon in the sky, they equated it with silver, a metal of the earth. There's a direct correlation. Curses by design have a built-in way to be rectified—in this instance, Lycaon's curse, as it is officially known — to become a hybrid of man and beast. Whoever created the curse was a lower-case *g* 'god,' or corrupt spirit who wanted to be seen as such. That entity chose the earthly reflection of the full moon to combat its spread. A gift, easy enough to be remembered over generations."

"A gift and a curse. The duality of nature." Mills recalled his conversation with Liam.

"Precisely. Our world is based on balance. Order and disorder. You can't have one without the other because of the fall." Elliot took the sheriff for a simple man on paper. He found himself pleasantly surprised with the conversation—for an old man thrown into chaos.

"You just nonchalantly mentioned the fall of mankind and Noah's flood," Mills said.

"Almost every culture on earth has its own flood myth. Doesn't seem like much of a myth, does it?" Elliot asked.

"Last question: Is true evil real?" Mills asked.

"Carl, you already know. We all know this to be true. In the last twenty-five years, countries around the world have stopped calling evil what it is. People have started making excuses for it. A cabal serving demons of the old world is making the rules. Humanity has to wake up. They're losing a battle for their very souls."

Deputy Sparts came to speak with them. He carried a revolver in a plastic evidence bag.

"Sheriff, I've brought in Brett Adams. He murdered Thomas Morro tonight. Naked and unarmed," Keith said.

This caught Verdun's attention. The Brett Adams he read so much about. "I'd much like to speak with the boy."

"Brett lost his mother tonight, Keith. His father is here. Send both of them to us, and leave the gun," Mills requested.

A few minutes later, Brett and his father entered the office.

"Does your son know?" Carl asked Michael.

"Not yet," Michael said.

"Know what?" Brett asked.

"I need to hear in your words what you did tonight, Brett." Elliot wanted information before the boy had an emotional breakdown.

"Who are you?" Brett asked.

"Someone you can trust with the truth," Elliot replied.

"That's why we're all here, but no one will believe me," Brett said.

"Son, I understand why you didn't tell your story. I saw a werewolf tonight," Mills said.

Brett looked surprised to hear this. "That's what attacked us out on Jackson Road. The more I think about it, there must be more than one. Tonight, I was at my girlfriend's house. My grandpa helped me forge silver bullets for that revolver you're holding. Four shots. I used two to kill a werewolf, which transformed into Thomas Morro after it died."

Elliot took the revolver from the sheriff. He opened the cylinder to have a look. The boy was telling the truth. Two spent casings and two silver bullets. From inside his jacket, he produced his journal, and began to jot down notes from the night so far. "Good boy. You have done a great service to your community tonight. Were you bitten? Anyone else?"

Brett avoided eye contact. "Cassie's dad, yeah. I don't know about her mom. She helped us escape."

"Thank you. I believe you and your father need to have a conversation. We'll reach out if there are more questions." Mills dismissed Brett and Michael.

"How many of them do you think are out there?" Mills asked Liam when the boy and his father had left the room.

"At a minimum, three. Upward of ten is possible after two full moon cycles. You have the original still unaccounted for. Has anyone reported a black wolf?" Elliot asked curiously.

"Brett encountered it at the cemetery. Liam and I at the reservoir. How does it fit into the picture?" Carl asked.

"The curse originates from that creature. When the curse is active, it tends to hang around, which is bad news; it can infect more people unrestricted by the full moon. It proves a theory I formulated," Elliot said.

A commotion ensued in the lobby of the police station. Elliot followed the sheriff to see what was going on. Zachery Grant and a host of men and women in black suits were gathered.

Zachery Grant exercised his authority, saying, "Carl, I think it's best you resign. Martial law is going to be the best path forward in the county. You've failed your constituents. We're aware you've been sneaking around, doing your own investigation. Look where that has gotten us—more dead bodies."

"Can I borrow your cell phone?" Elliot asked the sheriff.

Mills passed him the phone. "What have you done, Grant? Don't scapegoat me for your failure as an investigator. Two months, not a single answer."

Elliot drowned out the bickering as he placed a call. Someone answered on the other side. "Elliot Verdun, confirmation, green light for resolution." He ended the call and passed the phone back. "Alright everyone, I'm in command of the investigation going forward. You are all dismissed."

"Who the fuck are you?" Grant blasted.

Elliot couldn't help but smile. "As of thirty seconds ago, I am your superior." He enjoyed trivial banter in these situations.

"I'm going to need to see some identification," Grant demanded.

"I don't have any. Nor do I need to prove anything to you, a subordinate."

This enraged Grant. "Congratulations, you are under—" His declaration got cut short by a phone call. "Grant," he answered. "What? You can't be serious. Who is he? Yes ma'am. Bye."

"Short conversation," Elliot said, amused.

"What would you have us do?" Grant asked, defeated.

"Clean up the crime scenes. Report anything out of the ordinary. Then shut down every road in a twenty-mile radius around Mattfield. No one in, no one out. Communication cut off from the outside world. Constant patrols. An indefinite blockade. Until told otherwise."

"That's a lot of resources," Grant said.

"My word is the way, not a request. You answer to Sheriff Mills. Call him if you have a problem."

The black suits marched from the police station.

"Who did you call?" Mills asked.

"I'm not here on a whim. These jobs are meticulously planned. That's all I'm allowed to say on that," Elliot replied, noticing Brett Adams crying down the hall.

There was going to be a lot more tears before the end. People must die to stop the spread. A list of names grew in Elliot's notebook. Being pragmatic, it was safe to eliminate every potential carrier than risk the alternative.

Elliot awoke midafternoon. Everyone required rest from the previous night. In all likelihood, they would be on the defensive once again tonight, then a month of relative safety, with the intent of wrapping things up during the next full moon.

Mills slept in his chair.

"Time to get up," Liam said.

Groggily, Mills came to. "What's the plan?"

"This place called the Indian House. I'd like to see it." No sense in wasting daylight.

"Why? Won't the werewolves return tonight?" Mills asked.

"Probably, but not a guarantee. The moon is only technically full for a single night. The energy that fuels the curse can be enough for up to three days at the most. Recent history from your county is averaging two nights a month. It is safe to assume that will repeat. The rest I'll explain when we get there."

They drove out west of town, taking a winding gravel road up into the hills. The Indian House stood alone in the backcountry. "This is it. Haven't been down this road in years." Carl looked at the place with contempt.

"I appreciate that you've stuck with me so far. This is where things start to get difficult to wrap your mind around." Elliot admired the old stone homestead.

This got a laugh from the sheriff. "Surely not."

He wouldn't be laughing for long.

"What happened to the last family that lived here?" Liam asked.

"They vanished. First their boy. Raving lunatics, the Petersons were. I worked that case," Mills reminisced.

"Native Americans lived up here for a time preceding those events. There's an answer to everything on this property. A Drift," Elliot said.

"I've been all over this property. Saw nothing on these acres that can't be found on the surrounding hills. What is a Drift?" Mills asked.

"In layman's terms, a weak point between dimensions. Bastion called them portals over the centuries. When the US military claimed one at Groom Lake, we changed to their terminology. Entities and objects drift into our world through these weak points. Aliens is the correct term for anything foreign to our domain."

"What are you saying? The Peterson family was abducted? This is what Area 51 is all about?" Mills's mind unraveled just as Elliot predicted.

"Yes, most likely. My guess, they passed through the Drift going the other direction. It's not visible to the naked eye. There is no recorded account of someone returning from the other side. Yes, your government is well aware of the phenomenon. So were the Native Americans. The black wolf you encountered is from the Drift. He first needs to be ritually summoned, which the tribes knew how to do. Thus, Mattfield got the story of an undying man, bitten by the wolf known as Lycaon and sealed away in a cave northwest of town for over one hundred and fifty years. Until thieves at the Coal Creek Rock Quarry set him free—a theory of mine that fills in all the holes."

The sheriff sat flabbergasted. "Why are you sharing all of this with me?"

"Carl, you are a proud man. The elected protector of your community. You feel you've failed in your duty. I need you to trust me. To help me save lives. Besides, anyone you tell will think you're schizophrenic. Citizens in the west are conditioned to believe this is all nonsense. I'm giving you the reassurance that you have not failed. If we work together, you can retire a hero. Not a single person will thank you, or know what you have done. Which is like my entire life's work as a member of Bastion. What do you say?"

After a short pause, Mills replied, "I will follow your lead. How do we get this done?"

That commitment would be put to the test. "Sacrifice pieces to save the whole. Do you trust the Asian man?"

"I have a lot of respect for Liam. Sophisticated hunter by trade. He was calm under pressure at the hospital."

"A hunter—that we can use. What about at the police department?" Elliot asked.

"Keith and Erica will do as I ask. But I think my investigator, Jack, blames me for all of this." Mills hadn't spoken to Jack in weeks.

"Tonight we'll take Liam with us. I'd like to assess him myself. What we have discussed is privileged knowledge. It stays between us. That said, having a team may be the right course of action. To outnumber the werewolves. Be warned of the peril ahead. When the dust settles, we'll be lucky to lose just one."

"Whatever it takes," Mills said.

On return to the police station, Mills resumed his nap. Elliot would use the opportunity to initiate Liam. The man sat sharpening a knife in the hallway.

"That won't serve you well on this hunt." Verdun withdrew a concealed knife from his back. "Silver, it's the only way." He handed the knife to Gable.

"Silver. Werewolves. What a mess," Liam said.

"Keep that. A trained killer is an asset. Especially a man who does whatever it takes to get the job done." Elliot had seen through Gable.

Liam starred at him. "I don't want to be that man anymore."

"Guilt, the great deceiver. Anything you have done was for the right cause," Elliot said.

"There was a time I believed that lie. Now I wander the earth, seeking relief. You are living it. How did you decay this far from humanity?" Liam asked pointedly.

It wasn't often that someone saw past the exterior Elliot presented. Liam had shared experience. He saw the snake that hid inside. "For the greater good."

"Dangerous men tell themselves how righteous they are. The mirror tells the truth," Liam replied.

"Our reflections be damned. Mattfield needs dangerous men to save it from oblivion," Elliot said.

"If you're asking, this is where I'm supposed to be. To the bitter end."

With a nod, Verdun acknowledged the pledge of support. He went to sit alone, taking a few minutes to record the new developments in his journal. Elliot fell asleep with anticipation of seeing a werewolf for the first time.

31

JUST

The assailants made a grave mistake giving Dream Walker weeks to plan a defense. He knew they wanted to catch him off guard. To their detriment. As a special operator in the military, he knew meticulous planning secured victory.

Just after midnight, Sam and his cohorts descended upon his house. Lucas wore all black, his face painted to match. An unarmed shadow in the night.

The sound of wood splintering interrupted the quiet as the front door of his house burst open. Lucas waited patiently at the top of the stairs. A narrow passage upward would be the great equalizer. His attackers scurried into the home, fanning out.

"Go check upstairs," a man ordered.

Loud thuds from booted feet pounded against each stair. The masked man reached the top, armed with a handgun. No doubt they came to kill him this time. Lucas moved swiftly. With his left arm, he put the man in a tight choke hold. His right hand snapped the assailant's trigger finger backward. As much as his victim wanted to scream, there was no air to be had. He dragged the man from the hallway into a bedroom, out of sight. Gun swinging widely, Lucas used his right hand to disarm the attacker. It took under a minute for him to choke the man unconscious. Dream Walker produced black zip ties from a pocket, binding the man's wrists behind his back, then locking his ankles together. In a few seconds, he disassembled the handgun.

One down.

Feet hit the staircase. Lucas stayed low, creeping back into the hallway. Two masked individuals approached. Using the element of surprise, he appeared in front of the first man to reach the top, delivering a massive blow to the chest with his foot. Force from the kick rocketed the man backward into his compatriot. A crash shook the house as they rattled violently downward. They laid entangled in a heap at the foot of the stairs, groaning in pain.

It was now or never. Lucas gave pursuit down the stairs, seizing each of their handguns. Like the first, he dismantled them, their parts clattering to the floor. He checked the surroundings for other intruders. There appeared to be no one. Dream Walker zip-tied both of them, dragging one of his attackers to put distance between them. In a bid for answers, he ripped the mask off the one he'd been dragging.

A woman?

"Why did you wait so long?" Lucas asked.

"We had to heal from the first beating. Plus, we don't call the shots. The boss gave the order today," she replied.

"Who is the boss?" Lucas asked.

The floor creaked behind him. A maskless Sam had a rifle trained at his head. "You should've joined the team. No one likes a hero."

Dead to rights, Lucas thought.

He reflected on the dream walk. Some of the elements were present. Three other individuals. One being a woman. Gun pointed at his head. The setting didn't match, but it had been years without practice. Enough of the dream was present to know it had come to fruition. There was room for error, unless he was currently living a different version of those events. What if his dream had been the path of vengeance? By not going that route, had Lucas created a new version of events? Reinvigorated by the idea, he commanded his own fate.

Sam made a cocky mistake. He got closer with the gun, standing mere feet away. "Last words?"

"Who wants me dead?" Lucas asked.

"Judge Thomas gave the order. He oversees the drug trade in this part of the state," Sam explained.

"He's not going to like you ratting him out. Lucky for you, I'll take care of it," Lucas said. He struck his arm upward, raising the rifle's barrel into the air—just in time, as Sam pulled the trigger. Dry wall ceiling sprinkled down from the upward shot. Lucas wrestled the gun from Sam, bludgeoning his foe in the face with the rifle's stock.

"No more! I'm done!" Sam pleaded for mercy.

Instincts forged in military service made Lucas yearn to kill Sam.

Fair game, he took a shot at you. Self-defense in your own home, no less.

Lucas took deep breaths to regain calm. The great spirit gave him the knowledge to save life. His own included. "I'm going to bind you, like your friends. Sam, if you resist, I will snap your neck."

Sam yielded immediately. "I told you, I'm done."

Zip ties incapacitated his last assailant.

The police responded to the scene not long after to collect the intruders. "How the hell did you do this without getting shot?" one of them asked.

"When I set my mind to a task, failure isn't an option," Lucas said. A mentality built from years of high-pressure missions.

"Are you going to tell them who sent you?" Lucas asked Sam as he was being led from the house.

"I'll be dead before I can testify," Sam said.

"Take a plea deal. Do what's right for once in your life. Maybe things will play out differently than what you expect," Lucas said in parting.

Until Judge Thomas is taken down, Lucas would have to pay attention. The risk grew exponentially when he learned the truth.

Pulling out his cell phone, Dream Walker hit stop on the audio recording of events. Sam would have the chance to do the right thing. His confession would make it to the authorities one way or another.

Lucas made arrangements for an extended stay with his father, packing a few days of clothes and supplies. They hid his truck in an old building out behind his father's home. "Judge Thomas controls the drug trade? He profits from poisoning our people. Uses the law as a shield. This cannot stand," Paul said in disgust.

"Some people wear their masks well, Father. No evil goes unpunished. I will make sure of it," Lucas said.

Five days went by. Still no news of the judge's arrest. Police contacted Lucas to let him know his house had been burnt down, the responsible parties still at large. He couldn't stay hidden away. Dream Walker knew he was putting his father at risk.

News broke on Wednesday, October 8th, but not what they anticipated.

"Word is, more deaths out of Mattfield, Kansas," Paul informed his son. "Then the news abruptly stopped. Rumors say road blocks have locked down the entire county up there."

"Tell Nicolas and Gray Eyes to devise a plan for our people's protection. Call Judge Thomas to a meeting, as usual," Lucas said.

"I can't have that man in my home," Paul said.

"We have to prepare for what comes next. I have a plan," Lucas said. Cut the head off the snake. Save lives and families from drug addiction and certain death.

Thomas played his part well. Without hesitation, he accepted the invite to discuss the developments out of Mattfield. Was the judge unaware of Lucas knowing his guilt? It was safe to assume so. Sam kept his mouth shut about selling out his boss. Maybe that was a cry for help. To have someone else remove the threat.

Paul led the judge into the living room.

"More news, you say?" Thomas asked.

"All information flow has stopped. It appears the federal government has cut off cell and internet service from Linn County. They must finally be aware of what is at stake," Paul said.

"Oh my, are the others joining us?" Thomas said, taking a seat.

"Just me," Lucas answered, walking into the living room, a 9mm Taurus in hand.

"Why do you have a gun?" Thomas pretended to be confused.

Lucas played the audio of Sam's confession for the judge to hear.

"The man is a criminal and a liar!" Thomas grew angry.

"You are an old friend. I do not know you. The real you," Paul said.

"Paul? You believe this? I am a judge. I am the law. How would this benefit me?"

"Explain it to the police. They are on their way. Nothing will turn up when they search your home and office if you are innocent." Lucas had revealed his trump card.

Fear flashed in the judge's eyes. "Please, can we talk about this? Is it money you want? I can pay you."

"You already know I can't be bought," Lucas said.

Backed into a corner, the judge tried to draw a handgun from his belt. Lucas shot him twice in the chest. "It is finished."

Thomas's legs kicked a few times before going limp.

Paul lowered his head at the death of his friend.

"You should call the police. Give them my phone as evidence. I need to head north. Apparently, phones are no good there, anyways," Lucas said.

"Son, you just killed a judge. You cannot leave," Paul said, bewildered.

"The police could just as easily be corrupt. I've given much thought on what to do with my life. A soldier masquerading as a citizen. I'm meant for battle. Mattfield needs a warrior to defend against the shape-shifter."

No protest came from his father this time. Paul's face was riddled with sadness. "I will not stop you. A warrior, indeed."

"I need the box of silver weapons," Lucas said.

"Modern weapons would serve you better in this battle," Paul said.

"I'm going to honor our people. I mean to fight the old way," Lucas said.

For the first time in years, his father looked on Dream Walker with pride. "Very well."

They loaded the box into Lucas's truck.

Paul disappeared into the house before returning with a bow. "Take my bow. May it serve you well. Return home to me."

Pride welled up inside Lucas. He took the pristine bow fashioned from Osage Orange wood. "Thank you, Father. I will kill the shape-shifter and come home a hero of our people."

"You already have, son."

They embraced, a connection not shared since Lucas signed with the military.

Dream Walker drove his truck north toward Kansas, unsure of what lay ahead. Behind the wheel, he contemplated the events that set him on this path. This was his destiny. The great spirit gave him a chance to change his fortune. Lucas meant to repay that debt.

In the dead of night, he crossed the state line. A few hours to his destination, Dream Walker came to a four-way intersection, halting the truck at the stop sign. No traffic in sight. Perks of traveling on a weekday.

As Lucas prepared to take off, an animal startled him. A great horned owl fluttered out of the dark, landing on the hood of his truck. Mesmerized, Dream Walker admired the bird. It took flight, vanishing into the night sky. A clear omen of where this road led.

My mind is made up.

He willed himself to push the gas pedal. Lucas did not fear death. Onward to

Mattfield.

To end the curse of vengeance.

32

THE HUNTING PARTY

The doors of the black Cadillac swung open. A number of cars sat in the driveway. Mills took the lead, flanked by Verdun and Gable, furnished with silver ammunition by Bastion's liaison. Lloyd Glass crawled across the front lawn toward them.

"Monster! In the house!" Lloyd screeched, shirt splattered with blood. No light came from inside.

They entered through the open door of the two-story home. Mindy dropped from the banister of the second story, landing with a crash in front of them. Blood oozed in all directions upon the ornate rug. Claw marks cut fleshy canyons in her back. A werewolf peered down at them, snarling.

Police instincts kicked in. Mills snapped to target and fired. The beast, with nimble reflexes, moved from their sight.

"It has high ground. We should back out!" Liam shouted.

Elliot ignored the sentiment as he tactically ascended the staircase. Mills pushed farther into the home. Six bodies lay thrown about the living room and kitchen, glass strewn across the living room carpet where the beast had made its grand entrance through a large window. Blood dripped from the kitchen counters onto the wood floor.

Lloyd had hosted a party in full knowledge of the curfew. The foolish mayor had learned the hard way.

A boom shook the house. Mills turned to see the werewolf crouched over Mindy's dead body by the front door. He raised his gun as it bolted straight at him—not quick enough as he got knocked aside, slamming against the wall. The beast vanished out the broken window.

Verdun came to pull Mills back onto his feet. "You alright? It got the jump on me and went over the banister while I was checking a backroom."

"Twenty-one-foot rule. Couldn't get the gun up quick enough," Mills said.

"Well, it didn't attack you, thankfully. It must be aware we pose a threat." Elliot led him back outside.

Liam knelt down, tending to Lloyd.

"Is he hurt?" Mills asked.

"No, not his blood," Liam replied.

"Good, he's under arrest. Cuff him," Mills ordered.

"Is Mindy alright?" Lloyd whimpered.

"No, Lloyd. All your houseguests are dripping from the walls, as well. Your days of skating by the law are done. I'm sorry you chose to ignore the curfew. I'm sorry about Mindy. You will get plenty of time to think about it," Mills said bluntly.

Mills secured the mayor in Verdun's former cell. He noticed Verdun writing in his notebook. "What's that all about?"

"I record. Bit of a requirement. For training purposes, and to make sure everything gets squared away. Speaking of which, where would I find Annie Stafle?" Elliot asked.

"Best guess is with her sister. We had her here, but she made bail." Carl felt uneasy about the question. Verdun knew every detail of the last two months.

"I'm going to insist on ignoring your beliefs about unlawful detention going forward. The mayor should stay in a cell indefinitely," Elliot said.

"Fine by me," Mills agreed.

"We have a month to secure our victory. To select vantage points and set traps. Tie up loose ends. Prepare your deputies to be briefed. Schedule a town hall meeting for next week. The march to war is under way."

Erica approached them as their conversation wrapped up. "Sir, Keith reported to the southern blockade. A man was caught trying to bypass the guards into the county. This guy had some unusual belongings. They'll arrive shortly."

Intrigued by the development, Mills and Verdun waited in the lobby. Keith led in the handcuffed suspect: a middle-aged, tall, muscular Native American man.

"Blockades are a good sign not to trespass," Mills greeted their new prisoner. "What are you doing in my county?"

"I'm on a hunting trip. Are you the sheriff?" he asked.

"Yes, Sheriff Mills. What are you on the hunt for?"

"It is good to meet you in person. We spoke on the phone briefly a month ago. My name is Lucas Dream Walker of the Osage Tribal Nation. I come as an ambassador of my people. The elders believe we are responsible for the curse that has befallen your community."

"Sorry, Sheriff. He's a bit of a loon," Keith remarked.

This is the man who placed the phone call to him? An unexpected development. "Keith, fetch the man's belongings." Then to Lucas, "Your cryptic phone call came at a stressful time for me. It has yet to bear fruit."

Verdun studied the man. "Who's to say you are not the cursed? A Native American man would fit the profile."

"I came to save lives. If you don't want my help, so be it," Lucas said.

"To be clear, what did you mean when you said 'out of time'?" Mills asked.

"To say I was skeptical when this all began is putting it lightly," Lucas explained to the sheriff. "My elders recognized the signs early on. With each full moon, my belief in the curse got solidified. The warning I gave—that your suspect was born over a hundred and fifty years ago—of that I still have my doubts."

Keith came in carrying an old wooden box. "Shit's heavy, a bunch of Indian artifacts." He sat the box down and opened the lid. Aged silver arrowheads and knives filled the inside.

"You came prepared," Verdun said, rummaging through the box. Elliot took up a knife and handed it to Lucas. "Hold that."

Dream Walker realized the test. He cut his forearm with the blade. The silver had no effect on him besides drawing blood. "My elders say silver can kill the shape-shifter."

"Your elders aren't wrong, but it's not a shape-shifter problem we have. Not in the classical sense. We have a werewolf problem," Mills said.

"Werewolf?" Lucas said confused.

"Yes, and we will accept your aid. I can read a person. You have been to war. Served in combat, and taken lives. Be warned, this is nothing like war. An entirely new level of danger is at play," Elliot said.

Dream Walker, unshaken by the inherent risk, replied, "Sign me up."

"Call everyone into your office. Let's have that meeting," Verdun said to Mills.

Liam was the last one to arrive and join the group in the sheriff's office. "What's this about?"

"Get comfortable with everyone in this room," Mills addressed the newly gathered group. "We work as a team. Erica and Keith, Verdun will bring you up to speed."

Elliot moved to the center of the room. "We are going to make a last stand against a supernatural threat. For the uninitiated, we are dealing with werewolves. Yes, plural. In the range of three to ten. If you do not want to be a part of the fight, this is your last chance to walk away."

"What?" Erica said aghast.

"Sheriff, no offense, but is this a joke?" Keith asked.

"I've seen them," Mills said.

"Me, too," Liam added.

Verdun directed attention to the men in the room. "Deputies, your keeper of the peace, Carl Mills, hand-selected you two. Liam Gable, the hunter of man-eaters. Lucas Dream Walker, the veteran warrior. Myself, Elliot Verdun, a slayer of the supernatural. Monsters are real, werewolves are killing your people. Will you fight for them?"

Keith began to protest. "Is this drug-induced? I just—"

"I'll join," Erica cut him off.

"Really?" Keith said in shock.

"I trust Mills. He wouldn't make this up. Not to mention, it kind of makes sense. You shot Thomas Morro and he walked away."

"Then how did Brett Adams kill the man?" Keith asked.

"The boy used silver bullets." Mills produced a bullet from his pocket and tossed it to Keith.

"Silver ends the curse by death," Elliot told the room. "Werewolves can't heal from wounds inflicted by the metal. When killed by silver, the werewolf will return to human form. The curse only activates under the full moon. That's why DNA analysis has been misleading investigators. Werewolf blood inspected any time but under a full moon will simply appear human."

"It's not an infection detectable by a lab? You mean these people are literally cursed? As in witchcraft?" Keith asked.

"Yes, but we'll stick to our subject matter," Elliot said.

Mills sensed Keith's hesitation.

"Look, I'm in if Erica is," Keith said. "Sorry, it's just hard to believe without seeing one firsthand."

"All onboard? Perfect," Elliot said. "Deputies, you will serve as observers, and information gathers leading up to the full moon. On the night of, you will be on patrol. We need civilians confined inside, while also monitoring for the beasts' locations."

"Are we certain they'll come to Mattfield?" Mills asked.

"Yes. Everyone in the county will be gathered and safely locked in the high school. Werewolves take pleasure in sadistic murder. Bring all the available victims to town, and they will come looking. You will stand guard at the high school, Sheriff.

"Mr. Gable, I have a special task for you at the location known as the Indian House. You will be stationed there to hunt the black wolf. Many have tried to kill it over the ages. When the full moon returns, we will station you in a vantage point to shoot along Main Street. The courthouse tower should suffice. I wish you good fortune."

"Alright," Liam said.

"Dream Walker, you will hunt the rock quarry and surrounding areas. Hopefully within the month, you can kill the original host of the curse. On the full moon, you will position atop the businesses downtown. That creates a shooting gallery between Liam's and your position."

"Understood," Lucas said.

"That's everything for now. Arm yourselves with silver," Elliot said.

"What about you?" Mills asked.

"I have my responsibilities. Don't concern yourselves with others' tasks," Elliot said.

"Wait, don't we need a team name? I mean, a group of werewolf hunters. That's grounds for a team name," Erica said.

"This is life or death. You need to take this seriously," Elliot said, annoyed.

A team name gave comradery, to tie their missions together in a unified front. Although a silly suggestion, Mills wasn't opposed to the idea. This couldn't devolve into everyone for themselves. Verdun already warned him, those that joined their cause could die.

"She's right. Team names are important in battle," Lucas added.

"Silver Bullets?" Keith tossed out.

"The Hunting Party," Liam said.

That name stuck in the sheriff's mind. "The Hunting Party." He repeated the name aloud. Murmurs of agreement spread through the small room.

"Arrowheads signify the hunt to my people," Lucas said, giving his approval.

Elliot relented with his steadfast demeanor. A smile came to his face. "So be it. We are hence forth known as The Hunting Party."

A bittersweet moment of joy. Mills looked at the faces in the room. He couldn't help but wonder about each of their fates. There was hope they would all survive—however unlikely. Victory always exacts a cost.

How many of them would pay the ultimate price?

33

ORPHANS

Julia's Trailblazer came to a stop at a checkpoint heading north out of the county. Michael rolled down the window. "I have a house in the city. I'm taking these kids up there to stay."

Brett sat quietly next to Cassie in the backseat. They had leaned on each other over the last week, both having lost parents. Julia was the only parent Brett had a relationship with. Both orphans, as he saw it. Cassie ended up staying at his house. No other family was willing to take her in after what transpired.

His mind flashed to the silver knife. Grandpa Walt had asked Brett to return it to the Jones family—which Brett meant to do but hadn't got the chance. Since having the Governor confiscated, it was currently his only means of defense. Mr. Jones may be in need of it, as well. Selfishly, though, he wasn't willing to part with the heirloom. His primal drive to survive wouldn't allow it.

"I need you to turn your car around. County is under quarantine. There will be a town hall this evening. Sheriff Mills requests all citizens attend. Any questions you may have can be asked tonight," the officer said.

"Please, let us go. We've lost everything. Our phones aren't working, the internet is out. I need to get these kids to safety," Michael pleaded.

"I don't make the rules, sir. Just enforce them. You can turn around of your own accord, or we can arrest you and take you back," the officer warned.

Michael put the car in reverse. "We're prisoners. I'm going to find a way to get us out." He drove them back toward home.

Brett noticed a stark difference in his father, outside of mourning Julia's death. Michael desperately wanted to leave Mattfield. To the point of obsession.

"You know why they won't let us leave," Brett stated.

"They can't hold us hostage. It is un-American," Michael said.

"Give it up. We need to worry about staying alive." Brett had grown more irritable.

"What do you think I'm trying to do, Brett?" Michael fired back.

"Arguing isn't going to help," Cassie interjected.

"We'll go to the town hall, try and get answers," Michael promised.

"I already know what's going on," Brett said, looking out the window.

"What's that?" Cassie asked.

"The government, or whoever is in charge, won't let anyone leave. They know about the werewolves. We're in containment. To prevent the spread. I bet there's nothing they won't do to keep one from escaping."

"There can't be that many. Why would they want to put thousands of lives at risk?" Michael asked.

Because, Dad, there's probably one in our car. How else did Cassie recover from the attack? Just like Marcus, who is the only unaccounted-for person from the hospital.

Brett feared the worst for Cassie. He'd pressed her about what she remembered from the car wreck. She believed the crash knocked her unconscious. At least, that's what she said. Putting full trust in her words would be a mistake. He was resigned to keeping a watchful eye on Cassie for signs. So far, she did seem to be normal—besides the emotional damage suffered. They were all fighting their own struggles with that.

Brett made a conscious effort to go easier on his father. Vitriol was ever present. As a family, though, they had suffered a great deal, unable to lay Julia to rest. To have lost her while mourning Dalton . . . He was aware Michael had to be teetering on the edge of a complete breakdown.

Selfishly, Brett needed his father for protection—from the supernatural and, most pressingly, the human powers that be. A werewolf attack wasn't coming for a few more weeks. Those hunting the monsters posed a present danger. Did the rule of law even apply in a containment scenario? Brett had his doubts.

That evening, they reported to the town hall. Walt met up with them outside the courthouse. A stage set near the staircase, leading inside. Over a thousand people already stood by, waiting in confused anticipation.

Walt was disheveled, in rough shape from the sudden loss of his daughter. These unexpected losses in the family may very well be the death of him.

Brett went to give him a hug. "Hi, Grandpa."

"Are you holding up?" Walt's voice shook.

To Brett's own amazement, he was. The time to mourn their loses would come. Survival was the priority. "I'm okay. How are you?"

"Not okay. A grandson and a daughter. It's too much for my heart to handle." Walt spoke solemnly.

Murmurs erupted from the crowd as Sheriff Mills, flanked by a group of individuals, exited the courthouse and headed to the stage. Mills went to the microphone to address the gathered community.

"Good evening. Thank you all for being here. As many of you know, our county has been through a great deal of trials. The morgue hosts another slew of bodies from last week. All of our deceased are victims. We've paid a heavy toll."

"Why can't we leave!? We can't even contact our family members to let them know we're okay!" a man shouted. A multitude joined in jeering the sheriff.

"Please, have patience. Our county is locked down. State, federal, and military enforcement are doing this as a last resort. The curfew also remains in place. There's only one way to get through these trying times. That's together," Mills continued as the crowd grew restless.

"We are sheep to the slaughter! Who's next? Why are we getting punished because you can't catch a deranged mass murderer!" a woman yelled out.

"I'm going to protect all of you. In three weeks, Wednesday November the fifth, there is a plan in place. There is a credible threat the killer, or killers, will strike again. For your safety, everyone will gather at the high school in the afternoon. Prepare to stay for up to two days. That should be sufficient enough for us to flush out the killers, and restore peace to our community. Spread the word to anyone who skipped this town hall. You must comply—forcibly if that's the route you choose to go."

"You should resign!" another man shouted out, to applause from the crowd.

"I will. I give my word. Your loss in confidence does not go unrecognized. I will honor your wishes. These individuals on stage with me are the ruling authority here until further notice. We are approaching this as a team. Let me turn the microphone over to Mr. Verdun. He has some information, then you are free to go."

Brett recognized the mysterious man he encountered at the police station.

"Hello, citizens. I ask that you report any suspicious activity or behavior from those you encounter. That includes family and friends. If you have had a run in with a black wolf—whether sighting or physical encounter—I urge you to step forward. Your assistance will benefit everyone around you. Also, I'd like to have a word with Brett Adams. That is all."

Louder murmurs came from the crowd. Eyes darted to Brett. Soon he had the entire crowd staring at him. They parted out of his way as he walked to the stage. Another man made his way to the front of the crowd.

"Brett, thank you," Verdun said. He turned his attention to the other man. "Information regarding the wolf?"

"I got bit by that devil. Didn't think much of it. Looked worse than it was. Healed up pretty fast," the man answered.

"Your name?" Verdun asked.

"Xavier Hoff. How can I help?"

"You already did. I'll be in touch. You can go home." Verdun turned his attention back to Brett. "Join me inside for a minute."

From Verdun's tone, it wasn't a request.

Brett walked around the stage and into the courthouse. "What do you need from me?"

"This," Verdun held out the Governor revolver to him. "You did fine work with that. Best keep it close for what's to come."

A rush of relief fell over Brett as he took the gun. "I never thought I would get this back. Thank you."

"Killing a werewolf is no small thing. You very well may be the only living person to have done that. I applaud you. Mind if I ask you a few questions?" Verdun came across as polite.

"Yeah, sure," Brett said.

"I asked before, but I want to clarify. Be honest. Have you been bitten or scratched?" Verdun said.

"No, sir," Brett replied. He had suffered cuts to his chest homecoming night.

"What about the boy from the hospital, Marcus Jones?" Verdun pulled a notebook from his jacket.

Images came to mind of Marcus's bloody shoulder. "He was bitten at the quarry."

"Confirmation is good. Last question—about the girl, Cassie Meeks. I saw her with you in the crowd. Her father is missing, as you know. That's not a good sign. Was she bitten?"

Instinctually, Brett did his best to lie. "No." Even though he feared the worst, Brett wasn't about to give Cassie up.

His answer must not have been convincing. "Are you positive?" Verdun followed up.

For a man who came across nice, he had a foreboding essence about him. Brett sensed Mr. Verdun to be a dangerous man. "Positive. She wasn't bitten."

Verdun scribbled in his notebook. "Very well, you're free to go. We'll cross paths again."

Was that a promise or a threat? Brett tucked the gun in his waistband to hide it. He hurried out of the courthouse into the dispersing crowd. Overhearing mumbles and grumbles, people sneered at him as he passed. No doubt they associated Brett with all that had befallen the community. Not that long ago, they were cheering him on. Now a pariah to thousands. Judge as they may, none of them knew loss like Brett had suffered. It wouldn't be a surprise if a mob showed up at Brett's house with pitchforks.

"What did that guy want?" Michael inquired as Brett rejoined the group.

"He returned Grandpa's gun and asked me some questions," Brett said.

"With how things are playing out, why don't you hold onto that," Walt said.

"You're out of your mind, Walt. He's a senior in high school who killed a man with that gun a week ago," Michael said in shock.

"I killed a werewolf. I'm keeping the gun." Brett wasn't going to stand for being accused of murder.

"We'll see about that," Michael scoffed at the idea. "Let's go home."

At the house, Cassie sat with Brett on the couch. "What did he want to know?" Cassie asked.

"Nothing, really. He asked if I had been bitten, if Marcus had been bitten." Brett didn't know how to go about this subject with her.

"And me?" Cassie pressed.

Brett got the strange feeling Cassie was aware of what happened to her. "Yeah, you, too."

Fear flashed across her face before Cassie hid it. "Did that man say why he gave you back the gun?"

"For protection. It was a short conversation. I told him the truth. You and I were not bitten." A lie he felt Verdun saw right through.

"I think that man wants to hurt me," Cassie confided.

"I won't let him. I'm not going to lose anyone else," Brett promised her.

Cassie rested her head on his shoulder. "Do you think I'm a monster, Brett?"

The hair on the back of his neck stood up. He was being probed for answers. Was this being done innocently? It came across more as self-preservation. It was becoming apparent Cassie knew she was infected. Brett believed he would do what had to be done, if she, indeed, became a monster—to stop anyone else from suffering the same fate as his brother and mother.

"Of course not. I love you," Brett lied to his girlfriend.

"Good. I love you, too." Cassie nuzzled his shoulder.

There was no guide for what to do if your girlfriend has been bitten by a werewolf.

Keep your friends close and monsters closer, Brett.

Who knew the monster and friend were one and the same?

34

SHADOW OF DEATH

An old bur oak tree towered on the bluff. A perfect vantage point for a tree stand to hunt. Liam set about securing his stand to the tree fifteen feet in the air. Confident in his work, he scaled the ladder to have a view. The notorious Indian House was in sight. Wide open prairie provided three hundred yards to take a clean shot. Verdun had supplied silver .308 rounds for Liam's rifle. He caught a glimpse of a man standing alone out in the tall grass. He left the rifle leaning against the tree under the stand.

Why didn't I bring the gun? Liam thought. *Rookie mistakes like that can cause you to miss an opportunity.*

Swiftly, Gable scrambled down the ladder to the rifle, racking the bolt action to put a round in the chamber. He stalked out into the tall grass to get a closer look. Upon approach, Liam recognized the man, having just recently saved his life. "Lloyd?"

The mayor had a metal cuff around his left ankle, tethered by a ten-foot piece of steel cable to a stake driven into the rocky soil. "That nut job running the show tricked me into leaving my cell. Said he was going to set me loose. Then I woke up in this field. Chained like a damn dog. Can you get this off me?"

Liam stooped to inspect the mechanism. "I don't have anything with me to cut through this."

"Don't leave me. Please, you must stay," Lloyd pleaded.

"I'm not going to leave you. Let me grab my supplies. This is where I'll set up camp." Liam went back to his truck, well aware Verdun's intentions were for using the man as bait. Never again would Gable allow himself to use another to complete a hunt. This felt like the ultimate test.

Am I truly a reformed man?

A tent wouldn't offer much shelter, but it should suffice.

"Thank you," Lloyd said. He assisted Liam with setting up camp. "This stake is buried in rock. Any idea how to get me free? Something to pry it, perhaps?"

"Yes, but it will have to wait. Leaving you alone is too dangerous," Liam said.

"What is it you're doing at this forsaken place?" Lloyd asked.

"I'm on a wolf hunt," Liam said.

"For one of those things? Werewolves? Oh, Jesus, that psycho is using me as bait!" Lloyd began to panic.

"Look at me. Even if you were left here as bait, I would not use you as such. Keep your cool, and we'll both get through this." Gable tried his best to reassure the man.

The mayor started to whimper. "I've done so much wrong. This is my fault. But I don't want to die like this."

An all too familiar sentiment for Gable. "What did I say?"

"I'm sorry. You are a good man. How long will this take?" Lloyd asked.

A good man.

People tended to make that generalization about him. How wrong they were. Verdun was the only person that saw who Liam really was. "There is no way to tell. Three weeks at the most. Mattfield will need defending when the full moon returns."

Over the next two weeks, Lloyd's trust grew. Liam cooked and fed the man and provided fresh water. During the days, he gave overwatch from his tree stand, sitting silently in wait. Mayor Glass laid in the tent most of the daylight hours to avoid obstructing a shot. They chatted until bedtime each night. No one else ever showed up to check on them.

Gable found a fond appreciation for the squirrelly mayor. Underneath his drive and lust for power was a decent man. With each passing day removed from the world of politics, Lloyd's buried humanity shined through. Lloyd took notice of the change himself. Being out in nature worked wonders on the human soul.

Six days stood between them and the full moon. Still, Liam had zero sightings of the wolf. Of any animals in fact. This property was devoid of life, but a few unexplained incidents occurred in the night. What sounded like whispers in the distance. A red flash of light. Afraid of leaving the mayor alone in the dark, Liam chose not to pursue the strange occurrences.

"Running out of time on this. We need to strongly consider getting back to Mattfield." Lloyd expressed his anxiety over the full moon's approach.

Preparations in town should be near completion under the supervision of Lucas Dream Walker. The Hunting Party had full confidence in one another to complete their allotted tasks. "On the morning of the full moon, we'll leave this property," Liam said.

"You make the calls. Just going a bit stir crazy at this point," replied the mayor.

Liam walked to the tree stand to sit another ten-hour shift. Once seated in the stand, he soaked up the cool breeze. It dawned on him that today was Halloween. There wouldn't be any festivities this year with curfew. How time seemed to fly by in his later years. Winter was right around the corner.

He raised the rifle scope to make a scan of the surroundings. His eyes took in the prairie grass and distant tree line. As Liam rotated the scope past the camp site, he caught a glimpse of something beyond the tent. With a deep breath, he paused to refocus back on the camp. Something large hunkered down in the tall grass. Alarms went off in his head when he processed the black fur coat.

Rifle braced snug against his shoulder, he aimed to take the shot. His window had closed. The tent now obscured the view of the wolf. Lloyd's screams carried across the expanse of pasture. Liam descended the ladder, taking off at a full sprint toward the camp.

Gable took in the carnage as he ran up on the tent. Glass's severed foot above the steel clamp sat upright on the ground. Jagged bone protruded where the ankle had attached to the leg. Streaks of blood were smeared across the grass leading farther out into the prairie.

"Lloyd!" Gable hollered, chasing the blood trail.

"Help!" Lloyd called out in agony.

Liam found the man near the tree line. Blood oozed from the bloody stump of his left leg. Without thinking, Gable set the gun aside and unfastened his belt to make a tourniquet for the wound.

"Hang on! I have to slow the bleeding!" Sliding the belt underneath the mayor's mangled leg just below the kneecap, he pulled tight. Lloyd squealed in pain, causing him to breath laboriously. Liam secured the tourniquet. Grass shuffled behind him. At the last second, he drew the hunting knife from his belt as the black wolf charged. His left forearm was wedged in its mouth as the beast gnawed upon it. Shock set in as he repeatedly drove the knife into the wolf's neck. Hot blood ran from both their wounds. Just when he thought the beast wouldn't relent, the jaws released from his arm.

Cold red eyes backed away from him as the wolf shook its head, distressed. Army crawling across the ground, Gable reached his rifle. Déjà vu of his last tiger hunt. He raised the gun at the wolf. The black canine crouched to pounce as if realizing its mistake. "Go to hell!" Liam shouted as he pulled the trigger.

Kaboom! The gun echoed out across the isolated prairie.

Smoke emanated from the bullet hole in the wolf's chest. A clean shot through the vitals. The wolf opened its mouth to draw breath, exhaling black smoke as if its insides were aflame.

Liam got to his feet. He had never witnessed anything like this before. Soon, the black fur coat of the wolf began to deteriorate into fumes. Eyes once beady red turned to hot crackling coals. With a gust of fall wind, the black wolf dissolved away into the air. Where many had fallen short, Gable stood triumphant in slaying the otherworldly creature.

Rifle slung across his back, Liam dragged the maimed mayor back to his truck. He grabbed his police radio from inside. "Wolf down. The mayor is hurt, send medical."

Digging in his truck, he withdrew the first aid kit, first cleaning the torn flesh from the bite with alcohol. Using a needle and thread, he sewed up eight deep gashes, content the rest were mere flesh wounds. Liam wrapped the wound in gauze, securing it with tape, then changed into a long-sleeve green flannel shirt to conceal the bite. He wanted to gauge Verdun's reaction to see if revealing the bite was a good idea. He then twisted open his bottle of antibiotics tucked away for an occasion such as this. Early on, Liam learned to carry a ration of penicillin in case of a mauling-induced infection.

Lloyd came in and out of consciousness on the ground. "I'm alive," he said, astonished.

"You're going to be alright. Ambulance is on the way. Let me dress your wound." Liam knelt down to clean the stump. Sound from tires on gravel caught his attention. "Looks like the professionals will get to do that."

A black Cadillac parked behind Liam's truck. Verdun?

What about the ambulance? he thought.

Elliot got out to join them. "You called for an ambulance. Are you hurt?"

"No, Lloyd lost a foot. The one you tied down when you decided to use the man as bait," Liam said.

"Mr. Glass, I see you did your job well," Verdun said coldly.

On the ground, Lloyd got visibly frightened. "Stay away from me! What kind of monster are you!? I'm lucky to even be alive!"

"Wolf got to him before I could intervene," Gable said.

"Oh, that's a shame, but the wolf is dead?" Verdun said, unholstering a pistol.

"What the fuck are you doing!? I said stay away from me!" Lloyd screeched.

"I got the wolf. It burnt up, best I can describe," Liam said nervously. He anticipated what the drawn firearm was for.

"Fascinating. You're going to be a legend amongst my people. You don't understand the magnitude of what it is you've accomplished here." Verdun aimed the gun at the screaming mayor. Liam's ears rang from the gunshot. Lloyd collapsed in a heap.

"Was that necessary?" Gable asked.

"Unfortunately, yes. The wolf's bite spreads the curse," Verdun said.

"You guaranteed the outcome by tying the man down," Liam challenged.

"I used him as bait because I was going to have to kill him, regardless. It's the lesser evil to kill those who have had encounters than to let it spread further." Verdun didn't seem to be phased by shooting the man.

At least Gable felt guilt for his actions. "That's a lot of people in this town. You're going to kill them all?"

"I'm going to do what must be done. Judge, jury, and executioner. Know that I don't get sent places to prolong problems by showing mercy. The fact I'm here means this has gotten out of hand. We can end this in less than a week. A few will die to save millions."

"When you put it like that . . ." Liam said. He was learning just how far his companion was willing to go.

"That black wolf had a name: Lycaon. An ancient beast. Every spread of the curse starts from his mouth. Mr. Gable, you killed the father of werewolves. A crowning achievement in a life of service. Mattfield will be the last town to suffer this fate because of you." Verdun gave him a pat on the back.

"No more werewolves," Liam said, realizing the gravity of the situation.

"I'll let you in on a little secret. There are a handful, but they are a different breed entirely. Relegated to one continent when this is over. When Bastion takes care of that lot, there will never be another werewolf for the rest of time. Fingers crossed," Elliot said.

Pride welled up inside Liam. Whether deserved or not, he felt it. A form of redemption for his acts of wickedness. "I'll help Dream Walker finish preparation in town. I've decided this will be my last hunt." To live out his days on the farm was more than he deserved.

The bite on his arm pulsated with pain. In six days, the full moon would determine his ultimate fate.

35

GREEN PASTURES

In the pages of the journal are a list of names.

Lloyd Glass, the mayor of Mattfield. Home attacked, possible carrier of the curse. Used as bait for Lycaon. Suffered a bite to the leg. Neutralized with a silver bullet to the head, deceased. Lloyd, the second-to-last name recorded.

Xavier Hoff from the town hall was the latest addition.

Elliot had carefully planned for this day.

One day until the full moon. The Hunting Party was preoccupied. It was time to clean up.

The first name on the list read simply "Original." An unknown figure still in hiding. A problem for the full moon.

Marcus Jones's name was just below Original, confirmed carrier.

Brett Adams's name was written on the next line, status unknown.

Thomas Morro after that. Confirmed carrier, deceased. Killed with silver bullets by Brett Adams.

Annie Stafle, relations with Thomas Morro, possible carrier.

Paul Meeks, carrier.

Cassie Meeks, status unknown. Three months in, there could be more.

Liam Gable, status unknown.

Lucas Dream Walker, status unknown. Plenty of work yet to be done.

He stepped out of the black Cadillac, in front of a pleasant little muted green home in the countryside. Elliot knocked on the door. After a minute, the door swung inward. "Hey! I recognize you from the town hall. What brings you out here?" Xavier said in greeting.

"I'm following up on my investigation. Are you home alone by chance?" Verdun asked.

"Wife left me when the kids went off to college. Just me now," Hoff overshared.

Good, Elliot thought.

"I'm sorry to hear that."

"Don't miss her. Come on in." Hoff spun around to lead Verdun inside. When Xavier turned his back, Elliot drew a pistol. He shot Xavier in the back of the head. His lifeless body fell face-first onto the wood floor. Elliot walked back outside, shutting the door behind him.

He withdrew the notebook from inside his jacket.

Xavier Hoff, deceased. Silver bullet to the head, he scrawled.

Leaving Hoff's house, Elliot cruised by the Adams' country home.

The grandfather's truck is there today, he thought.

This would get volatile with an uncertain outcome. Too many variables and moving pieces. It would have to be his last stop. He couldn't afford the level of risk before the full moon. An ambush in the middle of the night would produce the highest odds for the desired outcome. Elliot decided to focus his attention on Annie Stafle. By days end, "deceased" will follow each person's name in his notebook.

Over the previous weeks, Elliot had thoroughly scouted out Mary Stafle's house, a small single-story red brick home on the outskirts of Mattfield. In no way confirmed, but it was everyone's belief that Mary was the only person who'd take her sister in. Elliot parked along the quiet street. Being in town, a firearm wasn't a safe option. Best to be discrete to avoid unwanted attention.

Sheriff Mills may protest to the methods of Bastion—most decent people revolt at the killing of peripheral connections on these jobs.

The tool for this circumstance fit neatly inside his jacket pocket.

A man opened the door as Elliot went up the steps of the porch. "Who are you?"

"I run the show. My charge is the protection of your community. Who are you?" Elliot asked to be polite. He was well aware of Mary's husband.

"Tony Fitzgerald. This is my house. What are you doing here? Matter of fact, you didn't answer my first question," Tony said cautiously.

"Your wife didn't take your last name? Strange custom for rural America. My name is Verdun. I'd like to speak with Annie. Is she here?" Elliot asked.

"We've both been divorced, but that's not any of your business, Verdun. If you get that menace out of my house, that would be great." Tony was no fan of his sister-in-law.

"I'll take care of it," Verdun said with a smile.

"Mary! Get your sister out here! Law wants to speak with her," Tony yelled into the house.

"I need to have a word with her inside, alone," Verdun said.

"Not my house. Take her to the police station," Tony said in defiance.

Elliot drew the pistol from his hip. "This should help you understand. I don't do requests."

Fitzgerald threw his hands up. "There's no need for that. Put the gun away!"

Mary came to the door. "What's the meaning of this? Tony has done nothing wrong!"

"Get your keys. Go for a long drive. It's a beautiful fall day. Go enjoy it," Elliot instructed.

"This is against our rights!" Tony yelled angrily.

"Yes, but I'm not law enforcement. Don't make a scene. Take your keys and go. This is the last chance you're going to get," Elliot said.

Tony grabbed his truck keys from a coat hanger inside the door. "I ain't getting shot over Annie."

"What do you want with my sister?" Mary asked.

Verdun shot her a glare.

Tony grabbed Mary by the wrist and pulled her out of the house. "Mary! The man means business. I will leave you here!" Tony pulled her off the porch toward his truck.

Elliot stood at the open front door as they pulled out onto the street and drove away. Mary stared at him the entire time.

The floor creaked as his black boots stepped inside the house. Elliot shut the door behind him before locking it. The scent from a pumpkin candle filled the room. "Annie? Are you home?"

"What do you want?" she called back.

"I came here to talk."

"Why did you send them away?" Annie asked.

"They don't know the things we do. About Thomas Morro. Those conversations are hard to have with nonbelievers around."

A door unlocked down the hallway. Annie revealed herself. "We can talk in the kitchen."

Verdun followed her to the compact kitchen.

She took a seat at the little dining room table wedged in the corner. "What do you want to know?"

Elliot once again pulled out his notebook. "For starters, I know quite a lot. About his condition. Can you fill in the blanks for me about the quarry?"

Annie nodded. "Stillman ran into financial trouble. Man worked a hard job in the oil field. Tom got acquainted with him at the bar in Red Hill one night. Neither one of them much liked the other. They ran around stealing shit. Anything that would make a quick buck at the junkyard. For Thomas, it was always about the thrill. He never cared much for money. Stillman was late the night they hit the quarry. It wasn't their original plan. They found boxes of dynamite when they got out there. Hit the jackpot, is what Thomas told me. But he couldn't help himself. Wanted to blow some up. Taped a few together in the bottom of Coal Creek. Accidentally blew open a cave. Excited at first. Until a monster came out of it."

Elliot scribbled down the important facts Annie revealed. "So, this whole thing started by a complete accident?"

"You tell me. Stillman was late. They go to the quarry instead. Blow open a cave with a monster inside. How unlucky do you have to be for all those things to happen?" Annie asked.

"The world is a mysterious place. We'll never know the secrets of it all. Not scientifically. There is a spiritual aspect humans do not take into consideration." Elliot finished writing the intel.

"Like ghosts? God and the devil? Thomas was on a bad path. It got him killed," Annie said.

"Why were you with him?" Elliot asked.

Her face showed that Annie had been thinking about this question a lot. "I don't know. He was always kind to me before the quarry. Even though I knew the man was no good. Being lonely leads you places you shouldn't go."

Verdun placed a hand on her shoulder. "In a way, you played the part meant for you in all of this."

"That doesn't make me feel better," Annie said as tears leaked from her eyes.

"Did you and Thomas have romantic relations?" Elliot asked.

"Are you asking me if I had sex with the man? Yeah, we're adults. We had sex," Annie said, getting upset.

Elliot wrote one last note in the book. He tucked it away into his interior jacket pocket. "Sorry, these questions can be like that. Tell me, how have you been feeling since Thomas's passing?"

Annie opened up about her emotional state, but he wasn't listening. Verdun fished silver wire from his pocket as she spoke, wrapping the ends around each of his leather gloved hands beneath the table.

Annie's voice cut off mid-sentence as Verdun lunged across the tabletop securing a loop around her neck. He rolled from his seat taking up position behind her as she squirmed. Bracing his foot against the back of the chair he pushed her torso against the table, pulling tightly with both hands simultaneously to get the maximum amount of force.

Annie clawed at the wire around her neck before flailing her arms about in distress. The sharp silver strand wire cut deep into the flesh. A red rain of blood spewed out onto the table. A splatter from the wound hit Elliot in the face. Warm blood dripped from his chin. Annie's body collapsed forward upon her death. Elliot shifted his hands back and forth using the wire as a saw. In less than a minute, Annie's severed head bounced off the table before rolling to a stop on the kitchen floor.

Messy business not using a gun, he thought.

His eyes set upon the four-burner propane kitchen stove. Elliot went to the living room to retrieve the still-lit pumpkin candle, setting it on the nook table in a pool of Annie's blood. At the stove, he turned all four knobs to release propane into the kitchen. An explosion would give cover for what transpired here.

He rushed from the house to the black Cadillac. The car sped forward as Verdun watched the rear-view mirror with anticipation.

The Cadillac came to a stop at a four-way intersection two blocks down the road. Tony and Mary's home erupted in a volcanic explosion. Black smoke and debris shot out in all directions. A shock wave sent a shudder through the car. This would preoccupy the first responders in the community, giving him plenty of time to target the Jones household.

So far, everything had gone according to plan. Elliot felt a growing confidence that this would all be over soon. He would return to Bastion triumphant, etching himself as the only living member to have slain an incursion of werewolves.

Christopher Jones lived in a more public part of town—in the vicinity of Main Street, the courthouse, and the police station. A quiet hit would be ideal, but Elliot's target was Marcus. His father wouldn't stand by quietly. This would require a gun. In order to not impede his plans for the Adams household, Verdun needed to secure the kills and distance himself from the scene.

A fire truck raced by on its way to the blown-up house. It was now, or never.

Shade from an old elm tree standing in front of the Jones home cast into the road. Verdun parked in the shadow. His feet met the asphalt. Brushing back his jacket, he drew the pistol from its holster. With a slight pull on the firearm's slide, Elliot made sure a silver bullet was chambered. Confidently, he strode to the door and gave a knock. Windows on the front of the house were shuttered, curtains on the inside.

No one answered the knock. He produced lockpick tools from his pocket, a skill not used often these days. Kneeling down, Elliot made quick work feeling the bolt lock turn to a stop. That was it. He twisted the door knob and pushed it inward, creeping inside like a silent assassin. To his shock, the door slammed shut behind him. Verdun spun around to feel the barrel of a gun press against his forehead.

Christopher Jones held him at gun point.

"Well done," Elliot said, holding his hands and gun up.

"Drop it," Christopher commanded.

There were no immediate solutions without getting killed. Elliot let his gun fall to the floor. "Take it easy."

"An armed man just broke into my home. You're telling me to take it easy?" Christopher said.

"We need to have a serious discussion about your son," Elliot said, growing anxious.

Marcus walked into the living room. "Dad, who is that?"

"I don't know. Get the zip ties in the kitchen drawer. We'll tie him up first, then find out what he wants."

"You need to listen to me. I don't have time for this," Elliot said.

"You're about to *make* time. Big miscalculation on your part coming in here like you did," Christopher scolded.

Marcus returned from the kitchen with a handful of zip ties.

"Put your hands behind your back," Christopher instructed.

Verdun relented, allowing the boy to zip-tie his wrists together, followed by his ankles. Once subdued, Christopher passed the gun to his son, proceeding to drag Elliot from the living room into a side room.

"Did you come here to kill my boy?" Christopher asked bluntly.

Elliot contemplated how to handle this conversation. The truth very well could lead to his execution. Lying had consequences, too.

Marcus was a monster. Tomorrow night, he would kill indiscriminately.

"Marcus is a werewolf. There's not much time left. He will kill you, and anyone else he sets his sights on when the full moon rises."

Shock spread across Christopher's face. "A werewolf? You are out of your damn mind."

"Tell that to the people he killed at the hospital. Four bodies. What Marcus is cursed with was designed to be merciless." Elliot chose honesty, but knew it would fall on deaf ears.

"Get comfortable. I'm not letting a psychopath like you go free. You'll see tomorrow that you're wrong." Christopher left the room.

"When you see for yourself, it will be too late!" Elliot shouted after him. Verdun's hope hinged on someone coming to rescue him. Maybe they would see the black Cadillac and be alerted to his location.

Marcus came to the doorway. "Heads up. I'm going to park your car out back."

Elliot slammed his head back against the wall. The mission's success hung on by a thread now. It was difficult not to envision a bleak outcome. Mattfield will become a graveyard. Ground zero for a plague of death that will branch out across the heartland. The weight of that defeat rested solely on Verdun's shoulders.

36

BESIDE THE
STILL WATERS

Tonight, the Hunting Party would make a stand against the werewolves.

Recent developments were giving Carl fits of anxiety. Verdun, who up to this point had led the charge in preparations was missing in action. Erica and Keith did a sweep in their squad cars, producing no leads. Annie Stafle's burnt remains were discovered after a devastating propane-fueled fire in what the fire department believed to be an intentional act. Xavier Hoff was discovered with a gunshot wound to the head. Mills deduced Verdun was the individual responsible. He was the only person with a reason to cause both of them harm. So where was he? Did the man go into hiding to avoid questions on his motive?

With Elliot out of the picture, Mills has been forced to take charge. Evacuations of citizens to the high school kicked off at daybreak. Fear permeated the citizens of Linn County and its communities. Most everyone would comply willingly, but some would refuse.

You can't save them all—an idea Mills had come to terms with.

Events over the past few months soured the close relationship the sheriff shared with his investigator, Jack. He had refused to take part in any conversations after the high schoolers were killed on Jackson Road. Carl left the man to assist the state and federal agents. It was past time to clear the air between the two of them. Jack's help at the high school was integral to managing the vast influx of county residents. They spoke privately in Mill's office.

"I could use your help on this, Jack. Those people taking shelter at the high school need you to step up," Carl opened the dialogue.

"How many people is that?" Jack replied. "Way beyond capacity of that school. Over four thousand, I estimate. A ludicrous proposition to cram people in like that. God forbid there is a fire, or any form of malintent."

"I know! We don't have the luxury of a good option. We're prisoners in this county until this is handled. The plan is set in motion. If we execute it properly, this can all be over tonight. No more living in fear or excess death," Carl said.

Jack lashed out with accusations. "Like Annie Stafle and Xavier Hoff? I went to those crime scenes. What a fucking mess. She was scorched, but had been beheaded before that. Murder and arson to cover the tracks. Hoff shot indiscriminately in the back of the head. Are you not going to pursue justice for them? For all the people who have died here? The hospital? You've lost control. Dare I say, complicit as things stand."

Finally, they were getting somewhere. Mills wasn't about to weather character assassination from a subordinate. "Tell me how you really feel. Seriously, I won't get mad. We need to get past this. So you can do your damn job and save lives."

"I think these murders broke you. Some outsider has been running the show. Given clearance above the federal agents, even? How does that make sense? Nothing has added up since Stillman's murder. The situation has only devolved from there. I'm certain Verdun is behind the murders. Yet you have acted as his lackey. I think you know that. Which makes you an accessory."

"Yeah, it's easy to make assumptions when you're not looking at the whole picture. You don't believe because you haven't been present to see what we're dealing with. Werewolves, Jack. They're real, and we have an infestation in this county. That is the truth. Plug that into your equation and see if things start adding up," Mills said.

"Werewolves?" Jack threw his hands up. "Is this an elaborate joke?"

"I don't have the luxury of naivety like you. I was at the hospital. At the Glass household. I've seen them—hell, even put bullets in one. Lend aid at the high school, Jack. I'll be there, as well. When the sun comes up tomorrow, and the dust settles, I give you my word, I will resign the office of sheriff. It's been three months, but it feels like I've aged a decade."

"Fine. I'll do security with you tonight. You will resign tomorrow, or I will. Enjoy your last day as sheriff," Jack said, leaving the office.

It was a promise Carl looked forward to keeping. A bitter end, but Mattfield needed Jack's help, and the community came first. One of his last acts made sure all of the safeguards were in place. That, Mills could live with.

A meeting of the Hunting Party was called. Erica, Keith, Lucas, and Liam joined him in the office.

"Where are we at?" Mills asked.

"Sir, the silver bullets are stored in Verdun's car. He hasn't distributed them yet. It was supposed to get done this morning. He's gone," Keith said.

"I have seven rounds left from the wolf hunt, but they're for my guns. I'll need them tonight," Liam said.

"We could have Walt make more, but there's little time. It's not like we can pick up the phone and call. He may have already reported to the high school," Mills said, dismayed by Verdun's disappearance.

"My plan remains the same," Lucas added. "I've fashioned my own arrows, and am armed with knives. I'm ready. A good balance with Gable. I will operate in silence."

Carl opened the top drawer of his desk, pulling out a magazine loaded with silver 9mm rounds, passing it off to Keith. "Let's pray Elliot shows back up. We stick to the plan. Take this, ten rounds. That's all I have," Mills said.

Chatter came across his radio. "Sheriff Mills," he answered. "What? I'll check it out, thanks." Carl ended the radio call. "Erica and Keith, I want you to get to the high school, get everyone inside. Then as planned, start your patrol."

"Who was that?" Erica asked.

"That was Patrick, a man was seen bathing in the Mattfield Reservoir. I'm going to go check it out. Jack has agreed to help at the school. I'll join him there when I get back. You two get going," Mills instructed.

"I'd better get some rest. We're in for a long night," Gable said. He departed with the two deputies.

Lucas drew a silver knife from his belt and offered the handle to Carl. "What's this for?" Carl asked.

"Just in case. You can't go unarmed against a shape-shifter," Lucas said.

"Better to be safe than sorry, I guess. Thank you." Mills took the knife.

"Be careful," Lucas advised. "Without Verdun here, we're already down an important man. We can't afford more lapses in security."

"I worry he made a miscalculation. My fear is he may already be dead," Mills confided.

"That's my fear, as well. We don't yet know what else may lie in store for us tonight. Take care, Sheriff. Victory depends on our preparation. Stick to the plan."

"There is no alternative. This must end tonight. I'd better get going," Mills said reluctantly.

He never envisioned Verdun, the self-proclaimed monster hunter, to not be in the fight. Without his leadership, hope was dwindling among the Hunting Party. None of them would admit it, but their faces said otherwise. Carl knew his did. Hours from sundown, the plan was living on a prayer.

Traffic on the roads ran in one direction toward the high school. Mills used the opportunity to speed out to the public entrance of the reservoir. He saw Martha's car in the line of vehicles. Carl had an uneasy feeling. What if someone carrying the curse reported to the school? The horrors that could unfold inside . . .

Don't think like that, he told himself. *The plan will work. It has to.*

The sheriff's truck zigged and zagged down the gravel entrance to the lake. Finally, the massive body of water came into view. An oddly calm day on the water's surface. It looked smooth as glass, a reminder that people should be out enjoying life. He desperately wanted to gift them back that liberty. Only a single white Suburban sat in the twenty-acre recreational area. Mills went straight to it.

"Are you the one who reported?" Mills asked, pulling up beside the SUV.

"Yes, sir. There was a naked man out here. You may still catch him if you're lucky," the man said. Carl recognized the fisherman as Phil Lacy.

"Get your ass to the school or I'll arrest you. Understood?" Mills commanded.

"Yes, sir. Thought I'd do some fishing while I waited for traffic to calm down. Don't want any trouble," Phil replied.

"Best get going, then," Mills finished.

The man tore off down the road.

Mills drove the sheriff's truck down to the boat ramp. No one in sight. He got out to have a look around, tucking the silver knife into his belt for good measure.

Carl scanned the shoreline, not expecting to find anyone now. To his surprise, a shirtless man stood in the tree line west of the boat ramp.

I'll be damned, he thought. *It's too late in the year for mushroom hunters.*

What on earth would someone be doing out in the brush? Liam had stumbled upon the encampment on this side of the lake. This man could be living off the grid. Wouldn't be the first time. But given the situation, Mills doubted that to be the case. His mind jumped to the only other conclusion. Armed with lead 9mm rounds in his handgun, Mills approached the suspect.

"What are you doing out here?" Mills asked as he got closer. The man didn't answer the question. He stood studying the sheriff. A ragged-looking white male probably in his forties, Mills guessed. A jumble of long, brown hair with a matching scraggly beard.

"Hey! I asked you a question!" Out of caution, the sheriff drew his sidearm.

"The wrong question. It's me who should be askin'. What brings you out here?" the man replied.

"I'm the sheriff," Mills said.

"You gonna shoot me, Sheriff? Why, we just met," the man said.

"If I have to," Mills said.

"Go ahead. Won't do you much good. But if it makes you feel more like a man, have at it."

"Why don't you come to the station with me? We can sort this out," Mills tried to reason.

"Station? You go on ahead. I'll be coming to town after dark. You can buy me a drink," the man said confidently in his thick southern drawl.

All at once, it became clear to Carl, wisdom shared by Lucas over the phone. *Out of place, out of time.* This man did not belong. Not in the sense that he wasn't from the area; he wasn't even from the modern world. Mills was engaging in conversation with a man from the 1800s. A living legend, at that—from a story almost as old as Mattfield itself. The one who kick-started the death of so many innocent lives then and now.

This was the undying man.

Chills ran down Carl's spine. After all this time, now the man showed himself. "What's your name?"

"Ain't polite to not introduce one's self first, Sheriff," the man said.

"Sheriff Carl Mills of Mattfield," he replied.

"I know who you are. Thomas told me all about things. Twenty twenty-five. I am a bona fide time traveler. Y'all don't even ride horses. What a time to still be alive," the man said.

"Your name!" Mills demanded as the tension built between them.

"Claude Previn. Back in my day, they called me the Scalper. Want to know how I earned that name?" Claude continued to taunt Mills.

He shuffled closer to Previn, keeping the gun aimed at him. A plan came to mind, reflecting on the exchange of gunfire with Morro. Gunfire didn't need to be fatal to subdue Previn. "I can guess how you got that name."

"I don't like to boast, but it is part of who I am—" Claude got cut off as Mills unloaded rounds into his chest. The man dropped to the ground in pain. "You shot an unarmed man!"

Without hesitation, Mills holstered the handgun and brandished the silver knife. He rushed Claude in an attempt to finish him. Lifting the knife above his head, Carl swung downward with a killing blow. Previn caught his wrist, redirecting the sharp blade. Carl stutter-stepped backward, the handle of the knife sticking out of the left side of his abdomen.

"No," Mills muttered, dropping onto a knee.

"Nothin' personal," Claude said, shaking his head. "I am a hard man to kill." He climbed back to his feet. Bullets cascaded from his gunshot wounds onto the ground. Mills watched wide-eyed as the wounds began to close. "I thought we were gonna be friends." Previn liked the sound of his own voice.

"Surviving for a hundred and fifty years must make you feel immortal," Mills said, wincing in pain.

"I try to stay humble. Say, that knife you got looks old. Where did you get it?" Claude asked, intrigued.

"A friend of mine. He is Osage," Mills said, trying to create an opening for attack.

"Shit, they still around? I'd sure like to pay them a visit. Thank them for what they gave to me. It was supposed to be punishment. Truth is, I like to kill. Don't care much what the skin color is," Claude said as he approached Mills. "Let me give you a hand."

Claude grabbed around Mill's shoulder and helped him to his feet. This was his last chance. In a final bid to kill the cursed man, he grabbed the knife handle and ripped the blade from his side. Blood flowed from the deep wound. Wrapping an arm around Claude, he held him tight. Bringing the knife in from the side, Carl tried to drive the blade in just below the ribs, but he was no match in strength. Previn head-butted the sheriff in the face, disorienting him. Mills stumbled away from the undying man, his back finding the bark from a tree looming overhead. His police uniform tore as he slid down the trunk back onto the ground. The sheriff's hand found the knife's handle protruding from his belly.

Claude paced back and forth, rubbing his forehead. "I ain't never killed a law-man. You have been stuck twice. You made me do this."

"Would you shut the hell up?" Mills said. Each breath brought a fresh wave of pain.

I failed the people I swore to protect.

It would take a miracle for Mattfield to pull through the coming attack. He thought of his wife. How heartbroken she would be. On the cusp of retirement, he'd died for nothing. How much time was left before dark? Carl was losing his senses.

If you are alive, the fight isn't done.

"Claude, can you do me a favor?"

"Depends," Claude said.

"Tell me your story," Mills asked. This man held the remaining answers to all of his questions. What he had to say played a part in the last chapter of the sher-iff's career. Carl found himself wanting to know the rest of the story. How they each reached these crossroads where their lives intersected. In a bid to distract Claude for time, he wanted to understand the man who took his life.

37

SINS OF THE PAST

"Forgive me. I don't remember dates in my life. If truly I was sealed away in that cave for a hundred and fifty years, well, that's like living three lifetimes.

"I had four siblings who died before they were eighteen. We grew up in central Missouri along the Current River. Pa died when I was eleven. We were a poor family before, but after his passing, we suffered greatly. When the Civil War broke out, I was the last living member of my immediate family.

"War wasn't good for much, but it filled your belly. I signed up at the beginning as a cavalry man. I was a fine soldier on horseback. Then for two years I was a prisoner of war before it ended. When it was said and done, most new friends I made were dead. Found out early on, people still paid good money for an Indian scalp in those days. Boy, I never had much, but that filled my pockets until they ran over. Biggest score my posse delivered came against the Osage. Men, women, and children. Didn't matter. Killed every last one of them. Went on the run from reprisal after that. No longer did I have to worry about where my next meal would come from. A bounty hung over my head. Funny thing is, there weren't many folks who were willing to pursue me for it. Most thanked God for my deeds against the savages, thanking God for cold-blooded murder.

"Spent a hard winter on the edge of the Rockies as I fled west. No bounty hunter ever caught up with me. That spring, I headed south into New Mexico. It was still untamed. Comanche ran wild down there. You learned to sleep with one eye open in Comancheria territory. Had my fair share of spats. Almost lost my life more than once. Fierce warriors, they are. Hell on horseback. There, my life took on a new purpose. A ragtag group of men offered me pay to assist them. A chief and his son, two Chinese twin brothers, and a bunch of white men with a freed slave. They sought revenge, each having been the victim of a baron gobbling up their lands. All of them lost their families to the baron's greed. I was repulsed by the inclusion of so many races I despised, the money was just too good to say no to. Plan was to get paid and then settle as far west as one could go. Hide away in California for the rest of my days.

"We struck against the baron. Hit him where he would feel it most. Burned the entire town he founded to the ground, and all his money with it to my displeasure. I struggle because I can't remember their names, faces, or what their voices sounded like. Just been too long. Our early success against the baron led to a colossal defeat. After pulling off that business, we sheltered in a cave for the night. Trouble was, we were followed. This became the first time I got trapped in a rock tomb. They snuck up on us in the dark. Blasted the entrance with dynamite. As the mouth of the cave came crashing down, the chief we rode with saved my life, in exchange for his own. For no reason. It was my time and he shoved me out of the way. A man I mistreated every chance I got died for me.

"A day of worming around in the dark, we found daylight, another way out, an escape from certain doom. I've forgotten a lot, but not what that chief did. How it changed me. My mind was filled with regret for the massacres I took part in. My heart saw Indians as human for the first time.

"After crawling free from that cave, the group wanted to press on against the baron. I'm sure they did. This is where I parted ways with them. I had escaped death more times than I can count. Evaded justice for all my sins. Years spent on the run. Finally, I was ready to face judgment—not by turning myself over to the law, or allowing bounty hunters to capture me, though. I had earned a fate far worse than the gallows. The Osage deserved that honor. Retribution for their slain. My mind was made up to deliver myself into their hands, to let them strike down the feared Scalper. To pay respect to the chief who gave his life for mine.

"I rode east against the current of settlers heading west in their wagon trains. Anticipation for what awaited me haunted every mile, riding horseback through hundreds of miles in the great grass sea. Many frigid nights on the cold plains. Indians at that time were being forced toward Oklahoma. The US government contained natives to plots of land while Catholic missionaries tried to civilize them. Kansas hosted the final stop for many tribes on their way south.

"I arrived in Mattfield as the weather warmed. Met with hatred as a former Confederate soldier—not unfounded, given the recent memory of the bloody border war with Missouri. There was a moment when I believed the people of Mattfield would hang me themselves. But enough level heads in leadership prevailed for my sake. Spent one night in town. At the saloon, I gathered information. A band of Osage camped on a bluff southwest of the town. My final test of resolve. Do I go through with it? I drank heavily to temper my nerves. Rode out late in the day to meet them.

"When I dismounted my horse, I was disarmed and taken hostage. A handful of them recognized me, saved me from having to introduce myself. Bound with rope between two poles, I awaited death. They sat around a bonfire in talk. It was clear there was dissent about what should be done with me. I didn't speak the language, but I have thought about their conversation. What was said. They carried on for hours. Night came and still I remained strung up. The full moon that night must have provided them with inspiration for my punishment.

"'Why have you come?' their chief asked me.

"'Atonement, to pay for my wicked deeds,' I replied.

"'You turn yourself over freely?' The chief could hardly believe the circumstances.

"'Yes. Do what you will with me,' I said.

"The chief sat quiet, then said, 'Death would be a kindness to you. We do not wish to give you that.'

"'Torture me first, then,' I told the chief.

"'My people you have killed. Your people you will kill,' the chief stated.

"'I'm done killing. That's why I'm here. No more runnin' for me,' I said.

"Out of the shadows, an enormous black wolf walked amongst the gathered tribe.

"'The wolf will set you on your new path. We curse you to walk the earth. Wherever you go, death will follow like a shadow. White man will suffer as we have. You will kill as the wolf does. You will look to your end. Death will not find you.'

"The wolf came toward me. My heart pounded in my chest. 'Take your justice against me! Just kill me!'

"The Indians rose in unison to watch as the wolf drew out its approach before halting in front of me.

"'You do not get to speak to my people of justice,' the chief insisted.

"Red eyes pierced through me, jagged teeth bared as it lunged. Sharp, agonizing pain tore into my side. I screamed. Then it was over. One bite and the beast strolled away, disappearing into the night.

"When I awoke the next morning, there was no bite mark. At first, I thought it had all been a dream. Dried blood remained on my side. Had I lost my senses? The chief came to me. He unsheathed a knife and held its blade in my face. I expected to meet my end, but instead the man cut me free, making the simple request that I remain in Mattfield a while. Another brought me my horse and sent me on my way. I chose to honor his wish. To make the nearby town my temporary home.

"I took up honest work shoeing horses. Residents of Mattfield slowly warmed to me being around. That was, until the full moon. Turning into a monster is hard to explain. To this day when it happens, I black out. Awake the next morning naked. No memory of what happened. Sometimes two nights in a row. I didn't understand what was going on. My subsequent trial led to answers. The Osage had made me immortal.

"Panic spread through Mattfield after my first transformation. Four citizens were brutally slaughtered. One young man walking home his drunk uncle. Town folk placed blame on Missouri and even the Osage. Fear does that to the mind. Causes you to look for enemies. Being a former Confederate, some fingers pointed my way. Tension hung thick over the town. The doctor concluded they had all been killed by an animal.

"The month after, I killed seven more when I turned. This time, there were witnesses who saw a wolf man. A tracker led them straight to where I slept in a stable. I was Claude again, but hadn't woken yet. Becoming a monster exhausts the body. They gave me a beating during my arrest. Held court on Main Street. Everyone showed up to see the monster. Most were disappointed. In my defense, I didn't think there was enough evidence to convict me. Judge found me guilty for eleven murders. Blood for blood. Law needed to place blame to calm the population.

"New gallows were constructed on the lawn of the courthouse. It was a public celebration when they hung me. I had made my peace. There was no escaping the hangman. My neck broke when I dropped. Dying was like falling asleep. Except I came back. Few stories existed of someone surviving a hanging. It scared them all. Whispers of me being in league with the devil circulated. A mob dragged me down to the river to drown me. Worked in the Salem witch trials. Not for Claude Previn. For the second time that day, I was put to death. Stone tied to my feet and thrown into the river. My fingertips clawed at the surface just out of reach. Next memory, I was throwing up water on the river bank. I'd died twice for my crimes. To the satisfaction of nobody.

"Put in a cell for a few days. Deprived of food and drink. When they brought me out, a pyre had been constructed. That was the worst death of all. Feeling your flesh melt from the bones. The smell of your own burning meat. Finally, the ropes that held me in the fire burnt loose. Not more than a skeleton, I walked from the pyre into a hail of bullets from those who watched in horror. Yet when I rose again, my body had healed.

"At their wit's end, they decided on permanent imprisonment. A posse rode me out to a crevasse in an open field. Must've been thirty feet down. Unceremoniously tossed in like a sack of potatoes. I crawled into a passage way at the bottom. You couldn't tell from the surface, but this was a cave system. The escape in New Mexico gave me hope of finding another way out. Thunder rang out as dust clouded my vision. Light had vanished completely. Using dynamite, they had collapsed the crevasse.

"From what I've gathered, this became my tomb for over a hundred and fifty years. Thirst and hunger caused endless suffering. A torture no human being deserves, no matter their wicked deeds. In the dark, I went mad over and over. Constantly my body and mind would be restored by the curse. Essentially finding myself in purgatory. Lost all sense of time. How long would this torment continue?

"To my shock, one morning I awoke in the daylight. Had to convince myself this wasn't heaven. I alone understand what hell is. An eternity alive in the pitch-black earth.

"I stumbled upon this lake. Set up camp and drank water until I vomited. Made a spear and ate raw bass. Deprived of humanity, I now lived like the beast lurking inside me. There was something strangely different. My mind felt connected to another, who would reveal himself to be Thomas. A man who now shared in my affliction. Thomas told me how I was set free, that he had been bitten by a werewolf. Just as my curse came from the jaws of the wolf, so did his from mine. We became friends until his death. At least I assume—because the connection we shared is gone and Thomas never returned to our camp. There are others I feel the connection with now. We have yet to meet."

Mills shifted in pain as he rested against the tree. "Thank you. That's a lot to take in. If you would have let me, you could finally rest in peace."

"You think I want to die after being locked in a cave? I was dead to this world. My sole purpose is to survive." Claude found himself offended by the remark.

Sticks cracked behind him. He spun around as an arrow cut his cheek. An Indian stood twenty feet away. Flashbacks of the red-eyed wolf ran across his mind. "Who are you?"

The Indian stood tall as a warrior. "Lucas Dream Walker of the Osage. I'm here to collect the sheriff."

"Osage!" Claude raged. "Your people made me what I am!"

Lucas reached into his quiver, producing another arrow. "I listened to your story. You were a monster long before my people cursed you. Two wrongs don't equal justice. That is why you must die, shape-shifter." Dream Walker nocked his arrow and started to draw back the bow string.

Claude snarled, "We'll see about that. After I kill you, I'll find your tribe and finish what I started." Unarmed, he would have to wait until the full moon to stand a chance. Taking off at a sprint, Claude weaved his way between the trees as he ran away. Another arrow whizzed by, slicing into his left bicep. These minor cuts from the arrows burned. He now understood the people had developed a way to kill the cursed. Some sort of metal or poison.

Claude paused in a clearing to see the setting sun. Soon the beast would come forth. He sensed the others were already in close proximity to each other. Tonight, they would join together. Mattfield would fall prey to their malice.

A debt was owed for the sins of the past.

38

LOOK INTO MY EYES

Brett grabbed his favorite black coat out of his closet, stuffing it into his school backpack. He reached between the mattress and box spring of his bed, quickly transferring the Governor from its hiding place, burying the gun within his coat to conceal it. Once more under the mattress, he revealed Marcus's silver knife, tossing it loosely on top before zipping up the backpack.

"Ready?" Michael called from downstairs.

He slung the backpack across his shoulders. "Good to go." Brett descended the staircase to join his father and Cassie by the door. "We need to stop by the Jones house on our way to the school."

"Son, is it really necessary?" Michael asked.

"I'm not asking. If you won't stop by there, I'll go myself," Brett said.

"No, I'll take you. Five minutes, then we report to the school. With all the people going, we need to find a place to settle in for the night," Michael replied.

Cassie looked at Brett with distrust. Their relationship had continued to grow more awkward as the full moon got closer. It went unsaid between them, but trust was definitely dwindling. Brett had been convinced that she was well aware of her condition. Cassie could sense he meant to stop her if she started to transform.

His father pulled into the shade of a tree in front of the Jones residence. "Five minutes, Brett. I mean it."

"Be right back," Brett promised. Backpack in tow, he went to the front door and knocked.

It took a minute for Christopher to crack the door open. "Brett? What are you doing here?"

"I've been meaning to return Marcus's knife. It belongs with your family," Brett said.

The door sprung open. "Come inside."

"I can't stay long," Brett said.

"Understood. I know everyone is heading to the high school," Christopher replied.

Brett shot a look toward his father waiting in the car. He stepped inside the Jones residence. All the windows had been covered with dark curtains. "When are you going to the school?"

Christopher came across distraught. "We're not. Stay here. Let me go to the basement and get Marcus. He's been sleeping most of the day." He left Brett standing alone in the living room.

A murmur caught his attention. "Hello?" Brett said softly. The sounds were coming from a side room. Putting his ear to the door to listen, the murmurs grew more intense. He paused to listen for Christopher, then let himself into the dark room. Verdun sat on the floor bound and gagged. "Holy shit!" Brett let out in surprise as he rushed to the man's side.

A creak came from a staircase somewhere below the floorboards. "He's coming back."

Without time to think, Brett swung the backpack off. Pulling the knife out, he put it in Verdun's hands, secured behind the man's back. "The knife is silver. Will you be able to get free?"

Verdun gave a nod.

Brett rushed from the room, quietly shutting the door again. He took deep breaths to calm himself.

Marcus walked into the living room, a face he'd last visited in the hospital. Emotions overcame him as their eyes met. Face-to-face with the boy who saved his life—the boy who'd murdered his mother.

"Dad told me everything, how you came to visit. I'm so sorry about Dalton, and then your mother. You have suffered so much. Glad to see you're still standing." Marcus couldn't hold back his emotions, either.

Regardless of what has transpired, he knew Marcus acted selflessly to protect him. Brett walked to Marcus, embracing him. "I gave up, and you saved my life. No matter what, I will always love you for that."

"Thank you," Marcus said in tears. "Stay inside tonight. Things are going to get bad."

"I know," Brett acknowledged. He released Marcus, and headed for the front door.

"We are all connected, Brett. Cassie is one of us. I know you love her. She is dangerous. A monster like me," Marcus said.

That confirmed what Brett had already accepted. He turned to look at Marcus. "I feel like I have a monster inside me, as well. I plan on doing what I have to. To keep others safe."

Marcus looked saddened by this revelation. "Monsters don't protect others, Brett. That's what heroes do."

"You don't have to be a werewolf to be a monster. There is nothing heroic about killing," Brett stated.

"Sometimes we don't get to choose. Kill or be killed. We forget how the world really is," Marcus replied.

"Welcome to Mattfield," Brett said solemnly. "Goodbye, Marcus."

He understood Verdun would likely kill his friend.

"Do whatever you have to," Marcus said in parting. "If you have regrets later, that means you're alive. Best of luck, man."

It was difficult for Brett to separate the human element from the people he knew were werewolves. They were decent human beings. Young and full of life. None of them deserve this fate. Neither did anyone else the monsters had killed. He found it difficult to justify this fight as purely between good and evil. All but one or two days a month these monsters remained human. If only there was another way.

Hundreds of vehicles overflowed from the parking lot into the ditches and road side. To Brett's surprise, most citizens had obeyed the order to spend the night in containment. Likely out of fear. Most remained unaware of what had befallen the county. They believed a group of murderers were running amuck. No fans of the government, they banded together to protect their families. A quarter-mile line filed toward the school's entrance. Walt stood to the side, awaiting them.

"Think this is going to work?" Walt asked as he joined them.

"It better. They can't keep us contained much longer before the shooting starts," Michael said.

Half an hour later, they made it inside. Marcus's uncle, Jack, gave orders where to go. "Classroom is set aside for you guys. No one else is allowed to join. List doesn't specify, but there is some concern. Dinner will be served in the cafeteria this evening. Send someone to get food. Other than that, I don't want any of you breaking containment. Understood?" Jack instructed.

"Alright," Michael agreed.

Jack passed him a key to the biology classroom. They were separated from the influx of people heading into the gymnasium.

"What's with the special treatment?" Walt asked.

"I've been around a lot of the death. They're either afraid for my safety or concerned one of us could be a monster," Brett replied.

Smart move on their part. This put distance between Cassie and a mass casualty event. Cold tile floor in the classroom would be their home for the night. No need for getting comfortable, anyways. Soon there would be running and screaming. He stood as the last safeguard, which meant he would be forced to kill the girl he loved—a thought up until now Brett had been avoiding. Cassie was the first girl he felt truly in love with.

Was he capable of doing what must be done?

There wasn't much comfort to be found in their private classroom. Brett seated himself in a corner next to Cassie. "How are you feeling?"

"I miss my parents. It feels like I'm falling, reaching out to grab on to anything that might slow me down. That night was the most scared I have ever been. Until today because now I know what's out there. What if they come back?" Cassie shared.

Why did she insist on lying to him? Brett took her hand. "Look into my eyes," he insisted. Cassie met his stare. "Remember what you said to me at the homecoming dance? Before any of this shit? Your eyes can't hide the truth from me. I can see your demons. Grab on to me. We'll get through this together."

"Are you afraid?" Cassie asked.

"Yes, but not of you. I love you. Ours is probably the worst love story ever. How you can even look at me, I will never understand. What happened to you and your parents is my fault. All my fault. To my brother, to my mother. That's who I am now. The guy that got everyone he cared about killed. Yet here I am, still standing. And for what? Marcus saved my life. Your mother saved our lives. The punishment just keeps intensifying. Stuck living in a hell," Brett said, pouring out his heart.

"Don't be like that. You haven't killed anyone. Nobody saw werewolves coming," Cassie pointed out.

"Marcus said it was destiny that we were there. My mom believed it was God's will. Truth is, it was my failures as a brother, a son, and a boyfriend. I'm the common denominator in this torment," Brett said.

"What about Sheriff Mills? Thomas Morro? LaVern Stillman? Nat Fuller? Mrs. Glass? Did you play a role in those, too? There are a lot of pieces. You aren't looking at the whole picture," Cassie rebuked him.

Yes, but how did his actions effect the others? This wasn't the first time he had thought about them. "You're right. This isn't just about me. They're going to war tonight, and I'm sitting in a classroom, even though I'm the only one of them who has ever killed a werewolf."

"You should go, then. Help them fight," Cassie encouraged.

"My part in this is here with you," Brett said.

Cassie gave him a smile. "I love you."

They both knew what was left unsaid between them. Their time together was coming to an end. A sense of calm before the storm. Brett meant to enjoy every last second by her side. They were both frightened that this would be their last night on Earth. Cassie rested her head on his shoulder. He relaxed his body against the wall and closed his eyes.

"Brett?" Michael startled his son awake. "Hey, your grandpa and I are going to get us all food. You two stay here. We'll be back shortly."

Brett nodded. Panic took over inside. How could he fall asleep? Cassie was no longer seated beside him.

Michael and Walt shut the door behind them as they left. Then he saw her standing by the only tall, narrow window in the room. "Cassie?" Brett called out anxiously.

"I didn't want to wake you. It's almost time," she replied. Cassie had her back turned to him, her attention focused to the sky.

Bolting from the floor to his backpack sitting atop a biology table, Brett dug inside for the Governor.

"He gave me permission to turn you," Cassie said.

"What?" Brett exclaimed. "Who gave you permission?"

"I don't know exactly, but he gives us orders. Tonight, we finish those hunting us. Then nothing will stand in our way. My father is alive. I'll get to see him again. You and I can be together forever. Don't you want that?" Cassie said.

He drew the revolver from the backpack. His thumb clicked back the hammer. "I don't want to become the thing that murdered my family. I'm sorry," Brett said to her. He squeezed the trigger. The hammer snapped forward, anticipation for the explosive shot that never came.

Don't fail now, Brett thought.

Repeatedly, his thumb pulled back the hammer and he squeezed the trigger. Nothing. Cassie held a hand out to her side and dropped the silver bullets onto the floor.

"I knew there was a chance you might deny me. Abandon your love for me. So I took precautions. He said immortality is not for everyone, Brett. We have to live with the choices we make," Cassie said. Her voice became demonic in nature. "You have chosen death." Cassie's body writhed as her transformation began.

Unsure of how quickly it took, Brett jumped into action. He lowered his shoulder, slamming into her at full force. The delivered hit knocked her through the window, shattering the glass. Inadvertently, he had only the wall to stop his remaining momentum. From the tile floor, he peered out to see Cassie's elongated clawed fingers digging into the grass. She grew rapidly as brown fur sprouted across her body. Brett scrambled around the floor for the silver bullets. Roars echoed into the room from Cassie. Brett spotted a bullet just a few feet away. With a shaky hand, he scooped it up. "Come on, come on!" Brett yelled aloud in frustration as he fumbled to open the Governor's cylinder.

A familiar clawed hand jutted into the room, narrowly grabbing him. Cassie had completed her transformation. Her snarling face fixed on Brett from outside. Jaws snapped enthusiastically, wanting to tear into his flesh. Her head smashed against the narrow window. To Brett's relief, due to the beast's size, it couldn't squeeze inside.

This was it. The cylinder popped ajar. He dropped the bullet in, then closed the gun. Brett stood and aimed directly at her head. "I love you."

Multiple shots rang out through the night. In the blink of an eye, Cassie disappeared just as he pulled the trigger. A round tore from the revolver, spraying dirt into the air. He had missed. Brett located the other silver bullet. As he retrieved the round from the floor, a man appeared in the window. "Brett, what the fuck is going on. What was that?"

Brett turned to see Jack Jones outside. "Werewolf. Get inside! Unless you have silver, your gun isn't going to kill it," Brett told the man. Jack squeezed through the broken window into the classroom.

"This is not happening. I owe Mills an apology. He was supposed to be here tonight." Jack struggled as he tried to comprehend the situation.

"Which way did it go?" Brett asked.

"It took off into the dark. Headed in the direction of town," Jack said.

"You need to secure this window. Get everybody who's in a room with a window to the gym or auditorium. Any access to the outside is not safe," Brett instructed. He dumped the spent round from the revolver. The brass case rang as it hit the tile floor.

He loaded the last silver bullet into the Governor. One final shot.

"You're a kid. Why do you have a gun?" Jack said in disbelief.

"To kill werewolves," Brett said. He headed toward the door to the hallway.

"Where the hell are you going?" Jack asked.

There wasn't time to explain. "My last answer works for that question, too."

"Hey! Nobody leaves! You hear me!?" Jack hollered.

Brett was already sprinting down the hallway toward the cafeteria.

Michael saw him coming with the gun in hand. "Brett! Put the gun away! Have you lost your mind?" his father scolded as he held a tray of food in each hand.

"Where are the car keys?" Brett asked.

"In my coat pocket. What are you doing?" Michael asked, annoyed.

"We were attacked in the classroom," Brett informed his dad.

"Where's Cassie? Is she alright? Are you hurt?" Michael spouted off rapid-fire questions.

With lightning reflexes, Brett reached into Michael's coat pocket, retrieving the keys. "She's gone."

Walt approached with two more trays of food. "You shouldn't have that gun out. I taught you firearm responsibility."

"I have to go," Brett said. He jogged away from them toward the school entrance. They couldn't convince him to stay so why bother arguing?

A loud clattering sound came from behind him. Michael must've dropped the trays.

"Brett!" his father cried aloud as Brett pushed through the front doors to the outside.

At a sprint, he made it to his mom's Trailblazer.

Cassie is out there somewhere. I have to find her before she hurts someone. For Dalton. For my mother. For Marcus, and everyone who has suffered.

Failure meant death. Down to his last silver bullet, Brett had literally one shot at success.

This ended tonight.

39

KARMA

At dusk, Gable took up position in the bell tower of the courthouse. Worry set in amongst the deputies after Mills failed to return from the reservoir. Verdun also had yet to return. Dream Walker was still missing, too.

"Stick to the plan. Everything else is out of our control," Liam told Keith and Erica as they set out on their patrol.

The Hunting Party had dwindled down to three members—not to mention the fact Liam had been bitten himself, a secret not shared with the others. To his surprise, the bite wound never healed. It gave him hope that killing the black wolf nullified the spread, but there was only one way to be certain. Gable mentally prepared to take his own life if he felt drawn to the full moon's power. Rifle under the chin tilted slightly to the back would put a silver bullet through his brain.

As the sun vanished across the western horizon, its counterpart rose above Mattfield. Liam gazed at the full moon's shine. He felt nothing at all. No change in attitude or consciousness. Gable let out a sigh of relief. Did this make him the first person to escape the curse? His mind flashed back to the madness he'd suffered in Nepal. Cursed to wander the earth carrying the sin of murder. Maybe a human couldn't carry two curses. Were his good deeds outweighing the evil he wrought. Doubt overcame him. If the feeling of guilt lingered, forgiveness wouldn't be achieved. And Liam would never forgive his own actions; that was for a divine judge to decide.

Gun in hand, he maneuvered around the bell atop the tower, eyes fixated on the ground for movement. Besides a few trees obscuring Main Street, his shooting lanes were wide open. Still no confirmation that any of the others were in their positions. The courthouse tower was easily defendable thirty feet in the sky. Safety became peril on the ground.

Toward the police station, Liam registered movement in the dark.

Here we go.

It appeared to be a person at full sprint. Shouldering the rifle, he directed his aim. Another, much larger, shadowy figure came into view: a werewolf in pursuit.

Who is it chasing? he wondered.

An opportunity came for a clean shot. In the midst of Liam's kill box, the werewolf paused. To his shock, the beast seemed to look right at him. A fatal mistake. He pulled the trigger. Flames erupted from the barrel. Squeals of pain came from the wounded creature below. It crawled across the grass. Gable lined up another shot, but lost the kill shot behind a tree. "Damn!" he lamented.

No other signs of movement came from the surrounding area. He considered his limited options. Leaving the tower came with inherent risk. The Hunting Party's goal was to eradicate the werewolves. What if his shot wasn't fatal? Animals tend to run a short distance when wounded before lying down to die. There was no way to be sure from the bell tower. Liam knew he had to be certain. Letting a werewolf survive put everyone in danger.

He set a timer on his smartwatch. Three minutes to confirm or finish the kill. A short interval would reduce his risk of vulnerability. When the time ran out, no matter what, he would return to his post.

Gable hit the start button for the watch to begin its countdown. He glided down the three flights of stairs back to the courthouse's main floor. The front door sat adjacent to the foot of the staircase. Cracking the door, Liam squeezed out into the night. Hunter instincts took over. Rifle at the ready, he walked down the steps to the grass, hyper-aware of what may be lurking nearby. There was no tactical advantage on the ground.

Stay calm, he told himself.

Silently, Liam moved farther away from the structural safety the courthouse provided. He reached the tree that had obscured his follow-up shot. Fresh blood glinted on the brown grass. A shiver went through his body. His hot breath fogged the air. The temperature had continued to steadily drop absent sunshine.

An old gazebo sat to his right. Across Main Street, he spotted the wounded creature's outline in the dark. Audible grunts came from the beast as it laid in the shadow of a church. Fifty yards, roughly, an easy enough shot. Gable knelt down to deliver the killing blow.

The sound of a pump-action shotgun being cycled startled him. A figure emerged from the far side of the gazebo.

Liam glanced at the black man holding him at gun point. He chose to remain aimed at the injured werewolf. "You shouldn't point guns at people. What are you doing out here?"

"That's my son you mean to kill. You already shot him," the man said.

"Your son? I saved your life," Liam said.

"Yes, his name is Marcus," the man continued.

The boy from the hospital. "I was at the hospital, you know. That's not your son. He is gone," Liam said.

"No! I've been with him for a month! He'll snap out of this!" Christopher shouted defiantly.

Liam's watch let out a beep. Time was up. "Given the chance, that thing will rip you to pieces, but I don't doubt your sincerity, sir. Walk away and let me do my job," Liam pleaded.

"Do you have children?" Christopher whimpered.

"No," Liam answered.

"Then you can't understand! He's all I have left."

Too much attention was being drawn to them by the hysterical father. "Lower your voice. There are more of them out here. I'm not asking permission. Remember your son for who he was. End of conversation," Liam said sternly.

"Shoot, and I will kill you," Christopher replied.

Damned if you do, damned if you don't. "I'm sorry," Liam said. He zeroed his sights and pulled the trigger. The werewolf, Marcus, collapsed dead on the church lawn. A flash blinded him from the side. The man had kept his word. In shock, Liam felt bird shot rip into his left arm and torso. He was no longer able to hold his gun to defend himself, his jacket now permeated with blood from the shotgun's close-range blast. Pain pulsated through his body as he curled on the ground. The man cycled the shotgun, ejecting the spent shell.

Taking a few steps closer, Christopher pointed the gun at Liam's head. "This is for my boy!"

Just then, steamy breath engulfed Christopher's head. He spun on his heel. In the commotion, another werewolf had rushed their position. The shotgun barrel was stuffed against the creature's stomach. A muffled shot punched a hole through its abdomen. Both arms grabbed Jones by the shoulders, lifting him into the air.

Liam was rendered helpless, watching in horror as the werewolf's gaping mouth tore into Christopher's collar bone. Blood ran from his elevated feet, soaking the grass.

Using his right arm, Liam dragged his body backward, but there was no use trying to escape; the fool had doomed them both.

After Liam had crawled ten feet, the werewolf tossed Christopher's body aside. Its attention then turned to Liam. Had Christopher not shot him, he could've easily killed another werewolf. Liam stopped his retreat. The monster seemed to relish his surrender, taking its time as it moved in for the kill.

"Come on!" Liam shouted.

A gunshot rang out from somewhere behind him. Blood spurted from where the werewolf's right eye had been a second before. Its dead body tipped to the side, crashing onto the ground. Toward the road, Liam saw Sheriff Mills and Dream Walker had come to his rescue.

Hope renewed in Liam. Mattfield may yet be saved.

40

TRAVELER IN THE MIST

Duct tape screeched as Lucas ran the roll around Sheriff Mills's bloody torso. "Just need to slow the bleeding. I'll get you to the hospital. Stay awake. You're going to be okay."

"Hospital may not be safe for all we know. We aren't going to make it out of here alive if we don't leave now. It's dark; his transformation may already be done," Mills said.

Lucas looked to the bright full moon in the east. "Alright, let's move." He helped the sheriff into the passenger seat of the police truck. A wolf's howl called from the trees where he'd discovered Mills. Dream Walker got behind the wheel.

"One way in, one way out. Don't let up," Mills instructed.

Plumes of dust clouded the air as Dream Walker sped down the gravel road. He saw the werewolf in his peripheral vision out the driver's side window. Stepping on the gas, the truck accelerated. "He's chasing us."

"Guess we'll find out how fast they are," Mills said.

Where the gravel met pavement, Lucas slammed the brakes, sliding the truck onto the blacktop. Minus a few slight curves, there was no slowing them down. "Home stretch. Are you okay?"

"No," Mills replied bluntly.

"A few more minutes. Just hang in there," Lucas said.

Mills sighed. "Werewolves are attacking my county. I'm not about to die from a knife wound. That'd just be embarrassing."

Humor, the great equalizer. Lucas smiled at the remark. Older generations were built different. Quitting was never an option.

They made it to the edge of town without another sighting of the werewolf. "Looks like we lost him."

"He's on his way. Stick to the plan," Mills said.

"You're going to die if I don't get you to the hospital," Lucas said.

"Do your part. I'll drive myself. You've seen combat; the others need your experience." Mills remained stubborn.

Shaking his head, Lucas gave up. "Have it your way. We'll get you in the driver's seat on Main Street."

Lucas turned onto Main Street. Up ahead, he saw the old brick buildings loom on both sides of the road. During the few weeks of preparation for tonight, a revelation had dawned on him. He hadn't escaped his fate from the dream walk. The great spirit had shown Lucas a glimpse of what awaited in Mattfield. Reflecting on the statue, he now knew the names of the men etched in stone with him. They were gathered together to do battle side by side: The Hunting Party. Dream Walker had been shown a vision of the future. Now it must come to fruition.

Amidst the downtown buildings, a familiar face dug in the trunk of his black Cadillac. "Verdun! Thank God, the man's alive." Mills's hope flourished.

Lucas put the windows down as he stopped the truck behind Elliot. "Where have you been?"

"Hostage. The Adams boy helped me escape. I thought the entire mission failed in my absence." Elliot loaded a scoped rifle, handing it to Mills. "You look terrible, Sheriff. Are you alright?"

Mills received the firearm through the truck window. "Met a werewolf, the original. I'll give you the details later. I need to go to the hospital."

"Bitten?" Verdun asked pointedly. A shot rang out in the direction of the courthouse. "Sounds like Liam is having some luck. The gun I gave you is a three-oh-eight, five rounds, sighted in at four hundred yards. Use the shots wisely."

"I was stabbed, twice. I had a silver knife, got overpowered," Mills explained.

"Best case scenario, I assure you," Elliot said.

"We'll go check on Liam. Do you want a ride?" Lucas asked.

"I work alone—protocol. It's a few blocks. I'm heading there now," Elliot said, revealing a lever-action rifle from the trunk.

Lucas felt the gun looked familiar. "Suit yourself."

Another shot echoed from the courthouse. Lucas put the truck in gear, taking off. A flash came from the lawn of the courthouse as they approached. "What the hell's going on? Who's outside?"

Mills readied the rifle to his bloodied side. "Don't get too close until we know what we're dealing with."

Not particularly keen to take the fools-rush-in approach, the warrior in Lucas itched for battle, but the soldier wished to protect his comrade. He parked the truck a hundred yards away from the scene. One man crawled upon the ground as a werewolf struggled with another. "That's Liam!" Lucas yelled.

Mills kicked open his door, resting the rifle in the passenger's side window frame. As he lined up the shot the werewolf was now fixated on Liam. A shock wave went out from the powerful .308 as he fired a shot. The recoil caused Carl to wince in pain. "Headshot. Let's go get him."

"You sure?" Lucas asked. Just then, the werewolf toppled over. "Forget I asked."

The police radio came alive with chatter. "Sheriff, this is Jack. Are you there?"

Mills snatched up the radio. "I'm here. How are things at the school?"

"Sheriff, I shot at a werewolf. I mean, that's what I saw. The Adams boy got in a vehicle and took off. Cassie Meeks is missing. That thing could still be hanging around. Looked to me like it took off toward town," Jack relayed.

"Alright, stay vigilant. Surviving the night out there is all that matters," Mills said.

"Carl, I'm sorry I didn't trust you," Jack said, his voice emotional.

"Conversation for another day, Jack. I gotta go." Mills set the radio down. "The Meeks girl, she's one of them. I'm in no condition to continue on."

What went unsaid, Lucas understood. "We'll handle this. You are no good to anyone dead." He got out, securing his bow and quiver from the back seat.

"Take the radio, and good luck," Mills said with gratitude. "In case I don't make it, know that I appreciate what you've done here. It takes a real man to put his life on the line for others. It takes a hero to do that for people he has no loyalty to."

Lucas looked to the sheriff with admiration. "My purpose in life has been to protect the innocent. I knew that early on. To my detriment, mostly. It doesn't matter to me what happened in centuries past. My people didn't deserve their suffering back then. Your people don't deserve this. It does not take a hero to see that. So I traveled here to kill the shape-shifter my people created out of vengeance. I don't fault my ancestors, for those days were harsh, but if we continue to carry the wrongs of the past, we have no future. Bitterness and hatred destroy the soul. Forgive, but never forget. Understand what has been and what can be. That's how we unite. History as our lesson. We are all one tribe."

Lucas helped the wounded man to the driver's seat. The sheriff drove away toward the hospital.

Dream Walker saw that Elliot had come to Liam's side while he'd been speaking with the sheriff. He hustled over to join them. "Are you alright? We need to get him inside. Sitting ducks out here."

"I've been shot," Liam said, gripping his bloody arm.

Using the radio left to him, Lucas called: "Keith, Liam has been shot at the courthouse. He's going to need a ride to the hospital."

Static blared from the radio. "Hang tight. On our way," Erica answered.

"I need to assess how bad it is," Lucas said.

"I'm fine," Liam assured.

"You are not. A close-quarter round from a shotgun can be fatal. Let the man have a look," Elliot said, concerned in a brief glimpse of his humanity.

Unsheathing a silver knife from his waste, Lucas cut Liam's shirt at the shoulder, then ripped it off, revealing the shredded flesh. He noticed a bandage on the man's forearm.

"When did you get wounded before?" Verdun asked, noticing it, as well.

Worry flashed on Liam's face. "H-hunting the wolf," he stuttered.

Another blast of static came from the radio. Erica's voice came across again: "Guys, we have eyes on a werewolf in the downtown area heading your way. We're going to engage."

Lucas looked over his shoulder. "That's three blocks from here."

"Go. I'll tend to this. That should be the last of the beasts," Elliot said.

"No, an incident got reported from the high school, as well. The Adams boy gave pursuit. Last update we got," Lucas shared.

Elliot contemplated this. "Liam says there are two werewolves dead here. If neither are the original, we're dealing with at a minimum two more."

He slid the knife back in its sheath. "About to be one fewer."

"Take a gun," Elliot said.

The thought had crossed his mind. "Our fates have been decided. I'll go out on my own terms."

"Are you insane?" Liam asked.

"I trust the great spirit. We will have victory," he said with confidence.

Lucas departed, leaving the men to ponder his words. He ran like the wind down Main Street. Anticipation grew for the battle ahead. These past few months rekindled the pride for his Osage heritage. Set to walk in the path set by his ancestors, guided by the hands of the great spirit, leading the charge into the unknown. A traveler in the mist.

The police cruiser sat horizontally across Main Street. Keith and Erica were outside, firing upon the monster. Their missed shots whizzed by him and ricocheted off the asphalt. Being down range was a death sentence. He kept his course, though, never catching a stray bullet. It was as if Lucas had an aura of protection around him. At thirty yards, he drew an arrow from his quiver.

He'd arrived too late to save the deputies, who were overwhelmed. Keith's body was flung backward, smashing into the side of the police car.

Erica, a fresh magazine in her pistol, came to his defense. She dumped rounds rapidly into the monstrous creature at point blank, to no avail. The werewolf stooped low, then brought its clawed hand rushing upward, delivering a fatal blow that impaled her. In its triumph, the beast held Erica high in the air, wriggling its fingers protruding from her back.

Lucas let an arrow fly, slashing off the left ear of the distracted creature. It gave a menacing snarl as it tossed Erica's lifeless body to the ground.

He nocked his next arrow as they exchanged glares. The werewolf stomped a foot forward, issuing a hair-raising roar. Lucas drew back and released his second arrow. To his shock, the monster almost caught it mid-flight. Lucky for him, the arrow ripped through the palm of its right hand. It gave a snort, studying the situation.

Dream Walker quickly nocked a third arrow. Without warning, the werewolf then charged straight at him. Drawing back his third shot, Lucas rushed forward. Every move had to be precise to survive in hand-to-hand combat. He would have to inflict a more grievous wound.

At ten yards, the werewolf launched forward into the air to tackle him. With his momentum, Lucas dropped into a baseball slide. His third arrow pierced the beast's belly as it glided overhead. Dream Walker dug his heals into the pavement to pop back onto his feet in one swift motion, spinning around to face his freshly wounded foe.

With its uninjured hand, the werewolf ripped the blood-soaked arrow from its stomach, tossing it aside. Lucas reached for a fourth, but the beast'd had enough. It came at him with a wild swing of its paw. Reflexively, Dream Walker used his father's bow to block. Impact from the hit snapped his weapon in half. A follow-up swing from the clawed hand forced him to roll to the side. He unsheathed the two silver knives from his belt, using the reverse knife grip technique. An easy stab is off the table this way, but any blow delivered would cause catastrophic damage.

Within striking distance of the creature's prolonged arms, Lucas stood his ground, weaving like a boxer to avoid the slash of its claws. At the opportune moment, he delivered a slice to its chest with his right-hand blade. This sent the werewolf into a fury. Its left leg rose up, nimbly delivering a powerful blow to his chest. The impact robbed him of breath, his ribs cracking. Dream Walker soared backward, bouncing violently off the pavement. Most of the arrows left in the quiver scattered.

Gasping for air, Dream Walker clambered to stand up. His assailant closed the gap, taking another swipe. Ducking the blow unsuccessfully, claws tore across his back. Adrenaline masked the pain.

Knives still clutched tightly, Lucas saw an opportunity to finish the fight. The werewolf took a kill shot, windmilling its arm downward. He dove past the beast, neatly avoiding the razor claws. From behind, Dream Walker drove the knives inward with all the physical strength he could muster, feeling them sink into the flanks of the werewolf's abdomen. A torturous scream split the night, reverberating between the buildings. It twirled around with a backhanded slap that sent him airborne yet again. Metal dented under his back as Lucas landed on the police car hood.

Pommels from the silver knives protruded from the creature's sides. In a fit of rage, it contorted violently. Fresh wounds kept the beast distracted. Lucas slid his feet back onto Main Street. His fingers grasped the last arrow from the quiver. Battling exhaustion and injury, Dream Walker broke the arrows shaft across his knee, tossing the fletched half aside. The werewolf didn't appear to tire—otherworldly stamina that couldn't be matched.

Armed only with six inches of wooden arrow shaft tied to an antique silver arrowhead, this was his last stand.

A path to victory was made clear for him.

I accept my fate.

Glancing at the full moon, he took a deep breath of cool autumn air. Arrowhead wielded in his right hand, he rushed in for the kill. The werewolf took a step to meet him. They went for the kill simultaneously. Lucas brought his left arm up in defense. Dagger claws sliced clean through the bone below the elbow, severing off his forearm. Dream Walker drove the arrowhead straight through the werewolf's throat. Clawing at its neck in distress, blood drooled from its jaws. The monster toppled to the ground as it writhed.

Lucas fell to his knees. He had no energy left to tie a tourniquet. Blood oozed from his severed stump. The werewolf went limp as it succumbed to the silver-inflicted wounds.

A warrior's death.

Dream Walker awaited his turn for eternal rest.

41

PRIDE

Brett Adams provided the silver knife that facilitated Verdun's escape. All Verdun had to do was wait. At dusk Marcus began his transformation, and Elliot cut himself free. With Christopher distracted, he dove through a window, shattering it. Preparation was everything for survival. A spare key magnetically attached under the driver's wheel well made for a quick getaway in the black Cadillac. The full moon hung overhead as Verdun drove to Main Street. Valuable time had been lost. There would be more werewolves to contend with than Elliot had envisioned.

As he began arming himself the injured Sheriff Mills arrived with Dream Walker. Providing the sheriff with a rifle, Elliot went on foot taking the dark alleyway down to the courthouse. He determined the area secure before approaching the bloodied Liam who laid injured on the ground. Dream Walker had joined them shortly, inadvertently revealing a bite Liam had concealed from Elliot. As Dream Walker raced toward downtown to assist the deputies, Elliot was left to deal with Liam.

"Tell me," Elliot said.

"The black wolf attacked camp. I got bit. Then I killed the wolf. My wound never healed. It's a full moon, but I didn't become one of them," Liam said.

This was a peculiar development. "Keeping that a secret put this entire night in jeopardy."

"Maybe so, but it worked out," Liam reminded him.

Elliot stood up to check out the other bodies. A middle-aged white male wasn't far from Liam. Gunshots erupted from the downtown area. He needed to wrap this up and get moving. The man who'd held him hostage lay bitten on the ground.

"It feels good to be on this side of the gun," Elliot said.

"My son didn't deserve to die," Christopher said, struggling.

"I'll take your word for it. This naked white man, the werewolf that bit you?" Elliot asked.

"Paul Meeks. His daughter went to school with my son. I should've killed you!" Christopher barked.

"Yes," Elliot replied slinging the gun across his back. He revealed the Jones's family heirloom from inside his jacket.

Christopher was shocked to see Elliot in possession of the silver knife. "That has been in my family for a very long time. Give it to me."

Elliot knelt down as if to hand over the knife. "As you wish," Elliot said, tightly grabbing Christopher's bloody shoulder as he plunged the silver blade between the man's ribs into his heart.

"The boy's body is across the street," Liam said not acknowledging the execution.

"I saw that. You've done your fair share to save this town. I'm sorry it ends this way," Verdun said, strolling back to him.

"Are you going to kill me? What about The Hunting Party? The Adam's boy? Where does it end?" Liam asked.

There was no need to draw out the conversation. "When the threat is neutralized."

"You're going to die then?" Liam asked.

"I know that you die, Liam," Elliot said.

"Look at me. I'm not one of them! Why did you let Mills go if you plan on murdering us all? That's your plan, isn't it? From one killer to another—you can't hide your intentions from me," Liam said.

"That's a risk I'm not willing to take. I would've been met with resistance. It will be easier to finish up with Dream Walker and you out of the way," Elliot explained.

Liam realized there was no reason to argue. His mind was made up. "I fear what awaits me on the other side, but it's what I deserve. They haunt my dreams. Maybe I'll get to haunt yours."

"We're different in that regard. Mine don't haunt me. I kill to save lives." Elliot cycled the lever, and took aim at Gable.

"I made the same excuse. The real difference is, I realized I was wrong," Liam said, shutting his eyes.

This was a man Elliot admired and understood. It was the heaviest pull of the trigger he could remember.

Liam fell back lifeless upon the courthouse lawn.

In his notebook, he wrote hastily to record the courthouse scene and kills. Enthused by the progress, he repeatedly wrote the word "deceased" beside names recorded in the notebook. His attention then turned to downtown.

As he got closer, he saw an intense struggle taking place between man and beast. Why had Lucas been so naive as to not use a firearm? Foolish, to say the least. The black Cadillac gave Elliot cover to observe the struggle at a safe distance without being noticed, deciding it best to let the fight play out to its inevitable conclusion.

Dream Walker held his own in hand-to-hand combat, fighting with animosity that rivaled that of his apex foe. In a final exchange of blows, Lucas suffered grievous injury. A poetic trading of lives. The werewolf collapsed to the ground, succumbing to its silver-inflicted wounds.

Elliot felt euphoric about how this night was panning out. Normally, he was responsible for the monster deaths. Mattfield had produced a host of willing sacrifices for their community. A pleasant change to be out of harm's way. All the glory would still be his. He wouldn't let anyone else survive to say otherwise. As usual, history would be written by the victor.

Dream Walker knelt on his knees as if in prayer.

"Masterclass of a fight," Elliot said to the Osage warrior.

"It is done," Lucas said in anguish. Blood pooled beneath him from the amputation.

"You did this community a great service. No need for you to suffer until death." Elliot shouldered the rifle, the barrel inches from Lucas's head.

Lucas's eyes fixated on the rifle, then he gave a nod of approval. Fear wasn't in his nature.

"Very well."

Elliot clicked back the hammer and pulled the trigger. Dream Walker's lifeless body fell sideways onto the asphalt.

Going to inspect the deputies, he found Keith still alive. Elliot leaned the officer forward to inspect for werewolf-related injuries. To his surprise, the man seemed unscathed.

"Having trouble breathing. I think my ribs are busted. Probably a concussion. Erica, is she—" Keith said under duress.

It didn't take a medical degree to see the hole punched through her sternum was fatal. "She's dead."

"No. I was knocked unconscious. I failed her. It should be me," Keith cried.

Elliot assessed the situation. "You loved her."

Keith nodded. "Yes, but I never told her. I was afraid."

"She gave her life so you could live, it appears," Elliot told the deputy.

A distant gunshot split the night air. Verdun looked south toward the edge of town.

"I don't know if I can live with myself," Keith said.

The deputy's firearm laid on the ground a few feet away. Verdun scooped it up and made sure it was loaded. He took Keith's hand, pressing the pistol into his palm. "There is no shame in that. Join her." Elliot walked away, leaving the wounded man to his own devices. He didn't see a reason to kill deputy Sparts. Instead, he sowed the seeds of chaos. Let the man determine his own fate. An inconsequential servant of the cause.

Getting behind the wheel of the Cadillac, Elliot drove south down residential streets. The last unaccounted piece was Brett Adams. If he could find and kill the boy, this case would come to an assured end. Verdun thought it safe to imagine being on a plane bound for Bastion headquarters before sunrise. A success of this magnitude would solidify Elliot's place as a legend among his peers. Nothing would prevent his ascension to leader of the organization.

Hawes's moral compass tied the hands of Bastion's members. That would soon change. Evil must be fought on level ground. No restraint, no remorse, and no quarter for those who stand between eradication of the wicked.

4 2

THE FALL

Coming into town, Brett saw the newly transformed Cassie. With only one silver bullet left, he couldn't get led into a trap. If he ended up faced with multiple werewolves—game over. Devising a way to draw Cassie's attention to keep her away from downtown Mattfield, a crazy thought came to mind.

What other choice do I have?

Brett accelerated his mother's car. Cassie's monstrous new appearance trotted along the roadside in the ditch. With a jerk of the steering wheel, Brett intentionally wrecked this time. His mom's Trailblazer became a missile. Leaving the highway, he plowed straight into her, sending the werewolf flying out of sight. The car's momentum launched it out of the ditch, farther away from the road, brought to rest when it plowed into a towering tree hard enough to deploy the airbag, which knocked him silly.

The driver's door screeched open as he exited, shaken up. Steam poured into the air from the smashed radiator.

What a stupid idea, Brett thought.

On foot in the dark with a werewolf—for the third time. All of a sudden, he was regretting his actions.

Morro took two shots to kill. To head toward town was the safest choice.

Use your shot in self-defense if necessary.

Stranded out here unsure of Cassie's location heightened his anxiety. Brett kept the highway in sight without leaving the trees' cover.

No matter what anyone else told him, there was nothing to shake the guilt he felt. The more time he sat idle, lost in thought, the more his guilt grew. In reality, he never gave Mattfield a fair shot. His mother had retreated home as an escape, to recover from a broken heart. Dalton gave her the support she deserved. Brett rubbed salt in the wound without remorse at every opportunity, ostracizing his family and crippling their ability to heal.

His peers sensed that Brett didn't want to belong. A self-proclaimed outsider, reacting maliciously when all they wanted was for him to be one of them. The entire ploy of going down Jackson Road was out of spite and revenge. One by one, they paid the ultimate price for it. Brett failed to save a single person. Payback felt so petty when others suffered worse than you anticipated, which was almost certainly the case each time one sought to get even for a perceived wrong. Innocent lives got caught in the crossfire. Dalton never did anything wrong without Brett's influence.

Two wrongs created a domino effect that spiraled toward destruction until someone was willing to forgive. Still, Brett persisted in his bitterness. An argument with his father led to his mother's death. Instead of being there to save her, he sought refuge with Cassie. Even worse, that hatred toward Michael killed Cassie's parents and turned her into a monster. Alone in the dark described more than his current situation. Brett's actions brought him here. And now Cassie had to die for those mistakes like so many before her. She would be the last. Hate could no longer be the driving force behind his decisions, to persist when everyone around him perished, left wondering if he would ever be able to live with himself. . . .

A distant howl snapped him back to reality. Crossing the highway, Brett found himself on the southern edge of Mattfield. Light from the full moon illuminated the enormous steel grain silos. This compound would provide shelter until sunrise. Steel caged ladders ran up the side of the massive grain bins to catwalks suspended forty feet above the ground. Conserving energy for the climb, Brett jogged down the Ag Co-op's gravel drive toward the nearest ladder.

Suddenly, Cassie burst forth from the trees in pursuit. Brett found a new gear at a dead sprint, but was no match for a werewolf's innate speed on open terrain. He slammed into the ladder, skipping rungs as he reached the steel cage ten feet up. To his surprise, the cage had a padlocked door preventing unsupervised climbers. Cassie reached up to drag him down. Her claws barely missed their full grab, cutting into his left ankle as they glanced off. Using one hand to cling onto the ladder, Brett drew the Governor.

Fearing the wild inaccuracy his shot would have in this situation, he concentrated on lining up the sights. With a cacophonous boom, the last silver bullet was expended.

Whimpers of pain came from Cassie. There was no way to be certain his shot landed as more than a mere flesh wound. Using his upper body strength, Brett hoisted himself onto the outside of the steel cage. Carefully choosing his holds and footing, he scaled the ladder's cage upward. Adrenaline coursed through his veins. A mere forty feet made him realize the pure insanity of free solo climbers.

Feeling relieved when his feet touched down on the catwalk at the top, he had a moment of reprieve to inspect his throbbing ankle. Blood stuck his blue jeans to the injury like glue.

A vibration went up through the ladder as metal clanked below. Brett looked over the side of the minimally railed catwalk. Cassie had ripped open the ladder cage, her werewolf body crammed in the cage, shimmying higher.

Brett never imagined the possibility. Frantically, he scoured the catwalk for options. No tools, weapons, or other way of escape. Taking a leap of faith from this height was suicide. he backed to the end of the catwalk as she neared the top. Maybe he could just squeeze past her, get inside the ladder cage.

With a bum ankle, sure.

Like a game of chess, the current situation put him in check. Cornered, in wait of the queen to end their game.

Arms emerged from the ladder cage. Grotesque claws he had become all too familiar with gripped the railing. Soon, her entire brown fur body slithered onto the catwalk. She rose up, immense. If not for the murderous intention,

Brett could almost appreciate the majesty of these monsters.

"Cassie, if you're in there, please . . ." Brett said.

Those predator eyes lacked humanity. She took a step closer with a taloned foot.

Brett found himself becoming emotional. There was no escape from this. Nor did he deserve to keep skirting consequences. Tears filled his eyes. "Cassie, I love you. I am so sorry this happened to you. This is my fault. My family, your family, and your friends. I was so angry. I became a monster myself. The worst kind. I was in control. I blamed my dad for my choices. It was all me. I know that now."

Marcus plummeting into the quarry flashed in his mind.

Brett lowered his shoulder, bursting forth headlong at Cassie, her wingspan too great to overcome. A clawed hand wrapped around his throat lifting his feet from the catwalk deck. Feet dangling, he struggled for air. Hot breath preceded the puncture of teeth sinking deep into Brett's rib cage. "No!" he gurgled.

Somewhere in the dark below, a loud pop ended their struggle. Cassie's bite relaxed as his feet suddenly dropped back onto the catwalk. Brett saw the life leave her eyes. Blood erupted in waves from a bullet hole in the side of her wolf-like head. Brett struggled to free his throat from the dead grip of her hand. When she toppled sideways, he inadvertently got dragged over the rails with her dead weight, directly on top of the werewolf as they fell back to Earth. He landed on top of her when they smashed into the ground.

When he opened his eyes again, he was lying on his back in the dirt, Cassie's werewolf body a few feet away. She started the process of reverting back to human, just as Morro had. Brett's body felt broken when he attempted to move, unable to look at Cassie's dead face as it became more recognizable.

He managed to turn his head. A pair of black boots strode toward him.

"It's a real shame. Sorry I waited for her to take a chomp of you before I shot. You're on my list of names. Regardless, I was going to have to kill you, Brett. This makes it easier for both of us. I can say you carried the curse, and you don't have to live with all the awful things that have happened," Verdun said confidently. "This is Cassie. See, we didn't know about her. I'm over seventy-five percent sure she's the last one. Well, minus you, that is." The man had his notebook out, scribbling inside.

"Please," Brett murmured.

Verdun ignored his plea. He snapped shut the notebook and tucked it away. In a single motion, he retrieved the rifle slung across his back and cycled the lever. "Last words? I don't usually do this, but you caught me in a good mood. We achieved something in this town that has been plaguing humanity for generations. You are the last feral werewolf. Think of that. Your death will make the history books. What an honor to be in your midst."

This man fights for the greater good?

Brett's pain had started to alleviate. The curse was healing his body. "You're a psychopath."

"Come on, I want something good to write. Don't make me have to fabricate the whole thing," Verdun said.

Faced with the inevitable, Brett decided to give the man what he wanted. Words he needed to say. An opportunity he looked forward to, that seemed out of reach. "Tell my father I forgive him, that I'm sorry."

A smile spread across Verdun's face. "I shall tell him. I plan on seeing your father and the sheriff to wrap up business on my way out of town." Elliot took aim.

Brett laid motionless, staring down the barrel. He thought of being reunited with Dalton, his mother, and Cassie. Should they be so lucky. Never one to take religion seriously, he found himself wondering if God would forgive him in this late hour.

The final shot fired in Mattfield went off with a crack. Its repercussions ignited a spark that carried nine thousand miles.

43

DUST IN THE WIND

Mattfield waited with bated breath each full moon. Those days came and went with no incident. Mattfield's trauma led to a mass exodus of the population. Whispers of monsters permeated the news cycle. Highly experienced with cover-ups, the military came in to do clean-up. Martial law was enacted for a short term. Rumors of a chemical spill that caused mass hysteria became the dominant story. There was no evidence left to suggest werewolves had ever walked the Earth.

Actual eye witnesses were few and far between. Anyone who spoke out had their reputation annihilated. It was an event in due time that would rival the Roswell crash—a vast conspiracy theory with even less evidence that it happened at all. Upon death, werewolves became human once more. Impossible to claim something as real when the evidence destroys itself.

Resigned to retire in peace, Mills vowed to never speak publicly about it.

The torch passed to Jack Jones, who stepped into the role of sheriff, which was met enthusiastically by the public. Though the man had a change of heart at the end, his pushback and vitriol toward Mills during the events solidified his popularity. Privately, they mended their relationship. In the best interest of the county, Jones continued to criticize the previous leadership. As much as it hurt him, Carl gave his blessing to do so.

He'd given his constituents everything in the fight. Almost paid with his life, having undergone emergency surgery and spending eleven days in the hospital battling an infection from his stab wounds.

His tenure as sheriff closed with a whimper instead of an earned celebration. When resigning leadership, he made a final request: for a statue to be made in honor of those who gave their lives to be built next to the 'Welcome to Mattfield' sign. Actions that would never be recognized. Heroes to the bitter end. With Jack's help, the statue got approval. People would look upon their faces etched in stone and wonder who they were. Guardians of the innocent. Erica being a local hero, received a flower bed memorial to honor her memory on the court house lawn.

Carl stuck around town until the statue's unveiling. To little fanfare, he gave the dedication speech:

"We all dream. Of what tomorrow holds, the future, and our descendants. This statue represents individuals who surrendered their dreams. Not in a bid to gain power, money, or recognition. No, they came from different walks of life. From far and wide, they gathered here. In our darkest hour. When all hope was gone. It is my greatest honor to dedicate this statue to their memory, as a reminder of their love poured out for their fellow man. May we each strive to show no fear in the face of evil. To never forget that love is still the answer more than hate will ever know."

Box in hand, Carl walked outside, loading it into the U-Haul. Martha was busy boxing up the kitchen. They had been steadily making progress over the last few days. Soon they would begin their three-day migration to their forever home in Florida. A for-sale sign stood along the road. He feared a quick sell wasn't in the cards, but financially, they would manage.

Carrying boxes was taking its toll. In his old age, the stab wounds were still presenting pain almost a year out—a small price to still be standing above ground.

An all too familiar black Cadillac pulled into the driveway.

So, the day has finally arrived.

Mills had anticipated this visit. Lately, he'd wondered if it was, indeed, coming. Today was as good a day as any.

A bald man with a gray beard got out of the car. "Going somewhere?" the man asked as he approached.

Carl greeted the man with a handshake. "We're moving to Florida to be near our grandkids. I'd introduce myself, but you know who I am."

"Do you know who I am?" the man asked.

"I know who you're with. You're here about Verdun," Mills said.

The man nodded, "Phillip Hawes, I'm the head of Bastion. There are some things I'd like to address, if you have the time." His tone was polite.

"Sure, we can inside." Mills led him into the kitchen. "Hey, Martha, I have some business. Do you mind running to the diner and grabbing lunch?"

"Hello. Yeah, I can do that. I'd offer to make coffee, but I've boxed up the maker," Martha said cheerily.

"That's okay, thank you," Hawes said.

Hawes took a seat at the dining room table. Martha grabbed her keys and left them alone. Mills retrieved the black notebook he had stashed away, handing it over to Hawes as he took a seat across the table. "Kept that safe. It took you longer than I expected to come looking."

Opening the book, Hawes started flipping through pages, reading. "Thank you for securing this. These are vitally important tools."

"He enlisted me to help," Mills said.

"Be glad it's me who made this trip. My organization has some bad eggs. When Elliot didn't return, this was the best-case scenario," Hawes said.

"I appreciate that," Mills said.

"Do you know what happened to him?" Hawes asked.

"Not for certain, but I think I have the gist of it. He suffered a fatal shot to the head. We buried him in the cemetery, no headstone yet. Best guess, Michael Adams killed him to protect his son. A lot of what Elliot did is recorded in there. Some revisionist history, to be sure. I filled in the missing blanks on the back pages of what I witnessed and uncovered," Mills shared.

Phillip nodded as he continued to read. "No incidents reported since that night. Case closed, then. It's impossible to replace a man of Verdun's caliber. Sad to see him murdered by a man when he faced monsters by trade. This Michael, do you know where he is?"

"In the pages I filled out, he bought two plane tickets to Australia before the dust settled. Out of fear, I assume, he fled with his son. I have no updates after that." Mills decided early on he would be as transparent as possible. These were dangerous people who would discover the truth whether he told them or not.

"Australia, now that *is* interesting. There were reported sightings of a creature in the Gibson Desert, but that was months ago. Do you believe the boy to have been bitten?" Hawes asked.

"I don't have proof either way. I'd hate for this to happen somewhere else. Is that something you can take care of?" Mills questioned.

"No, the risk on that continent is inherently more dangerous. In full transparency, a known pack of werewolves reside there, but not feral like what your community dealt with. Somehow they are able to maintain a form of control. Imagine your experience, but against human-level intelligence. We have a protocol. We don't hunt them because we can't afford to lose all our men. They rarely kill humans, and never spread the curse. A stalemate we've been comfortable with for a long time. It's possible they took care of the boy themselves," Hawes said.

Apex predators with heightened intelligence. Carl wished he could forget everything about the dark underbelly of the world around him. "What else do you want to know?"

"Your deputy, is he deceased?" Hawes asked.

"No, last I heard Keith took up work on a drilling rig in West Texas. Put himself in exile after his partner, Erica, died. A real shame—the young man had a bright future in law enforcement. I'm afraid he may never recover from the heartbreak." Carl had tried on numerous occasions to reach out, but never got a response from his former deputy.

"This property southwest of town—Elliot put it on our radar. From his notes, it appears he was for certain of the dangers there. By tomorrow, we'll have the land rights under our control. A group of contractors will have a high-voltage fence up within a few days. Locations like that must be secure to prevent further incidents." Hawes spoke of the infamous Indian House property. "Just reading, you encountered the man who started all this. What was he like?"

"Strangely human," Mills said of Claude Previn.

"Most monsters are. As a sheriff, you understand that," Hawes said.

There was one question Carl felt hanging over him the past year. "What about me? I've read the notebook. I know what Elliot had planned."

Phillip leaned back in his chair, rubbing his gray chin. "You, Mr. Mills, are free to live out your days. Enough time has passed to know you pose no threat. The work we do, sometimes these men get carried away in an abundance of caution. It's clear that your death would have been unfounded. So, my advice: Put this all behind you as best you can. Enjoy your grandkids. Feel safe knowing that men continue to fight evil wherever it may roam so your grandchildren can grow up naive, as you were before any of this."

The impending doom that had lingered for months dissipated. Carl let out a sigh of relief. "I will. Thank you for all that you do."

Hawes stood to leave. "You should've included yourself in that statue. In a generation, people will forget that you stood with them."

"I didn't earn the right to stand next to them in stone," Mills said.

"When I arrived, that statue told me all I needed to know about you. You were willing to give your life for the innocent, same as them. Heroes don't have to die, Mr. Mills," Hawes said.

"I'm alright with being forgotten. Same as you," Carl replied.

"All we are is dust in the wind." Hawes gave him a nod and left the house.

Their earthly possessions loaded, Carl and Martha departed, leaving the decades of memories made in their countryside home behind. They made one last pass down Main Street, heading east. For his entire life, this was all Carl knew. It was time to leave Mattfield behind. Today closed the chapter he thought retirement would.

Exiting town, he couldn't bring himself to look in the rear-view mirror. Bright blue sky and open roads beckoned them forward.

A fresh start lay just ahead.

EPILOGUE

9,000 MILES

Breath held, crosshairs aligned with the man's head, Michael pulled back on the trigger.

I have lost everything.

As the gun went off, he awoke. First light from the sun shone on the tent. Brett was still fast asleep next to him. Barefoot, he stepped outside onto the sand. Barren desert stretched as far as the eye could see in every direction.

Milling around camp, restless in the early morning, his dreams had been the same ever since taking Verdun's life. Michael cooked bacon and eggs over a portable camp stove. His mind captivated to find a solution, to save the last member of his family. Unhappy with the ideas he formulated, options were scarce, so leaps of faith would have to be taken.

They had been in remote Australia for almost a month, hiding out in the Gibson Desert. Tonight, the full moon would rise.

Brett popped out of the tent, giving a stretch. "That smells good."

Michael gave his son a smile. "Best I can do out here. Eat. We need to talk."

"About what?"

"The road ahead. For both of us. This is just a temporary solution. I can't let this be the rest of your life," Michael said.

Brett took a bite of bacon. "Do you think Mom will forgive us? I dreamed about her last night. They never let us bury her. She deserves better. To be next to Dalton."

This made Michael grow emotional. "Your mother would understand. Protecting you matters more than anything."

"I know that. I'm a monster now. Like, a real one. You saved my life, but I don't know if it was the right thing to do."

Michael remembered the promise he made to never abandon his family again. An impossible choice had to be made. "I won't surrender. Not until I'm sure there's no other way."

"I'm scared. What if I hurt someone. I don't want that." Brett had faced the werewolves over and over. He feared inflicting that on innocent people.

"That's why we're in the desert. There are communities, but as long as you can't reach them before sunrise, things should be fine. It's your responsibility to separate from civilization for the full moons, until I can fix this," Michael instructed.

Brett looked Michael in the eyes. "How can this be fixed? Dad, I'm cursed."

"My plan is to go to Europe. I have established a contact at the Vatican. They'll scour the archives. That man I shot carried a journal. He's part of a group called Bastion. I'm going to try and find them."

There was hesitation in Brett's voice. "Wouldn't Verdun have cured me if it was possible?" Then what Michael had said fully hit him. "You're going to leave me here alone?"

"Please, Brett. If I do nothing, eventually someone will die. It will be Mattfield all over again. This is the best I've come up with," Michael told his son. Inside it felt like he was abandoning Brett once again.

After a minute in contemplation, Brett relented. "Alright, I trust you. It's worth a shot. But what if there's no cure for this?"

"We cross that bridge when we get there. I'm your father. I will die trying to save you," Michael said.

"That man you killed. He asked me if I had any last words. I told him to let you know that I forgive you. I do forgive you, Dad. You need to forgive yourself, too." Brett wiped tears from his cheek.

Michael took those words to heart. "I will have time to work on that when you're better. I have to leave soon. Staying around close will only hinder our chances of finding a solution." He went and dug in the back of the Toyota 4Runner he'd rented. Brett's face lit up when he withdrew a football. "For old times' sake?"

"Just don't throw out your arm," Brett said.

"I'm not *that* old." Michael laughed.

They played catch together for over an hour, reminiscing about the newly minted Kansas City Chiefs dynasty. For a moment, they were able to forget the immense sadness that haunted them. A father playing catch with his son. This feeling would propel Michael in his mission.

"Football was going so well, I thought for sure I was going to play with Patrick Mahomes," Brett joked.

"That would've been something. You'd be like my second or third favorite Chiefs player," Michael replied.

This buckled Brett over in laughter. "Thanks, Dad."

After staying longer than anticipated, Michael loaded up to leave at noon. He refused to say goodbye to his son. "I'll see you soon, I promise." It was the best he had to offer.

As he drove away, Brett got smaller and smaller in the rear-view mirror. Michael sobbed uncontrollably for a while. Then he thought of his wife, Julia.

Be strong, fight for your family.

Determination kicked in.

Brett is not dead. He carries a heavy burden. You are the only person who can save him. This is what being a father means. Going to the ends of the earth for your children. You already killed a man. Where do you draw the line? Does a line even exist?

That was a question he hoped wouldn't get answered. How many would die so his son could live? Limits were bound to be tested on this journey.

It's hard to know what you're capable of until you're faced with the choice.

Michael feared losing his soul along the way.

Even so, that was a sacrifice he was willing to make.

ACKNOWLEDGEMENTS

My wife Anh, this has been a journey. Your reaction when you began to read the book for the first time is one of the most special moments of my life.

My parents Joe and Stacy, for a lifetime of love and support.

My daughter in Heaven, Eleanor. I love you.

My daughter Amelia, you can't read this until you're eighteen.

My sister, brother-in-law. my three nieces, and nephew, Uncle Dylan is an author.

To the towns where I grew up, Blue Mound and Mound City. There's no place like home.

To my teachers and coaches at Blue Mound Elementary, Jayhawk-Linn High School, FSCC and Pitt State University, thank you for the education and life lessons along the way.

To the JLHS Class of 2010, I don't miss high school, but I'm thankful it was with all of you. Can't forget Shelby.

Derek Willcut, thank you for being a part of the journey to get this done, we started in kindergarten now we're here.

Wyatt Jackson, I know you're used to the books with pictures, but I hope you like this one.

Steven Mann, it's because of you I'll need hearing aids in a few years.

Morgan Campbell, I almost made the monsters in this book a pack of gingers, you're welcome.

To my editor Brett Savory, thank you for the masterful work.

To Christian Storm, thank you for the exterior/interior design to elevate this book beyond my wildest dreams.

A special thank you to my Aunt Rebecca for the final proofread.

To my family and friends, we're just getting started.

ABOUT THE AUTHOR

Dylan Thyer grew up in the town of Blue Mound, Kansas. Drawing inspiration from not only rural life in southeast Kansas, but along with its deep history. Mound City, Kansas served as the template for Mattfield in the book, where Dylan went to high school and later owned his first home.

The first ideas for the story came to him at the age of seventeen. Those ideas would become the end to Part 1 of the story. Over the next fifteen years the story fleshed out to encompass a more complex narrative as life experience, reading, and continued learning refined it. For example, deciding to include Native American characters after reading books *Killers of the Flower Moon* by David Grann and *Empire of the Summer Moon* by S. C. Gwynne, which were influences for those aspects of the story.

At age thirty-two, Dylan wrote *Silver* in the span of four and a half months. A lifelong horror fan he was excited to add his voice to the genre. Being able to work with thoughts and ideas that interest him; from ancient and American history, folklore, religion, and morality.

A few examples of crafting the world of *Silver*: Mattfield got its name from Mattfield Greene a real Kansas town. The town Red Hill, is a play on Dylan's hometown, Blue Mound. Jackson Road in the story is a real road outside of Mound City, Kansas, but doubles as a shout out to Wyatt Jackson, a brother to the author. The surname Mills for the sheriff's name is used in remembrance of Kyle Mills who passed away in 2013. A few of the Native American characters got their names from actors that the author is a fan of: Mo Brings

Plenty (Yellowstone) and Michael Greyeyes (Fear the Walking Dead). The deputy Keith Sparts name comes from extended family, the Spartz. The film Dog Soldiers inspired the story's monsters. The film *The Ghost and The Darkness* inspired Liam Gable's profession. Michael Chrichton (*Jurassic Park/State of Fear*), Dylan's favorite author has multiple nods in the book. Inspiration was even drawn from a variety of music. Dylan is a lifelong fan of The Kansas City Chiefs, the same as main character Brett Adams. These are just a handful of insights on how this fictional world was born, along with the author's personal touches.